# 61 HOURS

www.rbooks.co.uk

# 61 HOURS

## Lee Child

BANTAM PRESS

LONDON · TORONTO · SYDNEY · AUCKLAND · JOHANNESBURG

TRANSWORLD PUBLISHERS
61–63 Uxbridge Road, London W5 5SA
A Random House Group Company
www.rbooks.co.uk

First published in Great Britain
in 2010 by Bantam Press
an imprint of Transworld Publishers

A CIP catalogue record for this book
is available from the British Library.

ISBNs 9780593057063 (cased)
9780593057070 (tpb)

Addresses for Random House Group Ltd companies outside the UK
can be found at: www.randomhouse.co.uk
The Random House Group Ltd Reg. No. 954009

The Random House Group Limited supports The Forest Stewardship
Council (FSC), the leading international forest-certification organization.
All our titles that are printed on Greenpeace-approved FSC-certified
paper carry the FSC logo. Our paper procurement policy can be
found at www.rbooks.co.uk/environment

Typeset in 11/14pt Century Old Style by
Kestrel Data, Exeter, Devon.
Printed in the UK by
CPI Mackays, Chatham, ME5 8TD.

11

**Mixed Sources**
Product group from well-managed
forests and other controlled sources
www.fsc.org   Cert no. TT-COC-2139
© 1996 Forest Stewardship Council
FSC

For my editor,
the irreplaceable Marianne Velmans

# 61 HOURS

# ONE

FIVE MINUTES TO THREE IN THE AFTERNOON. EXACTLY SIXTY-ONE hours before it happened. The lawyer drove in and parked in the empty lot. There was an inch of new snow on the ground, so he spent a minute fumbling in the foot well until his overshoes were secure. Then he got out and turned his collar up and walked to the visitors' entrance. There was a bitter wind out of the north. It was thick with fat lazy flakes. There was a storm sixty miles away. The radio had been full of it.

The lawyer got in through the door and stamped the snow off his feet. There was no line. It was not a regular visiting day. There was nothing ahead of him except an empty room and an empty X-ray belt and a metal detector hoop and three prison guards standing around doing nothing. He nodded to them, even though he didn't know them. But he considered himself on their side, and they on his. Prison was a binary world. Either you were locked up, or you weren't. They weren't. He wasn't.

Yet.

He took a grey plastic bin off the top of a teetering stack and folded his overcoat into it. He took off his suit jacket and folded it and laid it on top of the overcoat. It was hot in the prison. Cheaper to burn a little extra oil than to give the inmates two sets of clothes, one for the summer and one for the winter. He could hear their noise ahead of him, the clatter of metal and concrete and the random crazy yells and the screams and the low grumble of other disaffected voices, all muted by doglegged corridors and many closed doors.

He emptied his trouser pockets of keys, and wallet, and cell phone, and coins, and nested those clean warm personal items on top of his jacket. He picked up the grey plastic bin. Didn't carry it to the X-ray belt. Instead he hefted it across the room to a small window in a wall. He waited there and a woman in uniform took it and gave him a numbered ticket in exchange for it.

He braced himself in front of the metal detector hoop. He patted his pockets and glanced ahead, expectantly, as if waiting for an invitation. Learned behaviour, from air travel. The guards let him stand there for a minute, a small, nervous man in his shirtsleeves, empty-handed. No briefcase. No notebook. Not even a pen. He was not there to advise. He was there to be advised. Not to talk, but to listen, and he sure as hell wasn't going to put what he heard anywhere near a piece of paper.

The guards beckoned him through. A green light and no beep, but still the first guard wanded him and the second patted him down. The third escorted him deeper into the complex, through doors designed never to be open unless the last and the next were closed, and around tight corners designed to slow a running man's progress, and past thick green glass windows with watchful faces behind.

The lobby had been institutional, with linoleum on the floor and mint green paint on the walls and fluorescent tubes on the ceiling. And the lobby had been connected to the outside, with gusts of cold air blowing in when the door was opened, and salt stains and puddles of snowmelt on the floor. The prison proper was different. It had no connection to the outside. No sky, no weather. No attempt at décor. It was all raw concrete, already rubbed greasy where sleeves and shoulders had touched it, still

10

pale and dusty where they hadn't. Underfoot was grippy grey paint, like the floor of an auto enthusiast's garage. The lawyer's overshoes squeaked on it.

There were four interview rooms. Each was a windowless concrete cube divided exactly in half by a wall-to-wall desk-height counter with safety glass above. Caged lights burned on the ceiling above the counter. The counter was cast from concrete. The grain of the formwork lumber was still visible in it. The safety glass was thick and slightly green and was divided into three overlapping panes, to give two sideways listening slots. The centre pane had a cut-out slot at the bottom, for documents. Like a bank. Each half of the room had its own chair, and its own door. Perfectly symmetrical. The lawyers entered one way, and the inmates entered the other. Later they left the same way they had come, each to a different destination.

The guard opened the door from the corridor and stepped a yard into the room for a visual check that all was as it should be. Then he stood aside and let the lawyer enter. The lawyer stepped in and waited until the guard closed the door behind him and left him alone. Then he sat down and checked his watch. He was eight minutes late. He had driven slowly because of the weather. Normally he would have regarded it as a failure to be late for an appointment. Unprofessional, and disrespectful. But prison visits were different. Time meant nothing to prisoners.

Another eight minutes later the other door opened, in the wall behind the glass. A different guard stepped in and checked and then stepped back out and a prisoner shuffled in. The lawyer's client. He was white, and enormously overweight, marbled with fat, and completely hairless. He was dressed in an orange jumpsuit. He had wrist and waist and ankle chains that looked as delicate as jewellery. His eyes were dull and his face was docile and vacant, but his mouth was moving a little, like a simple-minded person struggling to retain complex information.

The door in the wall behind the glass closed.

The prisoner sat down.

The lawyer hitched his chair close to the counter.

The prisoner did the same.

Symmetrical.

The lawyer said, 'I'm sorry I'm late.'

The prisoner didn't answer.

The lawyer asked, 'How are you?'

The prisoner didn't answer. The lawyer went quiet. The air in the room was hot. A minute later the prisoner started talking, reciting, working his way through lists and instructions and sentences and paragraphs he had committed to memory. From time to time the lawyer said, 'Slow down a bit,' and on each occasion the guy paused and waited and then started up again at the head of the previous sentence with no change in his pace and no alteration to his singsong delivery. It was as if he had no other way of communicating.

The lawyer had what he considered to be a pretty good memory, especially for detail, like most lawyers, and he was paying a lot of attention, because to concentrate on the process of remembering distracted him from the actual content of the instructions he was getting. But even so some small corner of his mind had counted fourteen separate criminal proposals before the prisoner finally finished up and sat back.

The lawyer said nothing.

The prisoner said, 'Got all that?'

The lawyer nodded and the prisoner lapsed into a bovine still-ness. Or equine, like a donkey in a field, infinitely patient. Time meant nothing to prisoners. Especially this one. The lawyer pushed his chair back and stood up. His door was unlocked. He stepped out to the corridor.

Five minutes to four in the afternoon.

Sixty hours to go.

The lawyer found the same guard waiting for him. He was back in the parking lot two minutes later. He was fully dressed again and his stuff was back in his pockets, all reassuringly weighty and present and normal. It was snowing harder by then and the air was colder and the wind was wilder. It was going dark, fast and early. The lawyer sat for a moment with his seat heating and his engine running and his wipers pushing berms of snow left and right on the windshield glass. Then he took off,

12

a wide slow turn with his tyres squeaking against the fresh fall and his headlight beams cutting bright arcs through the white swirl. He headed for the exit, the wire gates, the wait, the trunk check, and then the long straight road that led through town to the highway.

Fourteen criminal proposals. Fourteen actual crimes, if he relayed the proposals and they were acted upon, which they surely would be. Or fifteen crimes, because he himself would then become a co-conspirator. Or twenty-eight crimes, if a prosecutor chose to call each separate issue a separate conspiracy, which a prosecutor might, just for the fun of it. Or just for the glory. Twenty-eight separate paths to shame and ignominy and disbarment, and trial and conviction and imprisonment. Life imprisonment, almost certainly, given the nature of one of the fourteen proposals, and then only after a successful plea bargain. A failed plea bargain was too awful to contemplate.

The lawyer made it around the highway cloverleaf and merged into the slow lane. All around him was the thick grey of falling snow in the late afternoon. Not much traffic. Just occasional cars and trucks going his way, some of them faster and some of them slower, answered by occasional cars and trucks going the other way, across the divider. He drove one-handed and jacked up off the seat and took out his cell phone. Weighed it in his hand. He had three choices. One, do nothing. Two, call the number he had been told to call. Three, call the number he really should call, which in the circumstances was 911, with hasty back-ups to the local PD and the Highway Patrol and the county sheriffs and the Bar Association, and then a lawyer of his own.

He chose the second option, like he knew he would. Choice number one would get him nowhere, except a little later, when they came to find him. Choice number three would get him dead, slowly and eventually, after what he was sure would be hours or even days of hideous agony. He was a small nervous man. No kind of a hero.

He dialled the number he had been told to dial.

He checked it twice and hit the green button. He raised the

phone to his ear, which in many states would be a twenty-ninth crime all its own.

But not in South Dakota.

Not yet.

Small mercies.

The voice that answered was one he had heard four times before. Coarse, and rough, and laced with a kind of rude animal menace. A voice from what the lawyer thought of as another world entirely. It said, 'Shoot, buddy,' with a smile and an overtone of cruel enjoyment, as if the speaker was enjoying his absolute power and control, and the lawyer's own consequent discomfort and fear and revulsion.

The lawyer swallowed once and started talking, reciting the lists and the instructions and the sentences and the paragraphs in much the same way they had been relayed to him. He started talking seven miles and seven minutes from a highway bridge. The bridge didn't look much like a bridge. The roadbed continued absolutely level but the land below it fell away a little into a wide shallow gulch. The gulch was dry most of the year, but in five months' time spring meltwater would rage through it in a torrent. The highway engineers had smoothed the gulch into a neat culvert and packed forty giant concrete tubes under the roadbed, all to stop the foundation getting washed away once a year. It was a system that worked well in the spring. It had only one drawback, which showed up in the winter. To counter it the engineers had placed signs ahead in both directions. The signs said: *Bridge Freezes Before Road.*

The lawyer drove and talked. Seven minutes into his monologue he reached the most obviously naked and blunt and brutal and egregious of the fourteen proposals. He recited it into the phone the same way he had heard it in the prison, which was neutrally and without emotion. The coarse voice on the other end of the phone laughed. Which made the lawyer shudder. A core moral spasm came up literally from deep inside him. It jerked his shoulders noticeably and ground the phone across his ear.

And moved his hand on the wheel.

His front tyres slipped a little on the bridge ice and he corrected clumsily and his rear tyres swung the other way and fishtailed once, twice, three times. He slid across all three lanes. Saw a bus coming the opposite way through the falling snow. It was white. It was huge. It was moving fast. It was coming straight at him. The back part of his brain told him a collision was inevitable. The front part of his brain told him no, he had space and time and a grass median and two stout metal barriers between him and any kind of oncoming traffic. He bit his lip and relaxed his grip and straightened up and the bus blew past him exactly parallel and twenty feet away.

He breathed out.

The voice on the phone asked, 'What?'

The lawyer said, 'I skidded.'

The voice said, 'Finish the report, asshole.'

The lawyer swallowed again and resumed talking, at the head of the previous sentence.

The man driving the white bus in the opposite direction was a twelve-year veteran of his trade. In the small world of his specialized profession he was about as good as it got. He was properly licensed and well trained and adequately experienced. He was no longer young, and not yet old. Mentally and physically he was up there on a broad plateau of common sense and maturity and peak capability. He was not behind schedule. He was not speeding. He was not drunk. He was not high.

But he was tired.

He had been staring into featureless horizontal snow for the best part of two hours. He saw the fishtailing car a hundred yards ahead. Saw it dart diagonally straight at him. His fatigue produced a split second of dull delay. Then the numb tension in his tired body produced an overreaction. He yanked the wheel like he was flinching from a blow. Too much, too late. And un- necessary, anyway. The sliding car had straightened and was already behind him before his own front tyres bit. Or tried to. They hit the bridge ice just as the steering told them to turn. They lost grip and skated. All the weight was in the rear of the bus. The huge cast iron engine block. The water tank. The toilet.

Like a pendulum, way back there. The rear of the bus set about trying to overtake the front of the bus. It didn't get far. Just a few crucial degrees. The driver did everything right. He fought the skid. But the steering was feather light and the front tyres had lost traction. There was no feedback. The back of the bus came back in line and then swung out the other way.

The driver fought hard for three hundred yards. Twelve long seconds. They felt like twelve long hours. He spun the big plastic wheel left, spun it right, tried to catch the skid, tried to stop it building. But it built anyway. It gathered momentum. The big pendulum weight at the back slammed one way, slammed the other. The soft springs crushed and bounced. The tall body tilted and yawed. The back of the bus swung forty-five degrees left, then forty-five right. *Bridge Freezes Before Road.* The bus passed over the last of the concrete tubes and the front tyres bit again. But they bit while they were turned diagonally towards the shoulder. The whole bus turned in that direction, as if following a legitimate command. As if it was suddenly obedient again. The driver braked hard. Fresh snow dammed in front of the tyres. The bus held its new line. It slowed.

But not enough.

The front tyres crossed the rumble strip, crossed the shoulder, and thumped down off the blacktop into a shallow ditch full of snow and frozen mud. The underbody crashed and banged and scraped on the pavement edge for ten long feet before all momentum was spent. The bus came to rest at an angle, tilted a little, the front third in the ditch, the rear two-thirds still on the shoulder, and the engine compartment hanging out in the traffic lane. The front wheels hung down to the limit of their travel. The engine had stalled out and there was no sound beyond hot components hissing against the snow, and the air brake gently exhaling, and the passengers screaming, then gasping, then going very quiet.

The passengers were a homogeneous bunch, all except for one. Twenty white-haired seniors plus a younger man, in a bus that could seat forty. Twelve of the seniors were widowed women.

16

The other eight made up four old married couples. They were from Seattle. They were a church group on a cultural tour. They had seen the Little Town on the Prairie. Now they were on the long haul west to Mount Rushmore. A side trip to the geographic centre of the United States had been promised. National parks and grasslands would be visited along the way. A fine itinerary, but the wrong season. South Dakota weather in the winter was not famously hospitable. Hence the fifty per cent take up on the tickets, even though the tickets were cheap.

The odd passenger out was a man at least thirty years younger than the youngest of the others. He was sitting alone three rows behind the last of the seniors. They thought of him as a kind of stowaway. He had joined the bus that same day, at a rest stop just east of a town called Cavour. After the Little Town on the Prairie, before the Dakotaland Museum. There had been no explanation. He had just gotten on the bus. Some had seen him in prior conversation with the driver. Some said money had changed hands. No one was sure what to think. If he had paid for his passage, then he was more like a steerage passenger than a stowaway. Like a hitchhiker, but not quite.

But in any case he was considered a nice enough fellow. He was quiet and polite. He was a foot taller than any of the other passengers and evidently very strong. Not handsome like a movie star, but not ugly, either. Like a just-retired athlete, maybe. Perhaps a football player. Not the best dressed of individuals. He was wearing a creased untucked shirt under a padded canvas jacket. He had no bag, which was strange. But overall it was vaguely reassuring to have such a man on board, especially after he had proved himself civilized and not in any way threatening. Threatening behaviour from a man that size would have been unseemly. Good manners from a man that size were charming. Some of the bolder widowed ladies had thought about striking up a conversation. But the man himself seemed to discourage any such attempt. He slept through most of the drive time and all his responses to conversational gambits had so far been entirely courteous but brief, and completely devoid of substance.

But at least they knew his name. One of the men had intro-duced himself, on his way back down the aisle from the toilet. The tall stranger had looked up from his seat and paused, just a beat, as if assessing the costs and benefits of a response. Then he had taken the proffered hand and said, 'Jack Reacher.'

# TWO

REACHER WOKE UP WHEN THE MOMENTUM OF THE SKID SMASHED his head against the window. He knew where he was, instantly. *On a bus.* He spent the next split second calculating the odds. *Snow, ice, reasonable speed, not much traffic. We're going to either hit the divider or fall off the shoulder. Worst case, we're going to tip over.* OK for him. Maybe not so good for the old folks in front of him. But probably survivable. He was more worried about the aftermath. Twenty old people, shaken up, maybe injured, cuts, bruises, broken bones, stranded miles from anywhere in a gathering winter storm.

Not good.

Then he spent the next eleven and a half seconds holding on, gently resisting the alternating inertia of the fishtails. He was the rearmost passenger, so he was feeling it worst. The folks nearer the front were swinging through smaller arcs. But they were fragile. He could see their necks snapping from side to side. He could see the driver's face in the rear-view mirror. The guy was hanging in there. Not bad. But he was going to lose. A

19

luxury bus was a very unwieldy type of vehicle. *Be careful what you wish for.* He had been in Marshall, Minnesota, for no very memorable reason, and he had hitched a ride with a guy heading west to Huron, South Dakota, but for some private reason the guy wouldn't take him all the way and had dumped him at a rest stop outside of a place called Cavour. Which had seemed like bad luck, initially, because Cavour was not exactly teeming with transcontinental traffic. But two cups of coffee later a white luxury forty-seat bus had pulled in and only twenty people had gotten out, which meant empty places were there to be had. The driver looked like a straightforward kind of a guy, so Reacher had approached him in a straightforward kind of a fashion. Twenty bucks for a ride to Rapid City? The guy asked for forty and settled for thirty and Reacher had climbed aboard and been very comfortable all day long. But the comfort had come from soft springs and vague steering, neither one of which was doing anyone any favours at the current moment.

But seven seconds in, Reacher was getting optimistic. With no foot on the gas, the bus was slowing. Didn't feel like it, but it had to be true. Simple physics. Newton's Laws of Motion. As long as no other traffic hit them, they would wobble around for a spell and then come to rest, maybe side-on, maybe facing the wrong way, but still right side up and drivable. Then he felt the front tyres bite again and saw they were going to drive straight off the road. Which was bad. But the driver braked hard and held tight through a whole lot of thumping and banging and scraping and they ended up half on and half off the blacktop, which was OK, except they had their asses hanging out in the traffic lane, which was not OK, and there were suddenly no active mechanical sounds at all, like the bus was dead, which was definitely not OK.

Reacher glanced back and saw no oncoming headlights. Not right then. He got up and walked to the front of the bus and saw flat land ahead, all white with snow. No cliffs. No embankment. Therefore no danger from a weight transfer. So he ducked back and started encouraging the geezers to move up the bus towards the front. That way if an eighteen-wheeler slammed into them it might just shear off the rear of the bus without killing anyone. But the geezers were shaken and reluctant to move. They just sat there. So Reacher moved back up front. The driver was inert in his seat, blinking a little and swallowing down his adrenalin rush.

Reacher said to him, 'Good work, pal.'

The guy nodded. 'Thanks.'

Reacher said, 'Can you get us out of this ditch?'

'I don't know.'

'Best guess?'

'Probably not.'

Reacher said, 'OK, have you got flares?'

'What?'

'Flares. Right now the back of the bus is sticking out in the traffic lane.'

The guy was unresponsive for a moment. Dazed. Then he leaned down and unlatched a locker beside his feet and came out with three warning flares, dull red cardboard tubes with steel spikes on the end. Reacher took them from him and said, 'Got a first-aid kit?'

The guy nodded again.

Reacher said, 'Take it and check the passengers for cuts and bruises. Encourage them to move up front as far as they can. Preferably all together in the aisle. If we get hit, it's going to be in the ass.'

The driver nodded for a third time and then shook himself like a dog and got into gear. He took a first-aid kit from another latched compartment and got up out of his seat.

Reacher said, 'Open the door first.'

The guy hit a button and the door sucked open. Freezing air blew in, with thick swirls of snow on it. Like a regular blizzard. Reacher said, 'Close the door after me. Stay warm.'

Then he jumped down into the ditch and fought through the ice and the mud to the shoulder. He stepped up on the blacktop and ran to the rear corner of the vehicle. Blowing snow pelted his face. He lined up on the lane markers and ran thirty paces back the way they had come. A curved trajectory. Thirty paces, thirty yards. Ninety feet. Near enough to eighty-eight. Eighty-eight feet per second was the same thing as sixty miles an hour, and plenty of lunatics would be driving sixty even in a snowstorm. He leaned down and jabbed a flare spike into the blacktop. The crimson flame ignited automatically and burned fiercely. He continued the curve and ran another thirty paces. Used the second flare. Ran another thirty and used the third to complete a warning sequence: three seconds, two, one, *move the hell over.*

Then he ran back and floundered through the ditch again and hammered on the door until the driver broke off his medical ministrations and opened up. Reacher climbed back inside. He brought a flurry of snow in with him. He was already seriously cold. His face was numb. His feet were freezing. And the interior of the bus itself was already cooling. The windows all along one side were already pasted with clumps of white. He said, 'You should keep the engine running. Keep the heaters going.'

The driver said, 'Can't. The fuel line could be cracked. From where we scraped.'

Reacher said, 'I didn't smell anything when I was outside.'

'I can't take the risk. Everyone is alive right now. I don't want to burn them up in a fire.'

'You want to freeze them to death instead?'

'Take over with the first aid. I'll try to make some calls.'

So Reacher ducked back and started checking the old folks. The driver had gotten through the first two rows. That was clear. All four of the window-seat passengers were sporting Band-Aids over cuts from the metal edges around the glass. *Be careful what you wish for.* Better view, but higher risk. One woman had a second Band-Aid on the aisle side of her face, presumably from where her husband's head had hit her after bouncing around like a rag doll.

The first broken bone was in row three. A delicate old lady, built like a bird. She had been swinging right when the bus changed direction and swung left. The window had tapped her hard on the shoulder. The blow had bust her collar bone. Reacher could

22

see it in the way she was cradling her arm. He said, 'Ma'am, may I take a look at that?'

She said, 'You're not a doctor.'

'I had some training in the army.'

'Were you a medic?'

'I was a military cop. We got some medical training.'

'I'm cold.'

'Shock,' Reacher said. 'And it's snowing.'

She turned her upper body towards him. Implied consent. He put his fingertips on her collar bone, through her blouse. The bone was as delicate as a pencil. It was snapped halfway along its length. A clean break. Not compound.

She asked, 'Is it bad?'

'It's good,' Reacher said. 'It did its job. A collar bone is like a circuit breaker. It breaks so that your shoulder and your neck stay OK. It heals fast and easy.'

'I need to go to the hospital.'

Reacher nodded. 'We'll get you there.'

He moved on. There was a sprained wrist in row four, and a broken wrist in row five. Plus a total of thirteen cuts, many minor contusions, and a lot of shock reaction.

The temperature was dropping like a stone.

Reacher could see the flares out the rear side windows. They were still burning, three distinct crimson puffballs glowing in the swirling snow. No headlights coming. None at all. No traffic. He walked up the aisle, head bent, and found the driver. The guy was in his seat, holding an open cell phone in his right hand, staring through the windshield, drumming his left-hand fingertips on the wheel.

He said, 'We've got a problem.'

'What kind of a problem?'

'I called 911. The Highway Patrol is all either sixty miles north of here or sixty miles east. There are two big storms coming in. One from Canada, one off the Lakes. There's all kinds of mayhem. All the tow trucks went with them. They've got hundred-car pile-ups. This highway is closed behind us. And up ahead.'

*No traffic.*

23

'Where are we?'

'South Dakota.'

'I know that.'

'Then you know what I mean. If we're not in Sioux Falls or Rapid City, we're in the middle of nowhere. And we're not in Sioux Falls or Rapid City.'

'We have to be somewhere.'

'GPS shows a town nearby. Name of Bolton. Maybe twenty miles. But it's small. Just a dot on the map.'

'Can you get a replacement bus?'

'I'm out of Seattle. I could get one maybe four days after the snow stops.'

'Does the town of Bolton have a police department?'

'I'm waiting on a call.'

'Maybe they have tow trucks.'

'I'm sure they do. At least one. Maybe at the corner gas station, good for hauling broken-down half-ton pick-up trucks. Not so good for vehicles this size.'

'Maybe they have farm tractors.'

'They'd need about eight of them. And some serious chains.'

'Maybe they have a school bus. We could transfer.'

'The Highway Patrol won't abandon us. They'll get here.'

Reacher asked, 'What's your name?'

'Jay Knox.'

'You need to think ahead, Mr Knox. The Highway Patrol is an hour away under the best of circumstances. Two hours, in this weather. Three hours, given what they're likely dealing with. So we need to get a jump. Because an hour from now this bus is going to be an icebox. Two hours from now these wrinklies are going to be dropping like flies. Maybe sooner.'

'So what gets your vote?'

Reacher was about to answer when Knox's cell phone rang. The guy answered it and his face lightened a little. Then it fell again. He said, 'Thanks,' and closed the phone. He looked at Reacher and said, 'Apparently the town of Bolton has a police department. They're sending a guy. But they've got problems of their own and it will take some time.'

24

'How much time?'

'At least an hour.'

'What kind of problems?'

'They didn't say.'

'You're going to have to start the engine.'

'They've got coats.'

'Not good enough.'

'I'm worried about a fire.'

'Diesel fuel is a lot less volatile than gasoline.'

'What are you, an expert?'

'I was in the army. Trucks and Humvees were all diesel. For a reason.' Reacher glanced back down the aisle. 'Got a flashlight? Got an extinguisher?'

'Why?'

'I'll check the underbody. If it looks all clear I'll knock twice on the floor. You start up, if anything goes on fire I'll put it out and knock again and you can shut it down.'

'I don't know.'

'Best we can do. And we have to do something.'

Knox was quiet for a spell and then he shrugged and opened up a couple more compartments and came out with a silver Maglite and an extinguisher bottle. Reacher took them and waited for the door to open and climbed out into the spectral crimson world of the flares. Down into the ditch again. This time he trudged counterclockwise around the front of the bus because the oblique angle put more of the left side above the blacktop than the right. Crawling around in the freezing ditch was not an attractive prospect. Crawling around on the shoulder was marginally better.

He found the fuel filler door and sat down in the snow and then swivelled around and lay on his back and wriggled into position with his head under the side of the bus. He switched the flashlight on. Found the fat tube running from the filler mouth to the tank. It looked intact. The tank itself was a huge squared-off cylinder. It was a little dented and scraped from the impact. But nothing was leaking out of it. The fuel line running back towards the engine compartment looked OK. Snow soaked

25

through Reacher's jacket and his shirt and freezing damp hit his skin.

He shivered.

He used the butt end of the Mag-lite and banged twice on a frame spar.

He heard relays clicking and a fuel pump start up. It wheezed and whined. He checked the tank. Checked the line, as far as the flashlight beam would let him. He kicked against the snow and pushed himself further under the bus.

No leaks.

The starter motor turned over.

The engine started. It clattered and rattled and settled to a hammer-heavy beat.

No leaks.

No fire.

No fumes.

He fought the cold and gave it another minute and used the time to check other things. The big tyres looked OK. Some of the front suspension members were a little banged up. The floor of the luggage hold was dented here and there. A few small tubes and hoses were crushed and torn and split. Some Seattle insurer was about to get a fair-sized bill.

He scrabbled out and stood up and brushed off. His clothes were soaked. Snow swirled all around him. Fat, heavy flakes. There were two fresh inches on the ground. His footsteps from four minutes ago were already dusted white. He followed them back to the ditch and floundered around to the door. Knox was waiting for him. The door opened and he climbed aboard. Blowing snow howled in after him. He shivered. The door closed.

The engine stopped.

Knox sat down in his seat and hit the starter button. Way at the back of the bus Reacher heard the starter motor turning, churning, straining, wheezing, over and over again.

Nothing happened.

Knox asked, 'What did you see down there?'

'Damage,' Reacher said. 'Lots of things all banged up.'

'Crushed tubes?'

'Some.'

Knox nodded. 'The fuel line is pinched off. We just used up what was left in the pipe, and now no more is getting through. Plus the brakes could be shot. Maybe it's just as well the engine won't run.'

'Call the Bolton PD again,' Reacher said. 'This is serious.'

Knox dialled and Reacher headed back towards the passengers. He hauled coats off the overhead racks and told the old folks to put them on. Plus hats and gloves and scarves and mufflers and anything else they had.

He had nothing. Just what he stood up in, and what he stood up in was soaked and freezing. His body heat was leaching away. He was shivering, just a little, but continuously. Small crawling thrills, all over his skin. *Be careful what you wish for.* A life without baggage had many advantages. But crucial disadvantages, too.

He headed back to Knox's seat. The door was leaking air. The bus was colder at the front than the back. He said, 'Well?'

Knox said, 'They're sending a car as soon as possible.'

'A car won't do it.'

'I told them that. I described the problem. They said they'll work something out.'

'You seen storms like this before?'

'This is not a storm. The storm is sixty miles away. This is the edge.'

Reacher shivered. 'Is it coming our way?'

'No question.'

'How fast?'

'Don't ask.'

Reacher left him there and walked down the aisle, all the way past the last of the seats. He sat on the floor outside the toilet, with his back pressed hard against the rear bulkhead, hoping to feel some residual heat coming in from the cooling engine.

He waited.

Five minutes to five in the afternoon.

Fifty-nine hours to go.

27

# THREE

FORTY-FIVE MINUTES LATER THE LAWYER GOT HOME. A LONG, SLOW trip. His driveway was unploughed and he worried for a moment that his garage door would be frozen shut. But he hit the remote and the half-horsepower motor on the ceiling inside did its job and the door rose up in its track and he drove in. Then the door wouldn't shut after him, because the clumps of snow his tyres had pushed in triggered the door's child safety feature. So he fussed with his overshoes once more and took a shovel and pushed the snow back out again. The door closed. The lawyer took off his overshoes again and stood for a moment at the mud room door, composing himself, cleansing himself, taking a mental shower. Twenty minutes to six. He walked through to the warmth of his kitchen and greeted his family, as if it was just another day.

By twenty minutes to six the inside of the bus was dark and icy and Reacher was hugging himself hard and shivering violently. Ahead of him the twenty old people and Knox the driver were all doing pretty much the same thing. The windows on the windward side of the bus were all black with stuck snow. The windows on the leeward side showed a grey panorama. A blizzard, blowing in from the north and the east, driven hard and relentlessly by the winter wind, hitting the aerodynamic interruption of the dead vehicle, boiling over it and under it and around it and swirling into the vacuum behind it, huge weightless flakes dancing randomly up and down and left and right.

Then: faint lights in the grey panorama.

White lights, and red, and blue, pale luminous spheres snapping and popping and moving through the gloom. The faint patter of snow chains in the eerie padded silence. A cop car, coming towards them on the wrong side of the divided highway, nosing slow and cautious through the weather.

A long minute later a cop was inside the bus. He had come through the ditch and in through the door, but he had just gotten out of a heated car and he was wearing winter boots and waterproof pants and gloves and a parka and a plastic rain shield over a fur hat with ear flaps, so he was in pretty good shape. He was tall and lean and had lined blue eyes in a face that had seen plenty of summer sun and winter wind. He said his name was Andrew Peterson and that he was second-in-command over at the Bolton PD. He took off his gloves and moved through the aisle, shaking hands and introducing himself by name and rank over and over again, to each individual and each couple, in a manner designed to appear guileless and frank and enthusiastic, like a good old country boy just plain delighted to help out in an emergency. But Reacher was watching those lined blue eyes and thinking that his front was false. Reacher was thinking that Peterson was actually a fairly shrewd man with more things on his mind than a simple road rescue.

That impression was reinforced when Peterson started asking questions. Who were they all? Where were they from? Where had they started today? Where were they headed tonight? Did they have hotel reservations up ahead? Easy answers for Knox and the twenty old folks, a tour group, from Seattle, hustling from one scheduled stop at the Dakotaland Museum to the next at Mount Rushmore, and yes, they had confirmed reservations at a tourist motel near the monument, thirteen rooms, for the four married couples, plus four pairs who were sharing, plus four individuals who had paid a singles supplement, plus one for Knox himself.

All true information, but not exactly necessary, in the circumstances.

Peterson made Knox show him the motel paperwork.

Then he turned to Reacher. Smiled and said, 'Sir, I'm Andrew Peterson, from the Bolton PD, deputy chief. Would you mind telling me who you are?'

Plenty of heartland cops were ex-military, but Reacher didn't think Peterson was. He wasn't getting the vibe. He figured him for a guy who hadn't travelled much, a straight-arrow kid who had done well in a local high school and who had stuck around afterwards to serve his community. Expert in a casual way with all the local stuff, a little out of his depth with anything else, but determined to do his best with whatever came his way.

'Sir?' Peterson said again.

Reacher gave his name. Peterson asked him whether he was part of the group. Reacher said no. So Peterson asked him what he was doing on the bus. Reacher said he was heading west out of Minnesota, hoping to turn south before too long, hoping to find better weather.

'You don't like our weather?'

'Not so far.'

'And you hitched a ride on a tour bus?'

'I paid.'

Peterson looked at Knox, and Knox nodded.

Peterson looked back at Reacher and asked, 'Are you on vacation?'

Reacher said, 'No.'

'Then what exactly is your situation?'

'My situation doesn't matter. None of this matters. None of us expected to be where we are right now. This whole thing was entirely unpredictable. It was an accident. Therefore there's no connection between us and whatever it is that's on your mind. There can't be.'

'Who says I have something on my mind?'

'I do.'

Peterson looked at Reacher, long and hard. 'What happened with the bus?'

'Ice, I guess,' Reacher said. 'I was asleep at the time.'

Peterson nodded. 'There's a bridge that doesn't look like a bridge. But there are warning signs.'

Knox said, 'A car coming the other way was sliding all over the place. I twitched.' His tone was slightly defensive. Peterson gave him a look full of sympathy and empty of judgement and nodded again. He said, 'A twitch will usually do it. It's happened to lots of people. Me included.'

Reacher said, 'We need to get these people off this bus. They're going to freeze to death. I am, too.'

Peterson was quiet for a long second. *There's no connection between us and whatever it is that's on your mind.* Then he nodded again, definitively, like his mind was made up, and he called out, 'Listen up, folks. We're going to get you to town, where we can look after you properly. The lady with the collar bone and the lady with the wrist will come with me in the car, and there will be alternative transportation right along for the rest of you.'

The step down into the ditch was too much for the injured women, so Peterson carried one and Reacher carried the other. The car was about ten yards away, but the snow was so thick by then that Reacher could barely see it, and when he turned back after Peterson had driven away he couldn't see the bus at all. He felt completely alone in the white emptiness. The snow was in his face, in his eyes, in his ears, on his neck, swirling all around him, blinding him. He was very cold. He felt a split second of panic. If for some reason he got turned around and headed in the wrong direction, he wouldn't know it. He would walk until he froze and died.

But he took a long step sideways and saw the crimson haloes of the flares. They were still burning valiantly. He used them

31

to work out where the bus must be and headed for it. Came up against its leeward side and tracked around the front, back into the wind, through the ditch to the door. Knox let him in and they crouched together in the aisle and peered out into the darkness, waiting to see what kind of a ride had been sent for them.

Five to six in the evening.

Fifty-eight hours to go.

At six o'clock the fourteen criminal proposals finally made it to paper. The guy who had answered the lawyer's call was plenty bright in a street-smart kind of way, but he had always figured that the best part of intelligence was to know your limitations, and his included a tendency to get a little hazy about detail when under pressure. And he was going to face some pressure now. That was for damn sure. Turning proposals into actions was going to require the sanction of some seriously cautious people.

So he wrote everything down, fourteen separate paragraphs, and then he unplugged a brand-new untraceable pay-as-you-go cell from its charger and started to dial.

The ride that had been sent for them was a school bus, but not exactly. Definitely a standard Blue Bird vehicle, normal size, normal shape, regular proportions, but grey, not yellow, with heavy metal mesh welded over the windows, and the words *Department of Corrections* stencilled along the flanks.

It looked almost new.

Knox said, 'Better than nothing.'

Reacher said, 'I'd go in a hearse if it had a heater.'

The prison vehicle K-turned across all three lanes and sawed back and forth for a while until it was lined up exactly parallel with the dead bus, with its entrance step about halfway down the dead bus's length. Reacher saw why. The dead bus had an emergency exit, which was a window panel ready to pop out. Peterson had seen the ditch and the passengers and the panel, and had made a good decision and called ahead. Peterson was a reasonably smart guy.

Normally eighteen random seniors might have needed an

32

amount of coaxing before stepping through an open hatch into a blizzard and the arms of a stranger, but the bitter cold had quieted their inhibitions. Knox helped them up top, and Reacher lifted them down. Easy work, apart from the cold and the snow. The lightest among the passengers was an old guy not more than ninety-five pounds. The heaviest was a woman closer to two hundred. The men all wanted to walk the short distance between the two vehicles. The women were happy to be carried.

The prison bus might have been almost new, but it was far from luxurious. The passenger area was separated from the driver by a bright steel cage. The seats were narrow and hard and faced with shiny plastic. The floor was rubber. The mesh over the windows was menacing. But there was heat. Not necessarily a kindness from the state to its convicts. But the bus manufacturer had built it in, for the school kids that the vehicle was designed to carry. And the state had not ripped it out. That was all. A kind of passive benevolence. The driver had the temperature turned up high and the blower on max. Peterson was a good advance man.

Reacher and Knox got the passengers seated and then they ducked back out into the cold and hauled suitcases out of the dead bus's luggage hold. The old folks would need nightwear and prescriptions and toiletries and changes of clothes. There were a lot of suitcases. They filled the prison bus's spare seats and most of the aisle. Knox sat down on one. Reacher rode standing next to the driver, as close to a heater vent as he could get.

The wind buffeted the bus but the tyres had chains and progress was steady. They came off the highway after seven miles and rumbled past a rusted yield sign that had been peppered by a shotgun blast. They hit a long straight county two-lane. They passed a sign that said *Correctional Facility Ahead. Do Not Stop For Hitchhikers*. The sign was brand new, crisp and shiny with reflective paint. Reacher was not pleased to see it. It would make moving on in the morning a little harder than it needed to be.

The inevitable question was asked less than a minute later. A woman in the front seat looked left, looked right, looked a little

33

embarrassed, but spoke anyway. She said, 'We're not going to be put in *jail*, are we?'

'No, ma'am,' Reacher said. 'A motel, probably. I expect this was the only bus free tonight.'

The prison driver said, 'Motels are all full,' and didn't speak again.

Five to seven in the evening.

Fifty-seven hours to go.

The county two-lane ran straight for more than ten miles. Visibility was never more than ten yards at a time. The falling snow was bright in the headlight beams, and beyond it was guesswork. Flat land, Reacher figured, judging by the unchanging engine note. No hills, no dales. Just prairie, flattened further by what was surely going to be a whole extra foot of snow by the morning.

Then they passed a sign: *Bolton City Limit. Pop. 12,261.* Not such a small place after all. Not just a dot on the map. The driver didn't slow. The chains chattered onward, another mile, then another. Then there was the glow of a street lamp in the air. Then another. Then a cop car, parked sideways across the mouth of a side street, blocking it. The car had its red roof lights turning lazily. The car had been stationary for a long time. That was clear. Its tyre tracks were half full of fresh snow.

The bus clattered on for another quarter-mile and then slowed and turned three times. Right, left, right again. Then Reacher saw a low wall, with a loaf of snow on top and a lit sign along its length: *Bolton Police Department.* Behind the wall was a big parking lot half full with civilian vehicles. Sedans, trucks, crew-cab pick-ups. They all looked recently driven and recently parked. Fresh tyre tracks, clear windshields, melting slush on their hoods. The bus eased past them and slowed and came to a stop opposite a lit entrance lobby. The engine settled to a noisy idle. The heater kept on going. The police station was long and low. Not a small operation. The roof was flat and had a forest of antennas poking up through the snow. The lobby door was flanked by a pair of trash cans. Like two proud sentinels.

The lobby looked warm.

The prison driver hauled on a handle and opened the bus door and a guy in a police parka came out of the lobby with a snow shovel and started clearing the path between the trash cans. Reacher and Knox started hauling suitcases out of the aisle, out of the bus, into the police station. The snow was letting up a little but the air was colder than ever.

Then the passengers made the transfer. Knox helped them down the step, Reacher helped them along the path, the guy in the parka saw them in through the door. Some sat down on benches, some stayed standing, some milled around. The lobby was a plain square space with dull linoleum on the floor and shiny paint on the walls. There was a reception counter in back and the wall behind it was covered with cork boards and the cork boards were covered with thumbtacked notices of different sizes and types. Sitting in front of them on a stool was an old guy in civilian clothes. Not a cop. An aide of some kind.

The guy in the parka disappeared for a moment and came back with a man Reacher took to be Bolton's chief of police. He was wearing a gun belt and a uniform with two metal bars stuck through the fabric on both peaks of his shirt collar. Like an army captain's insignia. The guy himself was what Peterson was going to be about fifteen years into the future, a tall lean plainsman going a little stooped and soft with age. He looked tired and preoccupied, and beset by problems, and a little wistful, like a guy more content with the past than the present, but also temporarily happy, because he had been handed a simple problem that could be easily solved. He took up a position with his back against the counter and raised his hands for quiet, even though no one was talking.

He said, 'Welcome to Bolton, folks. My name is Chief Tom Holland, and I'm here to see that you all get comfortable and taken care of tonight. The bad news is that the motels are all full, but the good news is that the people of Bolton are not the kind of folks who would let a group of stranded travellers such as yourselves sleep a night on cots in the high school gymnasium. So the call went out for empty guest rooms and I'm glad to say we got a good response and we have more than a dozen people right here, right now, ready to invite you into their homes just like honoured visitors and long-lost friends.'

There was a little low talking after that. A little surprise, a little uncertainty, then a lot of contentment. The old folks brightened and smiled and stood taller. Chief Holland ushered their hosts in from a side room, five local couples and four local men and four local women who had come alone. The lobby was suddenly crowded. People were milling about and shaking hands and introducing themselves and grouping together and hunting through the pile for their suitcases.

Reacher kept count in his head. Thirteen knots of people, which implied thirteen empty guest rooms, which exactly mirrored the thirteen Mount Rushmore motel rooms on Knox's official paperwork. Peterson was a good advance man.

Reacher wasn't on Knox's official paperwork.

He watched as the lobby emptied. Suitcases were hoisted, arms were offered, the doors were opened, pairs and threesomes and foursomes walked out to the waiting vehicles. It was all over inside five minutes. Reacher was left standing alone. Then the guy in the parka came back in and closed the doors. He disappeared down a doglegged corridor. Chief Holland came back. He looked at Reacher and said, 'Let's wait in my office.'

Five to eight in the evening.

Fifty-six hours to go.

# FOUR

HOLLAND'S OFFICE WAS LIKE A THOUSAND REACHER HAD SEEN before. Plain municipal décor, tendered out, the job won by the underbidder. Sloppy gloss paint all over the place, thick and puckered and wrinkled, vinyl tile on the floor, a veneered desk, six last-generation file cabinets in an imperfect line against the wall under an institutional clock. There was a framed photograph centred on the cabinets under the clock. It showed Chief Holland as a straighter, stronger, younger man, standing and smiling with a woman and a child. A family portrait, maybe ten or more years old. The woman was attractive in a pale, fair-haired, strong-featured way. Holland's wife, presumably. The child was a girl, maybe eight or nine, her face white and indistinct and unformed. Their daughter, presumably. There was a pair of dice on the desk. Big old bone cubes, worn from use and age, the dots rubbed and faded, the material itself veined where soft calcium had gone and harder minerals had remained. But apart from the photograph and the dice there was nothing personal in the room. Everything else was business.

Holland sat down behind the desk in a worn leather chair. There was an undraped picture window behind his head, triple-glazed against the cold. Clean glass. Darkness outside. Snow on the outer sill, a heater under the inner sill.

Reacher took a visitor chair in front of the desk.

Holland didn't speak.

Reacher asked, 'What am I waiting for?'

'We wanted to offer you the same hospitality we offered the others.'

'But I was a harder sell?'

Holland smiled a tired smile. 'Not really. Andrew Peterson volunteered to take you in himself. But he's busy right now. So you'll have to wait.'

'Busy doing what?'

'What cops do.'

Reacher said, 'This is a bigger place than I expected. The tour bus GPS showed it as a dot on the map.'

'We grew. That GPS data is a little out of date, I guess.'

The office was overheated. Reacher had stopped shivering and was starting to sweat. His clothes were drying, stiff and dirty. He said, 'You grew because you got a prison built here.'

'How do you figure that?'

'New prison bus. New sign after the highway.'

Holland nodded. 'We got a brand-new federal facility. We competed for it. Everybody wanted it. It's like getting Toyota to open an assembly plant. Or Honda. Lots of jobs, lots of dollars. Then the state put their new penitentiary in the same compound, which was more jobs and more dollars, and the county jail is there too.'

'Which is why the motels are full tonight? Visiting day to-morrow?'

'Total of three visiting days a week, all told. And the way the bus lines run, most people have to spend two nights in town. Heads on beds six nights a week. Motel owners are like pigs in shit. And the diners, and the pizza parlours, and the shuttle bus people. Like I told you, jobs and dollars.'

'Where's the compound?'

'Five miles north. The gift that keeps on giving.'

'Lucky you,' Reacher said.

Holland was quiet for a beat. Then he said, 'I learned a long time ago, you don't look a gift horse in the mouth.'

The guy in the parka knocked and walked straight in and handed Holland a closed file folder. The clock on the wall showed eight in the evening, which was about right according to the clock in Reacher's head. Holland swivelled his chair and opened the file folder ninety degrees and kept it tilted up at an awkward angle, to stop Reacher seeing the contents. But they were clearly reflected in the window glass behind Holland's head. They were crime scene photographs, glossy colour eight-by-tens with printed labels pasted in their bottom corners. Holland leafed through them. An establishing shot, then a progressive sequence of close-ups. A sprawled black-clad body, large, probably male, probably dead, snow on the ground, blunt force trauma to the right temple. No blood.

In the tour bus Knox had closed his cell phone and said: *The town of Bolton has a police department. They're sending a guy. But they've got problems of their own and it will take some time.*

Holland closed the file. Said nothing. A reserved, taciturn man. Like Reacher himself. In the end they just sat opposite each other without speaking. Not a hostile silence, but even so there was an undercurrent to it. Holland kept his palm on the closed file and glanced from time to time between it and his visitor, as if he wasn't yet sure which represented his bigger problem.

Eight o'clock in the evening in Bolton, South Dakota, was nine o'clock in the evening in Mexico City. Seventeen hundred miles south, sixty degrees warmer. The man who had taken the call from the untraceable pay-as-you-go cell was about to make a call of his own, from his walled city villa to a walled rural compound a hundred miles away. There another man would listen without comment and then promise a decision within twelve hours. That was how it usually went. Nothing worthwhile was achieved without reflection and rumination. With reflection and rumination impulsive mistakes could be avoided, and bold strokes could be formulated.

Holland's office was quiet and still and the door was closed, but Reacher heard noise in the rest of the station house. Comings and goings, close to thirty minutes' worth. Then silence again. A watch change, he guessed. Unlikely timing for a three-shift system. More likely a two-shift system. The day watch clocking off, the night watch coming on, twelve hours and twelve hours, maybe half past eight in the morning until half past eight at night. Unusual, and probably not permanent. Probably indicative of some kind of short-term stress.

*They've got problems of their own.*

Andrew Peterson came back to the station house just before nine twenty in the evening. He ducked his head into Holland's office and Holland joined him in the corridor with the file of crime scene photographs. The impromptu conference didn't last long. Less than five minutes. Reacher assumed that Peterson had seen the dead guy in situ and therefore didn't need to study pictures of him. The two cops came back into the office and stood in the centre of the floor with quitting time written all through their body language. A long day, and another long day tomorrow, but until then, nothing. It was a feeling Reacher recognized from the years he had held a job. It was a feeling he had shared on some days. But not on days when dead guys had shown up in his jurisdiction.

Peterson said, 'Let's go.'

Twenty-five past nine in the evening.

Fifty-four and a half hours to go.

Twenty-five past nine in the evening in South Dakota was twenty-five past ten in the evening in the walled compound a hundred miles from Mexico City. The compound's owner was an exceptionally short man who went by the name of Plato. Some people assumed that Plato was Brazilian, and had followed the Brazilian habit of picking a short catchy name to stand in for whatever long

40

sequence of patronymics littered his birth certificate. Like the way the soccer star Edson Arantes do Nascimento had called himself Pelé. Or the way another named Ricardo Izecson dos Santos Leite had called himself Kaká. Others claimed that Plato was Colombian, which would have been in many ways more logical, given his chosen trade. Others insisted he was indeed Mexican. But all agreed that Plato was short, not that anyone would dare say so to his face. His local driver's licence claimed five feet three inches. The reality was five feet one in elevator shoes, and four feet eleven without them.

The reason no one dared mention his stature to his face was a former associate named Martinez. Martinez had argued with Plato and lost his temper and called him a midget. Martinez had been delivered to the best hospital in Mexico City, unconscious. There he had been taken to an operating room and laid on the table and anaesthetized. He had been measured from the top of his scalp downward, and where the tape showed four feet and ten inches, lines had been drawn on his shins, a little closer to his knees than his ankles. Then a full team of surgeons and nurses had performed a double amputation, neatly and carefully and properly. Martinez had been kept in the hospital for two days, and then delivered home in an ambulance. Plato had delivered a get-well gift, with a card expressing the wish that the gift be appreciated and valued and kept permanently on display. Under the circumstances the wish was correctly interpreted as a command. Martinez's people had thought the gift was a tank of tropical fish, from its size and apparent weight and because it was clearly full of sloshing liquid. When they unwrapped it they saw that it was indeed a fish tank. But it contained no fish. It was full of formaldehyde and contained Martinez's feet and ankles and part of his shins, ten inches' worth in total.

Thus no one ever again mentioned Plato's height.

He had taken the call from the walled villa in the city and had promised a decision within twelve hours, but it really wasn't worth investing that much time on a relatively minor issue concerning a relatively minor outpost of a large and complex international organization. So after just an hour and a half his mind was made

41

up: he would authorize the silencing of the witness. He would send his man in as soon as was practical.

And he would go one step further. He would add a fifteenth item to the list. He was a little dismayed that it had not already been proposed. But then, he was Plato, and they weren't.

He would break the chain, for safety's sake.

He would have the lawyer silenced, too.

# FIVE

PETERSON LED REACHER OUT INTO THE FREEZING NIGHT AND asked if he was hungry. Reacher said yes, he was starving. So Peterson drove to a chain restaurant next to a gas station on the main route out to the highway. His car was a standard police specification Ford Crown Victoria, with winter tyres on the front and chains on the back. Inside it smelled of heat and rubber and hamburger grease and warm circuit boards. Outside it had nearly stopped snowing.

'Getting too cold to snow,' Peterson said. Which seemed to be true. The night sky had partially cleared and a vast frigid bowl of arctic air had clamped down. It struck through Reacher's inadequate clothing and set him shivering again on the short walk through the restaurant lot.

He said, 'I thought there was supposed to be a big storm coming.'

Peterson said, 'There are two big storms coming. This is what happens. They're pushing cold air ahead of them.'

'How long before they get here?'

'Soon enough.'

'And then it's going to warm up?'

'Just a little. Enough to let it snow.'

'Good. I'll take snow over cold.'

Peterson said, 'You think this is cold?'

'It ain't warm.'

'This is nothing.'

'I know,' Reacher said. 'I spent a winter in Korea. Colder than this.'

'But?'

'The army gave me a decent coat.'

'And?'

'At least Korea was interesting.' Which needled Peterson a little. The restaurant was empty and looked ready to close up. But they went in anyway. They took a table for two, a thirty-inch square of laminate that looked undersized between them.

Peterson said, 'The town of Bolton is plenty interesting.'

'The dead guy?'

'Yes,' Peterson said. Then he paused. 'What dead guy?'

Reacher smiled. 'Too late to take it back.'

'Don't tell me Chief Holland told you.'

'No. But I was in his office a long time.'

'Alone?'

'Not for a minute.'

'But he let you see the photographs?'

'He tried hard not to. But your cleaning staff did a good job on his window.'

'You saw them all?'

'I couldn't tell if the guy was dead or unconscious.'

'So you suckered me with that jab about Korea.'

'I like to know things. I'm hungry for knowledge.'

A waitress came by, a tired woman in her forties wearing sneakers under a uniform that featured a knotted necktie over a khaki shirt. Peterson ordered pot roast. Reacher followed his lead, and asked for coffee to drink.

Peterson asked, 'How long were you in the army?'

'Thirteen years.'

'And you were an MP?'

Reacher nodded.

'With medical training?'

'You've been talking to the bus passengers.'

'And the driver.'

'You've been checking me out.'

'Of course I have. Like crazy. What else do you think I was doing?'

'And you want me in your house tonight.'

'You got a better place to go?'

'Where you can keep an eye on me.'

'If you say so.'

'Why?'

'There are reasons.'

'Want to tell me what they are?'

'Just because you're hungry for knowledge?'

'I guess.'

'All I'll say is right now we need to know who's coming and going.'

Peterson said nothing more, and a minute later dinner arrived. Plates piled high, mashed potatoes, plenty of gravy. The coffee was an hour old, and it had suffered in terms of taste but gained in terms of strength.

Peterson asked, 'What exactly did you do in the MPs?'

Reacher said, 'Whatever they told me to.'

'Serious crimes?'

'Sometimes.'

'Homicides?'

'Everything from attempted to multiple.'

'How much medical training did you get?'

'Worried about the food here?'

'I like to know things too.'

'I didn't get much medical training, really. I was trying to make the old folks feel better, that's all.'

'They spoke well of you.'

'Don't trust them. They don't know me.'

Peterson didn't reply.

Reacher asked, 'Where was the dead guy found? Where the police car was blocking the side street?'

'No. That was different. The dead guy was somewhere else.'

'He wasn't killed there.'

'How do you know?'

'No blood in the snow. Hit someone hard enough in the head to kill them, the scalp splits. It's inevitable. And scalps bleed like crazy. There should have been a pool of blood a yard across.'

Peterson ate in silence for a minute. Then he asked: 'Where do you live?'

Which was a difficult question. Not for Reacher himself. There was a simple answer. He lived nowhere, and always had. He had been born the son of a serving military officer, in a Berlin infirmary, and since the day he had been carried out of it swaddled in blankets he had been dragged all over the world, through an endless blur of military bases and cheap off-post accommodations, and then he had joined up himself and lived the same way on his own account. Four years at West Point was his longest period of residential stability, and he had enjoyed neither West Point nor stability. Now that he was out of the service, he continued the transience. It was all he knew and it was a habit he couldn't break.

Not that he had ever really tried.

He said, 'I'm a nomad.'

Peterson said, 'Nomads have animals. They move around to find pasture. That's the definition.'

'OK, I'm a nomad without the animals part.'

'You're a bum.'

'Possibly.'

'You got no bags.'

'You got a problem with that?'

'It's weird behaviour. Cops don't like weird behaviour.'

'Why is it weirder to move around than spend every day in the same place?'

Peterson was quiet for a spell and then he said, 'Everyone has possessions.'

'I've got no use for them. Travel light, travel far.'

46

Peterson didn't answer.

Reacher said, 'Whatever, I'm no concern of yours. I never heard of Bolton before. If the bus driver hadn't twitched I'd have been at Mount Rushmore tonight.'

Peterson nodded, reluctantly.

'Can't argue with that,' he said.

Five minutes to ten in the evening.

Fifty-four hours to go.

Seventeen hundred miles to the south, inside the walled compound a hundred miles from Mexico City, Plato was eating too, a rib eye steak flown in all the way from Argentina. Nearly eleven in the evening local time. A late dinner. Plato was dressed in chinos and a white button-down shirt and black leather penny loafer shoes, all from the Brooks Brothers' boys' collection. The shoes and the clothes fit very well, but he looked odd in them. They were made for fat white middle-class American children, and Plato was old and brown and squat and had a shaved bullet head. But it was important to him to be able to buy clothes that fit right out of the box. Made-to-measure was obviously out of the question. Tailors would wield the tape and go quiet and then call out small numbers with studied and artificial neutrality. Alteration of off-the-rack items was just as bad. Visits from nervous local seamstresses and the furtive disposal of lengths of surplus fabric upset him mightily.

He put down his knife and his fork and dabbed his lips with a large white napkin. He picked up his cell phone and hit the green button twice, to return the last call he had received. When it was answered he said, 'We don't need to wait. Send the guy in and hit the witness.'

The man in the city villa asked, 'When?'

'As soon as would be prudent.'

'OK.'

'And hit the lawyer, too. To break the chain.'

'OK.'

'And make sure those idiots know they owe me big.'

'OK.'

47

'And tell them they better not bother me with this kind of shit ever again.'

Halfway through the pot roast Reacher asked, 'So why was that street blocked off?'

Peterson said, 'Maybe there was a power line down.'

'I hope not. Because that would be a strange sense of priorities. You leave twenty seniors freezing on the highway for an hour to guard a power line on a side street?'

'Maybe there was a fender bender.'

'Same answer.'

'Does it matter? You were already on your way into town by that point.'

'That car had been there two hours or more. Its tracks were full of snow. But you told us no one was available.'

'Which was true. That officer wasn't available. He was doing a job.'

'What job?'

'None of your business.'

'How big is your department?'

'Big enough.'

'And they were all busy?'

'Correct.'

'How many of them were busy sitting around doing nothing in parked cars?'

'You got concerns, I suggest you move here and start paying taxes and then talk to the mayor or Chief Holland.'

'I could have caught a chill.'

'But you didn't.'

'Too early to say.'

They went back to eating. Until Peterson's cell phone rang. He answered and listened and hung up and pushed his plate to one side.

'Got to go,' he said. 'You wait here.'

'I can't,' Reacher said. 'This place is closing up. It's ten o'clock. The waitress wants us out of here. She wants to go home.'

Peterson said nothing.

48

Reacher said, 'I can't walk. I don't know where I'm supposed to go and it's too cold to walk anyway.'

Peterson said nothing.

Reacher said, 'I'll stay in the car. Just ignore me.'

'OK,' Peterson said, but he didn't look happy about it. Reacher left a twenty dollar bill on the table. The waitress smiled at him. Which she should, Reacher thought. Two pot roasts and a cup of coffee at South Dakota prices, he was leaving her a sixty per cent tip. Or maybe it was all tip, if Bolton was one of those towns where cops ate for free.

The Crown Vic was still faintly warm inside. Peterson hit the gas and the chains bit down and the car pushed through the snow on the ground. There was no other traffic except for snow-ploughs taking advantage of the lull in the fall. Reacher had a problem with snowploughs. Not the machines themselves, but the compound word. A plough turned earth over and left it in place. Snowploughs didn't do that with snow. Snowploughs were more properly bulldozers. But whatever, Peterson overtook them all, didn't pause at corners, didn't yield, didn't wait for green lights.

Reacher asked, 'Where are we going?'

'Western suburbs.'

'Why?'

'Intruders.'

'In a house?'

'On the street. It's a Neighbourhood Watch thing.' No further explanation. Peterson just drove, hunched forward over the wheel, tense and anxious. Reacher sprawled in the seat beside him, wondering what kind of intruders could get a police depart-ment's deputy chief to respond so urgently to a busybody's call.

Seventeen hundred miles south the man in the walled Mexico City villa dialled long distance to the United States. His final task of the day. Eleven o'clock local time, ten o'clock Central Time in the big country to the north. The call was answered and the man in the villa relayed Plato's instructions, slowly and precisely. No room for misunderstanding. No room for error. He waited for confirmation and then he hung up. He didn't call Plato back. No point. Plato didn't understand the concept of confirmation. For Plato, obedience followed command the same way night followed day. It was inevitable. The only way it wouldn't happen was if the world had stopped spinning on its axis.

# SIX

PETERSON HAD HIS DASHBOARD RADIO TURNED UP HIGH AND Reacher picked out four separate voices from four separate cars. All of them were prowling the western suburbs and none of them had seen the reported intruders. Peterson aimed his own car down the streets they hadn't checked yet. He turned right, turned left, nosed into dead ends, backed out again, moved on. There was a moon low in the sky and Reacher saw neat suburban developments, small houses in straight rows, warm lights behind windows, all the sidewalks and driveways and yards rendered blue and flat and uniform by the thick blanket of snow. Roofs were piled high with white. Some streets had been visited by the ploughs and had high banks of snow in the gutters. Some were still covered with an undisturbed fresh layer, deep but not as deep as the yards and the driveways. Clearly this current fall was the second or the third in a week or so. Roads were covered and cleared, covered and cleared, in an endless winter rhythm.

Reacher asked, 'How many intruders?'

Peterson said, 'Two reported.'

'In a vehicle?'

'On foot.'

'Doing what?'

'Just walking around.'

'So stick to the ploughed streets. Nobody walks around in six inches of snow for the fun of it.'

Peterson slowed for a second and thought about it. Then he turned without a word and picked up a ploughed trail and retraced it. The plough had zigzagged through main drags and cross streets. The snow had been sheared thin and low and white. The excess was piled high to the sides, still soft and clean.

They found the intruders four minutes later.

There were two of them, shoulder to shoulder in a close standoff with a third man. The third man was Chief Holland. His car was parked twenty feet away. It was an unmarked Crown Vic. Either navy blue or black. It was hard to say, in the moonlight. Police specification, with antennas on the trunk lid and concealed emergency lights peeping up out of the rear parcel shelf. The driver's door was open and the engine was running. Twin puddles of black vapour had condensed and pooled in the thin snow beneath the twin exhausts. Holland had gotten out and stepped ahead and confronted the two guys head on. That was clear.

The two guys were tall and heavyset and unkempt. White males, in black Frye boots, black jeans, black denim shirts, black leather vests, fingerless black gloves, black leather bandannas. Each had an unzipped black parka thrown over everything else. They looked exactly like the dead guy in the crime scene photographs.

Peterson braked and stopped and stood off and idled thirty feet back. His headlights illuminated the scene. The standoff looked like it wasn't going well for Holland. He looked nervous. The two guys didn't. They had Holland crowded back with a snow bank behind him. They were in his space, leaning forward. Holland looked beaten. Helpless.

Reacher saw why.

The holster on Holland's belt was unsnapped and empty, but there was no gun in his hand. He was glancing down and to his left.

He had dropped his pistol in the snow bank.

Or had it knocked from his hand.

Either way, not good.

Reacher asked, 'Who are they?'

Peterson said, 'Undesirables.'

'So undesirable that the chief of police joins the hunt?'

'You see what I see.'

'What do you want to do?'

'It's tricky. They're probably armed.'

'So are you.'

'I can't make Chief Holland look like an idiot.'

Reacher said, 'Not his fault. Cold hands.'

'He just got out of his car.'

'Not recently. That car has been idling in place for ten minutes. Look at the puddles under the exhaust pipes.'

Peterson didn't reply. And didn't move.

Reacher asked again, 'Who are they?'

'What's it to you?'

'Just curious. They're scaring you.'

'You think?'

'If they weren't they'd be cuffed in the back of this car by now.'

'They're bikers.'

'I don't see any bikes.'

'It's winter,' Peterson said. 'They use pick-up trucks in winter.'

'That's illegal now?'

'They're tweakers.'

'What are tweakers?'

'Crystal meth users.'

'Amphetamines?'

'Methylated amphetamine. Smoked. Or to be technically accurate, vaporized and inhaled. Off of glass pipes or busted

53

light bulbs or aluminum foil spoons. You heat it up and sniff away. Makes you erratic and unpredictable.'

'People are always erratic and unpredictable.'

'Not like these guys.'

'You know them?'

'Not specifically. But generically.'

'They live in town?'

'Five miles west. There are a lot of them. Kind of camping out. Generally they keep themselves to themselves, but people don't like them.'

Reacher said, 'The dead guy was one of them.'

Peterson said, 'Apparently.'

'So maybe they're looking for their buddy.'

'Or for justice.' Peterson watched and waited. Thirty feet ahead the body language ballet continued as before. Chief Holland was shivering. With cold, or fear.

Or both.

Reacher said, 'You better do something.'

Peterson did nothing.

Reacher said, 'Interesting strategy. You're going to wait until they freeze to death.'

Peterson said nothing.

Reacher said, 'Only problem is, Holland will freeze first.'

Peterson said nothing.

'I'll come with you, if you like.'

'You're a civilian.'

'Only technically.'

'You're not properly dressed. It's cold out.'

'How long can it take?'

'You're unarmed.'

'Against guys like that, I don't need to be armed.'

'Crystal meth is not a joke. No inhibitions.'

'That just makes us even.'

'Users don't feel pain.'

'They don't need to feel pain. All they need to feel is conscious or unconscious.'

Peterson said nothing.

Reacher said, 'You go left and I'll go right. I'll turn them around and you get in behind them.'

Thirty feet ahead Holland said something and the two guys crowded forward and Holland backed off and tripped and sat down heavily in the snow bank. Now he was more than an arm's length from where his gun must have fallen.

Half past ten in the evening.

Reacher said, 'This won't wait.'

Peterson nodded. Opened his door.

'Don't touch them,' he said. 'Don't start anything. Right now they're innocent parties.'

'With Holland down on his ass?'

'Innocent until proven guilty. That's the law. I mean it. Don't touch them.' Peterson climbed out of the car. Stood for a second behind his open door and then stepped around it and started forward. Reacher matched him, pace for pace.

The two guys saw them coming.

Reacher went right and Peterson went left. The car had been a comfortable seventy degrees. The evening air was sixty degrees colder. Maybe more. Reacher zipped his jacket all the way and shoved his hands deep in his pockets and hunched his shoulders so that his collar rode up on his neck. Even so he was shivering after five paces. It was beyond cold. The air felt deeply refrigerated. The two guys ahead stepped back, away from Holland. They gave him room. Holland struggled to his feet. Peterson stepped alongside him. His gun was still holstered. Reacher tracked around over the thin white glaze and stopped six feet behind the two guys. Holland stepped forward and dug around in the snow bank and retrieved his weapon. He brushed it clean and checked the muzzle for slush and stuck it back in his holster.

Everyone stood still.

The shaved snow on the street was part bright white powder and part ice crystals. They shone and glittered in the moonlight. Peterson and Holland were staring straight at the two guys and even though he was behind them Reacher was pretty sure the two guys were staring right back. He was shivering hard and his teeth were starting to chatter and his breath was fogging in front of him.

Nobody spoke.

The guy on Reacher's right was more than six feet tall and close to four feet wide. Some of the bulk was goose-feather insulation in the black winter parka, but most of it was flesh and bone. The guy on Reacher's left was a little smaller in both directions, and more active. He was restless, moving from foot to foot, twisting at the waist, rolling his shoulders. Cold, for sure, but not actively shivering. Reacher guessed the twitching was all about chemistry, not temperature.

Nobody spoke.

Reacher said, 'Guys, either you need to move right along, or one of you needs to loan me a coat.'

The two men turned around, slowly. The big guy on the right had a white slab of a face buried deep in a beard. The beard was rimed with frost. Like a polar explorer, or a mountaineer. The smaller guy on the left had two days of stubble and jumpy eyes. His mouth was opening and closing like a goldfish pecking at the surface. Thin mobile lips, bad teeth.

The big guy on the right asked, 'Who are you?'

Reacher said, 'Go home. It's too cold for foolishness on the street.'

No reply.

Behind the two guys Peterson and Holland did nothing. Their guns were holstered and their holsters were snapped shut. Reacher planned his next moves. Always better to be prepared. He anticipated no major difficulty. He would have preferred the bigger guy to be on his left, because that would have maximized the impact from a right-handed blow by allowing a marginally longer swing, and he always liked to put the larger of a pair down first. But he was prepared to be flexible. Maybe the jittery guy should go down first. The bigger guy was likely to be slower, and maybe less committed, without the chemical assistance.

Reacher said, 'Coat or float, guys.'

No answer from the two men. Then behind them Chief Holland

came to life. He stepped forward one angry pace and said, 'Get the hell out of my town.'

Then he shoved the smaller guy in the back.

The smaller guy stumbled towards Reacher and then braced against the motion and spun back and started to whirl a fast one-eighty towards Holland with his fist cocking behind him like a pitcher aiming to break the radar gun. Reacher caught the guy by the wrist and held on for a split second and then let go again and the guy staggered through the rest of his turn all unbalanced and uncoordinated and ineffectual and ended with a weak late swing that missed Holland entirely.

But then he turned right back and aimed a second swing straight at Reacher. Which in Reacher's opinion took the whole innocent-until-proven-guilty thing right off the table. He stepped left and the incoming fist buzzed by an inch from his chin. The force behind it spun the guy onward and Reacher kicked his feet out from under him and dumped him face down on the ice. Whereupon the bigger guy started wading in, huge thighs, short choppy steps, fists like hams, trumpets of steam from his nose like an angry bull in a kid's picture book.

Easy meat.

Reacher matched the guy's charge with momentum of his own and smashed his elbow horizontally into the middle of the white space between the guy's beard and his hairline. Like running full tilt into a scaffolding pipe. Game over, except the smaller guy was already up on his knees and scrabbling for grip, hands and feet, like a sprinter in the blocks. So Reacher kicked him hard in the head. The guy's eyes rolled up and he toppled sideways and lay still with his legs folded under him.

Reacher put his hands back in his pockets.

Peterson said, 'Jesus.'

The two guys lay close together, black humps on the moonlit ice, steam rising off them in a cloud. Peterson said nothing more. Holland stalked back to his unmarked car and used the radio and came back a long minute later and said, 'I just called for two ambulances.'

He was looking straight at Reacher.

Reacher didn't respond.

Holland asked, 'You want to explain why I had to call for two ambulances?'

Reacher said, 'Because I slipped.'

'What?'

'On the ice.'

'That's your story? You slipped and just kind of blundered into them?'

'No, I slipped when I was hitting the big guy. It softened the blow. If I hadn't slipped you wouldn't be calling for two ambulances. You'd be calling for one ambulance and one coroner's wagon.'

Holland looked away.

Peterson said, 'Go wait in the car.'

The lawyer went to bed at a quarter to eleven. His children had preceded him by two hours and his wife was still in the kitchen. He put his shoes on a rack and his tie in a drawer and his suit on a hanger. He tossed his shirt and his socks and his underwear in the laundry hamper. He put on his pyjamas and took a leak and brushed his teeth and climbed under the covers and stared at the ceiling. He could still hear the laugh in his head, from the phone call just before he spun out on the highway. A bark, a yelp, full of excitement. Full of anticipation. Full of glee. *Eliminate the witness*, he had recited, and the man on the phone had laughed with happiness.

Reacher got back in Peterson's car and closed the door. His face was numb with cold. He angled the heater vents up and turned the fan to maximum. He waited. Five minutes later the ambulances showed up, with flashing lights pulsing bright red and blue against the snow. They hauled the two guys away. They were still out cold. Concussions, and probably some minor maxillary damage. No big deal. Three days in bed and a cautious week's convalescence would fix them up good as new. Plus painkillers.

58

Reacher waited in the car. Thirty feet ahead of him through the clear frigid air he could see Holland and Peterson talking. They were standing close together, half turned away, speaking low. Judging by the way they never glanced back, Reacher guessed they were talking about him.

Chief Holland was asking: 'Could he be the guy?'

Peterson was saying, 'If he's the guy, he just put two of his presumptive allies in the hospital. Which would be strange.'

'Maybe that was a decoy. Maybe they staged it. Or maybe one of them was about to say something compromising. So he had to shut them up.'

'He was protecting you, chief.'

'At first he was.'

'And then it was self-defence.'

'How sure are you he's not the guy?'

'One hundred per cent. It's just not feasible. It's a million-to-one chance he's here at all.'

'No way he could have caused the bus to crash right there?'

'Not without running up the aisle and physically attacking the driver. And no one said he did. Not the driver, not the passengers.'

'OK,' Holland said. 'So could the driver be the guy? Did he crash on purpose?'

'Hell of a risk.'

'Not necessarily. Let's say he knows the road because he's driven it before, summer and winter. He knows where it ices up. So he throws the bus into a deliberate skid.'

'A car was coming right at him.'

'So he says now.'

'But he could have been injured. He could have killed people. He could have ended up in the hospital or in jail for manslaughter, not walking around.'

'Maybe not. Those modern vehicles have all kinds of electronic systems. Traction control, antilock brakes, stuff like that. All he did was fishtail around a little and drive off the shoulder. No big deal. And then we welcomed him with open arms, like the Good Samaritan.'

Peterson said, 'I could talk to Reacher tonight. He was a witness on the bus. I could talk to him and get a better picture.'

Holland said, 'He's a psychopath. I want him gone.'

'The roads are closed.'

'Then I want him locked up.'

'Really?' Peterson said. 'Tell the truth, chief, he strikes me as a smart guy. Think about it. He saved you from a busted nose and he saved me from having to shoot two people. He did us both a big favour with what he did tonight.'

'Accidentally.'

'Maybe on purpose.'

'You think he knew what he was doing? Right there and then?'

'Yes, I think he did. I think he's the sort of guy who sees things five seconds before the rest of the world.'

'Are you serious?'

'Yes, sir. I've spent a little time with him.'

Holland shrugged.

'OK,' he said. 'Talk to him. If you really want to.'

'Can we use him for more? He's ex-military. He might know something.'

'About what?'

'About what's out there to the west.'

'You like him?'

'Doesn't matter if we like him. We can use him. It would be negligent not to, in the current circumstances.'

'That's an admission of defeat.'

'No, sir, it's common sense. Better to ask for help beforehand than get our asses kicked afterwards.'

'How much would we have to tell him?'

'Most of it,' Peterson said. 'Maybe all of it. He'd probably figure it out anyway.'

'Is this what you would do if you were chief?'

'Yes, sir, it is.'
Holland thought about it. Nodded.
'OK,' he said again. 'Good enough for me. Talk to him.'
Five minutes to eleven in the evening.
Fifty-three hours to go.

# SEVEN

PETERSON DROVE HOME IN HIS SQUAD CAR. WHICH REACHER thought was unusual. In his experience town cops dumped their squads in a motor pool and rode home in their personal vehicles. Then the next watch climbed in and drove away while the motors and the seats were still warm. But Peterson said the Bolton PD had a lot of cars. Every member of the department was issued with one. And every member of the department was required to live within ten minutes' drive of the station house.

Peterson lived within two minutes' drive, a mile out of town to the east, in a house sitting on a remnant of an old farm. The house was a solid wooden thing shaped like a pound cake, painted red with white trim, with warm yellow light in some of the windows. There was a matching barn. Both roofs were piled high with snow. The surrounding land was white and frozen and flat and silent. The lot was square. Maybe an acre. It was bounded by barbed wire strung on wizened posts. Maybe a foot of the fence showed above the fall.

The driveway was ploughed in a Y-shape. One leg led to the barn and the other led to the front of the house. Peterson parked in the barn. It was a big old open-fronted structure with three bays. One was occupied by a Ford pick-up truck with a plough blade on it, and one was full of stacked firewood. Reacher climbed out of the car and Peterson joined him and they backtracked down the ploughed strip and turned the tight angle and headed for the house.

The front door was a plain slab of wood painted the same red as the siding. It opened up just as Peterson and Reacher got close enough to touch it. A woman stood in the hallway with warm air and warm light behind her. She was about Peterson's age, well above medium height, and slender. She had fair hair pulled back into a ponytail and was wearing black pants and a wool sweater with a complex pattern knitted into it.

Peterson's wife, presumably.

All three of them paused in a mute pantomime of politeness, Peterson anxious to get in from the cold, his wife anxious not to let the heat out of the house, Reacher not wanting to just barge in uninvited. After a long second's hesitation the woman swung the door wider and Peterson put a hand on Reacher's back and he stepped inside. The hallway had a polished board floor and a low ceiling and wallpapered walls. On the left was a parlour and on the right was a dining room. Straight ahead in the back of the house was a kitchen. There was a wood stove going hard somewhere. Reacher could smell it, hot iron and a trace of smoke.

Peterson made the introductions. He spoke quietly, which made Reacher think there must be sleeping children upstairs. Peterson's wife was called Kim and she seemed to know all about the accident with the bus and the need for emergency quarters. She said she had made up a pull-out bed in the den. She said it apologetically, as if a real bedroom would have been better.

Reacher said, 'Ma'am, the floor would have been fine. I'm very sorry to put you to any trouble at all.'

She said, 'It's no trouble.'

'I hope to move on in the morning.'

'I don't think you'll be able to. It will be snowing hard before dawn.'

'Maybe later in the day, then.'

'They'll keep the highway closed, I'm afraid. Won't they, Andrew?'

Peterson said, 'Probably.'

His wife said, 'You're welcome to stay as long as you need to.'

Reacher said, 'Ma'am, that's very generous. Thank you.'

'Did you leave your bags in the car?'

Peterson said, 'He doesn't have bags. He claims he has no use for possessions.'

Kim said nothing. Her face was blank, as if she was having difficulty processing such information. Then she glanced at Reacher's jacket, his shirt, his pants. Reacher said, 'I'll head out to a store in the morning. It's what I do. I buy new every few days.'

'Instead of laundry?'

'Yes.'

'Why?'

'Because it's logical.'

'You'll need a warm coat.'

'Apparently.'

'Don't buy one. Too expensive, for just a few days. We can lend you one. My dad is your size. He keeps a coat here, for when he visits. And a hat and gloves.' She turned away and opened a closet door and leaned in to the back and wrestled a hanger off the rail. Came out with an enormous tan parka, the colour of mud. It had fat horizontal quilts of down the size of inner tubes. It was old and worn and had darker tan shapes all over it where patches and badges had been unpicked from it. The shapes on the sleeves were chevrons.

'Retired cop?' Reacher asked.

'Highway Patrol,' Kim Peterson said. 'They get to keep the clothes if they take the insignia off.'

The coat had a fur-trimmed hood, and it had a fur hat jammed in one pocket and a pair of gloves jammed in the other.

'Try it on,' she said.

64

It turned out that her father was not Reacher's size. He was bigger. The coat was a size too large. But too big is always better than too small. Reacher pulled it into position and looked down at where the stripes had been. He smiled. They made him feel efficient. He had always liked his sergeants. They did good work.

The coat smelled of mothballs. The hat smelled of another man's hair. It was made of tan nylon and rabbit fur.

'Thank you,' Reacher said. 'You're very kind.' He shrugged the coat off again and she took it from him and hung it on a hook on the hallway wall, just inside the entrance, next to where Peterson was hanging his own police-issue parka. Then they all headed for the kitchen. It ran left to right across most of the width of the house. There was all the usual kind of kitchen stuff in it, plus a beat-up table and six chairs, and a family-room area with a battered sofa and two armchairs and a television set. The wood stove was at the far end of the room. It was roaring like a locomotive. Beyond it was a closed door.

'That's the den,' Kim said. 'Go straight in.'

Reacher assumed he was being dismissed for the night, so he turned to say thanks once again, but found that Peterson was following right behind him. Kim said, 'He wants to talk to you. I can tell, because he isn't talking to me.'

The man who had been told to kill the witness and the lawyer set about cleaning the gun he had been given for the job. It was a Glock 17, not old, not new, well proved, well maintained. He stripped it, brushed it out, oiled it, and reassembled it. The cheeks of the grip were stippled, and there was some accumulated grime in the microscopic valleys. He worked it out with a Q-tip soaked in solvent. The maker's name was embossed near the heel, an overcomplicated and rather amateur graphic featuring a large letter G surrounding the rest of the word. It was easy to see the G merely as an outline, and therefore to overlook it. At first glance the name appeared to be LOCK. There was dirt over the whole thing. The man soaked the Q-tip again and started work and had it clean a minute later.

*   *   *

Peterson's den was a small, dark, square, masculine space. It was in the back corner of the house and had two outside walls with two windows. The drapes were made of thick plaid material and were drawn back, open. The other two walls had three doors in them. The door back to the family room, plus maybe a closet and a small bathroom. The remainder of the wall space was lined with yard-sale cabinets and an old wooden desk with a small refrigerator on it. On top of the refrigerator was an old-fashioned alarm clock with a loud tick and two metal bells. Out in the body of the room there was a low-slung leather chair that looked Scandinavian, and a two-seat sofa that had been pulled out and made up into a narrow bed.

Reacher sat down on the bed. Peterson took two bottles of beer from the refrigerator and twisted the tops off and pitched the caps into a trash basket and handed one of the bottles to Reacher. Then he lowered himself into the leather chair.

He said, 'We have a situation here.'

Reacher said, 'I know.'

'How much do you know?'

'I know you're pussyfooting around a bunch of meth-using bikers. Like you're scared of them.'

'We're not scared of them.'

'So why pussyfoot around?'

'We'll get to that. What else do you know?'

'I know you've got a pretty big police station.'

'OK.'

'Which implies a pretty big police department.'

'Sixty officers.'

'And you were working at full capacity all day and all evening, even to the point where the off-duty chief and the off-duty deputy chief had to respond to a citizen's call at ten o'clock in the evening. Which seems to be because most of your guys are on roadblock duty. Basically you've got your whole town locked down.'

'Because?'

'Because you're worried about someone coming in from the outside.'

Peterson took a long pull on his beer and asked, 'Was the bus crash for real?'

Reacher said, 'I'm not your guy.'

'We know you're not. You had no control. But maybe the driver is our guy.'

Reacher shook his head. 'Too elaborate, surely. Could have gone wrong a thousand different ways.'

'Was he really fighting the skid?'

'As opposed to what?'

'Causing it, maybe.'

'Wouldn't he have just killed the engine and faked a breakdown? Nearer the cloverleaf?'

'Too obvious.'

'I was asleep. But what I saw after I woke up looked real to me. I don't think he's your guy.'

'But he could be.'

'Anything's possible. But if it was me, I would have come in as a prison visitor. Chief Holland told me you get plenty of them. Heads on beds, six nights a week.'

'We know them all pretty well. Not too many short sentences out there. The faces don't change. And we watch them. Anyone we don't know, we call the prison to check they're on the list. And they're mostly women and children anyway. We're expecting a man.'

Reacher shrugged. Took a pull from his bottle. The beer was Miller. Next to him the refrigerator started humming. Warm air had gotten in when Peterson had opened the door. Now the machinery was fighting it.

Peterson said, 'The prison took two years to build. There were hundreds of construction workers. They built a camp for them, five miles west of us. Public land. There was an old army facility there. They added more huts and trailers. It was like a little village. Then they left.'

'When?'

'A year ago.'

'And?'

'The bikers moved in. They took the place over.'

67

'How many?'

'There are more than a hundred now.'

'And?'

'They're selling methamphetamine. Lots of it. East and west, because of the highway. It's a big business.'

'So bust them.'

'We're trying to. It isn't easy. We have no probable cause for a search out there. Which isn't normally a problem. A meth lab in a trailer, life expectancy is usually a day or two. They blow up. All you need to do is follow the fire department. All kinds of volatile chemicals. But these guys are very careful. No accidents yet.'

'But?'

'We caught a break. A big-time guy out of Chicago came west to negotiate a bulk purchase. He met with their top boy right here in Bolton. Neutral ground, and civilized. He bought a sample out the back of a pick-up truck in the restaurant parking lot, right where we had dinner.'

'And?'

'We have a witness who saw the whole transaction. The Chicago guy got away, but we grabbed the dope and the money and busted the biker. He's in the county lock-up right now, awaiting trial.'

'Their top boy? Didn't that give you probable cause to search his place?'

'His truck is registered in Kentucky. His driver's licence is from Alabama. He claims that he drove up here. He says he doesn't live here. We had nothing to link him to. We can't get a warrant based on the fact that he dresses like some other guys we've seen. Judges don't work that way. They want more.'

'So what's the plan?'

'We're going to roll him. We'll offer him a plea bargain and he'll give us what we need to clean out the whole mess.'

'Has he agreed?'

'Not yet. He's waiting us out. Waiting to see if the witness forgets stuff. Or dies.'

'Who's the witness?'

'A nice old lady, here in town. She's seventy-plus. Used to be a teacher and a librarian. Perfect credibility.'

'Is she likely to forget stuff or die?'

'Of course she is. That's how these people do it. They scare the witnesses. Or kill them.'

'Which is why you're worried about strangers coming to town. You think they're coming for her.'

Peterson nodded. Said nothing.

Reacher took a long pull on his bottle and asked, 'Why assume it will be a stranger? Couldn't the bikers come over and take care of it for themselves?'

Peterson shook his head. 'We're all over any biker who shows up in town. As you saw tonight. Everyone watches for them. So it won't be a biker. It would be self-defeating. Their whole strategy is to deny us probable cause.'

'OK.'

Peterson said, 'Someone else is on his way. Has to be. On their behalf. Someone we won't recognize when he gets here.'

# EIGHT

REACHER TOOK A THIRD LONG PULL ON HIS BOTTLE AND SAID, 'IT'S not the bus driver.'

Peterson asked, 'How sure are you?'

'How much money are these guys getting for their meth?'

'Two hundred bucks a gram, as far as we know, and we guess they're moving it in pick-up trucks, which is a whole lot of grams. They could be making millions.'

'In which case they can afford professionals. A professional hit man with a day job as a bus driver is an unlikely combination.'

Peterson nodded. 'OK, it's not the bus driver. Mr Jay Knox is innocent.'

'And you can vouch for all the prison visitors?'

'We watch them. They hit the motels, they get on the shuttle buses to the prison, they come back, they leave the next day. Any change to that pattern, we'd be all over them, too.'

'Where's the witness?'

'At home. Her name is Janet Salter. She's a real sweetie. Like a storybook grandma. She lives on a dead-end street, fortunately. We have a car blocking the turn, all day and all night. You saw it.'

'Not enough.'

'We know. We have a second car outside her house and a third parked one street over, watching the back. Plus women officers in the house, the best we've got, minimum of four at all times, two awake, two asleep.'

'When is the trial?'

'A month if we're lucky.'

'And she won't leave? You could stash her in a hotel. Maybe in the Caribbean. That's a deal I would take right now.'

'She won't leave.'

'Does she know the danger she's in?'

'We explained the situation to her. But she wants to do the right thing. She says it's a matter of principle.'

'Good for her.'

Peterson nodded. 'Good for us, too. Because we'll nail the whole lot of them. But hard on us, also. Because we're using a lot of resources.'

Reacher nodded in turn. 'Which is why you're pussyfooting. Why you're not confronting the bikers. Because an all-out war right now would stretch you too thin.'

'And because we have to sell this thing to a jury. We can't let defence counsel make out it's all part of a harassment campaign. Plus, the bikers aren't dumb. They keep their noses clean. Technically as individuals they haven't done anything wrong yet. At least not in public.'

'In fact the opposite seems to be true. I saw the photographs.'

'Exactly,' Peterson said. 'It looks like one of our good citizens beat one of theirs to death.'

The clock on the refrigerator ticked on and hit five to midnight. Fifty-two hours to go. Outside the window the moon had crept higher. The fallen snow was bright. The air was still. No wind. The cold was so intense Reacher could feel it striking through the farmhouse walls. There was a buffer zone about a foot deep, where the cold came creeping in before the heat from the iron stove overwhelmed it and beat it back.

Reacher asked, 'Is Chief Holland up to the job?'

Peterson said, 'Why do you ask?'

'First impressions. He looks a little overmatched to me.'

'Holland is a good man.'

'That's not an answer to my question.'

'Did you discuss your superiors when you were in the army?'

'All the time. With people of equal rank.'

'Are we of equal rank?'

'Approximately.'

'So what were your superiors like?'

'Some of them were good, and some of them were assholes.'

'Holland's OK,' Peterson said. 'But he's tired. His wife died. Then his daughter grew up and left home. He's all alone, and he feels a little beaten down.'

'I saw the photograph in his office.'

'Happier days. They made a nice family.'

'So is he up to the job?'

'Enough to ask for help when he needs it.'

'Who's he asking?'

'You.'

Reacher finished his Miller. He was warm, and comfortable, and tired. He said, 'What could I possibly do for him?'

Peterson said, 'There was an old army facility where they built the construction camp.'

'You told me that already.'

'We need to understand exactly what it was.'

'Don't you know?'

Peterson shook his head. 'It was put in a long time ago. There's a single stone building, about the size of a house.'

'Is that all?'

Peterson nodded. 'A long straight road leading to a single small building all alone on the prairie.'

'And it's the size of a house?'

'Smaller than this one.'

'What shape?'

'Square. Rectangular. Like a house.'

'With a roof?'

'Of course.'

'Because I'm wondering if it was a missile silo. There are plenty of them in the Dakotas.'

'It's not a silo.'

'Then it could be anything. Could be something they started and didn't finish.'

'We don't think so. There's a kind of folk memory with the older people. They say there were hundreds of engineers out there for months. And a security cordon. And a lot of coming and going. That's a lot of effort for a thing the size of a house.'

'I've heard of stranger things.'

'We need to know. Chances are we're going to need to go out there and make a hundred arrests. We need to know what we're dealing with.'

'Call somebody. Call the Department of the Army.'

'We have. We've called, the county board has called, the state government has called.'

'And?'

'Nobody ever got a reply.'

'How old are your older people?'

'Does that matter?'

'I'm asking when the place was built. Did they see all these engineers for themselves? Or just hear stories about them from their parents or grandparents?'

'The place is about fifty years old.'

'How long since soldiers were seen out there?'

'Never. The place was never used.'

Reacher shrugged. 'So it's an abandoned Cold War facility. Maybe never even completed. One day it seemed like a good idea, the next day it didn't. That kind of thing happened all the time, way back when, because strategy was fluid. Or because nobody had the faintest idea what they were doing. But it's no big deal. A stone house is going to be more resistant to small-arms fire than a hut or a trailer, but I'm assuming you're not planning on a shooting war out there anyway.'

'We need to know for sure.'

'I can't help you. I never served here. Never heard any talk.'

'You could make some back-channel calls. Maybe you still know people.'

'I've been out a very long time.'

'You could go west and take a look.'

'It's a stone building. Army stone is the same as anyone else's.'

'Then why the hundreds of engineers?'

'What's on your mind?'

'We're wondering if it's an underground facility. Maybe the stone building is just a stair head. It could be a warren down there. Their lab could be down there. Which would explain the lack of fires and explosions in the trailers. They could have turned the whole place into a fortress. There could be food and water and weapons down there. This whole thing could turn into a siege. We don't want that.'


Peterson stood up and stepped over to the desk and took two fresh bottles from the refrigerator. Which told Reacher they were only halfway through their conversation. Maybe only a third of the way through, if there was a six-pack in there.

Peterson said, 'There's more.'

'No kidding,' Reacher said.

'We've got their top boy locked up, but command and control is still happening. They're still functioning.'

'So he's got a deputy.'

'Gangs don't work like that.'

'So he's still communicating. Cell phone or smuggled notes.'

'Not happening.'

'You know that for sure?'

'Definitely.'

'Then it's through his lawyer. A private conference every day, they're pretending to discuss the case, your guy is really issuing verbal instructions, his lawyer is passing them on.'

'That's what we guessed. But that's not happening either.'

'How do you know?'

'Because they have concealed video and audio in the conference rooms.'

'For privileged discussions between lawyers and clients? Is that legal?'

'Maybe. It's a brand-new prison. And there's a lot of fine print in some of the new federal legislation.'

'He's not a federal prisoner.'

'OK, so no, it's probably not entirely legal.'

'But you're doing it anyway?'

'Yes,' Peterson said. 'And we haven't heard a single instruction or business detail. No notes passed, nothing written down.'

'You ever heard of the Fourth Amendment? This could screw your case.'

'We're not planning on using anything we hear. The prosecutor doesn't even know we're doing it. We just want advance warning, that's all, in the police department, in case they decide to move against the witness.'

'She'll be OK. You've got her buttoned up tight. It's only a month. You're on the hook for a little overtime, but that's all.'

'We competed for that prison.'

'Holland told me. Like a Toyota plant. Or Honda.'

'It was a give and take process.'

'It always is.'

'Correctional staff get tax breaks, we built houses, we expanded the school.'

'And?'

'Final item was we had to sign on to their crisis plan.'

'Which is what?'

'If there's an escape, we have a preassigned role.'

'Which is what?'

'The whole of the Bolton PD moves up to a prearranged perimeter a mile out.'

'All of you?'

'Every last one of us. On duty or off. Awake or asleep. Healthy or sick.'

'Are you serious?'

'It's what we had to agree. For the good of the town.'

'Not good,' Reacher said.

'Not good at all,' Peterson said. 'If that siren goes off, we drop everything and head north. All of us. Which means if that siren goes off any time in the next month, we leave Janet Salter completely unprotected.'

# NINE

REACHER FINISHED MOST OF HIS SECOND BEER AND SAID, 'THAT'S insane.'

'Only in reality,' Peterson said. 'Not on paper. The Highway Patrol is theoretically available to us as back-up. And the feds offered us witness protection for Mrs Salter. But the Highway Patrol is usually hours away all winter long, and Mrs Salter refused the protection. She says the bikers are the ones who should be locked up miles from home, not her.'

'Problem,' Reacher said.

'Tell me about it,' Peterson said.

Reacher glanced at the moonlit view out the window and said, 'But it's not exactly ideal escaping weather, is it? Not right now. Maybe not for months. There's two feet of virgin snow on the ground for five miles all around. If someone gets through whatever kind of a fence they have out there, they'll die of exposure inside an hour. Or get tracked by a helicopter. Their footsteps will be highly visible.'

Peterson said, 'No one escapes on foot any more. They stow away on a food truck or something.'

'So why form a perimeter a mile out?'

'Nobody said their crisis plan makes any sense.'

'So fake it. Leave some folks in place. At least the women in the house.'

'We can't. There will be a head count. We'll be audited. We don't comply to the letter, we'll get hit with federal supervision for the next ten years. The town signed a contract. We took their money.'

'For the extra cars?'

Peterson nodded. 'And for housing. Everyone lives within ten minutes, everyone gets a car, everyone keeps his radio on, everyone responds instantaneously.'

'Can't you stick Mrs Salter in a car and take her with you?'

'We're supposed to keep civilians away. We certainly can't take one with us.'

'Has anyone escaped so far?'

'No. It's a brand-new prison. They're doing OK.'

'So hope for the best.'

'You don't get it. We would hope for the best. If this was about random chance or coincidence, we wouldn't be sweating it. But it isn't. Because the same guy who wants us out of Janet Salter's house has the actual personal power to make that happen, any old time he wants to.'

'By escaping on cue?' Reacher said. 'I don't think so. I know prisons. Escapes take a long time to organize. He would have to scope things out, make a plan, find a truck driver, build trust, get money, make arrangements.'

'There's more. It gets worse.'

'Tell me.'

'Part two of the crisis plan is for a prison riot. The corrections people move in off the fence and we take over the towers and the gate.'

'All of you?'

'Same as part one of the plan. And prison riots don't take a long time to organize. They can start in a split second. Prisons are riots just waiting to happen, believe me.'

There was no third bottle of beer. No more substantive conversation. Just a few loose ends to tie up, and a little reiteration. Peterson said, 'You see? The guy can time it almost to the minute. The wrong thing gets said to the wrong person, a minute later a fight breaks out, a minute after that there's a full-blown riot brewing, we get the call, ten minutes after that we're all more than five miles from Janet Salter's house.'

'He's in lock-up,' Reacher said. 'The county jail, right? Which is a separate facility. Nobody riots in lock-up. They're all awaiting trial. They're all busy making out like they're innocent.'

'He's a biker. He'll have friends in the main house. Or friends of friends. That's how prison gangs work. They look after their own. And there are lots of ways of communicating.'

'Not good,' Reacher said again.

'Not good at all,' Peterson said. 'When the siren sounds, we leave the old-timer civilian on the desk, and that's it. He's supposed to call us back if there's a terrorist alert, but short of that, our hands are tied.'

'You expecting a terrorist alert?'

'Not here. Mount Rushmore has symbolic value, but that's Rapid City's problem.'

Reacher asked, 'Did you expand the police department too? Like the schools?'

Peterson nodded. 'We had to. Because the town grew.'

'How much did you expand?'

'We doubled in size. By which time we were competing with the prison for staff. It was hard to keep standards up. Which is a big part of Chief Holland's problem. It's like half of us are his from the old days, and half of us aren't.'

'I can't help him,' Reacher said. 'I'm just a guy passing through.'

'You can make those calls to the army. That would help him.

79

If we get through the next month, we're going to need that information.'

'I've been out too long. It's a new generation now. They'll hang up on me.'

'You could try.'

'I wouldn't get past the switchboard.'

'Back when I came on the job we had a special emergency number for the FBI office in Pierre. The system changed years ago, but I still remember the number.'

'So?'

'I'm guessing there's a number you remember, too. Maybe not for a switchboard.'

Reacher said nothing.

Peterson said, 'Make the calls for us. That's all, I promise. We'll handle the rest, and then you can get on your way.'

Reacher said nothing.

'We can offer you a desk and chair.'

'Where?'

'At the police station. Tomorrow.'

'You want me to come to work with you? To the police station? You don't quite trust me yet, do you?'

'You're in my house. With my wife and children sleeping in it.'

Reacher nodded.

'Can't argue with that,' he said.

But Kim Peterson wasn't sleeping. Not right then. Ten minutes after Andrew Peterson left him alone Reacher got tired of the stale hop smell from the four empty beer bottles, so he trapped their necks between his knuckles and carried them two in each hand out to the kitchen, hoping to find a trash bin. Instead he found Kim Peterson tidying her refrigerator. The room was dark but the light inside the appliance was bright. She was bathed in a yellow glow. She was wearing an old candlewick bathrobe. Her hair was down. Reacher held up the four bottles, as a mute inquiry.

'Under the sink,' Kim Peterson said.

Reacher bent down and opened the cabinet door. Lined up the bottles neatly with six others already there.

'Got everything you need?' she asked him.

'Yes, thanks.'

'Did Andrew ask you to do something for him?'

'He wants me to make some calls.'

'About the army camp?'

Reacher nodded.

'Are you going to do it?'

Reacher said, 'I'm going to try.'

'Good. That place drives him crazy.'

'I'll do my best.'

'Promise?'

'Ma'am?'

'Promise me, if he asks, would you help him any way you can? He works too hard. He's responsible for everything now. Chief Holland is overwhelmed. He barely knows half his department. Andrew has to do everything.'

There was a tiny bathroom off the den and Reacher used it to take a long hot shower. Then he folded his clothes over the back of the chair that Peterson had used and climbed under the covers. The sofa springs creaked and twanged under his weight. He rolled one way, rolled the other, listened to the loud tick of the clock, and was asleep a minute later.

Five to one in the morning.

Fifty-one hours to go.

# TEN

REACHER WOKE UP AT TEN TO SEVEN, TO A SILENT SEPULCHRAL world. Outside the den windows the air was thick with heavy flakes. They were falling gently but relentlessly on to a fresh accumulation that was already close to a foot deep. There was no wind. Each one of the billions of flakes came parachuting straight down, sometimes wavering a little, sometimes spiralling, sometimes sidestepping an inch or two, each one disturbed by nothing except its own featherweight instability. Most added their tiny individual masses to the thick white quilt they landed on. Some stuck to fantastic vertical feathered shapes on power lines and fence wires, and made the shapes taller.

The bed was warm but the room was cold. Reacher guessed that the iron stove had been banked overnight, its embers hoarded, its air supply cut off. He wondered for a moment about the correct protocol for a house guest in such circumstances. Should he get up and open the dampers and add some wood? Would that be helpful? Or would it be presumptuous? Would it upset a delicate and long-established combustion schedule and condemn his hosts to an inconvenient midnight visit to the woodpile two weeks down the road?

In the end Reacher did nothing. Just kept the covers pulled up to his chin and closed his eyes again.

Five to seven in the morning.

Forty-five hours to go.

Seventeen hundred miles to the south the day was already an hour older. Plato was eating breakfast in the smaller of his two outdoor dining rooms. The larger was reserved for formal dinners, and therefore little used, because formal dinners meant business dinners, and most of his current business associates were Russians, and Russians didn't much care for the evening heat a hundred miles from Mexico City. They preferred air conditioning. Plato supposed it was a question of what they were accustomed to. He had heard that parts of Russia were so cold you could spit, and the saliva would freeze and bounce off the ground like a marble. Personally he didn't believe it. He was prepared to accept that parts of Russia recorded very low temperatures, and certainly some of the extreme numbers he had seen in almanacs and weather reports might indeed freeze a small volume of organic liquid in the space and time between mouth and ground. But to survive in such an environment he was sure a human would have to wear a ski mask, possibly made from silk or a more modern synthetic material, and spitting was categorically impossible while wearing a ski mask. And he understood that in general extremely low temperatures went hand in hand with extremely low humidity, which would discourage spitting anyway, maybe even to the point of impracticability. Thus the anecdote was illustrative without being functionally true.

Plato was proud of his analytical abilities.

He was thinking about Russians because he had received an intriguing proposal from one of them, an hour ago by telephone. It was the usual kind of thing. A cousin of a friend of a brother-in-law wanted a bulk quantity of a certain substance, and could Plato help the man? Naturally Plato's first priority was to help

Plato, so he had viewed the proposal through that lens, and he had arrived at an interesting conclusion, which might, with a little honing and salesmanship, be turned into an advantageous deal. Dramatically advantageous, in fact, and completely one-sided in his own favour, of course, but then, he was Plato, and the unnamed Russian cousin wasn't.

There were three main factors.

First, the deal would require a fundamental shift in the Russian's initial baseline assumption, in that the bulk quantity would not be transported to the Russian, but the Russian would be transported to the bulk quantity.

Second, the deal would require complete faith on Plato's part in the notion that a bird in the hand was worth two in the bush.

And third, the deal would change things a little, up in South Dakota. Therefore the situation up there had to remain pristine, and viable, and immaculate, and perfectly attractive. Perfectly marketable, in other words. Which meant the witness and the lawyer had to be dealt with sooner rather than later.

Plato reached for his phone.

At fourteen minutes past seven the old farmhouse was still quiet. At fifteen minutes past, it burst into life. Reacher heard the thin beep and wail of alarm clocks through walls and ceilings, and then the stumbling tread of footsteps on the second floor. Four sets. Parents, and two children. Two boys, Reacher figured, judging by the uninhibited clumsiness of their progress. Doors opened and closed, toilets flushed, showers ran. Ten minutes later there was noise in the kitchen. The gulp and hiss of a coffee machine, the padded slam of the refrigerator door, the scrape of chair legs on floorboards. Again, Reacher wondered about applicable protocol. Should he just come out and join the family at breakfast? Or would that scare the children? He supposed it would depend on their ages and their constitutions. Should he wait to be invited? Or should he wait until the children had left for school? Would they be going to school at all, with a foot of new snow on the ground?

He showered fast and dressed in the tiny bathroom and made

the bed and sat on it. A minute later he heard the scrape of a chair and small fast feet on the boards and an inexpert knock on his door. It opened immediately and a boy stuck his head inside. The kid was maybe seven years old. He was a miniature version of Andrew Peterson. His face was equal parts resentment at being sent to do a chore, and apprehension for what he might find, and open curiosity about what he had actually found.

He stared for a second and said, 'Mama says come get a cup of coffee.'

Then he disappeared.

By the time Reacher got through the door both children had left the kitchen. He could hear them running up the stairs. He imagined he could see disturbances in the air behind them, dust and vortexes, like a cartoon. Their parents were sitting quietly at the table. They were dressed the same as the day before, Peterson in uniform, his wife in sweater and pants. They weren't talking. Any kind of conversation would have been drowned out by running feet above. Reacher took coffee from the pot and by the time he was back at the table Peterson had gotten up and was on his way out to the barn to start the pick-up to plough his way out to the street. His wife was on her way upstairs to make sure the children were ready. A minute later both boys ran down the stairs and crashed out through the door. Reacher heard the rattle of a heavy diesel engine and saw a glimpse of yellow through the snow. The school bus, apparently right on schedule, undeterred by the weather.

A minute after that, the house was completely silent. Kim didn't come back to the kitchen. Reacher got nothing to eat. No big deal. He was used to being hungry. He sat alone until Peterson stuck his head in the hallway and called for him. He took the borrowed Highway Patrol coat from the hook and headed out.

Five to eight in the morning.

Forty-four hours to go.

The lawyer was wrestling with his garage door again. There was a new foot of snow out on the driveway and it had drifted a little against the door, jamming it in its tracks. He had his overshoes on, and his shovel in his hand. The motor on the garage ceiling was straining. He grabbed the inside handle and jerked upward. The mechanism's chains bucked and bounced and the door came up in a rush and the peak of the snowdrift outside fell inward. He shovelled it back out and then started his car and got ready to face his day.

His day began with breakfast. He had taken to eating it out. In some ways, normal small-town behaviour. A coffee shop, some banter, some networking, some connections. All valuable. But not worth more than a half-hour's investment. Forty-five minutes at the most. Now he was spending at least an hour in his booth. Sometimes, an hour and a half.

He was afraid to go to work.

The message forms his firm used were yellow. Every morning his secretary handed him a wad. Most were innocent. But some said *Client requests conference re case # 517713*. There was no case with that number. No file. Nothing written down. Such a note was a code. An instruction, really, to head up to the prison and take mental dictation.

Most days he got no such note. Some days he did. There was no way of predicting it. It was a part of his morning ritual now, to stand in front of his secretary's desk, with his hand out and his heart in his mouth, waiting to see what his life would do to him next.

Reacher saw nothing on the ride downtown except snow. Snow on the ground, snow in the air. Snow everywhere. The world was slow and silent and shrunken. Traffic was light and was huddled together in narrow rutted lanes in the middle of roads. Small waffles of snow pelted up off tyres in cautious rooster tails. Small convoys joined up and crept along like slow trains, doing twenty miles an hour, or less. But Peterson's cruiser was warm and safe and solid. A heavy car on flat land, with chains on the back and winter tyres on the front. No problem.

By day through the snow the police station looked longer and lower than it had by night. It was a sprawling one-storey building built of white brick. It had a flat roof with microwave dishes and

86

radio antennas bolted to steel superstructures. It reminded Reacher of a classic State Police barracks. Maybe it had been built from a standardized blueprint. There were plenty of squad cars in the lot, still warm, just parked. Day watch personnel, presumably, coming in from home for briefing ahead of their eight-thirty start. There was a small front-loader working between the cars, bustling around on rubber caterpillar tracks, shovelling snow into a pile that was already eight feet high. Peterson seemed relaxed. Reacher figured he was feeling good about the snow. It limited fast access to anywhere, including Janet Salter's house. Intruders would wait for a better day. Stealthy approaches were hard to make through thigh-high drifts.

Reacher took the parka but left the gloves and the hat in the car. Too personal. He would replace them with items of his own. Inside the lobby there was a different old guy on the stool behind the counter. The day watch aide. Same kind of age as the guy the night before, same kind of civilian clothing, but a different individual. Peterson led Reacher right past him and down a corridor into a large open-plan squad room. It was full of noise and talk and men and women in uniform. They had go-cups of coffee, they were making notes, they were reading bulletins, they were getting ready to head out. There were close to thirty of them. A sixty-strong department, split equally between day and night duty. Some were young, some were old, some were neat, some were a mess. A real mixed bag. *We doubled in size*, Peterson had said. *It was hard to keep standards up*. Reacher saw the proof right there in front of him. It was easy enough to pick out the new hires from the old hands, and easy to see the friction between them. Unit cohesion had been disrupted, and professionalism had been compromised. Us and them. Reacher saw Chief Holland's problem. He was dealing with two departments in one. And he didn't have the energy for it. He should have retired. Or the mayor should have canned him, before the ink was dry on the prison deal.

But new or old, all the cops were punctual. By eight thirty the room was almost completely deserted. Clearly the roadblocks were eating manpower, and presumably snow days brought

87

fender benders by the dozen. Only two cops stayed behind. Both were in uniform. One had a name badge that said *Kapler*. The other had a name badge that said *Lowell*. Neither one was wearing a belt. No guns, no radios, no cuffs. Both were somewhere in their mid-thirties. Kapler was dark, with the remnant of a fading tan. Lowell was fair and red-faced, like a local boy. Both looked fit and strong and active. Neither looked happy. Kapler went clockwise and Lowell went counterclockwise and they emptied out-trays all around the room and carried the resulting piles of paper away through a blank door further down the corridor.

Reacher asked, 'What's that all about?'

Peterson said, 'Normal clerical duties.'

'While you're hurting for manpower? I don't think so.'

'So what's your guess?'

'Disciplinary. They did something wrong and they've been grounded. Holland took their guns away.'

'I can't talk about it.'

'Are they new or old?'

'Lowell has been here a spell. He's local. An old Bolton family. Kapler's new, but not too new. He came up from Florida two years ago.'

'Why? For the weather? I thought that worked the other way around.'

'He needed a job.'

'Because? What went wrong for him down there?'

'Why should something have gone wrong?'

'Because with the greatest possible respect, if you're in Florida law enforcement, South Dakota is the kind of place you go when you run out of alternatives.'

'I don't know the details. He was hired by Chief Holland and the mayor.'

'So what did Lowell do to deserve him as a partner?'

'Lowell's an odd duck,' Peterson said. 'He's a loner. He reads books.'

'What did they do to get themselves grounded?'

'I can't talk about it. And you've got work to do. Pick any desk you like.'

*       *       *

Reacher picked a desk way in the back corner. An old habit. It was a plain laminate thing, and the chair was adjusted for a small person. It was still warm. There was a keyboard and a screen on the desk, and a console telephone. The screen was blank. Switched off. The phone had buttons for six lines and ten speed dials.

Peterson said, 'Dial nine for a line.'

*I'm guessing there's a number you remember, too. Maybe not for a switchboard.*

Reacher dialled. Nine for a line, then a Virginia area code, then seven more digits. A number he remembered.

He got a recording, which was not what he remembered.

The recording featured a man's voice, speaking slowly and ponderously, with undue emphasis on his first three words. His message said, 'You have reached the Bureau of Labor Statistics. If you know your party's extension, you may dial it at any time. Otherwise, please choose from the following menu.' Then came a long droning list, press one for this, press two for that, three for the other thing, agriculture, manufacturing, non-food service industries.

Reacher hung up.

'You know another number?' Peterson said.

'No.'

'Who were you calling?'

'A special unit. An investigative department. Kind of elite. Like the army's own FBI, but much smaller.'

'Who did you get instead?'

'Some government office. Something about labour statistics.'

'I guess things change.'

'I guess they do,' Reacher said.

Then he said, 'Or maybe they don't. At least, not fundamentally.'

He dialled again. The same number. He got the same recording. *If you know your party's extension, you may dial it at any time.* He dialled 110. Heard a click and a purr and a new dial tone. A new voice, live, after just one ring.

89

It said, 'Yes?' A Southern accent, a man, probably late twenties, almost certainly a captain, unless the world had gone mad and they were letting lieutenants or NCOs answer that particular phone now, or, worse still, civilians.

Reacher said, 'I need to speak to your commanding officer.'

'Whose commanding officer?'

'Yours.'

'Who exactly do you think you're speaking with?'

'You're the 110th MP HQ in Rock Creek, Virginia.'

'Are we?'

'Unless you changed your phone number. There used to be a live operator. You had to ask for room 110.'

'Who exactly am I speaking to?'

'I used to work for the 110th.'

'In what capacity?'

'I was its first CO.'

'Name?'

'Reacher.'

Silence for a moment.

Reacher asked, 'Does anyone go ahead and actually choose from that menu?'

'Sir, if you worked for the 110th, you'll know that this is an active and open emergency channel. I'll have to ask you to state your business immediately.'

'I want to talk to your commanding officer.'

'Concerning?'

'A favour I need. Tell him to look me up in the files and call me back.' Reacher read out the number from a label stuck to the console in front of him.

The guy on the other end hung up without a word.

Five to nine in the morning.

Forty-three hours to go.

# ELEVEN

AT NINE THIRTY THE PHONE ON REACHER'S BORROWED DESK rang, but the call was not for him. He stretched the cord and passed the handset to Peterson. Peterson gave his name and rank and then listened for the best part of a minute. He asked whoever it was on the other end to stay in touch, and then he passed the handset back. Reacher hung it up. Peterson said, 'We need your information just as soon as you can get it.'

Reacher pointed at the console in front of him. 'You know how it is with kids today. They never write, they never call.'

'I'm serious.'

'What changed?'

'That was the DEA on the line. The actual Drug Enforcement Administration. The actual federal bureau. From Washington D.C. A courtesy call. Turns out they have a wiretap on a guy they think is a Russian dope dealer. New to the scene, trying to make a name, trawling for deals, out of Brooklyn, New York. A guy in Mexico called Plato just called him about a property for sale five miles west of a town called Bolton, in South Dakota.'

'A property for sale?'

'Those were the words they used.'

'So what is this? Real estate or dope dealing?'

'If there's an underground lab out there, then it's both, isn't it? And that's going to be the DEA's next question. It's a no-brainer. They'll be building their file and they'll call us to ask what exactly that place is.'

'Tell them to call the Department of the Army direct. Quicker all around.'

'But that would make us look like idiots. We can't admit we've had a place next to us for fifty years and we don't even know what it is.'

Reacher shrugged. Pointed at the phone again. 'You'll know as soon as I do. Which might be never.'

'You were their commanding officer? An elite unit?'

Reacher nodded. 'For a spell.' Then he said: 'Plato is a weird name for a Mexican, don't you think? Sounds more like a Brazilian name to me.'

'No, Yugoslavian,' Peterson said. 'Like that old dictator.'

'That was Tito.'

'I thought he was a South African bishop.'

'That was Tutu.'

'So who was Plato?'

'An ancient Greek philosopher. The pupil of Socrates, the teacher of Aristotle.'

'So what has Brazil got to do with all of that?'

'Don't ask,' Reacher said.

Kapler and Lowell came back to the squad room. They distributed memos still hot and curled from the photocopier, one into every in-tray, and then they slouched out again. Peterson said, 'That's their day's work done, right there. Now comes a five-hour lunch break, probably. What a waste.'

'What did they do?'

'I can't talk about it.'

'That bad?'

'No, not really.'

92

'So what was it?'

'I can't talk about it.'

'Yes you can.'

'OK, three days ago they were out of radio contact for an hour. Wouldn't say why or how or what they were doing. We can't allow that. Because of the prison plan.'

The phone rang again at twenty minutes to ten. Reacher picked it up and said, 'Yes?'

A woman's voice asked, 'Major Reacher?'

'Yes.'

'Do you know who I am?'

'Keep talking.'

'You taught a class in your last year in the service.'

'Did I?'

'About integrating military and federal investigations. I took the class. Don't you recognize my voice?'

'Keep talking.'

'What do you want me to say?' Right then Reacher wanted her to say plenty, because she had a great voice. It was warm, slightly husky, a little breathy, a little intimate. He liked the way it whispered in his ear. He liked it a lot. In his mind he pictured its owner as blonde, not more than thirty-five years old, not less than thirty. Probably tall, probably a looker. Altogether a terrific voice, for sure.

But not a voice he recognized, and he said so.

The voice said, 'I'm very disappointed. Maybe even a little hurt. Are you sure you don't remember me?'

'I need to speak to your CO.'

'That will have to wait. I can't believe you don't know who I am.'

'Can I take a guess?'

'Go ahead.'

'I think you're some kind of a bullshit filter. I think your CO wants to know if I'm for real. If I say I remember you, I fail the test. Because I don't. We never met. Maybe I wish we had, but we didn't.'

93

'But I took your class.'

'You didn't. You read my file, that's all. The course title was for public consumption only. The class was about screwing the feds, not cooperating with them. If you had been in the room with me, you'd know that.'

A smile in the voice. 'Good work. You just passed the test.'

'So who are you, really?'

'I'm you.'

'What does that mean?'

'I'm CO of the 110th Special Unit.'

'Really?'

'Really and truly.'

'Outstanding. Congratulations. How is it?'

'I'm sure you can imagine. I'm sitting at your old desk, right now, both metaphorically and literally. Do you remember your desk?'

'I had a lot of desks.'

'Here at Rock Creek.'

Actually Reacher remembered it pretty well. An old-style government desk, made of steel, painted green, the finish on the edges already worn back to bright metal by the time he inherited it.

The voice said, 'There's a big dent on the right-hand side. People say you made it, with someone's head.'

'People say?'

'Like a folk legend. Is it true?'

'I think the movers did it.'

'It's perfectly concave.'

'Maybe they dropped a bowling ball.'

'I prefer the legend.'

Reacher asked, 'What's your name?'

The voice said, 'Make one up for me.'

'What?'

'Let's keep this off the record. Give me a code name.'

'This is a private conversation.'

'Not really. Our system shows you're calling from a police station. I'm sure it has a switchboard and recording devices.'

Reacher said, 'OK, keep talking. I should try to make the name fit the person.'

'What do you want me to say?'

'Read the phone book. That would work for me.'

Another smile in the voice. 'People say the dent in the desk came from a colonel's head. They say that's why you got canned from the 110th.'

'I didn't get canned. I got new orders, that's all.'

'Only because no one liked that particular colonel. But you definitely walked the plank. That's what people say.'

'Amanda.'

'Amanda? OK, that's who I am. You need me again, call the number and ask for Amanda. Now, what can I do for you today?'

'There's a small town in South Dakota called Bolton. Roughly in the middle of the state, twelve or thirteen miles north of I-90.'

'I know where it is. Our system includes your coordinates. I'm looking at Bolton right now.'

'Looking at it how?'

'On my laptop. With Google Earth.'

'You guys have it easy.'

'Technology is indeed a wonderful thing. How can I help you?'

'Five miles west of town is an abandoned Cold War installation. I need to know what it was.'

'Can't you tell what it was?'

'I haven't seen it. And apparently there isn't much to see. It could be nothing. But I want you to check it out for me.'

'You sure it isn't a missile silo? The Dakotas are full of them.'

'They say it isn't a silo. Doesn't sound like one, either.'

'OK, hold on. I'm zooming and scrolling. According to the most recent image the only thing west of town looks like a prison camp. Fifteen huts and an older building, in two lines of eight. Plus a long straight road. Maybe two miles of it.'

'Does the older building look like a house?'

'From above it looks exactly like a house.'

'OK, but I need more than that.'

'You want me to come all the way up to South Dakota and go out there and look at it with you?'

'Since I'm stuck here in a snowstorm with nothing much else to do, that would be great. But a records check will do it. It'll show up somewhere. I need to know its purpose, its scope, and its architecture.'

'Call me back at close of business.'

Then there was a click, and the voice was gone.

Five to ten in the morning.

Forty-two hours to go.

# TWELVE

THE LAWYER PARKED HIS CAR IN HIS OFFICE LOT AND PUT ON HIS overshoes. He took them off again inside his building's lobby and placed them in a plastic grocery bag and carried the bag with his briefcase to the elevator. His secretary greeted him at her cubicle outside his door. He didn't answer. He didn't yet know whether it was or wasn't a good morning. He just held out his hand for his message slips.

There were eight of them.

Three were trivial inter-office issues.

Four were legitimate legal matters.

The last was a request for a client conference at the prison, on an urgent matter relating to case number 517713, at noon.

Reacher sat alone for a spell and then wandered out and found Peterson in an empty office off the corridor near the entrance to the squad room. The office had four desks boxed together in the centre of the space. The walls had long horizontal pin boards extending waist-high to head-high. Peterson was tacking yesterday's crime scene photographs to the boards. The dead guy, dressed in black. The establishing shot, the close-ups. Snow on the ground, blunt force trauma to the right temple. No blood.

Peterson said, 'We just got the autopsy report. He was definitely moved.'

Reacher asked, 'Were there other injuries?'

'Some perimortem bruising.'

'Are there bad parts of town?'

'Some are worse than others.'

'Have you checked the bars?'

'For what?'

'Newly cleaned floors, suspicious stains.'

'You think this was a bar fight?'

'Somewhere in the low rent district, but not in the war zone.'

'Why?'

'Tell me what the pathologist said about the weapon.'

'It was round, fairly smooth, probably machined metal or wood, maybe a fence post or a rainwater pipe.'

'Neither one of those,' Reacher said. 'A fence post or a rainwater pipe has a uniform diameter. Too wide to grip hard enough to swing hard enough. My guess is it was a baseball bat. And baseball bats are relatively hard to find in the winter. They're in closets or garages or basements or attics. Except sometimes they're under bars, where the bartender can grab them real quick. Not in the good part of town, of course, and in the war zone they'd probably want a shotgun.'

Peterson said nothing.

Reacher asked, 'Where do the prison guards drink?'

'You think it was one of them?'

'It takes two to tango. Prison guards are used to the rough and tumble.'

Peterson was quiet for a beat. 'Anything else?'

Reacher shook his head. 'I'm going out. I'll be back later.'

The snow was still heavy. Peterson's car was already just a humped white shape in the lot. Reacher turned up the hood of his borrowed coat and walked straight past it. He made it out to the sidewalk and peered left, peered right. The snow swirled around him and blew in under his hood and clogged his hair and his eyelashes and drifted down his neck. Directly opposite him was some kind of a public square or town park and beyond that was an array of commercial establishments. The distance was too great and the snow was too thick to make out exactly what they were. But one of them had a plume of steam coming out of a vent on the roof, which made it likely that it was either a dry cleaner or a restaurant, which made it a fifty-fifty chance that a late breakfast could be gotten there.

Reacher headed over, floundering through ploughed snow, slipping and sliding through the square. His ears and nose and chin went numb. He kept his hands in his pockets. The place with the steam was a coffee shop. He stepped inside, to hot wet air. A counter, and four tables. Jay Knox was alone at one of them. The bus driver. Judging by the state of his table he had finished a large meal some time ago. Reacher stepped up opposite him and put his hand on a chair back, ready to pull it out, like a request. Knox seemed neither pleased nor displeased to see him. Just preoccupied, and a little sullen.

Reacher sat down anyway and asked, 'You making out OK?'

Knox shrugged. 'They put me with some people.'

'And?'

'I suppose they're nice enough.'

'But you came out for a long slow breakfast.'

'I don't like to impose.'

'Didn't they offer?'

'I don't particularly like them, OK?'

Reacher said nothing.

Knox asked, 'Where did they put you?'

'With the cop who came to the bus.'

'So why are you here? Didn't the cop give you breakfast?'

Reacher didn't answer. Just said: 'Any news?'

'The tow trucks got here this morning. They pulled the bus off the highway. We're leasing a replacement out of Minneapolis. Should be here soon after the storm passes.'

'Not so bad.'

'Except that it will come with its own driver. Which means I'll be a passenger all the way back to Seattle. Which means I won't get paid, effective four o'clock yesterday afternoon.'

'Not so good.'

'They should do something about that damn bridge.'

'Have you seen anything of the passengers?'

'They're scattered here and there. One of them has her arm in a sling and one of them has a cast on her wrist. But generally they're not bitching too much. I don't think any of them has called a lawyer yet. Actually some of them are looking on the bright side, like this whole thing is a magical mystery tour.'

'Not so bad,' Reacher said again.

Knox didn't answer. Just got up suddenly and took stuff off a nearby hook and jammed a hat on his head, and wound a muffler around his neck, and struggled into a heavy coat, all borrowed, judging by the sizes and the colours. He nodded once at Reacher, a slightly bad-tempered farewell, and then he walked to the door and stepped out into the snow.

A waitress came by and Reacher ordered the biggest breakfast on the menu.

Plus coffee.

Five to eleven in the morning.

Forty-one hours to go.

The lawyer left his briefcase in his office but carried his overshoes in their grocery bag. He put them on in his building's lobby and retraced his steps through the lot to his car. He buckled up, started the engine, heated the seat, turned on the wipers. He knew that the highway was still closed. But there were alternative routes. Long, straight South Dakota roads, stretching all the way to the horizon.

He fumbled his overshoes off and put a leather sole on the brake pedal and moved the shifter to Drive.

Reacher was halfway through a heaping plate of breakfast when Peterson came in. He was dressed in his full-on outdoors gear.

100

It was clear that Reacher was supposed to be impressed by how easily Peterson had found him. Which Reacher might or might not have been, depending on how many other places Peterson had tried first.

Peterson put his hand on the chair that Knox had used, and Reacher invited him to sit with a gesture from his loaded fork. Peterson sat down and said, 'I'm sorry you didn't get breakfast at the house.'

Reacher chewed and swallowed and said, 'No problem. You're being more than generous as it is.'

'Kim suffers from loneliness, that's all. It isn't her favourite time of day, when the boys and I leave the house. She usually hides out in her room.'

Reacher said nothing.

Peterson asked, 'Have you ever been lonely?'

Reacher said, 'Sometimes.'

'Kim would say you haven't. Not unless you had sat on a back porch day after day in South Dakota and looked all around and seen nothing for a hundred miles in any direction.'

'Isn't she local?'

'She is. But being used to something doesn't mean you have to like it.'

'I guess not.'

'We checked the bars. We found one with a very clean floor.'

'Where?'

'North. Where the prison guards drink.'

'Any cooperative witnesses?'

'No, but the bartender is missing. Lit out in his truck yesterday.'

'OK,' Reacher said.

'Thank you,' Peterson said.

'You're welcome.' Reacher speared half a slice of bacon and a half-circle of set egg yolk and ate it.

'Any other thoughts?' Peterson asked.

'I know how the guy you put in jail is communicating.'

'How?'

'He made a friend on the inside. Or coerced somebody. Your

101

guy is briefing the second guy, and the second guy is briefing his own lawyer. Like a parallel track. You're bugging the wrong room.'

'There are dozens of lawyer visits every day.'

'Then you better start sifting through them.'

Peterson was quiet for a beat. 'Anything else?'

Reacher nodded. 'I need to find a clothing store. I more or less promised your wife. Cheap, and nothing fancy. You know somewhere like that?'

The clothing store that Peterson recommended was a long block west of the public square. It carried sturdy garments for sturdy farmers. There were summer and winter sections, without many obvious differences between the two. Some of the items were off-brand makes, and others had recognizable labels but visible defects. There was a limited choice of dull colours. Prices were low, even for footwear. Reacher started from the ground up with a pair of black waterproof boots. Then he started in on the garments. His rule when confronted with a choice was to take either olive green or blue. Olive green, because he had been in the army. Blue, because a girl had once told him it picked out his eyes. He went with olive green, because it almost matched his borrowed coat, which was tan. He chose pants with a flannel lining, a T-shirt, a flannel shirt, and a sweater made of thick cotton. He added white underwear and a pair of black gloves and a khaki watch cap. Total damage was a hundred and thirty bucks. The store owner took a hundred and twenty for cash. Four days of wear, probably, at the rate of thirty dollars a day. Which added up to more than ten grand a year, just for clothes. Insane, some would say. But Reacher liked the deal. He knew that most folks spent much less than ten grand a year on clothes. They had a small number of good items that they kept in closets and laundered in basements. But the closets and basements were surrounded by houses, and houses cost a whole lot more than ten grand a year, to buy or to rent, and to maintain and repair and insure.

So who was really nuts?

102

He dressed in a changing cubicle and dumped his old stuff in a trash barrel behind the counter. He jammed the hat on his head and tugged it down over his ears. He covered it with the borrowed parka's hood. He zipped up. He put on the gloves. He stepped out to the sidewalk.

And was still cold.

The air was meat-locker chilled. He felt it in his gut, his ribs, his legs, his ass, his eyes, his face, his lungs. Like the worst of Korea, but in Korea he had been younger, and he had been there under orders, and he had been getting paid. This was different. The snow danced and swirled all around him. A freshening wind pushed at him. His nose started running. His vision blurred. He took breaks in doorways. He turned a ten-minute walk to the police station into a twenty-minute winter odyssey.

When he arrived, he found full-on mayhem.

Five minutes before noon.

Forty hours to go.

It sounded like half the phones in the place were ringing. The old guy behind the reception counter had one in each hand and was talking into both of them. Peterson was alone in the squad room, on his feet behind a desk, a phone trapped between his ear and his shoulder, the cord bucking and swaying as he moved. He was gesticulating with both hands, short, sharp, decisive motions, like a general moving troops, as if the town of Bolton was laid out in front of him on the desk top, like a map.

Reacher watched and listened. The situation made itself clear. No rocket science was involved. A major crime against a person had been committed and Peterson was moving people out to deal with it while making sure his existing obligations were adequately covered. The crime scene seemed to be on the right hand edge of the desk, which was presumably Bolton's eastern limit. The existing obligations seemed to be slightly south and west of downtown, which was presumably where Janet Salter lived. The vulnerable witness. Peterson was putting more resources around her than at the scene, which indicated

103

either proper caution or that the victim at the scene was already beyond help.

Or both.

A minute later Peterson stopped talking and hung up. He looked worried. *Expert in a casual way with all the local stuff, a little out of his depth with anything else.* He said, 'We've got a guy shot to death in a car.'

Reacher said, 'Who?'

'The plates come back to a lawyer from the next county. He's had five client conferences up at the jail. All of them since we busted the biker. Like you said. He's their parallel track. And now their plan is made. So they're cleaning house and breaking the chain.'

'Worse than that,' Reacher said.

Peterson nodded. 'I know. Their guy isn't on his way. We missed him. He's already here.'

# THIRTEEN

TWICE PETERSON TRIED TO GET OUT OF THE SQUAD ROOM AND twice he had to duck back to answer a phone. Eventually he made it to the corridor. He looked back at Reacher and said, 'You want to ride along with me?'

Reacher asked, 'You want me there?'

'If you like.'

'I really need to be somewhere else.'

'Where?'

'I should go introduce myself to Mrs Salter.'

'What for?'

'I want to know the lie of the land. Just in case.'

Peterson said, 'Mrs Salter is covered. I made sure of that. Don't worry about it.' Then he paused and said, 'What? You think they're going to move on her today? You think this dead lawyer is a diversion?'

'No, I think they're breaking the chain. But it looks like I'm going to be here a couple of days. Because of the snow. If that escape siren goes off any time soon, then I'm all you've got. But I should introduce myself to the lady first.'

Peterson said nothing.

Reacher said, 'I'm trying to be helpful, that's all. To repay your hospitality.'

Peterson said nothing.

Reacher said, 'I'm not your guy.'

'I know that.'

'But?'

'You could be helpful at the crime scene.'

'You'll be OK. You know what to do, right? Take plenty of photographs and pay attention to tyre tracks and footprints. Look for shell cases.'

'OK.'

'But first call your officers in Mrs Salter's house. I don't want a big panic when I walk up the driveway.'

'You don't know where she lives.'

'I'll find it.'


In summer it might have taken ten minutes to find Mrs Salter's house. In the snow it took closer to thirty, because lines of sight were limited and walking was slow. Reacher retraced the turns that the prison bus had made, struggling through drifts, slogging through unploughed areas, slipping and sliding along vehicle ruts. It was still snowing hard. The big white flakes came down on him, came up at him, whipped all around him. He found the main drag south. He knew that ahead of him was the restaurant. Beyond that was the parked cop car. He kept on going. He was very cold, but he was still functioning. The new clothes were doing their job, but nothing more.

There were cars heading north and south, lights on, wipers thrashing. Not many of them, but enough to keep him on the shoulder and out of the tyre tracks, which would have been easier going. He guessed the roadway under the snow was wide, but right then traffic was confining itself to two narrow lanes near the centre, made of four separate parallel ruts. Each passing car confirmed the collective decision not to wander. With each passing tyre the ruts grew a little deeper and their side walls grew a little higher. The snow was dry and firm. The ruts were lined on the bottom with broken lattices of tread prints, smooth and greasy and stained brown in places.

Reacher passed the restaurant. The lunch hour was in full swing. The windows were fogged with steam. Reacher struggled on. Four hundred yards later he saw the parked cop car. It had pulled out of the southbound ruts and broken through the little walls and made smaller ruts of its own, like a railroad switch. It had parked parallel with the traffic and was completely blocking the side street. Its motor was turned off but its roof lights were turning. The cop in the driver's seat was not moving his head. He was just staring through the windshield, looking neither alert nor enthusiastic. Reacher slogged through a wide turn and approached him from his front left side. He didn't want to surprise the guy.

The cop buzzed the window down. Called out, 'Are you Reacher?'

Reacher nodded. His face felt too cold for coherent speech. The cop's name plate said *Montgomery*. He was unshaven and overweight. Somewhere in his late twenties. In the army his ass would have been kicked to hell and back a hundred times. He said, 'The Salter house is ahead on the left. You can't miss it.'

Reacher struggled on. There were no big ruts in the side street. Just two lone tracks, one car coming, one car going. The tracks were already mostly refilled with snow. The change of watch, some hours earlier. The night guy going home, the day guy coming in. The day guy had gunned it a little after the turn. His tracks slalomed through a minor fishtail before straightening.

The street curved gently and was lined on both sides by big old houses in big flat lots. The houses looked Victorian. They could have been a hundred years old. They had all been prosperous once and most of them still were. Clearly they had been built during an earlier boom. They predated the federal prison dollars by a century. Their details were obscured by snow, but they had heft and solidity and gingerbread trim. Peterson had called

Janet Salter a storybook grandma, and Reacher had expected a storybook grandma's house to be a small cottage with gingham curtains. Especially considering this storybook grandma had been a teacher and a librarian. Maybe Janet Salter had a different kind of story. Reacher was looking forward to meeting her. He had never known either one of his own grandmothers. He had seen a black and white photograph of himself as a baby on a stern woman's knee. His father's mother, he had been told. His mother's mother had died when he was four, before ever having visited.

The second cop car was parked up ahead. No lights. It was facing him. The cop inside was watching him closely. Reacher floundered onward and stopped ten feet short. The cop opened his door and climbed out and tracked around. His boots set powder flying and small snowballs skittering. He said, 'Are you Reacher?'

Reacher nodded.

'I have to search you.'

'Says who?'

'The deputy chief.'

'Search me for what?'

'Weapons.'

'She's more than seventy years old. I wouldn't need weapons.'

'True. But you'd need weapons to get past the officers in the house.'

This cop was a sharp-looking guy the right side of middle age. Compact, muscled, competent. A department of two halves, one better, one worse. A new hire at the end of the street, an old hand outside the house. Reacher planted his feet and unzipped his coat and stood with his arms held wide. Cold air rushed in under his coat. The cop patted him down and squeezed his coat pockets from both sides at once.

'Go ahead,' he said. 'They're expecting you.'

The driveway was long and the house was ornate. It could have been airlifted straight from Charleston or San Francisco. It had all the bells and whistles. A wraparound rocking-chair porch, dozens of windows, fish scale siding. It had turrets, and

108

more stained glass than a church. Reacher made it up the steps on to the porch and clumped across the boards and stamped the snow off his boots. The front door was a carved multi-panelled thing. It had a bell pull next to it, a cast weight on the end of a wire that looped over pulleys and entered the house through a small bronze eye. Probably ordered by mail from Sears Roebuck a century ago, and delivered by wagon in a wooden box packed with straw, and fitted by a man more used to cart wheels and horseshoes.

Reacher pulled on it. He heard a chime deep inside the house, delayed by a second, low and polite and sonorous. Another second later a policewoman opened the door. She was small and dark and young and was in full uniform. Her gun was in its holster. But the holster was unsnapped, and she looked to be fully on the ball. *Women officers in the house*, Peterson had said, *the best we've got, minimum of four at all times, two awake, two asleep.*

The woman asked, 'Are you Reacher?'

Reacher nodded.

'Come on in.'

The hallway was dark and panelled and fairly magnificent. There were oil paintings on the walls. Ahead was a substantial staircase that rose out of sight. All around were closed doors, maybe chestnut, each of them polished to a shine by a century of labour. There was a large Persian carpet. There were antiquated steam radiators connected with fat pipes. The radiators were working. The room was warm. There was a bentwood hat stand, loaded down with four new police-issue winter parkas. Reacher shrugged off his unzipped coat and hung it on a spare peg. It looked like he felt, an old battered item surrounded by current models.

The woman cop said, 'Mrs Salter is in the library. She's expecting you.'

Reacher said, 'Which one is the library?'

'Follow me.' The cop stepped ahead like a butler. Reacher followed her to a door on the left. She knocked and entered. The library was a large square room with a high ceiling. It had a fireplace and a pair of glass doors to the garden. Everything else was books on shelves, thousands of them. There was a second woman cop in front of the glass doors. She was standing easy with her hands folded behind her back, looking outward. She didn't move. Just glanced back, got a nod from her partner, and looked away again.

There was an older woman in an armchair. Mrs Salter, presumably. The retired teacher. The librarian. The witness. She looked at Reacher and smiled politely.

She said, 'I was just about to take some lunch. Would you care to join me?'

Five to one in the afternoon.

Thirty-nine hours to go.

# FOURTEEN

J ANET SALTER PREPARED THE LUNCH HERSELF. REACHER WATCHED
her do it. He sat in a spacious kitchen while she moved from
refrigerator to counter to stove to sink. The impression he
had formed from Peterson's casual description did not match the
reality. She was more than seventy years old, for sure, grey-
haired, not tall, not short, not fat, not thin, and she certainly
looked kind and not in the least forbidding, but as well as all of
that she was ramrod straight and her bearing was vaguely
aristocratic. She looked like a person used to respect and
obedience, possibly from a large and important staff. And
Reacher doubted that she was a real grandmother. She wore no
wedding band and the house looked like no children had set foot
in it for at least fifty years.

She said, 'You were one of the unfortunates on the bus.'

Reacher said, 'I think the others were more unfortunate than
me.'

'I volunteered this house, of course. I have plenty of space

111

here. But Chief Holland wouldn't hear of it. Not under the circumstances.'

'I think he was wise.'

'Because extra bodies in the house would have complicated his officers' operations?'

'No, because extra bodies in the house could have become collateral damage in the event of an attack.'

'Well, that's an honest answer, at least. But then, they tell me you're an expert. You were in the army. A commanding officer, I believe.'

'For a spell.'

'Of an elite unit.'

'So we told ourselves.'

'Do you think I am wise?' she asked. 'Or foolish?'

'Ma'am, in what respect?'

'In agreeing to testify at the trial.'

'It depends on what you saw.'

'In what way?'

'If you saw enough to nail the guy, then I think you're doing the right thing. But if what you saw was inconclusive, then I think it's an unnecessary risk.'

'I saw what I saw. I am assured by all concerned that it was sufficient to secure a conviction. Or to nail the guy, as you put it. I saw the conversation, I saw the inspection of the goods, I saw the counting and transfer of money.'

'At what distance?'

'Perhaps twenty yards.'

'Through a window?'

'From inside the restaurant, yes.'

'Was the glass clean? Steamed up?'

'Yes and no.'

'Direct line of sight?'

'Yes.'

'Weather?'

'Cool and clear.'

'Time?'

'It was the middle of the evening.'

'Was the lot lit up?'

'Brightly.'

'Is your eyesight OK?'

'I'm a little long-sighted. I sometimes wear spectacles to read. But never otherwise.'

'What were the goods?'

'A brick of white powder sealed tight in a wax paper wrap. The paper was slightly yellowed with age. There was a pictorial device stencilled on it, in the form of a crown, a headband with three points, and each point had a ball on it, presumably to represent a jewel.'

'You saw that from twenty yards?'

'It's a benefit of being long-sighted. And the device was large.'

'No doubts whatsoever? No interpretation, no gaps, no guess-work?'

'None.'

'I think you'll make a great witness.'

She brought lunch to the table. It was a salad in a wooden bowl. The bowl was dark with age and oil, and the salad was made of leaves and vegetables of various kinds, plus tuna from a can, and hard boiled eggs that were still faintly warm. Janet Salter's hands were small. Pale, papery skin. Trimmed nails, no jewellery at all.

Reacher asked her, 'How many other people were in the restaurant at the time?'

She said, 'Five, plus the waitress.'

'Did anyone else see what was happening?'

'I think they all did.'

'But?'

'Afterwards they pretended not to have. Those who dwell in the community to our west are well known here. They frighten people. Simply by being there, I think, and by being different. They are the *other*. Which is inherently disturbing, apparently. In practice, they do us no overt harm. We exist together in an uneasy standoff. But I can't deny an undercurrent of menace.'

113

Reacher asked, 'Do you remember the army camp being built out there?'

Janet Salter shook her head. 'Chief Holland and Mr Peterson have asked me the same question endlessly. But I know no more than they do. I was away in school when it was built.'

'People say it took months to build. Longer than a semester, probably. Didn't you hear anything when you were back in town?'

'I went to school overseas. International travel was expensive. I didn't return during the vacations. In fact I didn't return for thirty years.'

'Where overseas?'

'Oxford University, in England.'

Reacher said nothing.

Janet Salter asked, 'Have I surprised you?'

Reacher shrugged. 'Peterson said you were a teacher and a librarian. I guess I pictured a local school.'

'Mr Peterson has any South Dakotan's aversion to grandeur. And he's quite right, anyway. I was a teacher and a librarian. I was Professor of Library Science at Oxford, and then I helped run the Bodleian Library there, and then I came back to the United States to run the library at Yale, and then I retired and came home to Bolton.'

'What's your favourite book?'

'I don't have one. What's yours?'

'I don't have one either.'

Janet Salter said, 'I know all about the crisis plan at the prison.'

'They tell me it has never been used.'

'But as with all things, one imagines there will be a first time, and that it will come sooner or later.'

Plato skipped lunch, which was unusual for him. Normally he liked the ritual and ceremony of three meals a day. His staff duly prepared a dish, but he didn't show up to eat it. Instead he walked on a serpentine path through the scrub on his property, moving fast, talking on his cell phone, his shirt going dark with sweat.

His guy in the American DEA had made a routine scan through all their wiretap transcripts and had called with a warning. Plato didn't like warnings. He liked solutions, not problems. His DEA guy knew that, and had already reached out to a colleague. No way to stop the hapless Russian getting busted, but things could be delayed until after the deal was done, so that the money could disappear safely into the ether and Plato could walk away enriched and unscathed. All it would cost was four years of college tuition. The colleague had a sixteen-year-old and no savings. Plato had asked how much college cost, and had been mildly shocked at the answer. A person could buy a decent car for that kind of money.

Plato had only one remaining problem. The place in South Dakota was a multipurpose facility. Most of its contents could be sold, but not all of them. Some of them had to be moved out first. Like selling a house. You left the stove, you took the sofa.

He trusted no one. Which helped, most of the time. But at other times it gave him difficulties. Like now. Who could he ask to pack and ship? He couldn't call Allied Van Lines. FedEx or UPS were no good.

His reluctant conclusion was that if you wanted something done properly, you had to do it yourself.

Janet Salter patted the air to make Reacher stay where he was and started to clear the table around him. She asked, 'How much do you know about methamphetamine?'

Reacher said, 'Less than you, probably.'

'I'm not that kind of girl.'

'But you're that kind of librarian. I'm sure you've researched it extensively.'

'You first.'

'I was in the military.'

'Which implies?'

'Certain situations and certain operations called for what the field manuals described as alertness, focus, motivation, and mental clarity, for extended periods. The doctors had all kinds of pep pills available. Straight meth was on its way out when I came on the job, but it had been around before that, for decades.'

Janet Salter nodded. 'It was called Pervitin. A German refinement of a Japanese discovery. It was in widespread use during World War Two. It was baked into candy bars. *Fliegerschokolade*, which means flyers' chocolate, and *Panzerschokolade*, which means tankers' chocolate. The Allies had it, also. Just as much, actually. Maybe more. They called it Desoxyn. I'm surprised anyone ever slept.'

'They had morphine for sleeping.'

'But now it's controlled. Because it causes terrible damage to those who abuse it. So it has to be manufactured illegally. Which is relatively easy to do, in small home laboratories. But the manufacture of anything requires raw materials. For methamphetamine you need ephedrine or pseudoephedrine. You can buy it in bulk, if you can get past the regulations. Or you can extract it from over-the-counter decongestant medicines. To do that you need red phosphorus and iodine. Or lithium, from certain types of batteries. That's an alternative method, called the Birch reduction.'

'You can get it direct from acacia trees in west Texas,' Reacher said. 'Plus mescaline and nicotine. A wonderful tree, the acacia.'

'But this is not west Texas,' Janet Salter said. 'This is South Dakota. My point is, you can't make bricks without straw. If they're shipping out vast quantities of finished product, they must be shipping in vast quantities of raw materials. Which must be visible. There must be truckloads involved. Why can't Chief Holland get at them that way, without involving me?'

'I don't know.'

'I think Chief Holland has gotten lazy.'

'Peterson claimed they gave you the option of backing out.'

'But don't you see? That's no option at all. I couldn't live with myself. It's a matter of principle.'

'Peterson claims you were offered federal protection.'

'And perhaps I should have accepted it. But I much preferred to stay in my own home. The justice system is supposed to

116

penalize perpetrators, not witnesses. That's a matter of principle, too.'

Reacher glanced at the kitchen door. A cop in the hallway, a cop at the rear window, two more sleeping upstairs ready for the night watch, a car outside, another car one block over, a third at the end of the street. Plus alert townsfolk, and a paranoid police HQ. Plus snow all over the place.

All good, unless the siren sounded.

Reacher asked, 'Are you a grandmother?'

Janet Salter shook her head. 'We didn't have children. We waited, and then my husband died. He was English, and much older than me. Why do you ask?'

'Peterson was talking about your credibility on the stand. He said you look like a storybook grandma.'

'Do I?'

'I don't know. I guess I didn't have those storybooks.'

'Where were you raised?'

'On Marine Corps bases.'

'Which ones?'

'It felt like all of them.'

'I was raised here in South Dakota. My father was the last in a long line of robber barons. We traded, we bought land from the native inhabitants at twelve cents an acre, we bought thousands of government stakes through surrogates, we mined gold, we invested in the railroad. At insider rates, of course.'

Reacher said, 'Hence this house.'

Janet Salter smiled. 'No, this is where we came when we hit hard times.'

Out in the hallway the bell chimed once, quiet and civilized. Reacher stood up and stepped to the door and watched. The policewoman on duty was sitting on the bottom stair. She got up and crossed the dim space and opened the front door. Chief Holland came in, with a soft flurry of snow and a cloud of cold air. He stamped his feet on the mat and shivered as the warmth hit him. He took off his parka. The policewoman hung it up for him, right on top of Reacher's borrowed coat.

Holland crossed the hallway and nodded to Reacher and

pushed past him to the kitchen door. He told Janet Salter that he had no significant news for her, and that he was dropping by merely to pay his respects. She asked him to wait in the library. She said she would make coffee and bring it in. Reacher watched her fill an old percolator made of thick dull aluminum. It had a cord insulated with fabric. It was practically an antique. It could have been melted down from a surplus B-24 Liberator after World War Two. Reacher stood ready to help, but she waved him away and said, 'Go and wait with the chief in the library.' So Reacher joined Holland in the book-lined room and asked, 'How are things?'

Holland said, 'What things?'

'The car out on the eastern town limit. With the dead guy in it.'

'We're not sure if our initial assumption was correct. About breaking the chain, I mean. It could have been a simple robbery gone wrong.'

'How so?'

'The guy was a lawyer, but there was no briefcase in the car. You ever heard of that? A lawyer without a briefcase? Maybe someone took it.'

'Was there a wallet in his pocket?'

'Yes.'

'A watch on his wrist?'

'Yes.'

'Was he expected up at the jail?'

'Not according to the visitor lists. His client made no request. But his office claims he got a call.'

'Then it wasn't a simple robbery. He was decoyed out there. He had no briefcase because he wasn't planning on writing any-thing down. Not in his current line of work.'

'Maybe. We'll keep the line of inquiry open.'

'Who made the call to his office?'

'A male voice. Same as the first five times. From a cell phone we can't trace.'

'Who was the client he saw at the jail?'

'Some deadbeat simpleton we'll never get anything out of. We

118

arrested him eight weeks ago for setting fire to a house. We're still waiting for a psychological evaluation. Because he won't speak to anyone he doesn't want to. Not a word.'

'Sounds like your biker friend chose well.'

The percolator started burping and gulping out in the kitchen. It was loud. Reacher could hear it quite clearly. The smell of brewing coffee drifted in and filled the air. Colombian, Reacher figured, ground coarse, reasonably fresh. He said, 'Mrs Salter and I were talking about raw material supply to the lab you figure they've got out there.'

'You think we're negligent? You think we're putting her at risk when we have a viable alternative?'

'I didn't say that.'

'We've tried, believe me. Nothing comes through Bolton. We're damn sure of that. Therefore they're being supplied from the west. The Highway Patrol is responsible for the highway. We have no jurisdiction there. All we control is the county two-lane that runs north to the camp. We put cars there on a random basis. Literally random. I roll actual dice on my desk.'

Reacher said, 'I saw them there.'

Holland nodded. 'I do it like that because we can't afford for the pattern to be predictable in any way at all. But so far we haven't been lucky. They watch us pretty carefully, I suppose.'

'OK.'

'The trial will do it for us. Or the plea bargain the night before. It won't come any earlier than that. One more month, that's all.'

'Peterson told me there's no way to fudge the crisis plan.'

'He's right. We objected, of course, but the deal was done by the mayor. Lots of money, lots of strings attached. We'd have Justice Department monitors all over us for ever.'

'A gift horse.'

'More trouble than it's worth,' Holland said. 'But then, I don't own a motel.'

Plato's walled compound extended across a hundred acres. His walking path through the scrub was more than three miles long. He got his next idea at the furthest point from the house. It was characteristically bold. The DEA was going to bust the Russian. That was a given. Plato wasn't going to stand in their way. The agents had to see the guy take possession. But possession of what, exactly? Enough to make the charges stick, for sure. But not necessarily everything the guy was about to pay for. That would be excessively generous, under the circumstances. A small margin could be retained. A large margin, in fact. Possibly most of the agreed amount. Because what the hell could the Russian guy do? Rant and rave in a supermax cell somewhere, about the unfairness of life? He would be doing that anyway. So Plato could take the guy's money, and then sell the stuff all over again to someone else. Like selling a house, except this time you take the stove and the light bulbs and the glass from the windows.

The scheme would more than double his transportation problem, but he could deal with that. He was sure a solution would present itself. The details would fall into place.

Because he was Plato, and they weren't.

Janet Salter brought the coffee to the library on a silver tray. A china pot, some cream, some sugar, three tiny cups, three saucers, three spoons. Clearly the on-duty policewomen were not included. Probably there had been prior discussion about separation of professional and social obligations. Probably the policewomen were happy with the final outcome. Reacher had been in their situation many times. Always better to compartmentalize and focus.

Janet Salter poured the coffee. The cup was far too small for Reacher's hand, but the coffee was good. He sniffed the steam and took a sip. Then Chief Holland's cell phone rang. Holland balanced his cup and dragged the phone from his pocket and checked the window. He opened the phone one-handed and answered. He listened to the caller for eight seconds. Then he hung up and smiled, widely and gratefully and happily.

He said, 'We just caught the guy who shot the lawyer.'

Five minutes to two in the afternoon.

Thirty-eight hours to go.

# FIFTEEN

REACHER RODE BACK TO THE STATION WITH HOLLAND. THE unmarked Crown Vic churned its way out of the side street and locked into the established ruts and headed home smooth and easy. Peterson was waiting in the squad room. He was smiling, too, just as widely and gratefully and happily as Holland was. Reacher wasn't smiling. He had serious doubts. Based in bitter experience. A fast and easy resolution to a major problem was too good to be true. And things that were too good to be true usually weren't. A basic law of nature.

He asked, 'So who was the shooter?'

Peterson said, 'Jay Knox. The bus driver.'

Reacher got the story secondhand by standing off to one side and listening as Peterson briefed Holland. Forty minutes earlier a cop in a patrol car had seen a pedestrian floundering through deep snow alongside a rural road a mile out of town. Peterson named the cop in the car and called him *one of ours*. An old hand, presumably. From the good half of the department. Maybe someone Holland actually knew. As instructed, the cop in the car was operating at a level of high alert, but even so he thought the guy on foot was more likely a stranded driver than a murderer. He stopped and offered the guy a ride. There was something off about the guy's response. He was surly, and uncooperative, and evasive. The cop therefore cuffed him and searched him.

And found a Glock 17 nine-millimetre pistol in his pocket. It smelled like it had been recently fired and its magazine was one round short of full.

The cop arrested the pedestrian and drove him to the station. At the booking desk he was recognized as the bus driver. His hands and his clothing were swabbed for gunshot residue. The tests came up positive. Jay Knox had fired a gun at some point in the past few hours. His prints were all over the Glock. His rights had been read to him. He was in a holding cell. He hadn't asked for a lawyer. But he wasn't talking, either.

Holland left to take a look at Knox in his cell. It was an urge that Reacher had seen before. It was like going to the zoo. After a big capture people would show up just to stare at the guy. They would stand in front of the bars for a moment and take it all in. Afterwards they would claim there was something in the guy's face they always knew was wrong. If not, they would talk about the banality of evil. About how there were no reliable signs.

Peterson stayed in the squad room. He was tying up the loose ends in his head. Another urge Reacher had seen before. A dangerous urge. If you work backwards, you see what you want to see.

Reacher asked, 'How many rounds in the victim?'

'One,' Peterson said. 'In the head.'

'Nine millimetre?'

'Almost certainly.'

'It's a common round.'

'I know.'

'Does the geography work?'

'Knox was picked up about four miles from the scene.'

'On foot? That's too far, surely.'

'There has to have been a vehicle involved.'

'Why?'

'Wait until you see the photographs.'

The photographs were delivered thirty minutes later. They were in the same kind of file folder Reacher had seen the night before in Holland's office. They were the same kind of photographs. Glossy eight-by-tens, with printed labels pasted in their bottom corners. There were plenty of them. They were colour prints, but they were mostly grey and white. Snow on the ground, snow in the air. The camera shutter had frozen the falling flakes in strange dark suspended shapes, like ash from a volcano, like specks and impurities.

The first picture was an establishing shot taken from a distance, looking west to east. It showed a snowbound road with two pairs of ruts clustered close to the crown of the camber. A lone car was sitting dead centre in the westbound ruts. Its headlights were on. It hadn't veered or swerved. It had just rolled to a halt, like a train on a track.

The second picture had been taken about a hundred feet closer. Three things were apparent. First, there was a figure in the driver's seat. A man, held upright by a tight seat belt, his head lolling forward. Second, the glass in the rear passenger-side window was misted with a large pink stain. And third, there was absolutely nothing on the road itself except virgin snow and four wheel ruts. No other disturbance at all.

The third photograph confirmed that fact. For the third shot, the camera had ignored the car completely. The lens had been trained directly west to east along the road right above where the yellow line was buried under the snow. It was a featureless picture. Nothing to see. Passing tyres had dug trenches, the base of the ruts had been crushed downward, small side walls had been thrown upward, tiny avalanches had fallen outward from the top of the side walls, and those small fallen fragments had been smoothed over by a crust of fresh snow.

Nothing else.

'Good pictures,' Reacher said.

'I did my best,' Peterson said.

'Fine work.'

'Thank you.'

'No footprints,' Reacher said.

'Agreed,' Peterson said.

The fourth photograph was a close-up of one of the eastbound ruts. Nothing to see there either, except broken and confused pieces of tread marks, the same small waffles and lattices Reacher had seen all over town. No way to reconstruct anything worth sending to a lab.

The fifth picture was a close-up of the car, taken from the front right side. It was a small neat sedan, a make Reacher didn't recognize.

'Infiniti,' Peterson said. 'It's Japanese. Nissan's luxury division. That model has a V-6 engine and full-time four-wheel drive. There are snow tyres on it, all around. It's practical, and it's about as showy as a South Dakota lawyer wants to get.'

It was painted a light silver colour. It was basically clean, but grimed over by several recent winter trips. The way the light reflected off the snow and played over the paint made it look ghostly and insubstantial. The driver's window was all the way open. The dead guy was pinned upright against the seat back by the belt. Some snow had blown in on him. His chin was on his chest. He could have been asleep, except for the hole in his head.

The hole was the subject of photograph number five. It was in the centre of the guy's forehead. Like a third eye. Clearly the guy had been looking out the window, halfway between sideways and straight ahead. He had been shot right down his line of sight. He had been looking at the gun. The exit wound had spattered stuff all over the window diagonally behind him. His head had then slumped down and rotated back to a central position.

The rest of the photographs were of the body and the interior of the vehicle from every conceivable angle. *Take plenty of photographs*, Reacher had said, and Peterson had complied to the letter. There was a pair of rubber overshoes neatly placed in the passenger foot well. There was a small multi-purpose chrome hammer mounted centrally on the dash. Reacher had seen them advertised in mail order brochures on aeroplanes. They could tap the windshield out if the doors were jammed after a wreck. They had a blade concealed in the handle to cut seat belts. Ideal accessories for cautious, meticulous, organized people interested in cars. But Reacher wondered whether one had actually ever been used in earnest in the whole history of automotive transport. He suspected not.

The Infiniti's shifter was in Park. Its ignition key was turned to the run position. The tachometer showed an 800-rpm idle. The odometer showed fewer than ten thousand miles. Cabin temperature was set at sixty-nine degrees. The radio was tuned to a local AM station. The tick on the volume knob was all the way over at the eight o'clock position. Turned down low. The gas dial showed the tank to be close to full.

Reacher said, 'Tell me the story.'

Peterson said, 'OK, Knox is in a vehicle. He's driving. He's heading east. The lawyer is heading west. They're both driving slow, because the road is bad. Knox sees the lawyer coming. He winds his window down. Puts his arm out and flags the lawyer down. The lawyer slows and stops. He winds his own window down. Maybe he thinks that Knox is going to warn him about a danger up ahead. Driver to driver, like people do in adverse conditions. Instead, Knox shoots him and drives on.'

'Who found the body?'

'Another guy heading east. Maybe five or ten minutes after it happened. He slowed, took a look, and called us from a gas station two miles farther on. No cell phone.'

'Is Knox right-handed?'

'I don't know. But most people are.'

'Did you find a shell case?'

'No.'

'If Knox is right-handed, then he was shooting diagonally across his body. He would want reasonable arm extension. The muzzle was probably out the window, just a little. The ejection port on a Glock is on the right side of the gun. So he had to be very careful with his position. He had to keep the ejection port

125

inside the car. Kind of cramped. No opportunity to aim down the barrel. Yet he hit the guy right between the eyes. Not easy. Is Knox that good a shot?'

'I don't know.'

'You should try to find out.'

Peterson said, 'I figure the shell case hit the door frame or the windshield, at an angle, and bounced away inside Knox's vehicle.'

'So tell me about Knox's vehicle.'

'Prearranged. He got to town yesterday and met someone today. Maybe a biker. The biker handed over a vehicle, maybe a pick-up truck. Knox did the deed and returned the vehicle and was walking home when we arrested him.'

Reacher said nothing.

Peterson said, 'The people where we put him last night said he made a point of being out all day. They say he wasn't very good company. Like he had things on his mind.'

'I met him this morning in the coffee shop.'

'How was he?'

'Not very good company. He said because he wasn't getting paid as of yesterday. Maybe he was worried about losing his job.'

'He was nervous about his mission.'

'How did he know what the lawyer was driving?'

'Whoever delivered the car told him.'

'How did he know the lawyer was going to be on that road at that time?'

'Simple arithmetic. The decoy appointment was for noon. Easy enough to work backwards in terms of the clock. Easy enough in terms of location, too, given that everyone knew the highway was closed.'

'I just don't buy how he got here in the first place. It was way too complicated. And he said a car was heading straight at him. He couldn't prearrange that. He couldn't invent it, either. He had twenty-one potential witnesses on board.'

'None of them saw it.'

'He couldn't know that in advance.'

126

Peterson said, 'Maybe there really was a car coming at him. Maybe he made a split second decision to exploit it, instead of faking a breakdown nearer the cloverleaf. Was there any delay before he reacted?'

Reacher said, 'I don't know. I was asleep.'

Peterson said nothing.

Reacher said, 'I think you've got the wrong guy.'

'Not what cops like to hear.'

'I know. I was a cop. Doesn't make it any less true.'

'He had a gun in his pocket and he fired it.'

Reacher asked, 'Case closed?'

'That's a big step.'

'But?'

'Right now, yes, I think it is.'

'So put your money where your mouth is. Pull those cops out of Janet Salter's house.'

Peterson paused. 'Not my decision.'

'What would you do if it was?'

'I don't know.'

'Will Holland do it?'

'We'll have to wait and see.'

Five minutes to three in the afternoon.

Thirty-seven hours to go.

# SIXTEEN

OLLAND DIDN'T DO IT. NOT, HE SAID, BECAUSE HE BELIEVED Knox to be innocent. But because the stakes were high enough for the bad guys to justify a second attempt, and a third, and if necessary a fourth and a fifth. Therefore Janet Salter's protection would stay in place until the trial had run its course.

Then Jay Knox started talking, and things changed again.

Knox said he carried the gun for his own personal protection, and always had. He said he was down and depressed and frustrated about the incident with the bus, and annoyed that his employers were going to dock his pay. He didn't like the creeps he had been billeted with. He had lingered over his breakfast in the coffee shop as long as he could, but Reacher had disturbed him, so he had set out on a long angry walk. He was trying to burn off his feelings. But he had arrived at a small trestle bridge over an icy stream and seen a road sign: *Bridge Freezes Before Road.* He had lost his temper and pulled out the Glock and shot the

128

sign. For which he was prepared to apologize, but he added that pretty much every damn road sign he had seen in the area was pockmarked by bullet holes or shotgun pellets.

He remembered where the bridge was. He remembered where he had been standing. He was fairly exact about it. He could make a pretty good guess about where his spent shell case must have gone.

Peterson knew where the trestle bridge was, obviously. Its location made geographic sense, given the site of Knox's arrest. He figured that if Knox had really been out there, then his footprints might still be vaguely visible as smooth dents under the new accumulation. Certainly nobody else would have been walking there. Locals had more sense. He sent a patrol car to check. It had a metal detector in the trunk. Standard equipment, in jurisdictions that had gun crime and snow.

Ten minutes later the cop from the patrol car called in from the trestle bridge. He had found footprints. And he had found the shell case. It was buried in the snow at the end of a short furrow the length of a finger. It had hissed and burned its way in there. The furrow had been lightly covered by new fall, but was still visible, if you knew what you were looking for. And the cop confirmed that there was a new bullet hole in the warning sign, raw and bright, almost certainly a nine millimetre, in the space between the *F* of *Freezes* and the *R* of *Road*.

Peterson conferred with Holland and they agreed the man they were looking for was both still unidentified and already located in the vicinity.

And only halfway through his business.

Jay Knox was a free man five minutes later. But he was told his Glock would stay in the police station, just in case, until he was ready to leave town. It was a deal Knox agreed to readily enough. Reacher saw him walk out of the lobby into the snow, reprieved but still defeated, relieved but still frustrated. Peterson and Holland conferred again and put the department on emergency alert. Even Kapler and Lowell were sent back to active duty.

The entire force was ordered into cars and told to cruise the streets and look for odd faces, odd vehicles, odd behaviour, a mobile expression of any police department's primal fear: *there's someone out there.*

Peterson pinned the new crime scene photographs to the boards in the small office off the corridor outside the squad room. He put them on the wall opposite the pictures of the black-clad guy lying dead in the snow. Reacher found him in there. Peterson said, 'We just made fools of ourselves and wasted a lot of time.'

Reacher said, 'Not really a lot of time.'

'What would your elite unit do next?'

'We'd speculate about automobile transmissions and cautious people.'

'What does that mean?'

'Apart from Knox not being the guy, I think you were exactly right about how it went down. The absence of footprints in the snow pretty much proves it. Two cars stopped cheek to cheek, just shy of exactly level. The bad guy waved the lawyer down. The lawyer stopped. The question is, why did he stop?'

'It's the obvious thing to do.'

Reacher nodded. 'I agree, on a road like that. In summer, at normal speeds, it wouldn't happen. But in the snow, sure. You're crawling along, you figure the other guy either needs your help or has some necessary information for you. So you stop. But if you're the kind of guy who's cautious enough to fuss with overshoes and mount an emergency hammer on your dash and listen to AM radio for the weather report and keep your gas tank full at all times, then you're probably a little wary about that whole kind of thing. You'd keep the transmission in gear and your foot on the brake. So you can take off again right away, if necessary. Maybe you would open your window just a crack. But your lawyer didn't do that. He put his shift lever in Park and opened his window all the way.'

'Which means what?'

'Which means he was ready for a full-blown transaction. A conversation, a discussion, the whole nine yards. He turned his

130

radio down, ready for it. Which means maybe he knew the guy who stopped him. Which is possibly plausible, given the kind of people he seems to have been mixing with.'

'So what would you do now?'

'We'd already be tearing his life apart.'

'Difficult for us to do. He lived in the next county. Outside of our jurisdiction.'

'You need to get on the phone and cooperate.'

'Like you used to with the feds?'

'Not exactly,' Reacher said.

Plato finished his afternoon walk with a visit to his prisoner. The guy was chained in the open, by his ankle, to a steel post anchored deep in the earth. He was a thief. He had gotten greedy. Plato's operations were cash businesses, obviously, and vast quantities of bills had to be stored for long periods, in the ground, in cellars, hidden here and there, to the point where damp and rodent damage claimed a ballpark figure of ten per cent of incoming assets. A hundred grand out of every million just fell apart and rotted away. Except this guy's division was claiming wastage closer to twelve per cent. Which was an anomaly. Which on examination turned out to be caused by the guy skimming, a quarter-million here, a half-million there. To some extent Plato was tolerant of mistakes, but not of disloyalty.

Hence the guy, chained to the post by the ankle.

Winter weather a hundred miles from Mexico City was not fiercely hot. There were no biting insects in the air or in the ground, and the snakes were asleep, and the small night mammals were generally timid. So the guy would die of either thirst or starvation, depending on the rains.

Unless he chose not to.

There was a hatchet within easy reach. The blade was keen, and the guy's shin bone was right there. He hadn't used it yet. But Plato thought he would. It was usually about fifty-fifty. Proof of that proposition was all over the area, some widows, equal numbers of broken men hopping around on crutches.

\*     \*     \*

131

In the South Dakota squad room the clock ticked around to five to four in the afternoon. Thirty-six hours to go. Peterson said, 'Five to four here is five to five in the East. Close of business. Time to call your old unit back. We still need that information.'

Reacher wandered over to the desk in the corner of the squad room. He sat down. Didn't dial the phone. Close of business in Virginia was five o'clock, not five to. Precision was important. It had mattered to him, and he had no doubt it mattered to his current successor.

Peterson asked, 'What did you think of Mrs Salter?'

'She's probably very well read.'

'As a witness?'

'Excellent.'

'Is she holding up?'

'She's scared.'

'Can't blame her.'

'What about raw material supply to the lab? For that matter, what about intercepting the finished product as they ship it out?'

'We're trying. But to guarantee anything we'd have to be on that road all day and all night and all week.'

'With the right people, too,' Reacher said. 'Some of your guys look asleep at the switch. But whatever, you need to tell Mrs Salter you're doing everything you can. Right now she feels all the weight is on her shoulders.'

'We told her nothing is obligatory.'

'Some people see obligation in their own way.' Reacher picked up the phone. Hit nine for a line. Dialled the number he remembered and waited for the start of the recording. *If you know your party's extension, you may dial it at any time.* He hit 110. The same male voice answered. The captain, from the South. The same one-word greeting.

'Yes?'

Reacher said, 'Amanda, please.'

There was a click and a purr and a second of dial tone and the voice came on. Warm, husky, breathy, intimate. It said, 'You're a pain in the ass.'

Reacher said, 'Am I?'

'As if I don't have enough to do.'

'What's the problem?'

'Your place five miles west of Bolton isn't exactly front and centre in the records. There's nothing listed in the establishments register.'

'There wouldn't be. It's abandoned. Maybe never even used in the first place.'

'Was it sold?'

'I don't know. Maybe just yielded back. It's on what the cops here call public land.'

'I went back fifty years in the title register and found no transfers.'

'So maybe it's still ours.'

'In which case it would be costing us something. Biannual inspections and a little maintenance at the least. But there's no expenditure record.'

'There has got to be something. Not even the army builds places and then forgets all about them.'

'Is it fenced?'

'I don't know. I'm five miles away. Why?'

'Because not even the army builds places and then forgets all about them. Therefore the absence of records could mean it's on a different list. It could have been a secret installation.'

Reacher said, 'They all were.'

'Some more than others.'

'The old folks here remember a security cordon.'

'There was always a security cordon.'

'How secret could it be? They put construction workers on the site.'

'Secret then, abandoned now. Maybe because it was very weird. Which could be important to you. But if you really want to know, I'm going to have to do some digging.'

'Can you?'

'It'll cost you.'

'Cost me what?'

Warm, husky, breathy, intimate. 'I want to know the story behind the dent in the desk.'

'You don't have time. You've got enough to do.'

'Right now I'm just hanging out, waiting on a call.'

'Something interesting?'

'It's pretty good.'

'Tell me about it.'

'That's not the deal. This is about you telling me.'

'I don't want to talk through a switchboard.'

'You've got nothing to worry about. Obviously the colonel's head was righteous, or you would have been busted at the time. And the statute of limitations ran out long ago on damage to government property.'

'How hard will you dig?'

'As hard as you want me to.'

'When is your call coming through?'

'Soon, I hope.'

'Then we don't have time for the story. Get me what I need by tomorrow, and I'll tell you then.'

'You drive a hard bargain.'

'I was hoping for something for nothing.'

'At least give me a hint.'

'OK,' Reacher said. 'It wasn't a colonel. It was a one-star general.'


Plato decided on an early dinner, because he was hungry, because he had skipped lunch. So he showed up in his kitchen. It was something he liked to do occasionally. He felt it demonstrated solidarity with the people who worked for him. He felt it was inclusive and democratic. But it always came out feudal. His people would bob and bow and scrape and get all flushed and flustered. Probably because they were afraid of him. But they had no reason. He had never victimized his domestic staff. None of them had ever suffered. Not the current generation, anyway. Two of their predecessors were buried on the property, but no one presently in his employ knew anything about that.

He ordered a cold appetizer and a hot entrée and took a beer from the refrigerator and went to wait in the smaller outdoor dining area. He took out his cell and dialled the walled villa a hundred miles away in the city. He asked, 'How are we doing in South Dakota?'

The man in the villa said, 'The lawyer was taken care of six hours ago.'

'And the witness?'

'Not yet.'

'So when?'

'Soon.'

'How soon?'

'Very soon.'

Plato felt his blood pressure build behind his temples. He looked at the next twenty-four hours in his mind. He liked to think visually. He liked to see chronological intervals laid out in a linear fashion, like ticks on a ruler. He inspected them at close quarters, like a bird swooping low over the sea, and he filled some of them in, and left others blank. He said, 'Call the guy and tell him the thing with the witness can't wait.'

The man in the villa said, 'I will.'

Plato hung up and redialled. The airfield. He put his plane on standby. It was to be fuelled and ready for takeoff at a moment's notice. The flight plan should show Canada, but that would be a decoy. The reality would be seventeen hundred miles there and seventeen hundred miles back. Fuel was to be made available at the midpoint for the return leg.

Then he made a third call. He needed six men to go with him. Good men, but not so good he couldn't afford to leave them behind. If it came to that.

Which, he hoped, it would.


Reacher stopped thinking about the woman with the voice when he heard shouting in the police station lobby. One-sided shouting. A phone call. It had started out formal, gotten polite, then gotten a little defensive, and then gotten exasperated. It had ended with yelling. It had been followed by a three-way back and forth. The old guy from the desk to Holland's office, Peterson to

135

Holland's office, the old guy back to the lobby, Peterson back to the squad room.

Peterson said, 'Biker trouble. One of them just called. Three of their people are missing over here, and why aren't we doing anything about it?'

Reacher said, 'What did you tell them?'

'We said we're working on it.'

'And?'

'They said we better work harder, or they'll come to town and work on it themselves. They said they'll give us until tomorrow.'

Five to five in the afternoon.

Thirty-five hours to go.

# SEVENTEEN

PETERSON LEFT AGAIN AND REACHER SAT ALONE IN THE EMPTY squad room and looked out the window. It was still snowing. The flakes came down through pools of yellow sodium light. The sky was dark. The day was ending. Twelve thousand nearby souls were huddling in houses, staying warm, looking at the television, getting ready to eat. To the north the prison was seething. To the west the bikers were doing who knew what. And somewhere an unknown marksman was rehearsing a second shot.

Peterson came back and said, 'Chief Holland thinks they're bluffing. He says their whole strategy all along has been to stay inside the law and deny us probable cause.'

Reacher said nothing.

Peterson asked, 'What do you think?'

'Only one way to find out.'

'Which is what?'

'Reconnaissance.'

'You want us to go over there?'

'No, I'll go,' Reacher said. 'I need to see the place anyway. To find out what it is.'

'You have people working on that.'

'No substitute for a live eyeball.'

'You're just going to show up there?'

'I'll say I'm from the army. A biannual inspection of our property.'

'On your own?'

'Why not?'

'Won't work. They'll want to see ID.'

'They won't. These are not regular citizens.'

Peterson asked, 'When would you go?'

'As soon as possible,' Reacher said. 'No point in the dark. Let's say first light tomorrow.'

Peterson said the department had a spare unmarked car. Reacher could use it. First light would depend on the weather, but it would be somewhere between seven and eight o'clock. So Peterson said, 'I'll drive you home now. You should get some rest.'

Reacher shook his head. 'You should drive me to Janet Salter's instead. She has rooms to spare. She told me she volunteered them after the bus crash. Then she told me she knew about the crisis plan at the prison. It was like a coded message. She wants someone there who won't leave if the siren sounds. Imagine how that would feel.'

Peterson thought about it for a second, and nodded. Started to say something, and stopped. 'I was going to say I'll bring your bags over. But you don't have any.'

'Tell Kim I got new clothes. Tell her you saw me in them. I think she was a little worried. And tell her I'll look after her dad's parka. And tell her thanks again for her hospitality.'

It was still snowing but the roads between the police station and Janet Salter's house were still passable. They had been ploughed at least once during the day. The plough blades had thrown up steep banks either side, so that the wheel ruts were now four small trenches inside one giant trench. Sound was absorbed. The world was silent. The flakes came down invisible until they hit the headlight beams. They settled vertically and implacably ahead of the creeping car.

The way the ploughs had narrowed the roads meant that Peterson couldn't turn into Janet Salter's street. The parked cop car filled its whole width. The car's red lights turned lazily and made the falling flakes pink, like garnets, or blood spatter. Reacher climbed out of Peterson's ride and zipped up and squeezed awkwardly between the parked cruiser's trunk and the snow bank behind it. The cop in the cruiser paid no attention. Reacher trudged alone down the centre of the street. The tracks from the change of watch that morning were long gone, smoothed over and obscured. The air was bitter. A cold day was slipping away, and a savage night was moving in to replace it.

Reacher climbed up on Janet Salter's porch and pulled the bell wire. Pictured the cop inside getting up off her perch on the bottom stair and stepping across the Persian rug. The door opened. The cops had swapped their positions. This was the one from the library window. She was tall and had fair hair pulled back in an athletic ponytail. Her hand was resting on her gun. She was alert, but not tense. Professionally cautious, but happy about the tiny break in routine.

Reacher hung his borrowed coat on the hat stand and headed for the library. Janet Salter was in the same armchair as before. She wasn't reading. She was just sitting there. The other woman cop was behind her. The one that had been in the hallway earlier. The small, dark one. She was staring out the window. The drapes were wide open.

Janet Salter said, 'You had to rush off before you finished your coffee. Would you like me to make some more?'

'Always,' Reacher said. He followed her to the kitchen and watched her fill the antique percolator. The faucets over the sink were just as old. But nothing in the room was decrepit or dowdy. Good stuff was good stuff, however long ago it had been installed.

She said, 'I understand you'll stay here tonight.'

He said, 'Only if it's convenient.'

'Were you not comfortable at the Peterson place?'

'I was fine. But I don't like to impose too long.'

'One night was too long?'

'They have enough on their plate.'

'You travel light.'

'What you see is what you get.'

'Mr Peterson told me.'

'Told you, or warned you?'

'Is it a phobia? Or a philia? Or a consciously existential decision?'

'I'm not sure I ever inquired that deeply.'

'A phobia would be a fear, of course, possibly of commitment or entanglement. A philia would imply love, possibly of freedom or opportunity. Although technically a philia shades towards issues of abnormal appetite, in your case possibly for secrecy. We must ask of people who fly beneath the radar, why, exactly? Is radar in itself unacceptable, or is the terrain down there uniquely attractive?'

'Maybe it's the third thing,' Reacher said. 'Existential.'

'Your disavowal of possessions is a little extreme. History tells us that asceticism has powerful attractions, but even so most ascetics owned clothes, at least. Shirts, anyway, even if they were only made of hair.'

'Are you making fun of me?'

'You could afford to carry a small bag, I think. It wouldn't change who you are.'

'I'm afraid it would. Unless it was empty, which would be pointless. To fill a small bag means selecting, and choosing, and evaluating. There's no logical end to that process. Pretty soon I would have a big bag, and then two or three. A month later I'd be like the rest of you.'

'And that horrifies you?'

'No, I think to be like everyone else would be comfortable and reassuring. But some things just can't be done. I was born different.'

'That's your answer? You were born different?'

'I think it's clear we're not all born the same.'

Janet Salter poured the coffee, this time straight into tall china mugs, as if she thought silver trays and ceremony were inappropriate for an ascetic, and as if she had noticed his earlier discomfort with the undersized cup.

She said, 'Well, whatever your precise diagnosis might be, I'm glad to have you here. You're welcome to stay as long as you like.'

Five to six in the evening.

Thirty-four hours to go.

After the coffee was finished Janet Salter started to make dinner. Reacher offered to eat out, but she said it was as easy to cook for six as five, which told him the two cops on night watch would be getting up and forming a foursome for most of the evening. Which was reassuring.

With her permission he used the food preparation time to inspect the house. He wasn't interested in the first floor or the second floor. He wanted to see the basement. South Dakota had tornadoes, and he was pretty sure a house of any quality would have been planned with an underground safety zone. He went down a flight of stairs from a small back hallway off the kitchen and found a satisfactory situation. The prairie topsoil had been too deep for the excavation to reach bedrock, so the whole space was basically a huge six-sided wooden box built from massive baulks of timber banded with iron. The walls and floor were thick to provide stability, and the ceiling was thick to prevent the rest of the house from crashing through after a direct hit. There was a thicket of floor-to-ceiling posts throughout the space, not more than six feet apart, each one hewn and smoothed from the trunk of a tree. Four of them were panelled with wallboard, to form a furnace room. The furnace was a stained green appliance. It was fed by a thin fuel line, presumably from an oil tank buried outside in the yard. It had a pump and a complicated matrix of wide iron pipes that led out and up through the ceiling. An old installation. Maybe the first in town. But it was working fine. The burner was

141

roaring and the pump was whirring and the pipes were hissing. It was keeping the whole basement warm.

The stairs leading upward could be closed off at the bottom with a stout door that opened outward. It could be secured from the inside with an iron bar propped across iron brackets. It was a fine tornado shelter, no question. Probably an adequate bomb shelter. Almost certainly resistant to any kind of small arms fire. Reacher had seen .50 calibre machine guns chew through most things, but hundred-year-old foot-thick close-grain hardwood would probably hold up until their barrels overheated and warped.

He came back upstairs encouraged and found the night watch cops up and about. They were with their daytime partners in the kitchen. Janet Salter was moving around inside their cordon. There was an atmosphere of custom and comfort. Clearly the strange little household was becoming used to getting along together. The oven was on and it was warming the room. The glass in the window was fogged with moisture. Reacher stepped into the library and checked the view to the rear. Nothing to see. Just a vague sense of flat land receding into the frigid distance. The snow was easing. The falling flakes themselves seemed stunned by the cold.

Reacher turned back from the window and found Janet Salter stepping in through the door. She said, 'May we talk?'

Reacher said, 'Sure.'

She said, 'I know the real reason why you're here, of course. I know why you're inspecting the house. You have volunteered to defend me, if the siren should happen to sound, and you're making yourself familiar with the terrain. And I'm very grateful for your kindness. Even though your psychological imperatives may mean you won't be here for quite long enough. The trial might not happen for a month. How many new shirts would that be?'

'Eight,' Reacher said.

She didn't reply.

Reacher said, 'There would be no shame in bowing out, you know. No one could blame you. And those guys will get nailed for something else, sooner or later.'

'There would be considerable shame in it,' she said. 'And I won't do it.'

'Then don't talk to me about psychological imperatives,' Reacher said.

She smiled. Asked, 'Are you armed?'

'No.'

'Why not?'

'Do retired plumbers carry wrenches the rest of their lives?'

She pointed to a low shelf. 'There's a book that might interest you. A work of history. The large volume, with the leather binding.'

It was a big old thing about a foot and a half high and about four inches thick. It had a leather spine with raised horizontal ribs and a quaint title embossed in gold: *An Accurate Illustrated History of Mr Smith's & Mr Wesson's Hand Guns*. Which sounded Victorian, which did not compute. Smith & Wesson had made plenty of handguns in the late nineteenth century and the early twentieth, but not nearly enough to fill a book four inches thick.

Janet Salter said, 'Take a look at it.'

Reacher pulled the book off the shelf. It was heavy.

She said, 'I think you should read it in bed tonight.'

It was heavy because it wasn't a book. Reacher opened the leather-bound cover and expected to see faded pages with half-tone engravings or hand-tinted line drawings, maybe alternated with tissue paper leaves to protect the art. Instead the cover was a lid and inside was a box with two moulded velvet cavities. The velvet was brown. Nested neatly in the two cavities was a matched pair of Smith & Wesson revolvers, one reversed with respect to the other, cradled butt to muzzle, like quotation marks either end of a sentence. The revolvers were Smith & Wesson's Military and Police models. Four-inch barrels. They could have been a hundred years old, or fifty. Plain simple steel machines, chequered walnut grips, chambered for the .38 Special, lanyard eyelets on the bottom of the butts, put there for officers either military or civil.

Janet Salter said, 'They were my grandfather's.'

Reacher asked, 'Did he serve?'

'He was an honorary commissioner, back when Bolton first got a police department. He was presented with the guns. Do you think they still work?'

Reacher nodded. Revolvers were usually reliable for ever. They had to be seriously banged up or rusted solid to fail. He asked, 'Have they ever been used?'

'I don't think so.'

'Do you have any oil?'

'I have sewing-machine oil.'

'That will do.'

'Do we need anything else?'

'Ammunition would help.'

'I have some.'

'How old?'

'About a week.'

'You're well prepared.'

'It seemed the right time to be.'

'How many rounds?'

'A box of a hundred.'

'Good work.'

'Put the book back now,' she said. 'The policewomen need not know. In my experience professionals are offended by amateur plans.'

After dinner the phone rang. It was Peterson, at the police station. He told Janet Salter that the phone on the back corner desk had rung. The 110th MP. The woman wouldn't talk to him. She wanted Reacher to call her back.

Janet Salter's phone was in the hallway. It was newer than the house, but not recently installed. It had a push-button dial, but it also had a cord and was about the size of a portable typewriter. It was on a small table with a chair next to it. Like phones used to be, back when one instrument was enough for a household and using it was a kind of ceremony.

Reacher dialled the number he remembered. He waited for the recording and dialled 110.

'Yes?'

144

'Amanda, please.'

There was a click. Then the voice. No dial tone. She already had the phone in her hand. She said, 'Either you're crazy or the world is.'

Reacher said, 'Or both.'

'Whichever, I'm about ready to give up on you.'

'Why?'

'Because the place you're pestering me about doesn't exist.'

Five to seven in the evening.

Thirty-three hours to go.

# EIGHTEEN

REACHER MOVED ON THE HALLWAY CHAIR AND SAID, 'THE PLACE exists. For sure. I'd believe stone and eyewitness reports before I believed army paperwork.'

The voice said, 'But you haven't actually seen the stone for yourself.'

'Not yet. But why would anyone invent a story like that?'

'Then the place must have been unbelievably secret. They built it but never listed it anywhere.'

'And then they let a construction camp get built right over it? How does that work?'

'Everything changed, that's how. It was top secret fifty years ago, and it was totally defunct by five years ago. Typical Cold War scenario. Probably declassified in the early nineties.'

'I don't care when it was declassified. I just want to know what it is.'

'I could get on a plane. But you're closer.'

Reacher asked, 'How's your case?'

'Still waiting. Which doesn't encourage me. It will probably fall apart by morning.'

'You working all night?'

'You know how it is.'

'So use the down time. Check Congressional appropriations for me. The purpose will be redacted, but the money will be listed. It always is. We can make a start that way.'

'You know how big the defence budget was fifty years ago? You know how many line items there were?'

'You've got all night. Look for South Dakota involvement, House or Senate. I don't see any real strategic value up here, so it could have been a pork barrel project.'

'Checking those records is a lot of work.'

'What did you expect? A life of leisure? You should have joined the navy.'

'We have a deal, Reacher. Remember? So tell me about the one-star general.'

'You're wasting time.'

'I've got time to waste. Sounds like you're the one who hasn't.'

'It's a long story.'

'The best stories always are. Summarize if you like, but make sure you hit all the main points.'

'I'm on someone else's phone here. I can't run up a big bill.'

The voice said, 'Wait one.' There was a click and a second of dead air and then the voice came back. 'Now you're on the government's dime.'

'You could be working the money for me.'

'I am. I already put a guy on it thirty-five minutes ago. I maintain standards here, believe me. However good you were, I'm better.'

'I sincerely hope so.'

'So, once upon a time, what happened?'

Reacher paused.

'I went to Russia,' he said. 'Well after the fall of communism. We got a weird invitation to go inspect their military prisons. Nobody had the faintest idea why. But the general feeling was,

147

why not? So we flew to Moscow and took a train way east. It was a big old Soviet-era thing with bunks and a dining car. We were on it for days. The food was awful. But awful in a way that felt familiar. So one night I went for a stroll up and down the train and stopped in at the kitchen. They were serving us American MREs. Our very own meals, ready to eat.'

'U.S. Army rations? On a Soviet train?'

'A Russian train by then, technically. They had coal-fired stoves in the kitchen car. Samovars and everything. They were heating pans of water and ripping open MRE packs and mixing them together. They had boxes and boxes of them.'

'Did they try to hide them?'

'The cooks didn't know what they were. They couldn't read English. Probably couldn't read anything.'

'So how had our MREs gotten there?'

'That's tomorrow's instalment. You need to get back to work.'

'I'm just waiting on a call.'

'From where?'

'I can't say.'

'You know you want to tell me.'

'Fort Hood.'

'What about?'

'An infantry captain killed his wife. Which happens. But this wasn't any old wife. She had a job with Homeland Security. It's possible the guy has ties overseas. It's possible he was stealing documents from her and killed her to cover it up.'

'Where overseas?'

'What we call non-state actors.'

'Terrorists?'

'Terrorist organizations, anyway.'

'Nice. That's a Bronze Star right there.'

'If I get the guy. Right now he's in the wind.'

'Tell me if he heads for South Dakota.'

She laughed. 'How old are you, anyway?'

'Younger than your desk.'

\*　　\*　　\*

148

Five miles away in the prison mess hall all traces of the evening meal had been cleared away. But more than fifty men were still seated on the long benches. Some were white, some were brown, and some were black. All wore orange jumpsuits. They were sitting in three segregated groups, far from each other, like three island nations in a sea of linoleum.

Until a white man got up and walked across the room and spoke to a black man.

The white man was white in name only. His skin was mostly blue with tattoos. He was built like a house. He had hair to his waist and a beard that reached his chest. The black man was a little shorter, but probably heavier. He had biceps the size of footballs and a scalp shaved so close it gleamed.

The white man said, 'The Mexicans owe us two cartons of smokes.'

The black man didn't react in any way at all. Why would he? White and brown had nothing to do with him.

The white man said, 'The Mexicans say you owe them two cartons of smokes.'

No reaction.

'So we'll collect direct from you. What goes around comes around.'

Which was a technically acceptable proposition. A prison was an economy. Cigarettes were currency. Like dollar bills earned selling a car in New York could be used for buying a TV in Los Angeles. But economic cooperation implied the existence of laws and treaties and détente, and all three were in short supply between black and white.

Then the white man said, 'We'll collect in the form of ass. Something tender. The youngest and sweetest you got. Two nights, and then you'll get her back.'

In Janet Salter's house the four women cops were handing over. The day watch was going off duty, and the night watch was coming on. One of the night watch came out of the kitchen and took up her post in the hallway. The other headed for the library. The day watch climbed the stairs. Janet Salter herself said she

149

was headed for the parlour. Reacher guessed she wanted to spend some time on her own. Being protected around the clock was socially exhausting for all parties concerned. But she invited him in with her.

The parlour was different from the library in no significant way at all. Similar furniture, similar décor, similar shelves, thousands more books. The window gave a view across the porch to the front. It had almost stopped snowing. The cop in the car on the street had gotten out from time to time to scrape his windows. There was a loaf of snow a foot high on the roof and the hood and the trunk, but the glass was clear. The cop was still awake and alert. Reacher could see his head turning. He was checking ahead, in the mirror, half left, half right. Not bad, for what must have been the twelfth hour of twelve. The good half of the Bolton PD made for a decent unit.

Janet Salter was wearing a cardigan sweater. It was long on her and the pockets were bagged. By, it turned out, a rag and a can of oil. She took them out and put them on a side table. The rag was white and the can was a small old green thing with *Singer* printed on it.

She said, 'Go get the book I showed you.'

The night watch cop in the library turned around when Reacher came in. She was a small neat round-shouldered person made wider by her equipment belt. Her eyes flicked up, flicked down, flicked away. *No threat*. She turned back to the window. Behind her Reacher took the fake book off the shelf and hefted it under his arm. He carried it back to the parlour. Janet Salter closed the door behind him. He opened the leather box on the floor and lifted out the first revolver.

The Smith & Wesson Military and Police model had been first produced in 1899 and last modified three years later in 1902. The average height of American men in 1902 had been five feet seven inches, and their hands had been proportionately sized. Reacher was six feet five inches tall and had hands the size of supermarket chickens, so the gun was small for him. But his trigger finger fit through the guard, which was all that mattered. He pressed the thumb catch and swung the cylinder out. It was empty. He locked it back in and dry fired. Everything worked. But he felt the microscopic grind and scrape of steel that had been greased in the factory many decades earlier and never touched since. So he went to work with the rag and the can and tried again five minutes later and was much happier with the result. He repeated the process on the second gun. He capped the oil and folded the rag. Asked, 'Where is the ammunition?'

Janet Salter said, 'Upstairs in my medicine cabinet.'

'Not a logical place, given that the guns were in the library.'

'I thought I might have time, if it came to it.'

'Lots of dead people thought that.'

'You're serious, aren't you?'

'This is a serious business.'

She didn't answer. Just got up and left the room. Reacher heard the creak of the stairs. She came back with a crisp new box of a hundred Federal .38 Specials. Semi-wadcutters with hollow points. A good choice. She had been well advised by somebody. The 158-grain load was not the most powerful in the world, but the mushrooming effect of the hollow points would more than make up for it.

Reacher loaded six rounds into the first gun and kept the second empty. He said, 'Look away and then look back and point your finger straight at me.'

Janet Salter said, 'What?'

'Just do it. Like I'm talking in class.'

'I wasn't that kind of teacher.'

'Pretend you were.'

So she did. She made a good job of it. Maybe undergraduate students at Oxford University hadn't been exactly what the world imagined. Her finger ended up pointing straight between his eyes.

'Good,' he said. 'Now do it again, but point at my chest.'

She did it again. Ended up pointing straight at his centre mass.

'OK,' he said. 'That's how to shoot. The gun barrel is your finger. Don't try to aim. Don't even think about it. Just do it,

151

instinctively. Point at the chest, because that's the biggest target. Even if you don't kill him, you'll ruin his day.'

Janet Salter said nothing. Reacher handed her the empty gun.

'Try the trigger,' he said.

She did. The hammer rose, the cylinder turned, the hammer fell. Nice and easy. She said, 'I suppose there will be a certain amount of recoil.'

Reacher nodded. 'Unless the laws of physics changed overnight.'

'Will it be bad?'

Reacher shook his head. 'The .38 Special is a fairly friendly round. For the shooter, I mean. Not much bang, not much kick.'

She tried the trigger again. The hammer rose, the cylinder turned, the hammer fell.

'Now do it over and over,' he said.

She did. Four, five, six times.

She said, 'It's tiring.'

'It won't be if it comes to it. And that's what you've got to do. Put six rounds in the guy. Don't stop until the gun is empty.'

'This is awful,' she said.

'It won't be if it comes to it. It'll be you or him. You'll be surprised how fast that changes your perspective.'

She passed the gun back to him. He asked her, 'Where are you going to keep it?'

'In the book, I guess.'

'Wrong answer. You're going to keep it in your pocket. At night you're going to keep it under your pillow.' He loaded six rounds into it. Locked the cylinder in place and passed it back. He said, 'Don't touch the trigger until you're ready to kill the guy.'

'I won't be able to.'

'I think you will.'

She asked, 'Are you going to keep the other one?'

He nodded. 'I'll be sure to turn it in before I leave.'

Five to eight in the evening.

Thirty-two hours to go.

The prison siren started to wail.

# NINETEEN

THE SIREN WAS FIVE MILES AWAY TO THE NORTH, BUT ITS SOUND came through the frigid night very clearly. It was somewhere between loud and distant, somewhere between mournful and urgent, somewhere between everyday and alien. It shrieked and howled, it rose and fell, it screamed and whispered. It rolled across the flat land and down the silent snowy streets and shattered the crystal air it passed through.

The cops in the house reacted instantly. They had rehearsed, probably physically, certainly mentally. They had prepared themselves for the tough choice. The woman from the hallway ducked her head into the parlour. Conflict was all over her face. There was the sound of footsteps from the floor above. The day watch was scrambling. The woman from the library ran straight for her parka on the hat rack. Outside on the street the nearest cop car was already turning around. Broken slabs of snow were sliding off its roof and its hood and its trunk. The car from the mouth of the road was backing up fast. There were running feet on the stairs.

The woman from the hallway said, 'Sorry.'

Then she was gone. She grabbed her coat and spilled out the door, the last to leave. The cop cars had their doors open. Reacher could hear furious radio chatter. The cops from the house threw themselves into the cars and the cars spun their wheels and slewed and churned away down the street. Reacher watched them go. Then he stepped back and closed the front door. His borrowed coat had fallen to the floor in the scramble. He put it back on a hook. It hung all alone on the rack.

The siren wailed on.

But the house went absolutely silent.

The house stayed silent for less than a minute. Then over the sound of the siren Reacher heard the patter of chains on snow and the grind of a big engine revving fast and urgent in a low gear. He checked the parlour window. Bright headlights. A Crown Vic. Unmarked. Black or dark blue. Hard to say, in the moonlight. It crunched to a stop at the end of the driveway and Chief Holland climbed out. Parka, hat, boots. Reacher tucked his gun in his waistband at the back and draped his sweater over it. He stepped out to the hallway. He opened the front door just as Holland made it up on the porch.

Holland looked surprised.

He said, 'I didn't know you were here.'

Reacher said, 'It made more sense. There are empty beds here and Kim Peterson doesn't need protection.'

'Was this Andrew's idea or yours?'

'Mine.'

'Is Mrs Salter OK?'

'She's fine.'

'Let me see her.'

Reacher stepped back and Holland stepped in and closed the door. Janet Salter came out of the parlour. Holland asked her, 'Are you OK?'

She nodded. She said, 'I'm fine. And I'm very grateful that you came. I appreciate it very much. But really you should be on your way to the prison.'

154

Holland nodded. 'I was. But I didn't want you to be alone.'

'Rules are rules.'

'Even so.'

'I'll be fine. I'm sure Mr Reacher will prove more than capable.'

Holland glanced back at Reacher. Wretched conflict in his face, just like the cop from the hallway. Reacher asked him, 'What's happening up there?'

Holland said, 'Blacks and whites having at it. A regular prison riot.'

'First ever?'

'Correct.'

'Great timing.'

'Tell me about it.'

'Bottom line, what happens if you don't go?'

'The department is disgraced, and I get fired. After that, no one really knows.'

'So go.'

'I don't want to.' A simple statement. The way Holland said it and the way he stood there afterwards made Reacher think he had more on his mind than his duty to Mrs Salter. He wanted to stay indoors, comfortable, in the warm, where he was safe.

Holland was scared.

Reacher asked him, 'Have you ever worked a prison before?'

Holland said, 'No.'

'There's nothing to it. You'll be on the fence and in the towers. Anyone tries to get through, you shoot them dead. Simple as that. They know the rules. And they won't try, anyway. Not at a moment's notice in this kind of weather. They'll stay inside, fighting. They'll burn out eventually. They always do. You're going to get cold and bored, but that's all.'

'Have you worked prisons?'

'I've worked everything. Including personal protection. And with all due respect, I can do at least as good a job as you. So you should let me. That way everyone wins.'

'I don't know.'

'I can look after the situation here, you can take care of your people up there.'

'It could last for hours. Even days.'

'Actually it could last for weeks. But if it looks like it's going to, then you can regroup.'

'You think?'

Reacher nodded. 'You can't work around the clock for days on end. Not all of you. No one could expect that. You can establish some flexibility after the first panic is over.'

Holland didn't answer. Outside the siren suddenly died. It just cut off mid-wail and absolute silence came crashing back. A total absence of sound, like the air itself was refreezing.

Reacher said, 'That probably means you're all supposed to be up there by now.'

Holland nodded, slow and unsure, once, then twice. He looked at Janet Salter and said, 'At least come with me in the car. I need to know you're safe.'

Janet Salter said, 'That's not permitted, Chief Holland. Rules are rules. But don't worry. I'll be safe here, with Mr Reacher.'

Holland stood still a moment longer. Then he nodded a third time, more decisively. His mind was made up. He turned abruptly and headed out the door. His car was still running. A thin cloud of exhaust was pooling behind the trunk. He climbed in and K-turned and drove away and out of sight. White vapour trailed after him and hung and dispersed. The small sound of his chains on the packed snow died back to nothing.

Reacher closed the door.

The house went quiet again.

Tactically the best move would have been to lock Janet Salter in the basement. But she refused to go. She just stood in the hallway with her hand on the butt of the gun in her pocket. She looked all around, one point of the compass, then the next, as if she suddenly understood that the four walls that were supposed to protect her were really just four different ways in. There were doors and windows all over the place. Any one of them could be forced or busted in an instant.

Second best would have been to stash her in her bedroom. Second-floor break-ins were much less common than first-floor. But she wouldn't go upstairs, either. She said she would feel she had nowhere to run.

'You won't be running,' Reacher said. 'You'll be shooting.'

'Not while you're here, surely.'

'Twelve holes in the guy are better than six.'

She was quiet for a beat. She looked at him like he was an alien.

She asked, 'Shouldn't you be patrolling outside?'

'No.'

'Why not?'

'It would take me far too long to get from front to back, if I had to. And my finger wouldn't fit in the trigger guard with gloves on. And it's too cold to go out without gloves.'

'So we just wait in here?'

Reacher nodded. 'That's right. We wait in here.'

They waited in the parlour. Reacher figured it was the best choice. It overlooked the front, and given the snow on the ground, frontal approach was the most likely. And even if an actual approach was not attempted, the parlour was still the best room. The way it looked out under the lip of the porch roof and across the whole of its depth meant that a potential sniper would have to line up front and centre to get a shot. He would be spotted twenty paces before he even raised the rifle to his eye.

There were many other possible dangers. Bombs or fire bombs were top of the list. But if that kind of thing was coming their way, it didn't really matter which room they were in.

The clock ticked past nine and marked the end of their first hour alone. The street outside was deserted. Reacher made a careful sweep of the interior perimeter. The front door, locked. The first floor windows, all closed. The French doors in the library, locked. The back door, locked. Second storey windows, all good. Most of them were inaccessible without a ladder. The only viable possibility was a bedroom window at the front, which had the back edge of the porch roof directly under its sill. But there was a lot of snow out there. The porch roof itself would be slippery and treacherous. Safe enough.

The weather was changing. A light wind was getting up. The night sky was clearing. The moon was bright and stars were visible. The temperature felt like it was dropping. Every window Reacher checked had a layer of air in front of it that was pulsing with cold. The wind didn't help. It found invisible cracks and made invisible draughts and sucked heat out of the whole structure.

The wind didn't help safety, either. It made strange sounds. Rustling, cracking, crackling noises, the brittle chafing of frozen foliage, hollow clicks and clonks from frozen tree limbs, a faint keening from the weird shapes on the power lines. In absolute terms the sounds were quiet, but Reacher could have done without them. He was depending on hearing the soft crunch and slide of feet on snow, and the chances of doing that were diminishing. And Janet Salter was talking from time to time, which made things worse, but he didn't want to shut her up. She was nervous, understandably, and talking seemed to help her. He got back from a circuit of the house and she asked him, 'How many times have you done this kind of thing before?'

He kept his eyes on the window and said, 'Once or twice.'

'And clearly you survived.'

He nodded. 'So far.'

'What's your secret of success?'

'I don't like getting beaten. Better for all concerned that it just doesn't happen.'

'That's a heavy burden to carry, psychologically. That kind of burning need for dominance, I mean.'

'Are there people who enjoy getting beaten?'

'It's not black and white. You wouldn't have to enjoy it. But you could be at peace with whatever comes your way. You know, win some, lose some.'

'Doesn't work that way. Not in my line of work. You win some, and then you lose one. And then it's game over.'

'You're still in the army, aren't you?'

158

'No, I've been out for years.'

'In your head, I mean.'

'Not really.'

'Don't you miss it?'

'Not really.'

'I heard you on the phone, with the woman in Virginia. You sounded alive.'

'That was because of her. Not the army. She's got a great voice.'

'You're lonely.'

'Aren't you?'

She didn't answer. The clock ticked on. Nobody approached the house.

After an hour and a half Reacher had made four security sweeps and felt he knew the house pretty well. It had been built for an earlier generation, which had been in some ways tougher, and in some ways gentler. The windows had catches and the doors had locks, all solid well-machined pieces of brass, but nothing like the armour on sale at any modern hardware store. Which meant that there were forty-three possible ways in, of which fifteen were realistically practical, of which eight might be anticipated by a solo opponent of normal intelligence, of which six would be easy to defeat. The remaining two would be difficult to beat, but feasible, made harder by Janet Salter's wandering presence. Lines of fire were always complicated. He thought again about insisting she lock herself downstairs, but she saw him thinking and started talking again, as if to head him off. He was at the parlour window, craning left, craning right, and she asked, 'Was it your mother or your father who was a Marine?'

He said, 'Excuse me?'

'You told me you grew up on Marine Corps bases. I was wondering which of your parents made that necessary. Although I suppose it could have been both of them. Was that permitted? A husband and wife serving together?'

'I don't imagine so.'

'So which one was it?'

159

'It was my father.'

'Tell me about him.'

'Not much to tell. Nice guy, but busy.'

'Distant?'

'He probably thought I was. There were a hundred kids on every base. We ran around all day. We were in a world of our own.'

'Is he still alive?'

'He died a long time ago. My mother, too.'

'It was the same for me,' Janet Salter said. 'I made myself distant. I was always reading.'

He didn't reply, and she went quiet again. He watched the street. Nothing happening. He moved to the library and checked the yard. Nothing happening. The last of the cloud was moving away and the moon was brightening. It was a blue, cold, empty world out there.

Except that it wasn't empty.

But nobody came.


Hide and seek. Maybe the oldest game in the world. Because of ancient thrills and fears buried deep in the back of every human's brain. Predator and prey. The irresistible shiver of delight, crouching in the dark, hearing the footsteps pass by. The rush of pleasure in doubling back and wrenching open the closet door and discovering the victim. The instant translation of primeval terrors into modern-day laughter.

This was different.

There would be no laughter. There would be short seconds of furious gunfire and the stink of smoke and blood and then sudden deafened silence and a world-stands-still pause to look down and check yourself for damage. Then another pause to check your people. Then the shakes and the gulps and the need to throw up.

No laughter.

And this wasn't hide and seek. Nobody was really hiding, and nobody was really seeking. Whoever was out there knew full well where Janet Salter was. An exact address would have been provided. Maybe turn-by-turn directions, maybe GPS coordinates. And she was just sitting right there, waiting for him. No art. Just brutality. Which disappointed Reacher a little. He was good at hide and seek. The real-world version, not the children's game. Good at hiding, better at seeking. His former professional obligations had led him in that direction. He had been a good hunter of people. Fugitives, mainly. He had learned that empathy was the key. Understand their motives, their circumstances, their goals, their aims, their fears, their needs. Think like them. See what they see. *Be* them. He had gotten to the point where he could spend an hour with a case file, a second hour thinking, a third with maps and phone books, and then predict pretty much the exact building the guy would be found in.

He checked the view to the front.

No one there.

Just an empty white world that seemed to be frozen solid.

He glanced back at Janet Salter and said, 'I need you to watch the front for me.'

'OK.'

'I'll be in the hallway for a spell. Anyone comes in through the kitchen or the library, I can get them in the corridor.'

'OK.'

'Stay back in the shadows, but keep your eyes peeled.'

'OK.'

'You see anything at all, you call out to me, loud and clear, with concise information. Numbers, location, direction, and description.'

'OK.'

'And do it standing up.'

'Why?'

'So if you fall asleep on the job I'll hear you fall down.'

She took up a good position, well back in the room, invisible from outside, but with a decent angle. Her hand was still on the gun in her pocket. He stepped out to the hallway and moved the chair to the other side of the telephone table, so he could sit facing the rear of the house. He put his gun in his lap. Picked up the phone. Dialled the number he remembered.

161

'Yes?'

'Amanda, please.'

A pause. A click. The voice. It said, 'You have got to be kidding me. Two hours ago you gave me two weeks' worth of work, and already you're calling me for a result?'

'No, I'm not, but I can't give you two weeks anyway. I need something by tomorrow at the latest.'

'What are you, nuts?'

'You said you were better than me, and I could have done it in a day. So a night should be good enough for you.'

'What is that, psychology? You took motivation classes up at West Point?'

Reacher kept his hand on his gun and his eyes on the kitchen door. He asked, 'Did you catch your guy yet?'

'No, can't you tell?'

'Where are you looking?'

'All the airports, plus boats on the Gulf Coast between Corpus Christi and New Orleans.'

'He's in a motel a little ways north of Austin. Almost certainly Georgetown. Almost certainly the second motel north of the bus depot.'

'What, he's wearing a secret ankle bracelet I don't know about?'

'No, he's scared and alone. He needs help. Can't get it any-place except the overseas folks he's in bed with. But he's waiting to call them. They'll help him if he's clean, they'll ditch him if he's compromised. Maybe they'll even kill him. He knows that. A fugitive from the law, that's OK with them. A political fugitive, not so much. They'd worry about us tracking him all the way home, wherever home is. So he needs to know the news. He needs a media market that covers Fort Hood's business. If it stays a plain vanilla domestic homicide, he'll make the call. If it doesn't, he'll end up putting his gun in his mouth.'

'We haven't released the background.'

'Then he'll take a day or two to be sure, and then he'll call them.'

162

'But he could have gone anywhere for that. Waco, Dallas, Abilene, even.'

'No, he made a careful choice. Abilene is too far and too small. And Waco and Dallas are too patriotic. He thinks that TV and radio there might sit on the espionage angle. What is he, Fourth Infantry? Audiences in Waco and Dallas don't want to hear about a Fourth Infantry captain going bad. He knows that. But Austin is much more liberal. And it's the state capital, so the news stations are a little looser. He needs the real skinny, and he knows that Austin is where he's going to get it.'

'You said Georgetown.'

'He's afraid of the actual city. Too many cops, too much going on. He didn't drive, did he? Too afraid of cops on the highway. His car is still on the post, right?'

'Yes, it is.'

'So he took the bus from Hood and stopped short. Georgetown is right there, close to Austin, but not too close. He watched out the window, all the way in. One motel after another. He mapped them in his head. He got out at the depot and walked back the way he came. Didn't want unfamiliar territory. Didn't want to walk too far, either. Too exposed. Too vulnerable. But even so he didn't like the place nearest the depot. It felt too obvious. So he picked the second place. He's there right now, in his room with the chain on, watching all the local channels.'

The voice didn't answer.

Reacher said, 'Wait one.' He laid the phone gently on the table and got up. Checked the kitchen, checked the library. Nothing doing. He checked the parlour. Janet Salter was still on her feet, rock solid, deep in the shadows.

Nothing to see on the street.

No one coming.

Reacher went back to the hallway and sat down again in the chair and picked up the phone. The voice asked, 'Anything else?'

'Not that it matters, but he sat in the front third of the bus.'

'You're full of shit.'

'It was a kind of camouflage. He didn't want to give himself

163

away as a fugitive. He thinks bad boys sit in back. He's a Fourth Infantry captain. Probably a strait-laced kind of a guy. He remembers his school bus. The greasers sat in back. He didn't.'

No answer.

'Georgetown,' Reacher said. 'Second motel north of the bus depot. Check it out.'

No answer.

Reacher asked, 'Where are your nearest people?'

'I have people at Hood.'

'So send them down. It's about fifty miles. What can it cost you?'

No answer.

Reacher said, 'And don't forget, I need my information by tomorrow.'

He hung up. He put the chair back where it was supposed to be and stepped across the hallway and into the parlour. He checked the window.

Nothing to see.

No one coming.

Five to ten in the evening.

Thirty hours to go.

# TWENTY

The clock ticked on. Reacher took every completed minute to be a small victory. A prison riot could not last for ever. Its initial phase would be relatively short. Hostages would be taken, territory would be seized, a standoff would ensue. Tactical adjustments would be made. The corrections officers would regroup. The cops would be released from duty. Reacher knew that.

Therefore the guy knew that, too.

Reacher didn't understand why he didn't come. His target was an old woman in a house. What was he waiting for?

At half past ten Janet Salter volunteered to make coffee. Reacher wouldn't let her. Maybe that was what the guy was waiting for. The percolator needed water. Water came from the faucet. The faucet was over the sink. The sink was under the window. A preoccupied grey head two feet the other side of the glass might be a tempting target. So he made the coffee himself, after a duly cautious inspection of the vicinity. An unnecessary inspection, as it turned out. He stepped out the back door without coat, gloves, or hat. The cold hit him like a fist. It was raging. It was searching. It stunned him. Way below zero. Too far below to even guess at a number.

He stepped back in. Nobody was waiting out there for a target of opportunity. Impossible. After a minute you would be shaking too hard to see, let alone shoot. After an hour you would be in a coma. After two, you would be dead.

Which thoughts clarified things a little. There would be no long stealthy approach on foot through the snow. The danger would come from the front. The guy would have to drive up, jump out, and move fast. So after the percolator finished gulping and hissing Reacher poured two mugs and carried them back to the parlour, where he told Janet Salter they would alternate spells at the window, ten minutes on, ten minutes off, all through the next hour.

The next hour passed slowly. No one approached the house. The world outside was dead. Deep frozen. Nothing was moving, except the wind. It was blowing steadily out of the west. It was scouring powder into small stunted drifts and exposing ridges of ice that glittered blue in the moonlight. A spectral, elemental scene. Janet Salter did something with a dial on a wall and turned the heat up. Not good, in Reacher's opinion. Warmth made people sleepy. But he didn't want her to freeze. He had read about old folks, dead in their homes, overcome by hypothermia.

She asked, 'Have you ever been here in winter before?'

He said, 'I've never been here in any season.'

'North Dakota, perhaps?'

'I've been in the Dakota Building in New York City.'

'Which was named for here,' she said. 'At the time it was built, the city didn't extend much past 34th Street. It seemed lunatic to build fancy apartments all the way up on 72nd Street, and on the West Side, too. People said, you might as well put them in the Dakota Territory. The name stuck. The man who built it owned part of the Singer Sewing Machine Company, which brings us full circle, really, doesn't it, back to that can of oil.'

She was talking for the sake of talking. Reacher let her. He kept his eye on the street and filtered most of it out. She got into a long disquisition on the state's history. Explorers and traders, Lewis and Clark, the Sioux Nation, Fort Pierre, sodbusters and pioneers, the gold rush, Crazy Horse, Sitting Bull, Custer, the Black Hills, Wounded Knee, the Dust Bowl, some guy called Brokaw she claimed had been on network TV.

Five to eleven in the evening.

Twenty-nine hours to go.

Reacher completed his eighth circuit of the interior perimeter. He saw nothing to get concerned about. Nothing to see from any window except frozen moonlit emptiness. Nothing to hear except the rush of water in the heating pipes and a faint creaking as the ice outside got colder. It was clamping down. The earth was in its grip. He thought back to the sodbusters and the pioneers that Janet Salter had talked about. Why the hell had they stayed?

He was on his way back down the stairs when she called out.

She said, 'Someone's coming.'

She spoke loud and clear. But she added no information. No numbers, no location, no direction, no description. He stepped into the parlour and eased past her to the window. Saw a guy approaching on foot in the middle of the road, from the left. He was small, but swaddled in an enormous coat with a hood. He had a ski mask on. Plus a muffler, plus gloves, plus boots. Nothing in his hands. His hands were held out to the sides, for balance, and they were empty.

The guy moved on, slowly, tentatively, unsure of his footing. He stopped directly opposite the end of Janet Salter's driveway. Just stood there.

Reacher asked, 'Do you know who he is?'

She said, 'Wait.'

The guy turned around, a stiff and ungainly half-circle, and faced the other way. A dog trotted up to him. A big white thing. Lots of fur. The guy turned around again, and man and dog walked on.

Janet Salter said, 'A neighbour. A she, actually. Mrs Lowell. But it was hard to be sure, the way she was dressed.'

Reacher breathed out and said, 'Is she the cop's wife?'

'Ex-wife. Officer Lowell moved out a year ago. There was some kind of unpleasantness.'

'What kind?'

'I don't know.'

'I saw Lowell today. Peterson called him an odd duck. Said he read books.'

'He does. He comes over and borrows some of mine from time to time. My family and his go way back.'

'Do you know his partner?'

'Officer Kapler? I've met him, certainly.'

'And?'

'He moved here from Florida. Which struck me as odd.'

'Me too,' Reacher said. He stayed at the window and watched Mrs Lowell and her dog round a curve and move out of sight.

They didn't speak again for thirty minutes. The clock in Reacher's head ticked on towards midnight. He asked, 'Are you tired?'

Janet Salter said, 'I haven't really thought about it.'

'You could go to bed, if you like. I can take care of things down here.'

'Would you take care of things standing up? So if you fell asleep I would hear you fall down?'

Reacher smiled. 'I won't fall asleep.'

'And I won't go to bed. This is my responsibility. I shouldn't be involving you at all.'

'A problem shared is a problem halved.'

'You could be killed.'

'Unlikely.'

She asked, 'Are you married?'

Reacher kept his eyes on the window and said, 'No.'

'Were you ever?'

'No.'

'Were you an only child?'

168

'I had a brother two years older. He worked for the Treasury Department. He was killed in the line of duty.'

'I'm sorry.'

'Not your fault.'

'Do you always deflect sympathy that way?'

'Usually.'

'So you're the last of your family's line.'

'I suppose so. But it wasn't much of a line in the first place.'

'Just like me. Scoundrels, all of them.'

'Where were your gold mines?'

'The Black Hills. Why?'

'Peterson thinks the army place west of here could be mostly underground. I was wondering if there were old workings they could have used.'

'No mines here. Just prairie topsoil and rock.'

'Were your parents alive when you went off to college?'

'Why?'

'Because if they were, they probably wrote you with all the local news. Maybe rumour and gossip, too. They must have told you something about that place. Maybe not exact enough for your scholarly mind to pass on as fact, but you must have heard some little thing.'

'Nothing worth repeating.'

'Try me.'

'All I know is that it was built and never used. Apparently because its purpose was too revolting. There was a minor scandal about it.'

'What was its purpose?'

'I don't know. No one spoke of it to me.'

Five minutes to midnight.

Twenty-eight hours to go.

Nobody came.

A thousand miles away down in Texas two fast cars covered the fifty miles south from Hood in less than forty minutes. Six men in the cars, all warrant officers working for the 110th Special Unit, all currently W3s, all wanting to be W4s, all well aware

169

that this kind of assignment could get them their promotions. They pulled off the main drag south and wheeled through the centre of Georgetown and found the bus depot. It was middle-of-the-night quiet. Cool air, trash, the stink of spilled diesel. Nothing coming in, nothing going out. They parked their cars a block farther on next to pawn shops and bail bond offices and hustled back the way they had come. They counted the motels. The first was a brick place behind a parking lot that was covered with broken blacktop. The second was right next to it, set end-on to the street, made of red wood, twelve rooms, a sign on a pole advertising free cable and free breakfast and no vacancies.

An office, first door on the left.

A clerk in the office, half awake.

A pass key, in the desk drawer.

The six W3s split up, three to the rear, three to the front. One of the front guys stood back, ready for anything. The other two entered every room, bold as you like, guns drawn, for close-up in-their-face flashlight examinations of the somnolent forms they found.

All twelve rooms.

Their man wasn't there.


Reacher prowled through Janet Salter's house one more time. By that point he was totally accustomed to its sounds. The creak of the boards, the creak of the stairs, an occluded right-angle joint in a steam pipe that hissed louder than all the others, a window sash that trembled a little in its frame because of the freshening wind. The smell of the air was changing. Tiny eddying draughts were stirring odours out of the rugs and the drapes. They were not unpleasant. Just old. Dyed wool, dusty velvet, mothballs, beeswax furniture polish, cigar smoke, pipe tobacco. Ancient, deep aromas, like an olfactory portrait of how prosperous frontier families used to live. Reacher sensed them behind the local mineral smell from the new oil on the gun he was carrying with him everywhere.

He came back to the parlour. Janet Salter's gun was still in her

170

pocket. Her hand was still resting on its butt. He asked her, 'You still OK?'

She said with great formality, 'I have reached the conclusion that I am privileged.'

'In what way?'

'I'm experiencing the chance to live out my principles. I believe that ordinary citizens must confront wickedness. But I believe in due process, too. I believe in an accused's right to a fair trial and I believe in his right to confront the witnesses against him. But it's so easy to talk the talk, isn't it? Not everyone gets the opportunity to walk the walk. But now I am.'

'You're doing great,' Reacher said.

He eased past her to the window.

Saw the wild bounce of headlight beams on the street.

A car, coming on fast.

# TWENTY-ONE

I T WAS PETERSON, LEADING WHAT LOOKED LIKE MOST OF THE BOLTON PD. Six cars, seven, eight. Then a ninth. They jammed and slid and crunched to a stop all over the road. Twelve cops spilled out, then thirteen, fourteen, fifteen. They drew their weapons and formed up for an approach driven partly by desperate haste and partly by extreme caution. Because they had no idea what they were going to find.

Either tranquillity, or a double homicide.

Reacher stepped out to the hallway and lined up on the hinge side of the front door. He flung it open and stayed well out of sight. He didn't want to get fired on by mistake. Fifteen nervous cops made for an unpredictable situation.

He called, 'Peterson? This is Reacher. We're all clear.'

No answer.

He tried again. 'Peterson?'

Icy air flooded in. Peterson's voice came with it. 'Reacher?'

Reacher called back, 'All clear in here. Holster your weapons and come on in.'

172

They came in at a run, all fifteen of them, Peterson first, then the four women, then the three guys from the stake-out cars, then seven more bodies Reacher didn't know. They brought gusts and billows of freezing air in with them. They all had red, chapped faces. The warm inside air hit them and they all started wrenching open their parkas and pulling the gloves from their hands and the hats from their heads.

The four women formed up around Janet Salter like a cordon and bustled her off to the kitchen. Peterson ordered the three night watch cars to their positions and sent the remaining seven men back to the station. Reacher watched normality restored from the parlour window. Within five minutes all was as it had been five hours earlier.

Peterson asked, 'So what happened here?'

'Nothing at all,' Reacher said. 'What happened there?'

'A riot. Not that we saw much of anything. They shut it down very fast.'

'Because it was phoney. It was a diversion.'

Peterson nodded. 'But their guy never came here.'

'And the big question is, why the hell not?'

'Because he saw you.'

'But I didn't see him. Which begs another big question. If he's good enough to see me without me seeing him, why didn't he just go for it?'

'I have no idea.'

'I saw a woman with a big white dog.'

'When?'

'A little after eleven.'

'Mrs Lowell. She's a neighbour. She walks her dog every night.'

'You should have told me that. I might have shot her.'

'I'm sorry.' Peterson clamped his palms tight on his nose. It must have been hurting. His skin temperature had vaulted sixty degrees in sixty seconds. Then he ran his fingers through his hair. 'Bad thing to say, I guess, but I kind of wish the guy had come tonight. I'm not sure we can take another month of this.'

Reacher said, 'I don't think you'll have to. I think they're fresh out of diversions.'

'They can start another riot any old time they want to.'

'They can't. That's the point. Prison riots need a critical mass. About a third of the population would riot every day of the week, given the chance. Another third never would. It's the middle third that counts. The swing votes. Like an election. And they're spent now. Their passion has gone. It will take a year before they're back in the game.'

Peterson said nothing.

Reacher said, 'And your biker pal can't organize an escape fast enough. So you're in the clear now. You're safe.'

'You think?'

'You might never hear that siren again.'

Five to one in the morning.

Twenty-seven hours to go.


At a quarter past one the phone in the hallway rang. Janet Salter came out of the kitchen to answer it. She passed the receiver to Peterson. Peterson listened for a second and went to find Reacher in the parlour.

'It's the woman from the 110th MP,' he said. 'How does she know this number?'

'She has a caller ID system,' Reacher said. 'With coordinates. She's probably watching this house right now, on Google Earth.'

'But it's dark.'

'Don't ask me how it works.' He stepped out to the hallway and sat down in the chair. Picked up the receiver. Asked, 'You got my answers for me?'

The voice said, 'Not yet.'

'So why are you calling so late? I could have been fast asleep.'

'I just wanted to tell you I got my guy.'

'Was I right?'

'I'm not going to answer that question. I'm not going to give you the satisfaction.'

174

'So I was right.'

'Actually, not quite. He was in the third motel north of the bus depot.'

'Because the first two were close together? He had to go on to the third, for distance?'

'You're good.'

'I used to do this for a living.'

'I'm duly impressed.'

'How was he?'

'You tell me.'

Reacher said, 'He was awake. He had a loaded firearm and shoes on. His bag was packed and his jacket was on the back of a chair. He struggled for less than ten seconds and then he gave it up.'

'You're very good.'

'Not good enough to survive the general's head.'

'I still want to hear that story.'

'Then get me my answers. A fair exchange is no robbery.'

'We're close. We can see the money coming out of Congress. But we can't see it arriving at the Department of the Army. It's dropping out of sight somewhere along the way. We're narrowing it down. We'll get there.'

'When?'

'Give me the rest of the night. Call me at eight o'clock in the morning.'

'You're good, too.'

'I try.'

Reacher said, 'There's a local rumour about a scandal. Word on the street is the place was never used because its purpose was too revolting.'

'On the street?'

'In an old lady's parlour, anyway.'

'OK. But old ladies get revolted by all kinds of things.'

'I guess.'

'Anything else?'

'You can search with your Google thing, right?'

'That's what it's for.'

'Check a Florida cop called Kapler for me. He left the state two years ago. I want to know why.'

'Why?'

'I like to know things. He moved from Florida to South Dakota. Who does that?'

'First name?'

'I don't know.'

'That's helpful.'

'How many Florida cops called Kapler can there be?'

'Probably more than ten, and less than a hundred.'

'With employment problems two years ago?'

'Anything else?'

Reacher asked, 'What are you wearing?'

'What is this, a dirty phone call now?'

Reacher smiled. 'No, I'm just trying to picture the scene. For old times' sake. I know the desk. Same office?'

'I assume so. Upstairs, third on the left.'

'That's the one.' Reacher saw it in his mind. Stone stairs, a metal handrail, a narrow corridor floored with linoleum, lines of doors left and right with fluted glass windows in them, offices behind each one, each office equipped according to some complex DoD protocol. His had had the metal desk, two phones with a total of three lines, a vinyl chair on casters, file cabinets, and two visitor chairs with springy bent-tube legs. Plus a glass light shade shaped like a bowl and hung from the ceiling on three metal chains. Plus an out-of-date map of the United States on the wall, made after Hawaii and Alaska had joined the Union but before the interstate highway system had been completed.

Made, in fact, around the same time that the strange installation near Bolton, South Dakota, was being put in.

The voice said, 'I'm wearing my ACUs with a T-shirt. I've got the jacket on, because it's cold tonight.'

Reacher said, 'You're in Virginia. You don't know what cold is.'

'Quit whining. You're still in double figures up there. Negative, but hey. Minus eleven degrees. But the radar shows colder air moving in from the west.'

'How could it get colder?'

'You're going to get what Wyoming just had, that's how.'

'You talking to meteorologists?'

'No, I'm looking at the Weather Channel.'

'What did Wyoming just have?'

'They were thirty below zero.'

'Terrific.'

'You can take it. You're a big guy. Probably a Norseman way back, by the look of you.'

'What, Google Earth can see through roof tiles now?'

'No, there's a photo of you in your file.'

'What about you?'

'Yes, there's a photo of me in my file, too.'

'Not what I meant, smartass. I don't have your file.'

'I'm a one-eyed fifty-year-old hunchback.'

'I thought so, judging by your voice.'

'Asshole.'

'I'm thinking maybe five-six or five-seven, but thin. Your voice is all in your throat.'

'You saying I'm flat-chested?'

'34A at best.'

'Damn.'

'Blond hair, probably short. Blue eyes. From northern California.'

She asked, 'Age?'

Reacher had been thirty-two years old, the first time he sat behind that battered desk. Which was both old and young for a command of that importance. Young, because he had been something of a star, but old, too, in that he had gotten there a little later than a star should, because he wasn't an organization man and hadn't been entirely trusted. He said, 'You're thirty or thirty-one,' because he knew that when it came to a woman's age it was always better to err on the side of caution.

She said, 'Flattery will get you everywhere.' Then she said, 'Got to go. Call me later.'

*　　*　　*

The household got right back into its settled routine. Peterson left, and the two day watch women went up to bed. Janet Salter showed Reacher to the front upstairs room with the window over the porch roof. In principle the most vulnerable, but he wasn't worried. Sheer rage would overcome any theoretical tactical disadvantage. He hated to be woken in the night. An intruder came through that window, he would go straight back out like a spear.

Five to two in the morning.

Twenty-six hours to go.

# TWENTY-TWO

REACHER HAD PLANNED ON SLEEPING UNTIL EIGHT, BUT HE WAS woken at half past six. By Peterson. The guy came into the bedroom and some primal instinct must have made him pause and kick the bed frame and then step smartly back. He must have figured that was the safest thing to do. He must have figured if he leaned over and shook Reacher gently by the shoulder he could get his arm broken.

And he might have been right.

Reacher said, 'What?'

Peterson said, 'First light is less than an hour away.'

'And?'

'You need to get going.'

'Where?'

'The biker camp. Remember? You offered.'

Janet Salter was already in her kitchen. Reacher found her there. She was dressed for the day. She had coffee going. The old percolator was slurping and rattling. He said, 'I have to go out.'

She nodded. 'Mr Peterson told me. Will you be OK?'

'I hope so.'

'I don't see how. There are a hundred people out there, and all you have is a six-shooter.'

'We need information.'

'Even so.'

'I've got the Fourth Amendment. That's all the protection I need. If I get hurt or don't come back, the cops get probable cause for a search. The bikers don't want that. They'll treat me with kid gloves.'

'That's hard to imagine.'

'Will you be OK here?'

'I hope so.'

'If the cops leave again, take your gun and lock yourself in the basement. Don't open the door to anyone except me.'

'Should we have a password?'

'You can ask about my favourite book.'

'You don't have one. You told me that.'

'I know. So that will be the correct answer.' The percolator finished and Reacher poured a generous measure into one of six white mugs standing on the counter.

Janet Salter asked, 'Will the police leave again?'

'Probably not.'

'There could be another riot.'

'Unlikely. Prison riots are rare. Like revolutions in a nation's history. The conditions have to be exactly right.'

'An escape, then.'

'Even less likely. Escapes are hard. The prison people make sure of that.'

'Are you saying my problems are over?'

'It's possible.'

'So are you going to come back here or not?'

'I think the highway is still closed.'

'When it opens again, where will you go next?'

'I don't know.'

Janet Salter said, 'I think you'll head for Virginia.'

'She might be married.'

'You should ask her.'

Reacher smiled. Said, 'Maybe I will.'

Peterson briefed him in the hallway. He said the spare unmarked car was outside, warmed up and running. It was reliable. It had been recently serviced. It had a full tank. It had chains on the back and winter tyres on the front. There was no direct route to the camp. The way to go was to head south towards the highway, but turn west a mile short of the cloverleaf on the old road that ran parallel.

'The road the lawyer was killed on,' Reacher said.

'That was all the way to the east,' Peterson said. 'But still, perhaps you shouldn't stop if someone tries to flag you down.'

'I won't,' Reacher said. 'Count on it.'

He was to keep on the old road for five miles, and then make a right and head back north on a county two-lane that wandered a little for about eight miles before hitting the ruler-straight section that the army engineers had put in fifty years before. That section was two miles long, and it ran right up to the camp, where he would find the fifteen wooden huts and the old stone building, laid out in two neat lines of eight, running precisely east to west.

'The stone building is in the back left corner,' Peterson said.

Five to seven in the morning.

Twenty-one hours to go.

Seventeen hundred miles south it was five to eight in the morning. Plato had finished his breakfast and was about to break the habit of a lifetime. He was about to cut out his middleman in the walled city villa and call his guy in the States direct.

He dialled.

He got an answer.

He asked, 'Is the witness dead yet?'

There was a pause on the line. His guy said, 'You know there was always going to be a delay between the two.'

'How long has that delay been so far?'

His guy knew what to say. 'Too long.'

'Correct,' Plato said. 'I arranged a riot at the prison last night.'

'I know.'

'Evidently you didn't make use of it.'

'There was a man in the house.'

'And?'

'I had no instructions.'

'That's your answer? You needed instructions?'

'I thought perhaps there were complexities I wasn't grasping.'

Plato breathed out. 'How can I hurt you?'

His guy knew what to say. 'In ways I don't want to be hurt.'

'Correct,' Plato said. 'But I need you to be more specific. I need you to focus on what's at stake.'

His guy said, 'You'll kill the person nearest and dearest to me.'

'Yes, I will, eventually. But first there will be a delay, which seems to be a concept you're very familiar with. I'll cripple her and mutilate her and let her live for a year or so. Then I'll kill her. Do you understand me?'

'Yes, I do.'

'So for your own sake, get the job done. I don't care about bystanders. Wipe out the entire damn town if you have to. The entire state, for all I care. How many people live in South Dakota anyway?'

'About eight hundred thousand.'

'OK. That's your upper limit for collateral damage. Get it done.'

'I will. I promise.'

Plato hung up and poured himself another cup of coffee.


The spare unmarked was another dark Crown Vic. It smelled dusty and tired inside. Its heater was set to seventy degrees and the fan was blowing hard in a desperate attempt to get there. The weather was way down in a whole new dimension. The temperature was dropping fast. The ground was bone hard and the air was solid with microscopic nubs of snowflakes borne on the wind. They were chilled and shrivelled to sharp fragments. They hurled themselves against the windshield and made complex frozen traceries. The wipers wouldn't shift them. The blades just scraped over them. Reacher set the heater on defrost and waited until the blown air melted oval holes of clarity.

Then he left.

He K-turned across the width of Janet Salter's street. The ruts were frozen solid. The Crown Vic's tyres bumped up and down. The stake-out car at the end of the road backed up to let him squeeze by. He turned right and drove away from town. The wheel ruts that had been soft the day before were now as hard as concrete trenches. It was like driving a train on a track. He didn't need to steer. The chains on the back dug in and splintered the ice and the front tyres hammered left and right and kept him basically straight. The world outside was entirely white. There was pale light in the sky but no sun. The air was too full of ice. It was like dust. Like mist. The wind was blowing right to left in front of him. Small streamlined drifts had built up and frozen solid, against fence posts and power poles. The weird shapes on the power lines had shifted to the east, as if the whole world was tilted.

Reacher found the turn a mile short of the cloverleaf. Getting out of the frozen ruts was difficult. He had to slow to a walk and turn the wheel way over and churn his way out one tyre at a time, four separate climbs, four separate drops. He found new ruts running west and settled in for five more miles of autopilot. He repeated the escape manoeuvre at the next turn and headed north towards the camp. The new road was different. It hadn't seen much traffic. There were no established ruts. It was just a narrow ribbon of frozen snow. The front wheels skated and wandered a little. The blowing ice pattered left to right against the driver's window. The road humped and dipped and curved left and right for no apparent reason. The camber tilted one way, then the other. Not a great piece of civil engineering. Reacher slowed a little and concentrated hard. To slide into a ditch would be fatal. No chance of a tow before he froze. Even a blown tyre would be a disaster. The wheel nuts were probably frozen solid.

183

Five slow careful miles, then six, then seven. Then the horizon changed. Up ahead the road widened and straightened and flattened. Dramatically. Radically. In the murky distance it looked as broad and flat as a freeway. Maybe even broader and flatter. It looked like a sixteen-lane superhighway. It was a magnificent, surreal piece of road. It was built up slightly proud of the land around it, it was absolutely flat, and it was absolutely straight, for two whole miles.

And it was ploughed.

There was not a speck of snow on it. Just smooth grey concrete, scraped and brushed and salted. High piles of snow had been pushed to the sides, and smoothed, and shaped, so that the frozen prairie wind was launching off the western berm and not landing again until it was past the eastern. The tiny fragments of ice were howling past five feet in the air. The road surface itself was clear and dry, like the middle of summer.

Reacher slowed and bumped up on to it. The chains thumped and chattered. The front end tracked straight and true. He kept to a steady thirty and peered ahead. He could make out blond smudges on the horizon. Wooden huts, in a neat row. Two miles away. The car pattered and juddered. The chains were not good on dry concrete.

He kept on going.

Half a mile out he saw activity ahead. A hundred yards out he saw what it was. Pick-up trucks with plough blades lowered were grinding back and forth. A lot of them. Maybe thirty or forty. Beyond them bulky black-clad figures with shovels were working in a line. Other bulky figures were walking backwards, hurling stuff from their cupped hands in long arcs, like farm labourers feeding chaff to chickens. Salt, presumably. Or grit, or sand, or some other kind of de-icing chemical. Or all of the above. They were clearing the whole camp. They wanted the whole place immaculate. As good as the road.

The huts were raw lumber, bleached and faded a little, but not much. Not brand new, but not old either. On the left behind the first row of huts Reacher saw the roof of the old stone building. It

184

was tall and peaked and made of slate. It was covered with a foot of snow. It had twin ornate chimneys. The huts themselves were roofed with tarpaper. They had stove pipe vents. There were power lines running from gable to gable. There were concrete paths running from door to door. All were swept clear of snow. What had not been removed completely was piled neatly left and right. In front of the huts was a long line of shapes under black tarpaulins, side by side, like dominoes. Motorcycles, presumably. Big ones. Maybe thirty of them. Harleys, probably, laid up for winter.

Reacher slowed and came to a stop fifty yards out. People had stopped working and were staring at his car. Gloved hands were stacked on shovel handles. Chins were resting on the hands. The salt throwers had paused. One after the other the pick-up trucks came to rest. Their idling exhaust was carried away on the wind.

Reacher took his foot off the brake and inched forward. Nobody moved. Reacher kept on coming, ten yards, then twenty. He stopped again. He was close enough. He didn't switch off. The Crown Vic's dash was showing the outside temperature at twelve degrees below zero. If he switched the engine off he might never get it started again. He had read a book set above the Arctic Circle where you had to thaw the engine block with blowlamps.

He jammed his watch cap down on his ears and pulled his hood up. Zipped his coat to his chin. Put his gloves on, left and then right.

He climbed out of the car.

Twenty yards ahead the crowd had gotten larger. Men, women, and children. Maybe a hundred people in total. As advertised. They were all shapeless and hidden in coats and hats and mufflers. Their breath was condensing around their heads, an unbroken cloud that hung motionless and then rose and whipped away in the wind. The cold was stunning. It was getting worse. It seemed to attack from the inside out. Reacher was shivering after five seconds of exposure. His face was numb after ten. He walked ten paces and stopped. Olive green pants, a tan coat, an obvious police car behind him, South Dakota plates. Not even remotely convincing.

Twenty yards ahead a guy threaded through the crowd. Sidestepping, shuffling, leading with his left shoulder, then his right. Black coat, hat, gloves. His body language was like every interrupted workman in the world. Irritated, but curious. He swiped his padded forearm across his brow and paused and thought and moved forward again. He stepped out of the ranks and stopped a yard in front of the crowd.

Reacher said, 'Who the hell are you?'

The guy said, 'Piss off.'

Reacher stepped forward. One pace, two, three.

'You're not very polite,' he said.

'Show me where it says I have to be.'

'Well, you're walking around on my property.'

'How so?'

'I'm from the army. I'm here to check on our real estate. A two-year maintenance inspection. Your tax dollars at work.'

'That's a joke.'

Reacher said, 'Whatever, I need to take a look around.'

'I told you to piss off.'

'I know. But what are the odds I'm going to take you seriously?'

'You can't fight a hundred people.'

'I won't need to. Looks like two-thirds of you are women and children. That leaves maybe thirty guys. Or forty, say. But half of them look too fat to move. They pitch in, they're going to get all kinds of coronaries. The others, maybe half of them are pussies. They'll run away. That leaves maybe eight or ten guys, max. And one of me is worth eight or ten of you, easy.'

No answer.

'Plus, I'm from the army. You mess with me, the next guy you see will be driving a tank.'

Silence for a beat. Just the scouring howl of the wind, and the rattle of ice particles against wood. The guy in front looked at Reacher, at his clothes, at his car, and came to some kind of a decision. He asked, 'What do you need to see?'

186

Reacher said, 'The stone building.'

'That's not ours.'

'None of this is yours.'

'I mean, we're not using it.'

'You shouldn't be using anything.'

'Squatters' rights. It's an abandoned facility. We know the law.'

Reacher said nothing. Just stepped left and skirted the crowd. They all stood still and let him by. No move to block him. A policy decision. He glanced at the corner hut. It was a plain, utilitarian structure. Maybe fifty feet long, its blank slab siding pierced only by two small square windows. It had a door in its narrow end. All around it the snow had been cleared away meticulously. Directly behind it was the stone building. There was no snow around it, either. Just clear, swept paths.

Reacher turned around.

He said, 'If you're not using it, why clear the snow?'

The same guy came out of the crowd again.

He said, 'For the satisfaction of a job well done.'

The stone building was a strange little thing. It could have been copied from the plans for a small but fairly ornate and old-fashioned suburban house. It had all kinds of details and mouldings and curlicues and gables and rain gutters and eaves. Like a Gothic folly a rich man might put in his garden for guests.

But there were crucial differences, too. Where a guest house in a garden would have windows, the stone building had recesses only. Like an optical illusion. The right size and shape, but not filled with glass. Filled instead by unbroken expanses of stone, the same neat mortared blocks as the rest of the walls. There was a portico, but the front door under it made no attempt at illusion. It was just a meaty steel slab, completely plain. It had huge hinges. It would open outward, not inward. Like a blast door. A pressure wave outside would hold it shut, not burst it open. It had a handle and a keyhole. Reacher tried the handle. It didn't move. The keyhole was large. Smaller than the hole for a church key, bigger than the hole for a house key. The steel around it was rimed with frost. Reacher rubbed it away with his gloved thumb, and saw no nicks or scratches in the metal. The lock was not in regular use. No key had been inserted and withdrawn, day in and day out.

He asked, 'You know what this place is?'

The guy who had followed him said, 'Don't you?'

'Of course I do. But I need to know how our security is holding up.'

The guy said, 'We heard things.'

'From who?'

'The construction guys that were here before.'

'What things?'

'About atomic bombs.'

'They said there were nuclear weapons in here?'

'No. They said it was a clinic.'

'What kind of a clinic?'

'They said if we had been attacked in winter, in a city, like New York or Chicago, people would have been in coats and gloves, so only their faces would have been burned. You know, miles from the centre. Closer in, you would have been vaporized. But if you survived, you could come here and get a new face.'

'Like plastic surgery?'

'No, like prosthetics. Like masks. They said that's what's in there, thousands and thousands of plastic faces.'

Reacher walked on around the strange little structure. It was the same on all four sides. Heavy stone, fake windows, details, mouldings. A bizarre parody. Entertaining, but not instructive without getting inside. Which wasn't going to happen.

He walked away. Then on a sudden whim he stopped at the nearest hut. The first in the back row, which was in line with the second in the front row. The crowd had followed him in a long untidy straggle that looped all the way back to where he had started. Like a thin question mark, curling through the gaps and the passages. Steam hung above it. Nearest to him was the guy who had done all the talking. He was about six feet away.

Reacher pushed the hut's door. It swung halfway open.

The guy close to him said, 'That's not yours.'

188

'It's bolted down on army concrete. That's good enough for me.'

'You got no warrant.'

Reacher didn't answer. He was all done talking. It was too cold. His face was numb and his teeth were hurting. He just pushed the door all the way open and took a look inside.

The hut was dark. And warm. There was a paraffin stove going. Reacher could smell the sweet wet kerosene. There were twelve cots in the room, six to a side, and a boxed-in section at the far end that might have been a bathroom. Plain grey blankets on the cots, cardboard shipping cartons filled with folded clothes, burlap drapes at the small square windows.

There was a young woman sitting on the furthest cot on the right. No coat, because of the heat. No hat. She was maybe eighteen or twenty. She looked a little sullen and grimy, but behind that she was pretty. Long fair hair, strong vivid features. Tall, and slender. For a second Reacher thought he had seen her before. But he hadn't. She was a type, that was all. Like Kim Peterson. A South Dakotan. Wherever this bunch was from, they had picked up local recruits.

Reacher backed out and pulled the door shut behind him. Turned to the guy six feet away and said, 'Want to show me the other huts?'

'Whatever.' No reluctance. The guy just started his limbs moving inside his heavy clothing and trudged on down the paths and pushed open one door after another. Fourteen of the fifteen huts were the same. Rows of cots, crude drapes, paraffin stoves, grey blankets, shipping boxes, folded clothes. No benches, no work tables, no glass vessels, no gas rings, no laboratory equipment of any kind. No people, either. The girl in the first hut was the only one not outside and working. Maybe she was sick.

The last hut in the back row was a kitchen. It had two domestic stoves shoved side by side for cooking, and plain deal tables pushed against the walls for use as work surfaces, and crude shelves stacked with plates and bowls and mugs, and more shelves lined with a few meagre supplies. Jars almost empty of flour and sugar and coffee, single boxes of cereal and pasta standing alone in spaces that could have taken dozens.

There was no laboratory equipment.

Reacher hunched down in his coat and came out between two huts. His car was still there, idling faithfully. Beyond it the ploughed road narrowed into the distance, high, wide, and handsome. As flat as glass. Fifty summers, fifty winters, it hadn't heaved or cracked at all. The voice from Virginia had asked: *You know how big the defence budget was fifty years ago?* They had poured maybe four hundred thousand yards of concrete, and then forgotten all about them.

'Have a nice day,' Reacher said, and headed for his car.

Five minutes to nine in the morning.

Nineteen hours to go.

# TWENTY-THREE

THE DRIVE BACK WAS THE SAME AS THE DRIVE OUT, EXCEPT FOR A strange slow-motion near-collision at the first turn. Reacher had driven the wide ploughed road fast and the next eight narrow snow-bound miles slow, and then he had coasted and tried to work out a trajectory to get himself through the left turn and into the eastbound ruts on the old road that ran parallel with the highway. But at the same time a fuel tanker was trying to get out of those same ruts for a left turn of its own up towards the camp. It was a squat vehicle with a company name painted along its flank. Paraffin for the heaters, maybe, or gasoline for the pick-up trucks, or diesel for a generator. It changed down to a low gear and turned very early and came right across Reacher's lane. He braked hard, hoping his chains would bite, but the Crown Vic's onboard electronics wouldn't allow the wheels to lock. The car rolled on with all kinds of thumping and banging coming from the brake pistons. The fuel truck kept on coming. Reacher yanked the wheel. The front tyres lost their grip and skated. The Crown Vic's front left corner

191

missed the back of the truck by an inch. The truck roared on, low gear, walking pace, oblivious. Reacher watched it go in his mirror. He had ended up stationary at a right angle across the old road, with his front wheels in one of the eastbound ruts and his back wheels in one of the westbound. He had to rock between Drive and Reverse and hit the gas hard to break free.

But after that it was plain sailing all the way.

The cop in the stake-out car at the end of Janet Salter's street was Kapler. Better than Montgomery, from the day before. Kapler looked Reacher over very carefully and then backed up to let him by. Reacher parked nose to tail with the second stake-out car and hustled up the driveway. The day watch cop in the hallway let him in. He asked, 'All quiet?'

She said, 'So far.'

'Is Mrs Salter OK?'

'She's fine.'

'Let me see her.' Just like Chief Holland the night before, and just as pointless. If anything bad had happened, the cops wouldn't be sitting around doing nothing.

The day watch woman said, 'She's in the library.'

Reacher found her there, in her usual chair. This time she was reading, an old book with no dust jacket and a title too small to read from a distance. Her gun was still in her pocket. Reacher could make out its shape. She looked up and said, 'Kid gloves?'

He said, 'Plastic. Less classy than kid. But nothing to complain about.'

'Did you learn anything?'

'Plenty.'

He got back in the car and headed for the police station. Found Peterson in the squad room. Reacher said, 'Holland was right. They weren't coming over here. They were bluffing. Or someone was bluffing on their behalf. We have no idea who actually called here. Could have been the shooter himself, trying to create time and space, trying to point you in the wrong direction.'

192

'Well, whoever, they failed. And now we're going to bust them all.'

'Then you better do it quickly. They're about to move out.'

'They told you that?'

'Think back to that call from the DEA. Have you ever sold a house?'

'Once.'

'You cleaned it up, right? Made it look real good?'

'I painted the siding.'

'They've got the snow all ploughed. Everything is immaculate. They've got their stuff in shipping boxes. They've run down their food supplies to nothing. Whoever owns the place is selling it out from under them.'

'When are they going?'

'Soon.'

'Did they give you any trouble?'

'Not really.'

'Did they believe you were from the army?'

'Not for a minute. But they've been told to keep their noses clean, as of right now. The place needs to be a controversy-free zone. Whoever owns the place doesn't want the title damaged. So they didn't give me a hard time.'

'Nobody owns that place. It's all public land.'

'It makes a profit for somebody. Therefore somebody thinks he owns it. The bikers are his employees, that's all. Worker bees. And now they've got their marching orders. They're moving on to the next project.'

'Plato the Mexican.'

'Whoever.'

Peterson asked, 'Did you find a lab?'

Reacher said, 'I want to see the product from the restaurant parking lot.'

'Why?'

'Because that's the way my mind works. One step at a time.'

Peterson shrugged and led the way back to the corridor, around a corner, to an evidence room. There was a half-width counter outside it, unoccupied. Peterson stepped past it and took a bunch of keys from his pocket and unlocked the door.

'Wait there,' he said.

He went in and came out ten seconds later with a clear plastic evidence bag. It was big. Stapled to it was a chain-of-custody form with four separate dates and times and locations and signatures on it. Inside it was the package that Janet Salter had described. The brick of white powder, hard and smooth under the wax paper wrap. The picture stencilled on it, the crown, the headband, the three points, the three balls representing jewels.

Reacher asked, 'Did you test it?'

'Of course,' Peterson said. 'It's meth. No question. Just short of a kilo, very high purity, almost clinical. Good stuff, if you like that kind of thing.'

'Two hundred grand's worth, right there.'

'A million on the streets of Chicago, after they cut it and retail it.'

'Any idea what the picture means?'

'No. They always put some kind of logo on. This is a brand-conscious market.'

'You got the money in there too, that the Chicago guy paid?'

'Of course.'

'Can I see it?'

'Don't you believe me?'

'I just like looking at stuff like that.'

So Peterson ducked back in and came back out with another evidence bag. Same size. Same kind of form stapled to it. Full of bricks of bills, all banded together.

'OK?' Peterson asked.

'How long would it take you to earn that much?'

'After taxes? I don't want to think about it.'

'Is that really wax paper on the dope?'

'No, it's some kind of cellophane or glassine. It's a little yellowed because it's old stock. But it's proper pharmaceutical quality. This is a very high-end operation.'

'OK.'

'So did you find their lab?'

'No.'

'Did you see the stone building?'

'Only from the outside.'

'Do you know what it is?'

'No, but I know what it isn't.'

Reacher headed for the squad room. For the desk in the back corner. He picked up the phone, dialled nine for a line, and then the number he remembered.

'Yes?'

'Amanda, please.'

A click. A purr. The voice. It sounded tired. A little frustrated. It said, 'I could be in Afghanistan right now. In fact if you don't stop calling me I might just put in for a transfer.'

Reacher said, 'The food might be better. Can't beat a goat's eyeballs in yogurt.'

'You ever been there?'

'No, but I met someone who had.'

'I've got no news for you.'

'I know. You can't see the money hitting the Department of the Army.'

'I tried and failed.'

'You didn't. The money never went to the army.'

'Why not?'

'Garbage in, garbage out.'

'What does that mean?'

'We started with a false assumption. They told me about an army facility. A small stone building with a two-mile road. I just went out there. It's not a road. It's a runway. It's an air force place, not army.'

# TWENTY-FOUR

THE VOICE FROM VIRGINIA SAID, 'WELL, THAT CHANGES THINGS A little.'

Reacher said, 'There's another local rumour about prosthetic faces.'

'Yes, I saw a note about that. There's a file. Apparently the Pentagon got some calls from local folks in South Dakota. County and state government. But it's bullshit. The plastic face places were always nearer the metro areas. Why put one out in the middle of nowhere?'

'Why have them at all? If everyone is burned the same, why would anyone care?'

No reply.

Reacher asked, 'Do you know anyone in the air force?'

'Not for secrets.'

'Might not be a secret. Could be entirely routine. We're back at square one, as far as assumptions are concerned.'

'OK, I'll make some calls. But first I'm going to take a nap.'

'You can sleep when you're dead. This is urgent. The runway

196

is ploughed. Two whole miles. Nobody does that for fun. There-fore someone or something is due to show up. And I saw a fuel tanker. Maybe for the return trip. Maybe someone's planning on some heavy lifting.'

Silence for a beat. 'Anything else?'

He asked, 'Are you married?'

She asked, 'Are you?'

'No.'

'Were you ever?'

'No.'

'Why am I not surprised?'

She hung up.

Five minutes to ten in the morning.

Eighteen hours to go.

Peterson was two desks away, hanging up on a call of his own. He said, 'The DEA is blowing me off. Their guy wasn't interested.'

Reacher asked, 'Why not?'

'He said there's no lab out there.'

'How does he know?'

'They have satellites and thermal imaging. They've reviewed the data and can't see any heat. Therefore as far as they're con-cerned it's just a real estate deal. Until proved otherwise.'

'The lab is underground.'

'The DEA says not. Their imaging can see into basements. They say there's nothing down there.'

'They're wrong.'

'You didn't see a lab.'

'They have meth, they must have a lab.'

'We don't know that there's anything under the ground at all. Not for sure.'

'We do,' Reacher said. 'Nobody builds a two-mile runway for nothing. That's long enough to land any kind of plane. Any kind of bomber, any kind of transport. And nobody lands bombers or transports next to a building smaller than a house. You were right. The building is a stair head. Which means there's some-thing under it. Probably very big and very deep.'

'But what exactly?'

Reacher pointed at his phone. 'You'll know when I know.'

A half-hour later Peterson got a call to say that the highway had reopened. The weather radar was showing nothing incoming from the west except supercooled air, and all across the state the snowploughs and the salt spreaders had finished their work, and the Highway Patrol had conferred with the Department of Transportation, and traffic was flowing again. Then Jay Knox called to say he had been told the replacement bus was about three hours out. So Peterson lit up the phone tree and set up a two o'clock rendezvous for the passengers in the police station lobby. All twenty of them. The ladies with the broken bones were fit to travel. A two o'clock departure would get the group to Mount Rushmore a little less than two days late. Not bad, all in all, for South Dakota in the winter.

Then he looked at Reacher and asked, 'Are you going with them?'

Reacher said, 'I paid my money.'

'So are you going?'

'I'm a restless man.'

'Yes or no?'

'Depends what happens before two o'clock, I guess.'

What happened before two o'clock was that Janet Salter decided to go out for a walk.

Peterson took the call from one of the women cops in the house. Mrs Salter was going stir crazy. She had cabin fever. She felt cooped up. She was accustomed to taking walks, to the grocery, to the drugstore, to the restaurant, sometimes just for the fun of it. She had already been a prisoner in her own home for close to a week. She was taking her civic responsibilities seriously, but with responsibilities came rights, and stepping out like a free woman was one of them.

'She's crazy,' Reacher said. 'It's freezing cold.'

'She's a native,' Peterson said. 'This is nothing to her.'

'It must be twenty degrees below zero.'

198

Peterson smiled, like an insider against an outsider. He said, 'The coldest day we ever had was minus fifty-eight. Back in February of 1936. Then less than five months later in July we had the hottest day we ever had, a hundred and twenty exactly.'

'Whatever, she's still crazy.'

'You want to try to talk her out of it?'

Reacher tried. He drove over there with Peterson. Janet Salter was in her kitchen with the two day watch cops. Her percolator was all fired up. Reacher could smell fresh coffee and hot aluminum. She poured him a mug and said, 'The officers tell me you told Mr Peterson that the bikers are preparing to leave.'

Reacher nodded. 'That's how it looked to me.'

'Therefore it should be safe enough to take a little stroll.'

'The guy with the gun is not a biker. Never was.'

'But whoever he is, he won't be waiting outside. You said so yourself, last night. It's too cold.'

'It's also too cold to go for a walk.'

'Nonsense. If we keep up a brisk pace, we'll enjoy it.'

'We?'

'I certainly hope you'll accompany me.'

Five to eleven in the morning.

Seventeen hours to go.

Peterson improvised a plan that looked a lot like the Secret Service taking the president for a walk. He deployed the three stake-out cars to the town's southern, western, and eastern approaches, and told them to stand by to move like a rolling cordon if necessary. He and the two day watch women would be on foot, boxing in Mrs Salter at an appropriate tactical distance. Reacher would walk with her, always keeping himself between her and any passing traffic. A human shield, although Peterson didn't put it that way.

They all wrapped up in all the clothes they had and stepped through the door. The wind was steady out of the west. All the way from Wyoming. It was bitter. Reacher had been in Wyoming in the winter, and survived. He made a mental note never to risk

199

it again. Peterson ranged ahead and one of the day watch women trailed behind and the other kept pace on the opposite sidewalk. Reacher stayed at Janet Salter's shoulder. She had a scarf wrapped around the lower portion of her face. Reacher didn't. As long as the wind was on his back, the situation was tolerable. But when they turned and headed north to town, his nose and cheeks and chin went numb and his eyes started to water. He pulled his hood forward and shielded his face as much as was prudent. He felt he needed some kind of peripheral vision. The sidewalk was humped and ridged with glazed snow. Walking on it was difficult.

Janet Salter asked him, 'What are you thinking about?'

Her voice was muffled, literally. Her words came out thick and soft and then froze and whipped away on the wind.

'I'm thinking about February of 1936,' Reacher said. 'Minus fifty-eight degrees, the height of the Depression, dust storms, droughts, blizzards, why the hell didn't you all move to California?'

'Lots of folks did. The others had no choice but to stay. And that year had a warm summer, anyway.'

'Peterson told me. A hundred-seventy-eight-degree swing.'

'Did he tell you about the chinooks?'

'No.'

'Chinooks are hot winds out of the Black Hills. One day in January of 1943 it was minus four degrees, and then literally two minutes later it was plus forty-five. A forty-nine-degree swing in a hundred and twenty seconds. The most dramatic ever recorded in America. Everyone had broken windows from the thermal shock.'

'Wartime,' Reacher said.

'The hinge of fate,' Janet Salter said. 'That exact day the Germans lost control of the airfields at Stalingrad, many thousands of miles away. It was the beginning of the end for them. Maybe the wind knew.'

They trudged onward. Peterson stayed well ahead, one of the women cops stayed well behind, the other kept pace directly across the street. They got level with the restaurant parking lot. It was full of people heading in and out. Most of them were inadequately dressed and all of them looked thoroughly miserable.

'Prison visitors,' Janet Salter said. 'We seem to get more passing trade now than anywhere in the state except Mount Rushmore.' Which made Reacher think about the replacement bus from Minneapolis, due to leave town at two o'clock. He had no particular interest in oversized sculptures, but he knew there was a road there that led south. And south was Nebraska, then Kansas, then Oklahoma, then Texas, where it was warm. Or alternatively a person could turn left in Kansas, and then cross Missouri, and the southern tip of Illinois, and Kentucky, and end up in Virginia.

Janet Salter said, 'You're thinking about her, aren't you?'

Reacher said, 'No.'

He turned left and right from the waist. Scanned all around. There were more people up ahead than he had seen in a long time. And more cars. They were snuffling slowly along the frozen roads. Huge sheets of ice were creaking and cracking under their weight. Multiple threats, but all of them were trapped into ponderous slow motion by the weather. And there were cop cars among them. Every tenth or twelfth vehicle was a police cruiser, driving slow on a random endless loop, cautious and vigilant.

Reacher asked, 'Where are we going?'

Janet Salter asked, 'Where would you like to go?'

'This is your trip.'

'Bolton is a relatively dull town. We lack exciting destinations.'

'We could get lunch.'

'It's too early.'

'Brunch, then.'

'Brunch is a combination of breakfast and lunch, and I've already had breakfast. Therefore brunch is no longer an option today.'

'Cup of coffee?'

'Everywhere is full up. Visiting days are difficult. We'd never get a table for five.'

'Then let's head back.'

'Already?'

Reacher didn't answer. For a moment it looked like she would keep on going, maybe for ever, but then she stopped and nodded. Reacher tried to whistle ahead to Peterson, but his lips were too cold and cracked to make a sound. So they waited side by side until Peterson turned around to check. Reacher waved, everyone turned back, and the little procession retraced its steps, with the woman cop now in the lead and Peterson trailing behind.

Five minutes to noon.

Sixteen hours to go.


Seventeen hundred miles south it was lunch time. For the second day in succession Plato wasn't eating. And for the second time in succession he was breaking the habit of a lifetime. He was dialling his guy in South Dakota. And his guy was answering. Which annoyed Plato considerably, because it meant his guy had his phone switched on, which meant his guy wasn't at that very moment in the act of killing the damn witness.

His guy said, 'She wasn't in the house.'

Plato said, 'Find her.'


Heading back put the westerly wind on Reacher's other cheek, which was a wash in terms of comfort. Otherwise the inbound trip compared to the outbound was both better and worse. Better, because they were moving away from the populated areas, and fewer people meant fewer threats. Worse, because whatever threats remained were behind Reacher's back. He couldn't easily check over his shoulder. His torso tended to move independently inside the giant coat. A backward glance merely put his whole face inside his hood. So he was forced to rely on Peterson's vigilance behind him. He walked on, regarding each completed safe step as a separate minor triumph.

Janet Salter said, 'I'm sorry.'

'For what?'

'I was inconsiderate. I've put you all to a lot of trouble.'

202

'All part of a day's work. No reason why you shouldn't go out once in a while.'

They crunched onward, slipping and sliding occasionally, forming up in single file where the footstep trail narrowed around obstacles. Reacher had a high pile of ploughed snow between himself and the roadway. After most steps his left foot came down on its lower slope. It was like limping. He kept his eyes on the oncoming traffic. There wasn't much. A few pick-up trucks, a few old-model SUVs, a few salt-caked cars. Nothing to worry about. Then Lowell drove by in his squad car, and slowed in surprise, and waved. Janet Salter waved back. Lowell speeded up again. Then came nothing for a spell, and then came a big dark sedan, heading north towards them. A Ford Crown Victoria. Navy blue. Easy to be sure in the bright clear light. Chief Holland's car. The guy stopped the width of a traffic lane away and rolled down his window. He ignored Reacher completely. Looked straight at Janet Salter, some kind of concern in his face. She stopped and faced him. She said, 'I'm out for a walk. That's all. Nothing to worry about. Mr Peterson is doing a fine job.'

Holland said, 'You heading home now?'

'We're on our way.'

'Can I offer you a ride?'

'Thank you, but I would rather walk. A measure of fresh air and exercise was the point of this little adventure.'

'OK.'

'But please join us back at the house, for coffee, if you like.'

'OK,' Holland said again.

He checked his mirrors and U-turned across the width of the road. Frozen ruts splintered under his wheels. He got lined up in the southbound lane but didn't race on ahead. He kept pace instead, crawling slowly, holding a lateral line with himself on the left behind the wheel, then his empty passenger seat, then the berm of ploughed snow, then Reacher, then Janet Salter. His front tyres were made of hard winter compound, and they crunched and scrabbled slowly. He had chains on the back. Each link rotated into position and made its own distinct sound. He put his flashing lights on, to warn the traffic behind him of his low speed. He had strobes concealed in the rear parcel shelf, matched by more behind the radiator grille. Reacher guessed they would do the job. From a distance the unmarked car would look like a regular police cruiser.

Janet Salter said, 'This is ridiculous.'

Reacher said, 'He's just doing his job.'

'I don't like the attention.'

'You're important to him.'

'Only because he can use me.'

'You're a prominent citizen. You're the kind of person a chief of police worries about.'

Janet Salter said, 'The only prominent citizens in this town are the prison staff. Believe me. That's how it works now.'

They walked on, with the idling car crunching slowly alongside them. Where there were no buildings on their right the wind blew in hard and strong and uninterrupted, a mass of frozen air whistling relentlessly over the flat land, with nothing in its path to roil it up or make it turbulent. It was still carrying tiny spicules of ice. They came in horizontal and pattered against the side of Reacher's hood. They could have been airborne for hundreds of miles, maybe all the way from the Rocky Mountains.

Janet Salter asked, 'Are you cold?'

Reacher smiled, as much as his numb face would let him.

'I know,' he said. 'This is nothing.'

They got back in the house and peeled off layers and endured the pain of thawing. Reacher's ears burned and his nose and chin prickled and itched. Peterson and the two women cops had to have been feeling the same, but they showed no signs of distress. Probably a matter of local South Dakota pride. Chief Holland was entirely OK. He had been riding in a heated car, out of the wind. But still he gave a theatrical shiver as soon as he stepped into the hallway. Relief, Reacher figured, now that Janet Salter's exposure was over and they had gotten away with it.

The two women cops took up their established positions. Janet Salter went to work with her percolator. Reacher and Peterson and Holland watched her from the hallway. Then the phone rang. Janet Salter asked someone to pick it up. Peterson got it. He listened for a second and held the receiver out to Reacher.

'For you,' he said. 'It's the woman from the 110th MP.'

Reacher took the phone. Peterson and Holland trooped into the kitchen and left him alone. Instinctive politeness. Reacher put the phone to his ear and the voice from Virginia said, 'I called a guy in the air force.'

'And?'

'We're getting there. Slowly, but not because it's a secret. Quite the opposite. Because the place was abandoned and forgotten years ago. It fell off the active list when God's dog was still a puppy. Nobody can remember a thing about it.'

'Not even what it was?'

'All the details are archived. All my guy has seen so far is a report about how hard it was to build. The design was compromised several times during construction because of the kind of terrain they found. Some kind of schist. You know what that is?'

'Bedrock, I guess,' Reacher said. 'Probably hard, if it caused difficulties.'

'It proves they were excavating underground.'

'That's for sure. Not a bad result, for the first two hours.'

'One hour,' the voice said. 'I took a nap first.'

'You're a bad person.'

'Last time I checked, you're not my boss.'

'Anything else?'

'I got a hit on a Florida cop called Kapler. Miami PD, born there thirty-six years ago, upped and quit two years ago for no apparent reason. No health issues, not in debt. I'll get more when I'm in the Miami PD records.'

'You can do that with Google?'

'No, I'm using a few other resources. I'll let you know.'

'Thanks,' Reacher said. 'Anything else?'

There was a pause. 'My guy isn't talking.'

'From Fort Hood?'

'Not a word.'

'Where is he?'

'Back on post, in a cell.'

'Did he live on-post or off-post?'

'Off.'

'So he's looking at Texas law for the homicide or the Uniform Code for the treason. That's a rock and a hard place. Either way he's going to fry. He doesn't have an incentive to talk.'

'What would you do?'

'What's your goal?'

'The non-state actors. Who he's talking to, and how, and why.'

'The why is easy. He probably served in Iraq or Afghanistan and got seduced by all the humanitarian bullshit and made friends and got played like a fish. The how will be cell phone or e-mail or an encrypted web site. The who will be very interesting, I agree.'

'So how do I get him to talk?'

'Order him to. You outrank him. He's trained to obey.'

'That won't be enough. It never is.'

'Are his parents still alive?'

'Yes.'

'Siblings?'

'A younger brother, training with the navy SEALs.'

'That's good. That's close to perfect, in fact. You need to bring your boy north, and sit him down, and offer him a deal.'

'I can't do that.'

'You can, in terms of publicity. Tell him he's going to fry, no question, but for what is up to him. Domestic violence by returning officers is up what, a thousand per cent? Nobody condones it, but most folks kind of understand it. So tell him if he cooperates, that's all the world will know about him. But tell him if he doesn't cooperate, then you'll do the treason thing out in the open. His parents will be ashamed and mortified, his brother will have to quit the SEALs, his old high school will disown him.'

'Will that work?'

'All he's got left is his name. He's Fourth Infantry. That stuff matters over there.'

No reply.

206

'Believe me,' Reacher said. 'Let him get out with honour.'

'Domestic violence is honourable?'

'Compared to the alternative.'

'OK, I'll give it a try.'

'Don't forget about me,' Reacher said. 'I need to know what the air force built here. The scope, purpose and architecture, same as I always did. As soon as possible.'

'Anything else?'

'Are you married?'

She hung up without answering.

All six people that were awake and in the house had coffee. Janet Salter herself, Holland, Peterson, Reacher, and the two women cops. Maybe they joined in because they needed to get warm. They all got halfway through their first cup, and then Holland's cell phone rang. He balanced his mug and opened the phone one-handed and listened for a minute. Then he closed the phone again and stuffed it back in his pocket.

'Highway Patrol,' he said. 'The bikers are leaving. Right now. Thirty-six pick-up trucks just hit the highway.'

Five to one in the afternoon.

Fifteen hours to go.

# TWENTY-FIVE

REACHER RODE BACK TO THE STATION HOUSE WITH HOLLAND and got the story on the way. The Highway Patrol was out in force on the highway to check that there were no remaining weather problems. One of their number had been parked on the eastbound shoulder. He had been watching the traffic coming and going, but then in the left corner of his eye had seen a long fast convoy heading down the snowy ribbon that led from the construction camp. It was quite a sight. Between thirty and forty pick-up trucks driving nose to tail, each one with three people in the cab and a tarp-covered motorbike and piles of boxes strapped down in the load bed. They had slowed and turned and then streamed and snaked and swooped around the cloverleaf and merged on to the highway and accelerated west. Like a train, the officer had said. Like the Northern Pacific itself. The convoy looked a quarter-mile long and was taking twenty whole seconds to pass any given point.

The desk sergeant confirmed the news. Highway Patrol cruisers were calling in reports, one after the other. The convoy was now ten miles west of Bolton, and still moving fast. But not fast enough to get ticketed. They were holding to an easy sixty-five, driving straight and true, still steadfastly keeping their noses clean.

They used the office with the crime scene photographs. Four desks boxed together, four chairs. Holland and Peterson sat side by side, and Reacher sat facing Holland, with his back to the pictures of the dead guy dressed in black. He asked, 'You happy to just let them go?'

Holland asked, 'Why wouldn't I be?'

'They were selling meth.'

'This is a small town at heart,' Holland said. 'We operate under small town rules. If I see the back of a thing, that's generally as good as solving it.'

Peterson said, 'End of problem.'

'Not really,' Reacher said. 'They cleaned up and got out because the real estate closing is about to happen. And a closing needs a good title. Janet Salter is the last little smudge on it. She's in more danger now than she ever was. She's the only thing standing between someone and a lot of money.'

'Plato the Mexican.'

'Whoever.'

'We're doing everything we can,' Holland said. 'We have seven officers in place, and they're staying there. We'll be OK.'

'Unless the siren goes off again.'

'You say it won't.'

Reacher said, 'An educated guess is still a guess. Just remember, this is the time to start worrying, not to stop.'

Holland said, 'You see me relaxing, I hereby give you permission to kick my butt. We may have our problems, and we may not be the U.S. Army, but we've struggled along so far. You should remember that.'

Reacher nodded. 'I know. I'm sorry. Not your fault. It's the mayor's fault. Who would sign off on a plan like that?'

'Anyone would,' Holland said. 'Those are jobs that can't be shipped overseas. Which is the name of the game right now.'

The room went quiet for a moment.

Peterson said, 'The motels are all full.'

Reacher said, 'I know that.'

'So where is the bad guy sleeping?'

'In his car. Or in the next county.'

'Where is he eating?'

'Same answer.'

'So should we use roadblocks? There are only three ways in.'

'No,' Holland said. 'False premise. We set up a static perimeter, he might be already behind us. We have to stay mobile.' Then he went quiet again, as if he was running through a mental agenda and checking that all the items on it had been covered. Which they must have been, because his next move was to stand up and walk out of the room without another word. Reacher heard the slap of his boot soles against the linoleum and then the slam of a door. His office, presumably. Work to do.

Peterson said, 'We should get lunch. You could come back to the house. You could be company for Kim. She would like that.'

'Because she's lonely?'

'Yes.'

'Then you and I shouldn't be the only human specimens she sees all day. Go pick her up and we'll have lunch in town, the three of us.'

'Hard to get a table.'

'I'll wait on line while you're on the road.'

'Where?'

'The coffee shop where you found me yesterday. Across the square.'

Peterson said, 'But,' and then nothing more.

'I know,' Reacher said. 'I can see the police station from there. I can see when the bus is ready to leave.'

The walk across the square to the coffee shop was short, but it was straight into the wind. The blowing ice hurt for the first few steps, like tiny needles, but then Reacher's face went numb and he didn't feel them any more. The line for a table was out the door. Reacher took his place behind a woman and a child wrapped in

210

comforters that were probably borrowed from their motel beds. A guy commits a federal crime in Florida or Arizona, ends up in prison in South Dakota, the family has to follow. For the first year or two, anyway. After that, maybe not. A lot to lose.

The line moved slowly but steadily and Reacher got level with the steamed window. Inside he could see vague shapes bustling about. Two waitresses. Steady wages, maybe not much in tips. Families of prisoners didn't have much money. If they did, they weren't families of prisoners. Or, worst case, their guy was in a Club Fed somewhere, doing woodwork for a year, or reading books.

The mother and child squeezed their motel comforters in through the door. Reacher waited his turn on the sidewalk. He was pressed up against the building and out of the wind. Then a woman with three kids straggled out and Reacher ducked in. He waited at the register until a waitress glanced at him. He mouthed the word *three* and held up three fingers. The waitress nodded and swiped a rag across a table and beckoned him over. He dumped his coat on the back of a chair and peeled off his hat and gloves. He sat down and saw Peterson's car stop outside on the kerb, a long black and white shape through the fog on the glass. He saw Peterson cross the sidewalk. His wife wasn't with him. Peterson cut to the head of the line and stepped in through the door. No one complained. Peterson was in uniform.

Reacher stayed in his seat and Peterson shed his coat and sat down to an awkward silence that was broken only by the arrival of the waitress with an order pad in her hand. Not the kind of place that offered extra minutes for study of the menu. Peterson ordered a hamburger and water and Reacher got grilled cheese and coffee. Reacher was facing the window, and Peterson turned around to look at it, and then turned back with a satisfied smile.

'I know,' Reacher said. 'It's all steamed up. But a bus is a pretty big thing. I'll be able to make it out.'

'You won't leave.'

'I haven't decided yet.'

'Kim didn't want to come. She doesn't care much for crowds, either.'

'Crowds, or this kind of crowd?'

'Both.'

They were two people at a table for four, and the line was still out the door, but nobody wanted to sit with them. People came in, glanced over, maybe took half a step, and then stopped and looked away. The world was divided into two halves, people who liked cops and people who didn't. The military had been exactly the same. Reacher had eaten next to empty chairs, many, many times.

Peterson asked, 'What would you do, if you were me?'

'About what?'

'The department.'

'It's not yours.'

'I'm next in line.'

'I would start some serious training. Then I would renegotiate the deal with the prison. Their crisis plan is completely unsustainable.'

'It worked OK last night, apart from the thing with Mrs Salter.'

'That's the point. That's like saying it worked OK, except it didn't. You have to plan for the contingencies.'

'I'm not much of a politician.'

'Please tell me there's a review period built in.'

'There is. But they'll say it's rare that our help is needed. And if we get through this month with Mrs Salter we won't have any negatives to show them.'

There was no more conversation. Peterson kept quiet, and Reacher had nothing more to say. Without Kim there, the whole thing was a bust. But the food was OK. The coffee was fresh. No real alternative, given the turnover of customers. There were three flasks behind the counter and all three of them were constantly dripping and emptying. The sandwich was nicely fried, and Reacher was ready for the calories. Like throwing coal into a furnace. Being cold was like being on a diet. He understood why all the locals he met looked basically the same, all lean and fair and slender. Fair, because of their genetic inheritance. Lean and slender, because they were freezing their asses off for half the year.

First Reacher and then Peterson finished eating, and immediately they felt the covetous stares from the people lining up inside the door. So Reacher paid, and left a generous tip, which earned him a tired smile from the waitress. Then he and Peterson stepped out to the sidewalk, just in time to see a big yellow bus pull up in the police station lot.

Five to two in the afternoon.

Fourteen hours to go.

The bus was the same size and shape and style as the vehicle that had crashed two days earlier. Same amenities. It had blanked-out windows at the rear, where the washroom was. Same number of seats. Same kind of door. It had entered the lot from the north, so the door was facing away from the police station lobby. Reacher stood with Peterson in the square with the wind on his back and watched a thin line of wrapped-up old folks come out and walk around. There were all kinds of grateful farewells going on. The locals, shaking hands, getting hugged, giving out addresses and phone numbers. He saw the lady with the busted collar bone. She was in a coat with one empty sleeve. He saw the woman with the cracked wrist. She was cradling one hand and someone else was carrying her bag. Most of the others had their Band-Aids off. Their cuts were all healed up. The new driver was crouching down and slotting suitcases into the hold under the floor. The old folks were detouring around him one after the other and gripping the handrails carefully and climbing slowly up the step. Reacher saw them inside through the windows, white cotton-ball heads moving down the aisle, pausing, choosing their places, getting settled.

Last aboard was Jay Knox himself, once the driver, now just a passenger. He walked down the aisle and dumped himself in a window seat three rows behind the last of the seniors. Reacher's seat. Near the rear wheels, where the ride was roughest. No point in travelling, if you're not feeling it.

The new driver latched the hold compartments and bounced up the step. A second later the door sucked shut behind him. The engine started. Reacher heard the heavy diesel rattle. Heard the

213

air brake release and the snick of a gear. The engine roared and the bus moved away, out of the lot, on to the road. The icy wind battered at it. It headed south towards the highway. Reacher watched it go, until it was lost to sight.

Peterson clapped him on the back.

Reacher said, 'A viable mode of transportation just left town without me on it. I just broke the habit of a lifetime.'

Plato dialled his guy again. Direct. A risk, but he was enough of an analyst to know that caution sometimes had to be abandoned. To know that chronology couldn't be beaten. To know that timing was everything. The clock ticked on, whoever you were. Even if you were Plato.

His guy answered.

Plato asked, 'Do you have news for me?'

'Not yet. I'm sorry.'

Plato paused. 'It almost seems like it would be easier just to do the job than find new ways of delaying it.'

'It's not like that.'

'It seems like you're working very hard to save the wrong life.'

'I'm not.'

'Focus on the life you really want to save.'

'I will. I am.'

'You have a deadline. Please don't let me down.'

Reacher walked back to the station. Peterson drove. They met in the silent lobby and stood there for a second. They had nothing to do, and both of them knew it. Then Holland came out of his office and said, 'We should go up to the camp. To take a look around. Now that it's empty. While we've still got daylight.'

# TWENTY-SIX

THEY WENT IN HOLLAND'S CAR. IT WAS A BETTER FIT FOR THREE people than Peterson's cruiser, because it had no security screen between the front seats and the rear. Reacher rode in the back, sprawled sideways, comfortable, watching the roads he had driven that morning. Conditions were still bad. The wind was still strong. The snow was frozen so hard it looked like part of the earth, and it was being scoured into long sharp ridges and runnels. It was blinding white under the pale afternoon sun. Like the Ice Age.

They turned on to the old road parallel with the highway and again on to the wandering two-lane up towards the camp. The first eight miles were as bad as before. Icy humps and dips, reversed cambers, constant deviations from straight. Then, as before, the horizon changed. The clear grey concrete, massively wide, infinitely long, the aerodynamic berms of snow, the visible wind howling above the surface.

Holland slowed and bumped up on the new level and stopped and kept his foot on the brake, like a plane waiting to launch. He said, 'You see what you want to see, don't you? I was here a dozen times in my life and thought this was just a road. Kind of fancy, maybe, but I guess I figured hey, that's the military for you.'

'It used to be narrower,' Peterson said. 'That's what made it hard to see. The winds put dirt all over it. Only the middle part was ever used. These guys ploughed it for the first time in fifty years. Not just snow. They pushed the dirt off.'

'It's a piece of work,' Holland said. 'That's for sure.'

'That's for damn sure,' Reacher said. 'It's got to be a yard thick. By volume it's probably the largest manmade object in South Dakota.'

They all looked a minute longer and then Holland took his foot off the brake and the snow chains chattered and the car rolled on. Two whole miles. The tan shapes of the huts loomed up, with the slate roof of the stone building standing tall behind them, under its cap of snow. Holland parked about where Reacher had. The scene ahead was different. No people. No trucks. No bikes. Just the empty ploughed spaces, and the wooden huts all forlorn and abandoned among them.

They all got out of the car. Put their hats on, put their gloves on, zipped up their coats. The temperature was still dropping. Way below zero degrees, and the wind made it worse. The cold struck upward through the soles of Reacher's boots. His face went numb after seconds. Holland and Peterson were putting on a show of taking it in their stride, but Reacher knew they had to be hurting. Their faces were mottled red and white, and they were blinking, and they were coughing and gasping a little.

They all headed straight for the stone building. It looked no different from how it had in the morning. Partly forbidding, partly just plain weird. Peterson tried the door. It didn't move. He rubbed the new frost off the keyhole with his thumb, the same way Reacher had. He said, 'There are no scratches here. The lock wasn't in regular use.'

'Didn't need to be,' Reacher said. 'They unlocked it a year ago and relocked it this morning.'

'So where's the key?'

'That's a good question.'

Holland said, 'They took it with them.'

Reacher said, 'I don't think they did.'

'Why wouldn't they?'

'Because this place is getting sold. Wouldn't they have been told to leave the key for the new owner?'

'So where is it?'

'Under the mat, probably.'

'There is no mat.'

'Under a flowerpot, then.'

'What flowerpot?'

'Figure of speech,' Reacher said. 'People leave keys in pre-arranged locations.'

All three of them turned a slow circle, looking at everything there was to see. Which wasn't much. Just snow, and concrete, and the huts, and the building itself.

'What's it going to look like?' Peterson asked. 'Just a key?'

'Big,' Reacher said. 'It's a blast door, so the lock will be complex. Lots of moving parts. Hard to turn. So the key will be big and strong. Probably T-shaped, like a clock key, probably made out of some kind of fancy steel. Probably cost the Pentagon a thousand bucks all on its own.'

'Maybe they buried it in the snow. We have a metal detector in the car.'

'But I'm guessing the Russian guy from Brooklyn doesn't. Which means it isn't in the snow. That's no kind of customer relations. You can't ask a guy to dig around in a snow bank for an hour.'

'So where is it?'

There were stone ledges and carved mouldings and Gothic features all over the building. Eye-level and below was too obvious. Reacher walked a circuit and ran his hands along everything up to about eight feet off the ground. Nothing there. And anything higher would be inaccessible, unless the Russian was figuring on bringing a folding ladder.

Reacher stopped walking and looked around all over again and said, 'It has to be somewhere definite. Like under the third thing from the left or the fourth thing from the right.'

Peterson said, 'What kind of thing?'

'Hut, bed, anything.'

'Can't we just jimmy the door with a tyre iron?'

'It's a blast door. Designed to stand up to a big pressure wave.'

'But we'd be pulling outward, not pushing inward.'

'Pressure waves are followed by vacuums. Compression and then rarefaction. Compression pushes in, rarefaction sucks back out, and just as hard. Both ways around, that's a strong door.'

Peterson said, 'So we better start searching.'

'What's your lucky number?'

'Three.'

'So start with the third hut, under the third mattress.'

'Counting from where?'

Reacher paused. 'That's another good question. Front row, from the left, probably. But ultimately any counting system could be called subjective. And therefore potentially confusing. The only real objectivity would be in saying the nearest or the farthest.'

'From where?'

'Here. The locked door.'

'That's assuming it's in a hut at all.'

'It's not in the snow and it can't be in the building itself. What else is there?'

Peterson headed for the nearest hut. The first in the back row, opposite the second in the front row. The first one Reacher had checked that morning. The door was unlocked. Peterson pushed it open and stepped inside. Reacher and Holland followed him. The burlap drapes were still at the windows. Everything else portable was gone. There was nothing to see except the twelve cots, now stripped back to striped blue mattress ticking and dull iron frames. The place looked sad and abandoned and empty.

But it was warm.

The paraffin heater had its burner turned to the off position, but it was still giving out plenty of residual heat. It was glorious. Reacher stripped off his gloves and held his hands out to it. Simple physics meant that it had to be cooling all the time, and maybe in three hours' time it would be merely lukewarm, and three hours after that it would be stone cold, but right then it was completely magnificent. Still too hot to touch, in fact. The combination of cast iron and recent hydrocarbon combustion was a wonderful thing. Reacher said, 'You guys go search somewhere else. I'm staying right here.'

Peterson said, 'With a bit of luck they'll all be the same.'

They were. All three of them hustled to the farthest hut to check it out, and they found the same situation. Empty room, stripped beds, warm stove. They started the serious search right there. The warmth made them patient and painstaking. They checked every mattress, every cot frame, every nook, and every cranny. They checked the toilet tank in the bathroom area. They looked for loose boards, listened for hollows in the walls, and opened every bulkhead light fixture.

They found nothing.

Five to three in the afternoon.

Thirteen hours to go.

They searched the kitchen next. Reacher figured it was a strong possibility. A kitchen was an unambiguous location. A singularity. There was only one of them. Even more definite than the first hut or the last. But the key wasn't in it. The jars of flour and sugar and coffee were still there, but too empty to hide a metal object from even the most cursory of shakes. It wasn't shoved to the back of the shelves, it wasn't taped to the underside of a table, it wasn't in the cornflake dregs like a toy, it wasn't nested in a pile of bowls.

After the kitchen they worked back towards the stone building, hut by hut. They got better and faster at searching each step of the way, from sheer practice and repetition, because each hut was identical to all the others. They got to where they could have done it blindfold, or asleep. But even so, they got the same result everywhere. Which was no result at all.

They arrived back where they had begun, in the hut nearest the stone building. They were reluctant to start searching it, because they felt sure they would be disappointed, and drawing a blank in the last of fifteen places carried with it some kind of finality. Reacher walked through the space, stopping at the stove, moving on to the last bed on the right.

He said, 'There was a girl sitting here this morning.'

Holland stepped alongside him. 'What girl?'

'Just a biker, maybe nineteen or twenty. The only one I saw inside. The others were all out working on the snow.'

'Was she sick?'

'She looked OK to me.'

'Was she locked up?'

'No, the door was open.'

'Maybe she was guarding the key. Like that was her function.'

'Maybe she was. But where did she leave it?'

'What did she look like?'

'Tall and thin and blond, like the rest of you.'

'You think she was local?'

'Meth is a rural thing,' Reacher said. Then he thought: *Tall and thin and blond*. He asked, 'Are you getting a cell signal out here?'

'Sure,' Holland said. 'Flat land all around. Wind and dust and microwaves, they're all the same to us.'

'Let me use your phone.'

Holland handed it over and Reacher dialled the number he remembered.

'Yes?'

'Amanda, please.'

A click. A purr. The voice. It said, 'Where the hell are you?'

Reacher said, 'What? Now you're my mother?'

'I've been trying to get hold of you.'

'I'm out at the air force place. Trying to get in. Looking for the key. I need to know the top twenty ingenious places you've ever found a small hidden object.'

'VCR slot, kettle, shoe, inside a TV set, the battery compartment of a transistor radio, a hollowed-out book, cut into the foam inside the seat of a car, in a bar of soap, in a tub of cream cheese.'

220

'That's only nine. You're hopeless.'

'Give me time.'

'There isn't any of that kind of stuff here.'

'So what is there?'

Reacher walked around the hut and described everything he was seeing.

The voice said, 'The toilet tank.'

'Checked them all.'

'Any torn mattresses?'

'No.'

'Loose boards?'

'No.'

'So burn the place down and sift the ashes. An air force key is probably made of the same stuff as warheads. It would survive, easy.'

'Why were you trying to get hold of me?'

'Because I know what that place is.'

# TWENTY-SEVEN

PETERSON AND HOLLAND HAD HEARD THE THIN SQUAWK OF HER words from the earpiece. They stepped closer. Reacher sat down on the bed, where the biker girl had been. The voice on the phone said, 'That place was built as an orphanage.'

Reacher said, 'Underground?'

'It was fifty years ago. The height of the Cold War. Everyone was going nuts. My guy faxed me the file. The casualty predictions were horrendous. The Soviets were assumed to have missiles to spare, by the hundreds. A full-scale launch, they'd have been scratching their heads for targets. We ran scenarios, and it all came down to the day of the week and the time of the year. Saturday or Sunday or during the school vacations, it was assumed everyone would get it pretty much equally. But weekdays during the semester, they predicted a significant separation between the adult population and the juvenile, in terms of physical location. Parents would be in one place, their kids would be in another, maybe in a shelter under a school.'

'Or under their desks,' Reacher said.

'Wherever,' the voice said. 'The point is that the survival numbers two weeks after the launch were very skewed. They showed a lot more kids than adults. Some guy on House Appropriations started obsessing about it. He wanted places for these kids to go. He figured they might be able to get to undamaged regional airports and be flown out to remote areas. He wanted combination radiation shelters and living accommodations built. He talked to the air force. He scratched their backs, they scratched his. He was from South Dakota, so that's where they started.'

'The local scuttlebutt is about a scandal,' Reacher said. 'Building an orphanage doesn't sound especially scandalous.'

'You don't understand. The assumption was there would be no adults left. Maybe a sick and dying pilot or two, that's all. Some harassed bureaucrat with a clipboard. The idea was that these kids would be dumped out of the planes and left alone to lock themselves underground and manage the best they could. On their own. Like feral animals. It wasn't a pretty picture. They got reports from psychologists saying there would be tribalism, fighting, killing, maybe even cannibalism. And the median age of the survivors was supposed to be seven. Then the psychologists talked to the grown-ups, and it turned out that their worst fear was that they would die and their kids would live on without them. They needed to hear that things would be OK, you know, with doctors and nurses and clean sheets on the bed. They didn't want to hear about how things were really going to be. So there was a lot of fuss and then the idea was dropped, as a matter of civilian morale.'

'So this place just stood here for fifty years?'

'Something about the construction compromises made it useless for anything else.'

'Do we know what the compromises were?'

'No. The plans are missing.'

'So is the place empty?'

'They filled it with junk they needed to store and then they forgot all about it.'

'Is the stuff still in there?'

'I'm assuming so.'

'What is it?'

'I don't know yet. That's in another file. But it can't be very exciting. It's something that was already surplus to requirements fifty years ago.'

'Are you going to find out?'

'My guy has requested the file.'

'How's my weather?'

'Stick your head out the door.'

'I mean, what's coming my way?'

A pause. 'It'll be snowing again tomorrow. Clear and cold until then.'

'Where would a bunch of bikers have hidden a key?'

'I don't know. I can't help you.'

Five minutes to four in the afternoon.

Twelve hours to go.


Reacher handed the phone back to Holland. The light from the window was dimming. The sun was way in the west and the stone building was casting a long shadow. They set about searching the hut. Their last chance. Every mattress, every bed frame, the toilet tank, the floorboards, the walls, the light fixtures. They did it slowly and thoroughly, and got even slower and more thorough as they approached the end of the room and started running out of options.

They found nothing.

Peterson said, 'We could get a locksmith, maybe from Pierre.'

Reacher said, 'A bank robber would be better. A safe cracker. Maybe they've got one up at the prison.'

'I can't believe they never used the place. It must have cost a fortune.'

'The defence budget was practically unlimited back then.'

'I can't believe they couldn't find an alternative use for it.'

'The design was compromised somehow.'

'Even so. Somebody could have used it.'

'Too landlocked for the navy. We're close to the geographic centre of the United States. Or so they said on the bus tour.'

224

'The Marines could have used it for winter training.'

'Not with South in the name of the state. Too chicken. The Marines would have insisted on North Dakota. Or the North Pole.'

'Maybe they didn't want to sleep underground.'

'Marines sleep where they're told. And when.'

'Actually I heard they do their winter training near San Diego.'

'I was in the army,' Reacher said. 'Marine training makes no sense to me.'

They braved the cold again and took a last look at the stone building and its stubborn door. Then they walked back to the car and climbed in and drove away. Two miles along the runway, where battered planes were to have spilled ragged children. Then eight miles on the old two-lane, up which no adult would have come to the rescue. The Cold War. A bad time. In retrospect, probably less dangerous than people imagined. Some Soviet missiles were mere fictions, some were painted tree trunks, some were faulty. And the Soviets had psychologists too, preparing reports in the Cyrillic alphabet about seven-year-olds of their own, and about tribalism and fighting and killing and cannibalism. But at the time things had seemed very real. Reacher had been two years old at the time of the Cuban missile crisis. In the Pacific. He had known nothing about it. But later his mother had told him how she and his father had calculated the southern drift of the poisoned wind. Two weeks, they thought. There were guns in the house. And on the base there were corpsmen with pills.

Reacher asked, 'How accurate are your weather reports?'

Peterson said, 'Usually pretty good.'

'They're calling for snow again tomorrow.'

'That sounds about right.'

'Then someone's going to show up soon. They didn't plough that runway for nothing.'

\*　　\*　　\*

Far to the east and a little to the south a plane was landing on another long runway, at Andrews Air Force Base in the state of Maryland. Not a large plane. A business jet, leased by the army, assigned to an MP prisoner escort company. It was carrying six people. A pilot, a copilot, three prisoner escorts, and a prisoner. The prisoner was the Fourth Infantry captain from Fort Hood. He was in civilian clothes and was hobbled by standard restraint chains around his wrists and waist and ankles, all inter-connected. The plane taxied and the steps were lowered and the prisoner was hustled down them to a car parked on the apron. He was put in the back seat. Waiting for him there was a woman officer in a Class A army uniform. An MP major. She was a little above average height. She was slender. She had long dark hair tied back. Tanned skin, deep brown eyes. She had intelligence and authority and youth and mischief in her face, all at the same time. She was wearing ribbons for a Silver Star and two Purple Hearts.

There was no driver in the front of the car.

The woman said, 'Good afternoon, captain.'

The captain didn't speak.

The woman said, 'My name is Susan Turner. My rank is major, and I command the 110th MP, and I'm handling your case. You and I are going to talk for a minute, and then you're going to get back on the plane, and you're either going to head back to Texas, or straight over to Fort Leavenworth. One or the other. You understand?'

Her voice was warm. It was a little husky, a little breathy, a little intimate. All in her throat. It was the kind of voice that could tease out all kinds of confidences.

The infantry captain knew it.

He said, 'I want a lawyer.'

Susan Turner nodded.

'You'll get one,' she said. 'You'll get plenty. Believe me, before long you're going to be completely up to your ass in lawyers. It's going to be like you wandered into a Bar Association convention with a hundred dollar bill tied around your neck.'

'You can't talk to me without a lawyer.'

226

'That's not quite accurate. You don't have to say anything to me without a lawyer. I can talk to you all I want. See the difference?'

The guy said nothing.

'I have some bad news,' Susan Turner said. 'You're going to die. You know that, right? You are completely busted. You are more busted than the most busted person who ever lived. There's no way anyone can save you. That's exactly what you're going to hear from the lawyers. No matter how many you get. They're all going to say the same thing. You're going to be executed, and probably very soon. I won't give you false hope. You're a dead man walking.'

The guy said nothing.

Turner said, 'Actually you're a dead man sitting, at this point. Sitting in a car, and listening to me. Which you should do, because you've got two very important choices coming up. The second is what you eat for your last meal. Steak and ice cream are the most popular picks. I don't know why. Not that I give a shit about dietary issues. It's your first choice I'm interested in. Want to guess what that is?'

The guy said nothing.

'Your first choice is what you go down for. Either Texas will kill you for killing your wife, or Leavenworth will kill you for betraying your country. I'll be frank with you, in my opinion neither one does you much credit. But the Texas issue, maybe people will understand it a little bit. Combat stress, multiple tours of duty, all that kind of thing. All that post-traumatic stuff. Some people might even call you a kind of victim.'

The guy said nothing.

Turner said, 'But the treason issue, that's different. There's no excuse for that. Your mom and your dad, they're going to have to sell their house and move. Maybe change their name. Maybe they won't be able to sell, and they'll just hang themselves in the basement.'

The guy said nothing.

Turner said, 'Not much ceiling height in a basement. It'll be slow. Like strangulation. Maybe they'll hold hands.'

The guy said nothing.

Turner moved in her seat. Long legs, sheathed in dark nylon. 'And think about your kid brother. All those years of looking up to you? All gone. He'll have to leave the navy. Who would trust him on their team? The brother of a traitor? That's a life sentence for him, too. He'll end up working construction. He'll drink. He'll curse your rotten name every day of his life. Maybe he'll kill himself too. Gunshot, probably. In the mouth or behind the ear.'

The guy said nothing.

Turner said, 'So here's the deal. Talk to me now, answer all my questions, full and complete disclosure, all the details, and we'll keep the treason absolutely private.'

The guy said nothing.

Turner said, 'But if you don't talk to me, we'll do the investigation in public. Right out in the open. We'll tell CNN where your folks live, and we'll call the navy about your brother. Not the officers. We'll call his buddies first.'

Silence for a long moment.

Then the guy said, 'OK.'

'OK what?'

'OK, I'll talk to you.'

'OK you'll talk to me what?'

'OK, I'll talk to you, ma'am.'

Turner rolled her window down. She called out, 'Tell the pilot to go get his dinner.'

Plato put the phone down on his pilot. The guy had called to say the weather in the north was due to take a turn for the worse at some point within the next twenty-four hours. More snow. Which Plato already knew. He had satellite television. He had a huge mesh dish bolted to a concrete pad right next to his house. The dish was connected to a box, and the box was connected to an enormous Sony LCD screen on the end wall of the living room. It was tuned to the Weather Channel.

The Sony screen was not the only thing on the end wall. There were eighteen oil paintings next to it, all jostling for space. There were forty-three more on the two long walls. Twenty on the other end wall. A total of eighty-one works of art. Mostly second-rate pieces by fourth-rate painters. Or third-rate pieces by third-rate painters. Or fourth-rate pieces by second-rate painters. One was a Monet, supposedly, but Plato knew it had to be a forgery. Monet was a prolific artist. Widely distributed, often copied. Someone had once said that of the two thousand pictures Monet had painted in his lifetime, six thousand were in the United States alone. Plato wasn't a fool. He knew what he had. And he knew why he had it. He didn't much care for art. Not his thing. Each canvas was a souvenir, that was all, of a ruined life.

In the spaces between the paintings he had nailed small inverted horseshoe-shaped arrays of thin brass pins. Dozens of them, maybe even hundreds. He hadn't counted for a long time. Over each array was draped as many necklaces or bracelets as would fit. He had diamonds, emeralds, rubies, and sapphires. Gold chains, silver chains, platinum chains. He had earrings hung from single pins. He had finger rings looped over single pins. Wedding bands, engagement rings, signet rings, class rings, big diamond solitaires.

Hundreds and hundreds of them.

Maybe even thousands.

It was all a question of time.

It was a subject that interested him. It was dominated by class. How long could people last, after running out of cash, before they had to start selling their bodies? How many layers did people have, between defeat and surrender, between problem and ruin? For poor people, really no time at all, and no layers at all. They needed his product, so as soon as their meagre paycheques ran out, which was usually payday itself, they would start fighting and stealing and cheating, and then they would take to the streets, and they would do whatever it was they had to do. He got nothing but money from them.

Rich people were different. Bigger paycheques, which lasted longer, but not for ever. Then would start the slow depletion of savings accounts, stocks, bonds, investments of all kinds. Then desperate hands would root through drawers and jewellery boxes. First would come forgotten pieces, pieces that were not liked, pieces that had been inherited. Those items would find their way to him after long slow journeys, from nice suburbs in Chicago and Minneapolis and Milwaukee and Des Moines and Indianapolis. They would be followed by paintings snatched from walls, rings pulled from fingers, chains unlatched from necks. A second wave would follow, as parents were looted, then a third, as grandparents were visited. When nothing was left, the rich people would succumb, too. Maybe at first in hotels, fooling themselves, but always eventually out on the street, in the cold, kneeling in filthy alleyways, men and women alike, doing what needed to be done.

All a matter of time.

Holland parked in the lot and headed for his office. Peterson and Reacher headed for the squad room. It was deserted, as usual. No messages on the back corner desk, nothing in voice mail. Reacher picked up the phone and then put it back. He tapped the space bar on the keyboard and the computer screen lit up and showed a graphic of a police shield that had *Bolton Police Department* written across it. The graphic was large and a little ragged. A little digital. A tower unit a yard away was humming and whirring and chattering. A hard drive, getting up to speed.

Reacher asked, 'Have you got databases in here?'

Peterson asked, 'Why?'

'We could check on Plato. He seems to be the prime mover here, whoever he is.'

Peterson sat down at the next desk along and tapped his own keyboard. Clicked here, clicked there, typed a password. Then some kind of dialogue box must have come up, because Reacher saw him use his left forefinger on the shift key, his right forefinger on a capital *P*, then on a lower case *l*, then an *a*, a *t*, and an *o*.

Plato.

'Nothing,' Peterson said. 'Just a redirect to Google, who says he's a Greek philosopher.'

'Got a list of known aliases?'

Peterson typed some more. Nine keystrokes. Presumably *aka*, then a space, then *Plato*.

'South American,' he said. 'Citizenship unknown. Real name unknown. Age unknown. Believed to live in Mexico. Believed to own pawn shops in five United States cities, suspected narcotics trafficker, suspected involvement in prostitution.'

'Nice guy.'

'No arrest record. Nothing in Mexico, either.'

'Is that it?'

'The federal databases will have more. But I can't access them.'

Reacher picked up the phone again, and then put it back. Rock Creek had more on its plate than his trivial business. He wondered if he was becoming an embarrassment. Or a bore. Like the grizzled old noncoms who still lived close to army posts and sat in grunt bars all night, full of piss and wind and out-of-date bullshit and nonsense. Or like retired city cops, the ones who hadn't saved enough to move south, still patronizing the same old saloons and butting in on every conversation.

Peterson said, 'We could go up to the prison. It's in the federal system. They've got computers. I know some of the guys there.'

Five minutes to five in the afternoon.

Eleven hours to go.

# TWENTY-EIGHT

THE PRISON WAS FIVE MILES DUE NORTH, AT THE END OF A continuation of the same road that led up to town from the highway. The road was straight, as if a planner had laid a ruler on a map. It was ploughed and salted and pretty much clear from constant use. Visiting day. The shuttle buses had been busy.

The five miles took eight minutes. For the first seven Reacher saw nothing ahead except a late gloomy sky and ice in the air. Then he saw the prison. There was a diffuse glow on the far horizon that resolved itself into hundreds of separate puffballs of blue-white light high above a glittering razor-wire fence. The fence was long and maybe twelve feet tall. Maybe twelve feet thick. It had inner and outer screens of taut wire. The space in between was piled high with loose coils. More loose coils were fixed along the top. They were moving and swaying in the wind, flashing and winking in the light. The light came from stadium fixtures on tall poles set every thirty feet. Huge upside-down metal bowls in groups of four, with powerful bulbs

232

in them. There were watchtowers set every hundred feet, tall splay-legged structures with lit-up glassed-in cabins and outside walkways. There were searchlights on the walkways. The lights on the poles were blazing, and their glow came back up off the undisturbed snow seemingly twice as bright. Behind the fence was a three-hundred-yard expanse of lit-up snow-covered yard, and then huddled in the centre of the giant rectangle was a cluster of new concrete buildings. They covered an area the size of a large village. Or a small town. The buildings were all lit up, inside and out. They had small mean windows in heavy blank façades, like the portholes in the side of a ship. Their roofs were all covered with snow, like a thick uniform blanket.

'The gift horse,' Peterson said. 'The cash cow.'

'Impressive,' Reacher said.

And it was. As a whole the place was huge. Many hundreds of acres. The vast pool of bright light set against the prairie darkness made it look like an alien spacecraft, just hovering there, unsure whether to land or to whisk away again to a more hospitable location.

At its far end the road broadened out into a wide square plaza in front of the main gate. The plaza was lined at its edges with bus benches and trash cans. Peterson drove straight through it. The gate was really a tunnel, walled and roofed with wire, tall enough for prison buses, wide enough to form two separated lanes, one in, one out. Each lane had three gates forming two pens. Peterson drove into the first and was momentarily locked in, a closed gate behind him, a closed gate ahead. A guard in cold-weather gear came out of a door, looked them over, stepped back inside, and the gate ahead opened. Peterson rolled forward thirty feet. The whole procedure was repeated. Then the last gate opened and Peterson drove out and headed for the buildings on a thoroughfare that was both rutted by vehicles and beaten flat by footsteps. Clearly the shuttle buses discharged their passengers outside the gate. Reacher pictured the woman and the child he had seen at the coffee shop, wrapped in their borrowed motel comforters, trudging through the snow, trudging back.

Peterson parked as close to the visitor door as he could get.

Behind the door was an empty lobby, sad and institutional, with wet linoleum on the floor and mint green paint on the walls and fluorescent tubes on the ceiling. There was an idle X-ray belt and a metal detector hoop and three prison guards standing around and not doing much of anything. Peterson knew them. They knew him. A minute later he and Reacher had been hustled through a side door into a ready room. New construction, but it was already a little trashed and battered. It was hot. It smelled of old coffee, and new sweat, and wet wool coats, and cheap polyester uniforms. There were five low chairs in it, and a desk with a computer on it. A guard fired it up and typed in a password and then left the room.

'Federal prison, federal databases,' Peterson said. Those databases were evidently a little unfamiliar to him, because it took a whole lot of pointing and clicking and typing before he got anywhere. A whole lot of pursed lips and sudden inhalations and exhalations. But eventually he took his hands off the keyboard and sat back to read.

'Same stuff at first,' he said. 'South American, exact origins unknown, real identity unknown, exact age unknown but believed to be in his forties, believed to live in Mexico, pawn shops in Chicago, Minneapolis, Milwaukee, Des Moines and Indianapolis, suspected dope in the same five cities, suspected prostitution in the same five cities.'

Reacher asked, 'Anything new?'

'We didn't have the names of those cities before.'

'Apart from that.'

'Nothing proven. There's a standard warning about how tough he is. He made it to the top tier, and you don't do that by being a choirboy. They figure he must have killed hundreds of people. That seems to be an entry-level requirement. Des Moines doesn't impress anybody, but Chicago surely does. He's not an amateur.'

Then Peterson started clicking and scrolling again. More pursed lips, more deliberate breathing. He said, 'The guy owns his own plane.'

'So do plenty of people.'

234

'It's a Boeing 737. A regular airliner, converted for private use. Supposedly purchased from a bankrupt Mexican airline.'

Reacher said nothing.

Peterson clicked and scrolled.

'He's very small,' he said. 'Four feet eleven inches.'

'Really?'

'What are you?'

'Six feet five.'

'You've got eighteen inches on him. That's a foot and a half.'

Reacher said, 'He's practically a midget.'

Peterson said, 'Someone else once called him a midget, and woke up in the hospital with his legs cut off.'

Susan Turner made it back to her office in Rock Creek after a long slow drive through rush hour traffic. She parked in her reserved space and went in through the front door and up the stone stairs. The handrail was still metal. The second-floor corridor was still narrow. The floor was still linoleum. There were still lines of doors left and right, with fluted glass windows in them, with offices behind each one. All unchanged, she thought, since Reacher's day. Repainted, possibly, but not fundamentally altered. Each office was still equipped according to the current DoD protocol. Hers had the famous metal desk, three phones with a total of thirty lines, an ergonomic task chair on casters, file cabinets, and two visitor chairs with springy bent-tube legs. Her light shade was made of glass and shaped like a bowl and was hung from the ceiling on three metal chains. It was fitted with an energy-saving bulb. She had a desktop computer with a fast and secure government intranet connection. She had a laptop wirelessly connected to a separate network. She had an up-to-date map of the world on the wall.

She sat down. No messages. Nothing from the air force. Reacher hadn't called again. She plugged her digital voice recorder into her USB hub. Her conversation with her prisoner uploaded to an audio file. Voice recognition software would turn it into a written document. Both new files would be forwarded to the proper destinations. Arrests would be made in Texas and

Florida and New York City. A unit citation would follow, plus a Bronze Star recommendation for herself, like night follows day.

Reacher had won a Bronze Star, way back when. She knew that, because she had his personal file on her desk. It was a thick old thing, straining against a furred cardboard jacket. She had been through it many times. Jack-none-Reacher, born October 29th. A military family, but not a legacy career, because his father had been a Marine. His mother had been French. He had graduated West Point. He had served thirteen years. He had been an MP from the start, which as far as Susan was concerned put him on the side of the angels, but even so he had been in and out of trouble the whole time. He had said what needed to be said, and he hadn't cared who he said it to. He had done what needed to be done, and he hadn't cared who he did it to. He had cut corners, and cut heads. He had been busted back to captain for busting a civilian's leg. Demotion was always a coded message. *Time to move on, buddy.* But he had stayed in. He had stayed in and battled back to major again. Which had to be the biggest comeback of all time. Then he had led the 110th. Its first CO. Its founder, in effect.

Her predecessor, but no kind of role model.

Yet at intervals through his thirteen years he had won a Silver Star, the Defense Superior Service Medal, the Legion of Merit, a Soldier's Medal, a Purple Heart, and the Bronze Star. Clearly he had talent to burn. Which meant that with a more corporate attitude and an army father and an American mother, he could have been Chief of Staff by now.

A bizarre career.

The Silver Star and the Purple Heart came from Beirut. Reacher had been an army liaison officer serving with the Marine Corps at the time of the barracks bombing. He had been badly wounded in the attack, and then heroic in the immediate aftermath. All the other medal citations were redacted, which meant they involved secrets.

He had been hospitalized in Beirut and then airlifted to Germany for convalescence. His medical summary was in the file. He was a healthy person. The wound had healed fast and

236

completely. It had left what the army called a disfiguring scar, which implied a real mess. He was six feet five inches tall and at the time of the report from Germany had weighed two hundred and forty pounds. No internal weaknesses had been detected. His eyesight was rated excellent.

He had many formal qualifications. He was rated expert on all small arms. He had won an inter-service thousand-yard rifle competition with a record score. Anecdotally his fitness reports rated him well above average in the classroom, excellent in the field, fluently bilingual in English and French, passable in Spanish, outstanding on all man-portable weaponry, and beyond outstanding at hand-to-hand combat. Susan knew what that last rating meant. Like having a running chainsaw thrown at you.

A hard man, but intelligent.

His photograph was stapled to the inside cover of the file. It was a colour picture, a little faded by the intervening years. His hair was short and unruly. He had bright blue eyes, a little hooded. His gaze was direct and unflinching. He had two noticeable scars. One was at the corner of his left eye. The other was on his upper lip. His face looked like it had been chipped out of rock by a sculptor who had ability but not much time. All flat hard planes. He had a neck. Thick, for sure, but it was there. His shoulders were broad. His arms were long, and his hands were large.

His mouth was set in a wry smile that was halfway between patient and exasperated. Like he knew he had to get his picture taken, but like he had just gotten through telling the photographer the guy had three more seconds before his camera got rammed down his throat.

Jack-none-Reacher.

Altogether Susan felt that he would be interesting to know, possibly rewarding as a friend, certainly dangerous as an enemy.

She picked up her phone and dialled her guy in the air force. Asked him if there was news. There wasn't. She asked when it would come through. Her guy said soon. She said soon wasn't soon enough.

Her guy said, 'Trying to impress someone?'

237

She said, 'No,' and hung up.

The last page of Reacher's file was a standard cross-reference index that listed related mentions in other files. There were seventy-three citations. They were all classified, which was no big deal. Virtually all military paper was classified. The first seventy-two citations were dated at various points during his thirteen years of service and were classified at a level which would make them awkward for her to get hold of. Operational reports, obviously. The seventy-third citation was classified at a lower level, but it was ancient. Dated way back. So far back, in fact, that Jack-none-Reacher would have been just six years old at the time. A little boy. Which was strange. A contemporary report about family issues would be in the Marine Corps archives, not army. Because of his father.

So why was the army holding paper on a six-year-old kid?

She e-mailed the Human Resources Command for a one-time password that would grant her temporary access to the record.

The process for leaving the prison involved all the same moves in reverse, with the addition of a thorough physical inspection of the departing vehicle. Peterson stopped in the first locked cage and two guards came out with flashlights and one checked the trunk and the other checked the back seat. Then they swapped responsibilities and did it all over again. The centre gate opened and Peterson rolled forward into the second cage. A third guard checked their IDs and waved them away.

Peterson asked, 'What do you think?'

Reacher asked, 'About what?'

'Their security.'

'Adequate.'

'Is that all?'

'That's all it needs to be.'

'I think it's pretty good.'

'Human nature will get them in the end. They're only a year or so into it. All it will take is for two guards to get lazy at the same time. Bound to happen sooner or later. It always does.'

'Pessimist.'

'Realist.'

Peterson smiled and his car rolled on through the snow towards town.

Seventeen hundred miles south a small convoy of three black Range Rovers rolled through the heat towards Plato's compound. The trucks were all less than a month old, they all had blacked-out windows, and they were all the Sport model, which was really a rebodied Land Rover LR3 with a supercharged Jaguar engine under the hood. Fine trucks for rough but unchallenging roads, which were what Plato's part of the Michoacán was all about. Each truck was carrying two men, for a total of six. All of them were local thirty-somethings with twenty years' experience, all of them were dressed in dark suits, and all of them were heavily armed.

And all of them had worked for Plato before.

Which meant that all of them were a little afraid.

The three cars made the last turn and started the last dusty mile to the gate. All three drivers knew they were already being tracked with binoculars. They had passed the point of no return. They held a steady fifty and maintained a tight formation and then slowed far enough out to be unthreatening. People said Plato's gatemen had anti-tank missiles. Or rocket-propelled grenades, at the very least. Plus surface-to-air missiles for government helicopters. Maybe true, maybe not, but no one was in the mood to find out for sure.

The three cars stopped well short of the gate and the six men climbed out from behind their black windows and stood still in the early-evening heat. No one approached them. They knew that they were being identified at a distance. Beyond that there would be no intervention. They knew that their good behaviour was guaranteed not by a physical search, but by the fact that they all had sisters and mothers and grandmothers and female cousins all within easy reach. Watching a relative's skin being peeled off her face was not pleasant. Living with her afterwards was worse.

A gasoline engine started and a gear engaged and the

gate was driven back. A minute later the last of the cars was inside the compound and the gear reversed and the gate closed again.

Peterson let Reacher out at Janet Salter's house. It was his new default destination, night and day. He crunched up the driveway and the woman cop from the hallway let him in. Janet Salter was in the library, in her usual chair, in a pool of light, reading. The other woman cop was at the window, with her back to the room. Situation normal. All quiet.

Janet Salter held up her book and said, 'I'm reading Sherlock Holmes.'

Reacher said, 'The dog that didn't bark in the night?'

'Exactly.'

'I already thought about that. Your neighbour lives upwind. Doesn't mean no one was here, just because her dog didn't get a sniff.'

'There's a companion volume you should see, in the parlour,' Janet Salter said. She put her book down and got up out of her chair. Reacher followed her to the front room. She closed the door. Didn't show him a book. Instead she asked, 'Are the bikers really gone?'

Reacher said, 'Yes.'

'Are they coming back?'

'I don't think so.'

'So am I safe now?'

'Not really.'

'Why did Chief Holland let them go?'

'Small town rules,' Reacher said.

'Which now mean that if I go ahead and testify as planned, only one man will, as you put it, get nailed.'

'That's true.'

'Which absolutely wasn't the deal. The idea was to nail them all. Now they'll just become some other town's problem.'

'And then the next, and the next.'

'It isn't right.'

'It's how things work.'

'I mean it isn't right to put me at so much risk for so little reward.'

'You want to pull out?'

'Yes, I think I do.'

Five minutes to six in the evening.

Ten hours to go.

# TWENTY-NINE

JANET SALTER SAT DOWN IN A PARLOUR CHAIR. REACHER CHECKED the view from the window. Nothing there. Just the cop in his car, a good one, his head moving left, moving right, checking the mirror.

Reacher said, 'I think it's too late to make a practical difference.'

Janet Salter asked, 'Why?'

'You could talk to Holland right now, but Holland can't talk to the prosecutor before tomorrow, and the prosecutor can't file the papers until maybe the next day, and the news might take another day to filter through. But the bad guys are in a hurry. That place makes money for them. They can't afford any downtime.'

Janet Salter said, 'So I'm in, and I can't get out?'

'Hang tough,' Reacher said. 'You'll be OK.'

'I wouldn't have been OK last night, except for you. And you won't be here for ever.'

'I won't need to be,' Reacher said. 'The bad guys won't wait for ever.'

Janet Salter went to make dinner. She said cooking relaxed her. The night watch cops got up and came downstairs. The house felt safe. Dark and cold outside, bright and warm inside. Pots and pans on the stove top fogged the kitchen windows, so Reacher prowled between the library and the parlour and the hallway. He saw nothing from the windows except snow and ice and moving shadows. The wind was still blowing. Not ideal conditions for careful surveillance, but Reacher felt the situation was acceptable. Seven cops on the case, with himself as backup. Safe enough.

Then the phone rang.

Reacher was in the hallway at the time and Janet Salter called through from the kitchen and asked him to answer it. It was Peterson. He said, 'I have something I need you to see.'

'Where?'

'At the station, on a computer.'

'Can you bring it over?'

'No.'

'I can't leave here.'

'You said we might never hear that siren again. No escapes, no more riots.'

'An educated guess is still a guess.'

'I'll pick you up and bring you straight back.'

'You can't promise that. Suppose the siren sounds while I'm over there?'

'I'll still bring you back. I swear, on the lives of my children.'

'You'd get in trouble.'

'I'll fight it. And I'll win.'

'You should get the department, you know that?' Reacher said. 'The sooner the better.'

Peterson arrived five minutes later. He spoke to his people and then he found Janet Salter and told her he was borrowing Reacher for a quarter of an hour. He looked her in the eye and promised her that none of his officers would leave the house until Reacher was back. She was uneasy, but she seemed to believe

243

him. Reacher put his coat on and climbed into Peterson's car and five minutes after that he was back in the squad room.

Peterson sat down at a desk with a computer and started pointing and clicking and pursing his lips and inhaling and exhaling. He came up with a blank grey square in the middle of the screen. The square had a play arrow laid over its centre portion.

'Surveillance video,' Peterson said. 'From the prison interview room. It's digital. They e-mail it to us.'

'OK.'

'It's the biker and his lawyer. Earlier this afternoon. We never cancelled the surveillance. You know why?'

'Why?'

'Inefficiency.' Peterson moved the mouse and clicked on the play arrow. The grey square changed to a grainy colour picture of the interview room shot from above. The camera was presumably hidden in a light fixture, on the lawyer's side of the glass partition. It showed a man in a grey suit sitting forward in his chair with his elbows on the concrete counter and his face a foot from the glass. Opposite him on the other side of the barrier was a guy in an orange jumpsuit. He was tall and solidly built. He had long black hair and a greying beard. His pose mirrored his lawyer's. Elbows on the counter, face a foot from the glass.

Conspiratorial.

'Now listen,' Peterson said.

The lawyer said something in a whisper. Reacher couldn't hear it.

'Where's the mike?' he asked.

'In the light with the camera.' Peterson stabbed a key and the computer beeped the volume all the way up. Then he dragged a red dot backwards a fraction and the segment played again. Reacher craned closer. The audio quality was very poor, but this time the lawyer's sentence was at least intelligible.

The lawyer had said, 'You know, the ancient Greeks tell us that a six-hour wait solves all our problems.'

Peterson paused the replay. 'Ancient Greeks, right? Like ancient Greek philosophers? You said Plato was an ancient Greek philosopher. It's a code. It's a message.'

244

Reacher nodded. 'When was this?'

'Two o'clock this afternoon. So a six-hour wait would take us to eight o'clock. It's six o'clock now. Which gives them two more hours. They've already wasted two-thirds of their time.'

Reacher stared at the screen.

'Play it again,' he said.

Peterson dragged the red dot back. Hit play. The lawyer's head, moving forward an inch. The scratchy, whispery sound. *The ancient Greeks tell us that a six-hour wait solves all our problems.*

Reacher said, 'I don't hear it that way. He's not saying we have a six-hour period during which at some random point all our problems might be solved. I think he's saying that six hours from then something specific is going to happen in order to solve them.'

'You think?'

'Just my opinion.'

'What kind of thing will happen?'

'The siren will sound. It's their only way to get at Mrs Salter.'

'How can a lawyer make the siren sound?'

'He can't. But maybe they can together.'

'How?'

'What happens up there at eight o'clock? Are they eating? Feeding time at the zoo is always a good time for a riot.'

'They eat earlier.'

'TV time? An argument about CBS or NBC?'

'You said another riot won't happen.'

'Something is going to happen. That lawyer is talking about a future event with a fairly high degree of confidence.'

Peterson went pale. Papery white, under his reddened winter skin.

'Jesus,' he said. 'Eight o'clock is head-count time. They lock them in their cells for the night and check them off. Suppose that guy got out this afternoon and they don't know it yet? They're going to be one short. One minute past eight, they're going to hit the panic button.'

*　　*　　*

They drove straight back to Janet Salter's house. Dinner was almost ready. About ten minutes away. Spaghetti and sauce and cheese, with salad in the old wooden bowl. Janet Salter offered to set an extra place for Peterson. Peterson said yes. But nothing more. He just accepted the invitation and then stepped away from the kitchen activity and took Reacher by the elbow and dragged him into the parlour. He said, 'I'm staying right here when the siren goes off.'

Reacher said, 'Good.'

'Two are better than one.'

'Always.'

'Are you armed?'

'Yes. And so is Mrs Salter.'

'How will their guy arrive?'

'From the front, in a car. Too cold for anything else.'

'Anything we can do ahead of time?'

Reacher said, 'No.'

Peterson said, 'We could warn the prison, I suppose. If the siren went off right now, their guy might be out of position.'

'We don't want him out of position,' Reacher said. 'We want him walking up the driveway at two minutes past eight. Exactly when and where we expect him. You said it yourself, we need this thing to be over.'


Seventeen hundred miles south Plato came out of his house and found the three idling Range Rovers parked in a neat nose-to-tail line. The six men who had come with them were standing easy in pairs, heads up, sunglasses on, hands clasped behind their backs. Plato looked at them carefully. He knew them. He had used them before. They were solid but unspectacular performers. Competent, but uninspired. Not the best in the world. Second-rate, B-students, adequate. There were a lot of words with which to describe them.

He looked at the trucks. Three of them, all identical. British. Each the cost of a college education. Maybe not Harvard. He counted them from the front, one, two, three. Then from the back, three, two, one. He had to choose. He never occupied the same relative position in a convoy two times in a row. Too predictable. Too dangerous. He wanted a two-in-three chance of surviving the first incoming round, if there was to be one. He figured a second round would miss. The supercharged engines had great acceleration. Better than turbocharged. No lag.

He chose car number three. A double bluff, in a way. Slightly counterintuitive. If number one or number two was blown up, number three might get trapped by the flaming wreckage. He would be expected to expect that. He would be presumed to be in car number one, for that very reason. Which burnished his two-in-three chances a little. Convoys opened up at speed. Rack and pinion steering, fast reactions, number three's driver could swerve with plenty of time to spare.

He inclined his head, towards the third car. One of the men standing next to it stepped up smartly and opened the rear door. Plato climbed in. There was a step. Which was necessary, given his stature. He got settled on the rear seat. Cream leather, piped with black. An armrest on the door to his right, an armrest pulled down in the centre of the bench. Air conditioning, set low. Very comfortable.

The two men climbed into the front. Doors closed, a forward gear was engaged. The convoy moved off. The gate was grinding back as they approached it. They slowed, slipped through, sped up. They cruised through the first dusty mile.

Plato looked at the men in front of him.

Many words to describe them.

The best was: disposable.


Janet Salter's kitchen table was cramped for seven people. Peterson and the four women cops had guns on their hips, which made them wide. Reacher himself was not narrow, elbow to elbow. But perhaps as a consequence the atmosphere was cosy. At first Janet Salter was tense, as were Reacher and Peterson for other reasons. The four women cops were happy to talk. Then Janet Salter began to relax, and Reacher and Peterson took a mutual unspoken decision to save it for when it was going to count. They joined in. Everyone told stories. Janet Salter had attended

247

a small local elementary school, a long time ago. The farm boys had been sewn into their winter underwear in November and not released until March. By January the smell was awful. By February it was unbearable.

Peterson's experience had been different. He was half Janet Salter's age. His school was exactly the same as he saw in all the TV shows he watched. He felt part of America, until he looked at a map. Seven hundred miles from the nearest Major League team. A long way from anywhere. Something timid in his head had told him he would never leave. He confessed it quite openly.

Two of the women cops were from North Dakota. They had come south for jobs. And for warmer weather, one said with a smile. Their educations had been similar to Peterson's. Reacher didn't say much. But he knew what they were talking about. Lockers, the gym, the principal's office. He had been to seven elementary schools, all of them overseas on foreign bases, but all of them imported direct from the U.S. as standardized kits of parts. Outside he had been in the steamy heat of Manila or Leyte, or the damp cold of Germany or Belgium, but inside he could have been in North Dakota or South Dakota or Maine or Florida. At times he had been twelve thousand miles from the nearest Major League team. Something in his head had told him he would never stay still.

They had fruit for dessert and coffee and then they cleared the table and washed the dishes, all of them together, part professional, part collegial. Then the day watch women went off duty, and went upstairs. The night watch women headed for the hallway and the library. Janet Salter picked up her book. Reacher and Peterson went to the parlour to wait.

Five minutes to seven in the evening.

Nine hours to go.

# THIRTY

PETERSON KEPT CHECKING HIS WATCH. REACHER KEPT TIME IN his head. Seven o'clock. Five past. Ten past. A quarter past. No activity on the street. The view out from under the lip of the porch stayed the same. Snow, ice, wind, Peterson's parked car, the lookout police cruiser, its vigilant driver. Peterson took the Glock out of his holster and checked it over and put it back. Reacher had the Smith & Wesson in his trouser pocket. He didn't need to check it was there. He could feel its weight.

Peterson was at the window. Reacher sat down, in Janet Salter's chair. He was thinking about the runway, and the old stone building, and the wooden huts.

The first wooden hut, in particular.

He asked, 'Does Kim have a sister?'

Peterson said, 'No.'

'A niece or a cousin?'

'No nieces. Some cousins. Why?'

'That girl I saw in the hut, sitting on the bed. She looked

familiar. At first I thought I had seen her before. But I don't see how. So now I'm trying to pin it down. Either she was just a local type, or she looks like someone else I saw.'

'There's no real local type here.'

'You think? You and Chief Holland look the same.'

'He's older.'

'Apart from that.'

'A little, maybe. But there's no local type.'

'Then that girl looked like someone I saw. On my first night here, I think. And the only woman I saw on my first night here was Kim.'

'And the old ladies on the bus.'

'No resemblance.'

'The waitress in the restaurant?'

'Not her.'

'Kim doesn't have sisters. Or nieces. And I think all her cousins are boys.'

'OK,' Reacher said.

'Maybe you saw a guy. Brothers and sisters can look alike. Lowell has a sister who looks just like him. Remember him? The officer you met?'

'Tough on her,' Reacher said.

'What did this mystery girl look like anyway?'

'Tall and thin and blond.'

'We're all tall and thin and blond.'

'My point exactly.'

'But you can tell us apart.'

Reacher said, 'If I concentrate.'

Peterson smiled briefly and turned back to the window. Reacher joined him there. Twenty past seven. All quiet.

Far to the east and a little to the south Susan Turner dialled her phone again. Her guy in the air force answered on the first ring. He said he had been about to pick up the phone and call her himself. Because he had news. The relevant file had just come through.

'So what's down there under the ground?' Susan asked.

He told her.

'That's vague,' she said. 'Is there any way you can get more detail?'

'You told me this was private and off the record.'

'It is.'

'You sound like your next promotion depends on it.'

'I'm trying to help someone, that's all. And vagueness won't do it.'

'Who are you trying to help?'

Susan Turner paused.

'A friend,' she said.

'How good of a friend?'

'I don't know yet.'

'How good do you want him to be?'

'Good enough to be worth checking some more.'

Her guy said, 'OK, I'll check some more. I'll get back to you.'

At seven thirty Janet Salter started moving around. Reacher heard her in the hallway. He heard the cop on the bottom stair say that dinner had been great. He heard Janet Salter reply politely. Then she came into the parlour. Reacher wanted to put her in the basement, but he decided to wait until the siren sounded. That would be the time she would be most likely to comply, he thought, when she heard that banshee wail again.

She asked, 'What is about to happen?'

Peterson asked, 'Why do you think something is about to happen?'

'Because you're here, Mr Peterson, instead of being home with Mrs Peterson and your children. And because Mr Reacher has gone even quieter than usual.'

Peterson said, 'Nothing is going to happen.'

Reacher said, 'There's an eight o'clock head count up at the jail. We think they're going to come out one short. They're going to hit the panic button.'

'At eight o'clock?'

'Maybe one minute past.'

'An escape?'

Peterson said, 'We think it might have already happened. They'll find out when they count heads.'

'I see.'

'I won't leave,' Peterson said.

'I'm grateful for your concern. But I shall make you leave. You're our next chief of police. For the town's sake, nothing must stand in the way of that.'

'That's crazy.'

'No, it's how good decisions are made. One must take oneself out of the equation.'

'I can't do it.'

'A deal is a deal, even if Chief Holland didn't stick to his with me.'

'I won't go.'

'You will.'

The United States Air Force Security Forces were headquartered at Lackland Air Force Base in Texas. They had no direct equivalent of the army's MP Corps 110th Special Unit. The closest they came was the Phoenix Raven programme, which was an integrated set of specialized teams. One of those teams was led by a guy who had just gotten off the phone with Susan Turner in Virginia, and gotten back on the phone with a file clerk a thousand miles away in a records depository.

The clerk said, 'What I gave you is all I have.'

'Too vague.'

'It is what it is.'

'There has got to be more.'

'There isn't.'

'How hard have you looked?'

'Staring at a piece of paper won't make words appear on it.'

'Where did the delivery originate?'

'You want me to trace one particular cargo flight from fifty years ago?'

'Can you?'

'Not a hope. I'm sorry, major. But we're talking ancient history here. You might as well ask me what Neanderthal Man had for lunch a million years ago last Thursday.'

By ten to eight Janet Salter's house had gone absolutely silent. Some kind of drumbeat of dread had passed between one inhabitant and the next. The cop in the hallway had gotten up off the bottom stair and was standing behind the door. The cop in the library had stepped closer to the window. Peterson was watching the street. Janet Salter was straightening books on the parlour shelves. She was butting their spines into line. Small, nervous, exact movements with the knuckles of her right hand.

Reacher was lounging in a chair. Eyes closed. Nothing could happen before the siren sounded.

The clock ticked on.

Five to eight in the evening.

Eight hours to go.

# THIRTY-ONE

THE CLOCK IN REACHER'S HEAD HIT EIGHT EXACTLY. NOTHING happened. The world outside stayed icy and quiet. Nothing to hear except the sound of the wind, and the brush and rattle of frozen evergreens, and the creaking and stirring of tree limbs, and the primeval tectonic shudders as the earth itself got colder.

One minute past eight.

Nothing happened.

Two minutes past eight.

Nothing happened.

No sound.

No siren.

No one came.

Peterson glanced at Reacher. Reacher shrugged. Janet Salter looked out the window. No action on the street. The cop in the hallway moved. Reacher heard the boards creak under her feet.

Three minutes past eight.

Nothing happened.

Four minutes past.

Five.

Six.

Seven.

Nothing happened.

No sound, no siren.

Nothing at all.

At a quarter past eight they gave it up and stopped worrying. Peterson was certain the head count could not have been delayed. Prisons ran on strict routines. If the cells weren't locked for the night at eight exactly, there would be entries to be made in operational logs, and reports to be filed in triplicate, and supervisors called upon to explain. Way too much trouble for any reason short of a riot in progress, and if a riot was in progress the siren would have sounded anyway. Therefore the bid had failed. Or the lawyer had been blowing smoke.

All clear.

'You sure?' Reacher asked.

'Absolutely,' Peterson said.

'So prove it. Put your money where your mouth is.'

'How?'

'Go home.'

And Peterson did. He spun it out until twenty past, and then he put his coat on and crunched down the driveway and climbed in his car and drove away. Janet Salter stopped straightening books and started reading one instead. The cop in the hallway went back to her perch on the bottom stair. The cop in the library stepped back from the glass. Reacher sat in the kitchen and tried to decide whether to disturb Janet Salter by asking permission, or whether just to go ahead and make more coffee himself. He knew how to work a percolator. His mother had had one, even though she was French. In the end he went ahead and fired it up unbidden. He listened to it gulp and hiss and when it quieted down he poured himself a mug. He raised it in a mock salute to his reflection in the window and took a sip.

\*     \*     \*

255

At eight thirty the phone rang in the hallway. The cop got up from the bottom stair and answered it. It was for Reacher. The voice from Virginia. The cop put two forked fingers under her eyes and then pointed them at the door. *You watch the front, and I'll give you some privacy.* Reacher nodded and sat down and picked up the phone.

The voice said, 'Forty tons of surplus aircrew requirements left over from World War Two.'

'That's vague.'

'Tell me about it. My guy did his best for me, but that's all he knows.'

'What kind of surpluses did they have after World War Two?'

'Are you kidding? All kinds of things. The atom bomb changed everything. They went from having lots of planes carrying small bombs to a few planes carrying big bombs. They could have had forty spare tons of pilots' underwear alone. Plus they changed from prop planes to jets. They got helmets. It could be forty tons of those old-style leather hats.'

'I wish I had one of those right now.'

'Quit whining.'

'What's the temperature here?'

A pause. 'Minus fourteen degrees.'

'Feels worse.'

'It's going to get worse. The Weather Channel radar looks horrible.'

'Thanks for sharing.'

'Hey, you asked.'

'Hats and underwear?'

'Got to be something to do with a generational change of equipment or a reduced number of aircrew. Or both.'

'Anything on the size or architecture of the place itself?'

'That stuff disappeared a long time ago.'

'OK,' Reacher said. 'Thanks.'

'My guy talked. From Fort Hood. Like you said he would.'

'I'm glad.'

'I owe you.'

'No, we're even.'

'No, I do. It's my first major score.'

'Really? How long have you been in the job?'

'Two weeks.'

'I had no idea. You sound like you've been there for ever.'

'I'm not sure that's a compliment.'

'It was meant as one,' Reacher said.

'Then I thank you.'

'You should be out celebrating.'

'I sent my people out.'

'Good move. Give them all the credit. They'll appreciate it, but the brass will always know who really did the work. You'll win both ways around.'

'Is that how you did it?'

'Always. I made out that I did nothing much. A lot of the time that was true, of course.'

'Not what your file suggests.'

'You still looking at that old thing?'

'It's a saga.'

'Not fair. This is a very asymmetrical relationship in terms of information.'

'Dude, life sucks.'

'What did you just call me?'

'I was trying to sound blond and Californian.'

'I see.'

'Do you?'

'You're not blond or Californian.'

'Is that OK?'

'Brunette could work for me. Brown eyes?'

'You got it.'

'Long hair, right?'

'Longer than it should be.'

'Excellent.'

'You want to revisit the A-cup thing too?'

'Got to be honest. I'm just not hearing it.'

She laughed. 'OK, I confess. You're right.'

'Height?'

'Five feet seven.'

'Pale or dark?'

'Neither, really. But I tan well.'

'You want to see South Dakota in the winter?'

She laughed again. 'I prefer the beach.'

'Me too. Where are you from?'

'Montana. A small town you never heard of.'

'Try me. I've been to Montana.'

'Hungry Horse?'

'Never heard of it.'

'Told you,' she said. 'It's near Whitefish.'

'You like the army?'

'Did you?'

'You've got my file,' Reacher said.

'And half the time I'm thinking, man, if you hated it that bad, you should have just gotten out while the getting was good.'

'I never hated it. Not for a minute. I just wanted to fix what was wrong with it.'

'Above your pay grade.'

'I learned that, eventually.' Reacher looked around the hallway. The closed door, the dark panelling, the oil paintings, the Persian carpet. The rare woods, the wax, the polish, the patina. He had all the information he was ever going to get from or through the 110th. No real reason to keep on talking.

The voice asked, 'What are you doing in South Dakota anyway?'

He said, 'I was on a bus that crashed. I got hung up here.'

'Life is a gamble.'

'But the deck is stacked. No bus that I was on ever crashed in a warm place.'

'You behaving yourself up there?'

'Why wouldn't I be?'

'These files get tagged if an outside agency asks to take a look. You know, the FBI or a local police department or something. And yours is tagged to hell and back. Folks have been all over you for the last twelve years.'

'Anything from here in the last two days?'

'A transcript went out to someone called Thomas Holland at the Bolton PD.'

'The Chief of Police. Probably routine. He wanted to know I was qualified, because he wanted my help. Back when he thought the stone building was an army place. Any follow-up?'

'No.'

'That's because I'm behaving myself.'

A long pause.

Time to go.

He asked, 'What's your name?'

'Does it matter?'

'I could find out. The way the army is now, you're probably on a web site somewhere.'

'Are you kidding? The 110th? No way. We don't exist.'

'So what's your name?'

'Susan.'

'Nice name.'

'I think so too.'

Another long pause.

Time to go.

He asked, 'Is your air force guy at Lackland?'

'Yes. Talking to their records guys in Colorado.'

'Ask him to try one more time. Obviously that stuff was flown in. There has to be a cargo manifest somewhere.'

'I'll try.'

'Call me back?' he asked.

'You bet,' she said.


Reacher went back to the kitchen and took another cup of coffee. The house was quiet. No significant sound from the outside. No significant sound from the inside either, except for the subliminal vibe of calm alert people concentrating hard on the business at hand. It was the kind of silence Reacher had heard a hundred times before. He carried his mug to the parlour and found Janet Salter reading there. She looked up from her book and said, 'You're drinking coffee.'

Reacher said, 'I hope you don't mind.'

'Not at all. But doesn't it keep you awake?'

He nodded. 'Until I want to go to sleep.'

'How was she?'

'Who?'

'The woman in Virginia.'

'She was fine.' Reacher stepped to the window and took a look at the street. Snow, ice, the parked cruiser, frozen foliage moving stiffly in the wind. A little moonlight, a little high cloud, a distant orange glow from vapour lamps on the streets to the north and the east. He said, 'All quiet.'

Janet Salter asked, 'Do you think the state penitentiary and the federal prison have the same lock-down time as the county jail?'

'I imagine so.'

'Then we're safe for a spell, aren't we? Heads have been counted and there's no opportunity for mass disturbance until the morning.'

'In principle.'

'But?'

'Hope for the best, plan for the worst.'

'Is that your motto?'

'One of many.'

'What are the others?'

'Never forgive, never forget. Do it once and do it right. You reap what you sow. Plans go to hell as soon as the first shot is fired. Protect and serve. Never off duty.'

'You're as hard on yourself as you are on others.'

'Cruel but fair.'

'I can't stand this kind of tension much longer.'

'I hope you won't have to.'

'For the first time in my life I'm afraid. It's a very elemental thing, isn't it?'

'It's a choice,' Reacher said. 'That's all.'

'Surely everyone's afraid of death.'

'That was another motto. I'm not afraid of death. Death's afraid of me.'

'You sound like you were trying to convince yourself.'

260

'We were. All the time. Believe me.'

'So you are afraid of death.'

'We all have to go sometime. Depends what form it takes, I guess.'

Janet Salter went quiet for a moment. Then she said, 'I met my successor at Yale two years ago. At a library conference. It was an interesting experience. I imagine you feel the same way, talking to the woman in Virginia.'

'She isn't my successor. Not directly. There could have been six or seven other people in between me and her. Maybe more. It's a distant connection. Almost archaeological.'

'Is she better than you?'

'Probably.'

'That's how I felt, too. At first I was depressed about it. Then I realized actually I should feel encouraged about it. Progress is being maintained. The world is still moving forward.'

'How long have you been retired?'

'A little more than ten years.'

'So you got back here before the prison was built.'

'Years before. It was a different town then. But not too different, I suppose. The real change is still to come. We're still in a transitional phase. The real change will come when we get used to it. At the moment we're a town with a prison in it. Soon we'll be a prison town.'

'So what was it like?'

'Gentle,' Janet Salter said. 'Quiet. Half the size. No fast food, only one motel. Chief Holland was a young man with a family. Like Andrew Peterson is now. I don't know why, but that symbolizes the change for me. Everything felt cheerful and young and lighthearted. Not old and tired and bitter, like it is now.'

'What happened to Holland's wife?'

'Cancer. But mercifully quick. Their daughter Liz was fifteen at the time. Which could have been awkward, but she seemed to handle it quite well. She was named for her mother. Her mother went by Betty, and she went by Liz. They were very similar in every way. Which could have been awkward for the chief, too,

261

but he got past it. He was already involved in the early stages of planning the prison by then, which took his mind off it.'

'And what was the Lowell divorce all about?'

'I told you, I don't know. But the fact that no one speaks of it invites speculation, doesn't it?'

'His fault or hers?

'Oh, his, I think.'

'Peterson said he has a sister who looks just like him.'

'In a way. Much younger than him. More like a niece.'

'Are you going to stay here, even when it's a prison town?'

'Me? I'm far too old to start over somewhere else. What about you?'

'I couldn't stay here. It's too cold.'

'Eventually you'll want to stay somewhere.'

'Hasn't happened so far.'

'See how you feel thirty years from now.'

'That's a far horizon.'

'It will come faster than you expect.'

Reacher put his empty mug on a low table. He wasn't sure whether to stay in the room or to leave her alone to read. He wasn't sure which she would prefer.

'Sit,' she said. 'I'll have plenty of time to read after all this fuss is over.'

He sat.

She asked, 'Are you warm enough?'

He said, 'I'm fine.' Which he was. The ancient radiator under the window was putting out plenty of heat. The hot water in the pipes was coursing around the house relentlessly. He could hear it. He could hear the occluded right-angle joint at the top of the stairs, hissing a little louder than the others. He pictured the burner in the basement, roaring, and the pump, running hard. Unlimited heat, available around the clock. Much better than the arrangement in Andrew Peterson's farmhouse. The old iron wood stove, banked and cooling all night, barely warm by morning.

He stared into space for a second.

He said, 'Stupid.'

Janet Salter asked him, 'Who or what?'

'Me.'

'Why?'

'I need to make a phone call.' He got up and stepped out to the hallway. Spoke to the cop sitting on the bottom stair. Said, 'I need Andrew Peterson's home number.'

The cop said, 'I'm not sure I'm at liberty to give it to you.'

'Then dial it for me. I won't look.'

She dialled it for him. Checked that she was getting ring tone, and then handed the receiver to him. Kim Peterson answered. Reacher introduced himself and said, 'I'm very sorry to disturb you, but I need to speak with Andrew.'

'He just got home.'

'I know. I'm sorry. But it's important.'

There was a long delay. Maybe Kim had to go drag Peterson out of his den. But he came on the line eventually.

'Problem?' he asked.

'The opposite,' Reacher said. 'I know where the key is. For the stone building.'

Five to nine in the evening.

Seven hours to go.

# THIRTY-TWO

REACHER STAYED ON THE LINE AND PETERSON SPENT A MINUTE talking to himself about what to do next. Like he was thinking out loud. He said, 'The prison was locked down an hour ago, so the siren is not going to sound. It can't, really, can it? There's no opportunity. The guy could come without the siren, I suppose, but in that case we'll still have plenty of bodies in the way. Four in the house, three on the street. All of them are good people. I made sure of that. So right now it doesn't really matter whether you're there or not, does it? You're superfluous. In a temporary sense. So it's safe enough for you to come out. Do you agree?'

'Safe enough,' Reacher said.

'I'll pick you up in ten minutes.'

Reacher went back to the parlour. Janet Salter looked up at him. He told her he was going out, and where, and why. He said, 'If the cops have to leave, what do you do?'

She said, 'Lock myself in the basement.'

'With?'

'My gun.'

'When?'

'Straight away, I suppose.'

'Correct,' Reacher said. 'Straight away, immediately, instantly, no delay at all, before the cops are even out through the door. You lock yourself in, and you stay there until I get back.'

'With the password.'

'Correct,' Reacher said again. 'And even if the cops don't actually leave, you go down there if you sense any kind of commotion at all. Any kind of uneasiness, any kind of extra nervousness, any kind of heightened alert, OK?'

'You think the man might come with the police still in the house?'

'Hope for the best, plan for the worst. If the cops get a bad feeling, they won't tell you right away. They won't want to look stupid afterwards, if it turns out to be nothing. So it's up to you to figure it out. Trust your gut. Any doubt at all, get the hell down there, fast. A stray bullet can kill you just the same as one that was aimed.'

'How long will you be gone?'

'Two hours, maybe.'

'I'll be fine.'

'You will if you do what I say.'

'I will. I promise. I'll go down and lock the door and wait for the password.'

Reacher nodded. Said nothing.

Safe enough.


Reacher went out to the hallway and climbed into his giant coat. Checked the pockets for hat and gloves and gun. All present and correct. The telephone rang. The woman from the bottom stair answered it. She handed the receiver to Reacher without a word.

'Yes?' he said, expecting Peterson.

The voice from Virginia said, 'We got a partial cargo manifest.'

'And?'

'And I'm going to spend the rest of my life paying off the favour. You know how hard it must have been to find? An irrelevant piece of paper from fifty years ago?'

'They've got clerks, the same as we did. What else have they got to do?'

'They claim plenty.'

'Don't believe them. What's on the manifest?'

'Forty tons of war surplus flown in from the old Eighth Air Force bases in the United Kingdom. From the old World War Two bomber fields in East Anglia. They closed a bunch down in the middle fifties. Runways weren't long enough any more.'

'Does it specify what kind of surplus?'

'Yes and no. Generically it says aircrew requirements, and specifically there's a manufacturer's name that no one remembers, and a code that no one understands any more.'

'Not even the Lackland guys?'

'Not even them. This is ancient history we're dealing with here.'

'The way I remember my ancient history, we didn't bring World War Two surplus back from Europe. We either junked it over there or sold it off over there. Kept the money in the local currencies and used it for Fulbright scholarships. Two birds with one stone. We got rid of a lot of old crap and we spread peace and brotherhood and understanding all at the same time. Through educational exchange.'

'Those were the days.'

'What was the code?'

'N06BA03.'

'Means nothing to me.'

'Means nothing to anyone. Could be underwear. Or hats.'

'We wouldn't have flown forty tons of underwear or hats all the way back from Europe. No sense in that. Cheaper just to give them away, or burn them.'

'So maybe it was something we couldn't give away. Or sell. Or burn. For security reasons. Sidearms, maybe. I think World

War Two pilots carried them. In case they were shot down over enemy territory.'

'What was the manufacturer's name?'

'Some outfit called Crown Laboratories.'

'Say again?'

'Crown Laboratories.'

Reacher said, 'Oh, shit.'

'What?'

'Forty *tons*? They have got to be kidding me.'

'Reacher, what?'

'I got to go.'

As soon as he saw the leading edge of Peterson's headlight beams on the street he stepped out the door and crossed the porch and hustled down the driveway. The cold hit him like a hammer. Peterson's tyres crunched and crackled over the frozen snow. The car pulled up and Reacher climbed in. The heater was blowing lukewarm air. Reacher kept his hat and gloves on. Peterson K-turned and bounced across the ruts and headed back to the main drag. Turned right and drove south, slower than he would in summer, faster than he would in traffic. There was nothing else on the road. Only nine in the evening, but the whole state seemed closed up for the night. People were all huddled inside, and Peterson's car was the only thing moving across the landscape.

They made the turn ten miles later and drove on, parallel with the highway. The cloud was thin and high and there was plenty of moonlight. There was still ice on the wind, coming steadily at them out of the west. It crusted on the windshield, a thin abrasive layer that the wipers couldn't shift. Like diamond dust. Peterson put the heater on defrost and ducked his head to look through warmed circles that got smaller with every mile.

They turned right again on the wandering county two-lane. Now the wind was on their left hand side and the screen cleared again. The old runway loomed up ahead, grey and massive in the night. It was still clear. They bumped up on it and the tyre chains ground and rattled.

They drove two fast miles.

Saw red tail lights ahead.

A parked car. Its tail lights faced them and beyond its dark end-on bulk was a pool of white from its headlights. There was a swirl of exhaust from its pipes, pooling, eddying, drifting, then blowing away.

Peterson slowed and put his lights on bright. The parked car was empty. It was a Ford Crown Victoria. No markings. Either dark blue or black. Hard to say, in the glare.

'Chief Holland's car,' Peterson said.

They parked alongside it and climbed out into the stunning cold and found Holland himself at the first hut's door. Fur hat, zipped parka, thick gloves, heavy boots, moving stiff and clumsy in all the clothing, his breath clouding in front of him.

Holland wasn't pleased to see them.

He said, 'What the hell are you doing here?'

He sounded angry.

Peterson said, 'Reacher figured out where the key is.'

'I don't care who figured out what. You shouldn't have come. Neither one of you. It's completely irresponsible. Suppose the siren goes off?'

'It won't.'

'You think?'

'It can't. Can it? The cells are locked and the head counts are done.'

'You trust their procedures?'

'Of course.'

'You're an idiot, Andrew. You need to stop drinking the damn Kool-Aid. That place is a complete mess. Especially the county lock-up, which is what we're interested in right now. If you think they do a proper head count every night, then I've got a beachfront lot to sell you. Fifty bucks an acre, about a mile from here.'

'It's a brand new place.'

'Brand new metal and concrete. Same old human beings working there.'

'So what are you saying? The head count could be faulty?'

'I'm saying dollars to doughnuts there was no head count at all. I'm saying at five to eight they sound a horn and expect everyone to wander home and then at eight the cell doors lock up electronically.'

'Even if that's true, there's no danger until morning.'

'They do night patrols, son. Ten scheduled, one an hour. I'm guessing they skip nine of them. But at some point they walk around with flashlights, checking beds, doing what they were supposed to do at eight o'clock.'

'Are you serious?'

'Human nature, Andrew. Get used to it.'

'Should we go back?'

Holland paused a beat. 'No, we have to go back that way anyway. Worst case, Mrs Salter will be alone for five minutes. Maybe ten. It's a gamble. We'll take it. But I wish you hadn't come in the first place.'

Reacher asked, 'Why are you here?'

Holland looked at him. 'Because I figured out where the key is.'

'Good work.'

'Not really. Anyone with a brain could figure it out on a night like this.'

'Where is it?' Peterson asked.

It was inside the paraffin stove in the first hut. A fine hiding place, with built-in time-delayed access. Too hot to think about searching earlier, now cool to the touch. Like Peterson's own banked wood stove. The voice from Virginia had said, *Burn the place down and sift the ashes. An air force key is probably made of the same stuff as warheads. It would survive, easy.* And the voice had been right. The key had survived. It was fine. It had been dropped on the burner core and it had heated and cooled with no bad consequences. It was a large T-shaped device about three inches across. Complex teeth, the dull glitter of rare and exotic metal. Titanium, maybe.

From way back, when paranoia permitted no sceptical questions about cost.

Reacher fished it out of the stove. He handed it to Holland. Holland carried it to the stone building's door. He slipped it into the lock. Turned it. The lock sprang back.

# THIRTY-THREE

REACHER TRIED THE HANDLE. IT TURNED DOWNWARD SIXTY degrees with a hefty motion that was halfway between precise and physical. Like an old-fashioned bank vault. The door itself was very heavy. It felt like it weighed a ton, literally. Its outer skin was a two-inch-thick steel plate. Inset by two inches in every direction on the back was a ten-inch-deep rectangular protuberance that socketed home between the jambs and the lintel and the floor saddle. The protuberance was like a welded steel box. Probably packed with ceramics. When closed, the whole thing would make a seamless foot-thick part of the wall. The hinges were massive. But not recently oiled. They shrieked and squeaked and protested. But the door came open. Reacher hauled it through a short two-foot arc and then slipped in behind it and leaned into it and pushed it the rest of the way. Like pushing a broken-down truck.

Nothing but darkness inside the stone building.

'Flashlights,' Holland said.

Peterson hustled back and visited both cars and returned with

271

three flashlights. They clicked on one after the other and beams played around and showed a bare concrete bunker maybe twenty feet deep and thirty feet wide. Two storeys high. The stone was outside veneer only. For appearances. Underneath it the building was brutal and utilitarian and simple and to the point. In the centre of the space it had the head of a spiral stair that dropped straight down through the floor into a round vertical shaft. The air coming up out of it smelled still and dry and ancient. Like a tomb. Like a pharaoh's chamber in a pyramid. The hole for the stairwell was perfectly circular. The floor was cast from concrete two feet thick. The stairs themselves were welded from simple steel profiles. They wound round and down into distant blackness.

'No elevator,' Peterson said.

'Takes too much power,' Reacher said. He was fighting the pedantic part of his brain that was busy pointing out that a spiral was a plane figure. Two dimensions only. Thus a spiral staircase was a contradiction in terms. It was a helical staircase. A helix was a three-dimensional figure. But he didn't say so. He had learned not to. Maybe Susan in Virginia would have understood. Or maybe not.

'Can you imagine?' Holland said, in the silence. 'You're seven years old and you're looking to head down there and you know you won't be coming back up until you're grown?'

'If you got here at all,' Reacher said. 'Which you wouldn't have. The whole concept was crazy. They built the world's most expensive storage facility, that's all.'

Close to the stairwell shaft there were two wide metal ventilation pipes coming up through the floor. Maybe two feet in diameter. They came up about a yard and stopped, like broad chimneys on a flat roof. Directly above both of them were circular holes in the concrete ceiling. One shaft would have been planned as an intake, connected to one of the building's fake chimneys, fitted with fans and filters and scrubbers to clean the poisoned air. The other would have been the exhaust, to be vented up and out through the second fake chimney. An incomplete installation. Never finished. Presumably the fake chimneys were capped

272

internally. Some temporary fix that had lasted fifty years. There was no sign of rain or snow inside the bunker.

Reacher stepped over to one of the pipes and shone his flashlight beam straight down. Like looking down a well. He couldn't see bottom. The pipe was lined on the inside with stainless steel. Smooth and shiny. Efficient air movement. No turbulence. No furring, no accumulation of dirt. Regular cleaning had not been on the agenda. There would have been no one left alive to do it.

Reacher stepped back and leaned over the stair rail and shone his flashlight beam straight down the stairwell. Saw nothing except stairs. They wound on endlessly, wrapped around a simple steel pipe. No hand rail on the outer circumference. The space was too tight.

'This place is very deep,' he said.

His voice echoed back at him.

'Probably needed to be,' Holland said.

The stairs had once been painted black, but their edges were worn back to dull metal by the passage of many feet. The safety rail around the opening was scuffed and greasy.

Peterson said, 'I'll go first.'

Five to ten in the evening.

Six hours to go.

Reacher waited until Peterson's head was seven feet down, and then he followed. The stairs were in a perfectly round vertical shaft lined with smooth concrete. Space was cramped. There had been construction difficulties. The voice from Virginia had read him notes from faxed files: *The design was compromised several times during construction because of the kind of terrain they found.* Clearly the terrain had meant they hadn't drilled beyond the bare minimum. The diameter was tight. Reacher's shoulders brushed the concrete on one side and the central pipe on the other. But it was his feet that were the major problem. They were too big. A helical staircase has treads that narrow from the outside to the inside. Reacher was walking on his heels the whole way. Coming back up, he would be walking on his toes.

They went down, and down, and down, Peterson first, then

273

Reacher, then Holland. Fifty feet, then seventy-five, then a hundred. Their flashlight beams jerked and stabbed through the gloom. The steel under their feet clanged and boomed. The air was still and dry. And warm. Like a mine, insulated from the surface extremes.

Reacher called, 'See anything yet?'

Peterson called back, 'No.'

They kept on going, corkscrewing down, and down, and down, their flashlight beams turning perpetually clockwise, washing the trowelled concrete wall. They passed through strange acoustic nodes where the whole shaft resonated like the bore of an oboe and the sound of their feet on the metal set up weird harmonic chords, as if the earth's core was singing to them.

Two hundred feet.

Then more.

Then Peterson called, 'I'm there, I think.'

Reacher clattered on after him, two more full turns.

Then he came to a dead stop, deep underground.

He sat down, on the second to last step.

He used his flashlight, left, right, up, down.

Not good.

He heard the voice from Virginia in his head again: *Something about the construction compromises made it useless for anything else.*

Damn straight they did.

The stairwell shaft ended in an underground chamber made of concrete. It was perfectly circular. Like a hub. Maybe twenty feet in diameter. The size of a living room. But round. Like a living room in a movie about the future. It had eight open doorways leading off to eight horizontal corridors, one at each point of the compass, like bicycle spokes. The corridors were dark. Deep in shadow. The doorways were straight and square and true. The chamber's floor was hard and flat and dry and smooth. The walls were hard and flat and dry and smooth. The ceiling was hard and flat and dry and smooth. Altogether the whole place was a neat, crisp, exact piece of construction. Well designed, well engineered, well built. Ideal for its intended purpose.

Which was an orphanage.

For children.

What made it useless for anything else was that the ceiling was only five feet six inches above the floor. That was all. Bad terrain. The round chamber and the accompanying spoked corridors had been burrowed laterally into a thin and ungenerous seam between upper and lower plates of unyielding hard rock. The low ceiling was a necessary concession to reality. And a professional disappointment, probably. But theoretically adequate for a pack of unaccompanied kids, all runty and starving. Reacher could picture the engineers confronting the unexpected problem, poring over geological surveys, looking up tables of average height versus age, shrugging their shoulders, revising their plans, signing off on the inevitable. Technically acceptable, they would have said, which was the only standard military engineers understood.

But the place was not acceptable for anything else, technically or otherwise. Not even close. Not acceptable for Marine training or any other kind of military purpose. Not acceptable for any kind of full grown adult. Peterson had advanced maybe ten feet into the space and he was buckled at the knees and his head was ducked way down. He was crouching. His shoulders were on the ceiling. He was waddling painfully, ludicrously stooped, like a Russian folk dancer.

And Peterson was three inches shorter than Reacher.

Reacher stood up again. He was on the bottom step. Nine inches above the round chamber's floor. Its ceiling was level with his waist. His whole upper body was still inside the shaft.

Not good.

Holland came on down and crowded in behind him. Said, 'We won't hear the siren way down here.'

'Does your cell phone work?'

'Not a chance.'

'Then we better be quick.'

'After you,' Holland said. 'Mind your head.'

Reacher had a choice. He could shuffle along on his knees or scoot along on his butt. He chose to scoot on his butt. Slow and

275

undignified, but less painful. He snaked downward off the last stair like a clumsy gymnast and sat down and scuttled a cautious yard, heels and knuckles and ass, like a kid playing at being a crab. Ahead of him the two ventilation shafts came down through the low ceiling and ended a stubby foot below the concrete. Three separate parallel bores, one wide for the stairs, two narrow for the pipes, all ending the prescribed distance below the surface in a ludicrous horizontal slot burrowed laterally and grudgingly into the rock.

Reacher said, 'I was already taller than this when I was seven.'

His voice came back to him with a strange humming echo. The acoustics were weird. The concrete he was sitting on was neither warm nor cold. There was a faint smell of kerosene in the air. And a draught. Air was coming down the stairwell shaft and circulating back up through the ventilation shafts. A venturi effect. The stone building's door was open more than two hundred feet above them and the wind was blowing hard across it and sucking air out of the bunker. The same way a spray gun sucks paint out of a reservoir or a carburettor sucks gas out of a fuel line. But nature abhors a vacuum, so some circulatory layer was feeding air right back in, just as fast.

'Move,' Holland said.

Reacher scuttled another yard. Holland ducked down and stepped off the last stair and came after him, crouching like Peterson, spinning slowly, playing his flashlight beam around a whole wide circle.

'Eight doorways,' he said. 'Eight choices. Which one has the lab?'

The same strange, humming echo, like Holland's voice was everywhere and nowhere.

Reacher said, 'There is no lab.'

'Has to be. Where there's meth there's a lab.'

'There was a lab,' Reacher said. 'Once upon a time. But it wasn't here. It was a big place in New Jersey or California or somewhere. It had a sign outside.'

'What are you talking about?'

276

Reacher played his flashlight beam low across the floor. Started at the bottom step and followed a faint track of dirt and scuffs that curled counterclockwise across the concrete to a doorway more or less opposite where he was sitting. South, if he was north, or north, if he was south. He had been turned around so many times by the staircase he had lost his bearings.

'Follow me,' he said.

He scooted off. He found it faster to turn around and travel backwards. Push with his feet, pivot on his hands, dump down on his ass, and repeat. And repeat. And repeat. It was warm work. He pulled off his hat and his gloves and unzipped his coat. Then he resumed. Holland and Peterson followed him all the way, bent over, crouching, waddling, always in his view. He could hear knee joints popping and cracking. Ligaments, and fluid. Holland's, he guessed. Peterson was younger and in better shape.

He made it to the doorway and swivelled around and shone his flashlight down the length of the corridor. It was a tunnel maybe a hundred feet long, perfectly horizontal, like a coal seam. It was five feet six inches high, and about the same in width. The left hand half was an unobstructed hundred-foot walkway. The right hand half was built up into a long low continuous concrete shelf, a hundred feet long, about two feet off the floor. A sleeping shelf, he guessed. He imagined bedrolls laid head to toe all along its length, maybe twenty of them. Twenty sleeping children. Five feet each.

But the place had never been used. There were no bedrolls. No sleeping children. What was on the shelf instead was the war surplus flown back fifty years earlier from the old U.S. bomber bases in Europe. Aircrew requirements. Hundreds and hundreds of bricks of white powder, wrapped smooth and tight in yellowing glassine, each packet printed with the crown device, the headband, the three points, the three balls representing jewels. A registered trademark, presumably, for a now defunct but once entirely legitimate and government-contracted outfit called Crown Laboratories, whoever and wherever they had been.

Peterson said, 'I don't believe it.'

The packs looked to be stacked ten high and ten deep in groups of a hundred and there were maybe a hundred and fifty groups along the whole length of the shelf. A total of fifteen thousand, minus those already removed. The stack was a little depleted at the near end. It looked like a brick wall in the process of patient demolition.

Holland asked, 'Is this forty tons?'

'No,' Reacher said. 'Not even close. This is only about a third of it. There should be another two stacks just like this.'

'How many packs in forty tons?' Peterson asked.

'Nearly forty-five thousand.'

'That's insane. That's forty-five billion in street value.'

'Your granddaddy's tax dollars at work.'

'What was it for?'

'World War Two aircrew,' Reacher said. 'Bombers, mostly. None of us have any idea what that war was like for them. Towards the end they were flying twelve-hour trips, sometimes more, Berlin and back, deep into Germany, day after day after day. Every trip they were doing stuff that had never been done before, in terms of precision and endurance. And they were in mortal danger, every single minute. Every second. Casualties were terrible. They would have been permanently terrified and demoralized, except they were always too exhausted to think. Pep pills were the only way to keep them in the air.'

'These aren't pills.'

'Delivery method was up to the medical officers. Some made it up into pills, some preferred drinking it dissolved in water, some recommended inhaling it, some liked suppositories. Probably some prescribed all four ways at once.'

'I had no idea.'

'It was general issue, like boots or ammunition. Like food.'

'Can't have been good for them.'

'Some of the planes had little wires soldered near the end of the throttle travel. The last quarter inch. War boost, it was called. If you needed it, you hauled the throttle back and busted the wire and got maximum power. It strained the engine, which wasn't good, but it saved your life, which was good. Same exact principle with the dope.'

'How much did they get through?'

'Way more than we can guess. The air force in Europe was hundreds of thousands strong back then. And demand was pretty strong, too. It was a tough gig. I'm sure I would have snorted my body weight before my first tour was half done.'

'And this much was left over?'

'This could have been a month's supply. Suddenly not needed any more. Shutting down production was pretty haphazard at the end.'

'Why is it here?'

'Couldn't just junk it. Couldn't sell it. Certainly couldn't burn it. The whole of Europe would have gotten high as kites off the smoke.'

They went quiet. Just stared.

Then Holland said, 'Let's find the rest.'

The rest was shared between the next two tunnels to the left. The same hundred-foot shelves, the same meticulous stacks of packets, the same dull flashlight reflections off the yellowed glassine. A full fifteen thousand bricks in the second tunnel, another full fifteen thousand in the third.

Holland dropped to his knees. Clenched his fists. Smiled wide.

'Close to ninety thousand pounds, all told,' he said. 'The damn DEA will have to listen to us now. This has got to be the biggest drug bust in history. And we did it. Little old us. The Bolton PD, in South Dakota. We're going to be famous. We're going to be legends. No more poor relations. The damn prison staff can kiss my ass.'

'Congratulations,' Reacher said.

'Thank you.'

'But it's not all good. Plato found it a year before you did.'

'How?'

'Rumour and logic, I guess. He knew it had been used in the war, and he knew there was likely to be surplus stock some-where, so he tracked it down. He's probably got guys in the air force. That's probably why we found the cargo manifest. It was on top of a pile somewhere, because someone else had been looking for it already.'

Peterson said, 'I can't believe the bikers left it all sitting here. The temptation to take some with them must have been huge.'

Reacher said, 'I get the impression that if Plato tells you to leave something, you leave it.' He shuffled a little further into the tunnel, picturing a long line of sweating men fifty years ago passing the two-pound packets hand to hand to hand and then stacking them neatly like craftsmen. Probably the shortest guys had been detailed for the work. He didn't know what the air force's height requirement had been fifty years earlier. But probably some of the guys had been standing straight, and some of them hadn't. They had probably roped the packs down the ventilation tubes in kitbags. Five or ten at a time, maybe more. Trestles and pulleys on the surface. Some kind of an improvised system. Too laborious to carry them all down the stairs one by one. Probably the bikers had brought them back up the same way. The fact that the ventilation pipes were unfinished and open at both ends must have been too obvious to ignore.

He shuffled a little further in and made another discovery.

There was a lateral link feeding sideways off the main tunnel. Like part of a circle's circumference butting up against its radius. He squeezed down it and came out in the next tunnel along. He shuffled deeper in and found two more lateral links, one to the left, one to the right. The whole place was a warren. A maze. There was a total of eight spokes, and three separate incomplete rings. Each ring had its own curved shelf. Lots more linear feet for sleeping children. Lots of corners. Some turned only left, some turned only right. There were no four-way junctions. Everything was a T, upright at the far end of the spokes, rotated randomly left or right at the other turns. A bizarre layout. The plan view on the blueprint must have looked like a Celtic brooch. Maybe there had been more construction compromises than just the ceiling height. Possibly the whole thing was supposed to be like an odd truncated underground version of the Pentagon itself, but rounded off, not angular, and with some of the links between rings and spokes not made.

The wedges of solid rock separating the spokes and the rings had been hollowed out in ten separate places. Bathrooms, maybe, never installed, or kitchens, never installed, or storerooms for subsistence rations, never supplied. Everything was faced with smooth crisp concrete. It was dry and dusty. The air smelled old. The whole place was absolutely silent.

Peterson called, 'Take a look at this.'

Reacher couldn't locate his voice. It came through all the tunnels at once, from everywhere, humming and singing and fluttering and riding the walls.

Reacher called, 'Where are you?'

Peterson said, 'Here.'

Which didn't help. Reacher threaded his way back to the main circular hall and asked again. Peterson was in the next tunnel along. Reacher scooted over and joined him there. Peterson was looking at a fuel tank. It was a big ugly thing that had been welded together out of curved sections of steel small enough to have been dropped down the ventilation shafts. It was sitting on a shelf. It was maybe forty feet long. It was big enough to hold maybe five thousand gallons. It was sweating slightly and it smelled of kerosene. Not original to the place. The welds were crude. Technically unacceptable. Air force mechanics would have done better work.

Peterson stooped forward and rapped it with his knuckles. The sound came back dull and liquid. Reacher thought back to the fuel truck that had nearly creamed him in the snow at the bottom of the old county two-lane.

'Great,' he said. 'We're two hundred feet underground with five thousand gallons of jet fuel in a home-made tank.'

'Why jet fuel? It smells like kerosene.'

'Jet fuel is kerosene, basically. So it's one or the other. And there's way more here than they need for the heaters in the huts. And they just got it. After they already knew they were leaving. And after ploughing the runway. So a plane is coming

281

in. Probably soon. It's going to refuel. Holland needs to tell the DEA about that. They're going to need to be fast.'

'It won't come in the dark. There are no runway lights.'

'Even so. Time is tight. How far away is the nearest DEA field office?'

Peterson didn't answer. Instead he asked, 'How did they fill a tank all the way down here?'

'They backed the fuel truck to the door and dropped the hose down the air shaft.'

'That would need a long hose.'

'They have long hoses for houses with big yards.'

Then Holland called out, 'Guys, take a look at *this*.'

His voice reached them with a strange hissing echo, all around the circular room, like a whispering gallery. He was in a tunnel directly opposite. Reacher scooted and Peterson stooped and scuffled and they made their way over to him. He was playing his flashlight beam close and then far, all the way down the hundred-foot length and back again.

It was like something out of a fairy tale.

Like Aladdin's cave.

# THIRTY-FOUR

HOLLAND'S FLASHLIGHT BEAM THREW BACK BRIGHT REFLECTIONS off gold, off silver, off platinum. It set up glitter and refraction and sparkle off brilliant diamonds and deep green emeralds and rich red rubies and bright blue sapphires. It showed old muted colours, landscapes, portraits, oils on canvas, yellow gilt frames. There were chains and lockets and pins and necklaces and bracelets and rings. They were coiled and piled and tangled and tossed all the way along the shelf. Yellow gold, rose gold, white gold. Old things. New things. A hundred linear feet of loot. Paintings, jewellery, candlesticks, silver trays, watches. Small gold clocks, tiny suede bags with drawstrings, a cut-glass bowl entirely filled with wedding bands.

'Unredeemed pledges,' Peterson said. 'In transit, from Plato's pawn shops.'

'Barter,' Reacher said. 'For his dope.'

'Maybe both,' Holland said. 'Maybe both things are the same in the end.'

They all shuffled down the tunnel. They were unable to resist.

The shelf was a hundred feet long and maybe thirty-two inches wide. More than two hundred and fifty square feet of real estate. The size of a decent room. There was no space on it large enough to put a hand. It was more or less completely covered. Some of the jewellery was exquisite. Some of the paintings were fine. All of the items were sad. The fruits of desperation. The flotsam and jetsam of ruined lives. Hard times, addiction, burglary, loss. Under the triple flashlight beams the whole array flashed and danced and glittered and looked simultaneously fabulous and awful. Someone's dreams, someone else's nightmares, all secret and buried two hundred feet down.

A hundred pounds' weight, or a thousand.

A million dollars' worth, or ten.

'Let's go,' Reacher said. 'We've got better things to do. We shouldn't waste time here.'

The climb back to the surface was long and hard and tiring. Reacher counted the steps. There were two hundred and eighty of them. Like walking up a twenty-storey building. He had to take each step on his toes. Good exercise, he guessed, but right then he wasn't looking for exercise. The air got colder all the way. It had been maybe thirty degrees underground. It was about minus twenty on the surface. A fifty-degree drop. One degree every five or six steps. Fast enough to notice, but no sudden shock. Reacher zipped his coat and put on his hat and his gloves about a third of the way up. Holland surrendered next. Peterson made it halfway up before he succumbed.

They rested inside the stone building for a minute. Outside the moonlight was still bright. Peterson collected the flash-lights and shut them down. Holland stood with his hand on the stair rail. He was red in the face from exertion and breathing hard.

Reacher said to him, 'You need to make a call.'

'Do I?'

'The siren could have come and gone while we were down-stairs.'

'In which case we're already too late.' Holland pulled out his

284

cell and dialled. Identified himself, asked a question, listened to the reply.

And smiled.

'All clear,' he said. 'Sometimes you gamble and win.'

Then he waited until Peterson left to carry the flashlights back to the cars. He watched him go and turned back to Reacher and said, 'You and I figured out the key. You knew the meth was there. But I want to give Andrew the credit. He's going to be the next chief. A thing like this, it would help him with the guys. And the town. A thing like this, it would set him up right.'

'No question,' Reacher said.

'So would you be OK with that?'

'Fine with me,' Reacher said.

'Good.'

Reacher pushed the door closed against the yowling hinges and Holland locked it up and pocketed the key. They walked together back to the cars and Holland pulled his right glove off in the freezing air and offered his hand to Peterson. Peterson snatched his own glove off and shook.

'Now listen up,' Holland said.

He leaned into his car and unhooked his radio mike from the dash and pulled it out all the way until the cord went straight and tight. He thumbed the key and called in an all-points code and spoke.

He said, 'Ladies and gentlemen, tonight Deputy Chief Peterson broke open what I'm sure will prove to be our country's largest ever drug bust. Start of business tomorrow he'll be calling the DEA in Washington with the details and about thirty seconds after that this department will be among the most celebrated in the nation. He has my congratulations. As do you all. Just another fine night's work in a long and distinguished tradition.'

He clicked off and tossed the mike on his seat.

Peterson said, 'Thank you, chief.'

Holland said, 'You're welcome. But you still shouldn't have come.'

Five minutes to eleven in the evening.

Five hours to go.

Seventeen hundred miles south Plato's three-car convoy waited at an inconspicuous gate in a hurricane fence around an airfield. The gate was a battered, saggy affair, chained and padlocked. The fence was matted with trash and weeds at its base. But the airfield itself was fit for its purpose. It had been military, then civilian, then military again, then civilian again. It had a long runway and hangars and offices and apron parking for hobby planes. They were all lined up neatly, hooded and blinded in the dark by canvas covers.

Plato's was not a hobby plane. It was a Boeing 737. The largest craft on the field by far. It was twenty years old and Plato was its third owner. Not that anyone knew. Only geeks could date planes, and geeks knew better than to broadcast their conclusions. Plato told the world it had been custom built for him a year ago, up there in Washington state. In reality it had been flown to a facility in Arizona and stripped back to its aluminum skin and the paint had been replaced by a grey-tinted wash that made the bare metal look dark and shiny and evil. People who owed him services regularly spent days and weeks going over it with clay bars and carnauba wax. It was polished like a show car. Plato was proud of it. He was the first in his family to own a Boeing.

A dusty pick-up truck with one headlight drove around the perimeter track inside the fence and stopped short of the gate. A guy got out and clicked open the padlock and clattered the chain out of the way. He lifted and pulled and swung the gate open. The three-car convoy drove through.

Plato was Plato and Range Rovers were Range Rovers, so they didn't stick to the perimeter road. Instead they drove in a straight line, across bumpy grass, across smooth taxiways, across the runway, across the apron. They held a wide respectful curve around the Boeing and parked side by side between two Cessnas and a Piper. The six men climbed out and formed a loose cordon. Plato got out into it. He was in no danger, but it helped to appear as if he was, in terms of both caution and reputation. There was an old-fashioned set of rolling stairs set next to the Boeing's forward door. The word *Mexicana* was still visible on it, peeled and fading. Three men went up. After a minute one stuck his head back out and nodded. All clear.

Plato went up and took his seat, which was 1A, front row on the left. Leg room against the bulkhead was not an issue for him. The old first class cabin was intact. Four rows of four wide leather seats. Behind them economy class had been removed. There was just empty space back there. The plane was rated for a hundred and eighty passengers, and twenty years ago an average passenger was reckoned to weigh two hundred pounds including checked bags. Which gave a total lift capacity of thirty-six thousand pounds, which was about sixteen tons.

Plato sat while his men inspected their equipment. It had been supplied and loaded on to the plane by a guy who owed Plato a favour. Therefore it was all present and correct, on pain of death. But his guys checked anyway. Cold-weather clothing, aluminum ladders, flashlights, automatic weapons, ammunition, some food and water. Anything else necessary would be supplied at the destination.

The pilots had finished their pre-flight checks. The first officer stepped out of the cockpit and waited in the aisle. Plato caught his eye and nodded. Like a guy telling a butler when to serve the soup. The first officer went back to the flight deck and the engines started up. The plane taxied, lined up with the runway, paused, shuddered against the brakes, rolled forward, accelerated, and then rose majestically into the night.

Reacher rode back to town in Peterson's car. Holland followed them in his own car. Reacher got out at the end of Janet Salter's street and waved them both away. Then he eased past the parked cruiser and walked through the snow to the house. Janet Salter was still up when he walked in. She looked him up and down and side to side like she was inspecting him for damage. Then she asked, 'Successful?'

Reacher said, 'So far so good.'

'Then you should call the girl in Virginia and tell her. You were awfully abrupt before. You hung up on her, basically.'

'She's probably off duty. It's late.'

'Try her.'

So Reacher wrestled his way out of his coat and hung it up and sat down in the hallway chair. He dialled the number he remembered. Asked for Amanda.

She was still on duty.

He said, 'N06BA03 is clearly a pharmaceutical code for methamphetamine.'

She said, 'Forty tons?'

'Almost intact.'

'Jesus.'

'That's what we thought.'

'What are you going to do?'

'Nothing. The local cops are on it.'

'What does forty tons look like?'

'Repetitive.'

'How the hell can forty tons of methamphetamine get lost in the system?'

'I don't know. Stuff gets lost all the time. Shit happens. Maybe they weren't very proud of it. Values change all of a sudden, wartime to peacetime. Maybe that's why they hid it behind the code. And as soon as everyone forgot what the code meant, they forgot the stuff was there. Out of sight and out of mind.'

She didn't reply.

He said, 'Thanks for your help, Susan.'

'You're most welcome.'

'Tell your buddy at Lackland there are records clerks taking money for combing the archives. That stuff wasn't found by accident. Maybe you can pay off the favour that way.'

'Bronze Stars all around. Anything else?'

'Nothing on Kapler?'

'He resigned for no reason. That's all there is. Which is strange, I agree, but there's no hard data anywhere. Either he's clean, or someone cleaned up after him.'

'OK,' Reacher said. 'Thanks.'

'Anything else?'

Reacher said, 'No, I guess we're all done here.'

She said, 'So this is goodbye?'

He said, 'I guess it is.'

'It's been nice talking to you.'

'For me too. Stay lucky, Susan. And thanks again.'

'You bet.'

She hung up. He sat in the chair for a moment with his eyes closed and the receiver on his lap. When it started beeping at him he put it back in the cradle and got up and walked to the kitchen.

Janet Salter was in the kitchen with a book under her arm. Reacher found her there. She was filling a glass with water from the tap. She was on her way to bed. Reacher stood aside and she passed him and headed for the stairs. Reacher waited a moment and went to make one last check of the house. The cop in the library was standing easy, six feet from the window, alert and implacable. The cop in the hallway was in the telephone chair, sitting forward, her elbows on her knees. Reacher checked the view from the parlour and then headed upstairs to his room. He kept the lights off and the drapes open. The snow on the porch roof was thick and glazed and frozen. The street was empty. Just the parked cruiser, the cop inside, and ruts and ice and the relentless wind.

All quiet.

In Virginia Susan Turner's desktop computer made a sound like a bell. The secure government intranet. An incoming e-mail. The temporary password, from the Human Resources Command. She copied and pasted it to a dialogue box in the relevant database. The ancient report came up as an Adobe document. Like an online photocopy. The seventy-third citation from the cross-reference index in the back of Jack Reacher's service file.

It was the history of an experiment run by an army psychological unit, of which she knew there had been many, way back when. So many, in fact, that they had mostly sat around on their fat butts until inspiration had struck. This bunch had been interested in genetic mutation. The science was well understood by that point. DNA had been discovered. Then anecdotal evidence had come in about a kids' movie being shown on service bases. It was a cheap SF flick about a monster. Some rubber puppet filmed in extreme close-up. The creature's first appearance was held to be a cinematographic masterpiece. It came up out of a lagoon. Shock was total. Children in the audience screamed and recoiled physically. The reaction seemed to be universal.

The psychologists agreed that to recoil from a source of extreme danger was a rational response derived from evolution. But they knew about mutation. Giraffes were sometimes born with longer or shorter necks than their parents', for instance. Either useful or not, depending on circumstances. Time would tell. Evolution would judge. So they wondered if children were ever born without the recoil reflex. Counterproductive, in terms of the survival of the species. But possibly useful to the military.

They sent prints of the movie to remote bases in the Pacific. Army, navy, air force, and Marine Corps, because they wanted the largest possible test sample. The Pacific, because they wanted children not yet exposed to the movie, or even rumours of it. They set up inconspicuous cameras above the cinema screens. The cameras were focused on the front rows of the audience. The shutters were triggered by the film sprockets, timed to snap just after the monster emerged from the murk. Hundreds of children were invited to showings in batches, four- to seven-year-olds, which was an age group apparently considered mature in terms of emotional response but not yet socialized out of honest and unguarded expression.

There was a long illustrative sequence of still photographs in the document. A little blurred, a little dark, but they all showed the same thing. Small children, eyes wide, mouths open, slamming back against their seats, some of them launching themselves right over their seat backs, arms thrown up around their heads, ducking away in fear and panic.

Then came an exception.

One photograph was focused on a front row of fifteen seats.

Fifteen children. All boys. They all looked about six years old. Fourteen of them were slamming backward. One was jumping forward. He was larger than the others. He had short tousled hair, light in colour. He was diving up and out, trying to get to the screen. His right arm was raised aggressively. There was something in his hand.

Susan Turner was pretty sure it was an open switchblade.

The aggressive boy was not formally named in the document. He had been studied briefly but then his father had been cut new orders and the boy had gotten lost in the system. The experiment had petered out shortly afterwards. But the results gleaned to that point had been retained as a completed file. The aggressive boy had been labelled with long words, none of which meant anything to Susan.

The last page of the file was its own cross-reference index. There were no backward links to any other personnel file than Reacher's.

Susan returned to the technical preamble. The delay between the appearance of the monster and the click of the shutter had been set at eighteen frames, which was three-quarters of a second. She was impressed. Not so much with the forward leap. She knew people like that. She was one herself. But for a six-year-old to have gotten a switchblade up and open in his hand in less than a second was something else.

Janet Salter's house stayed all quiet for less than ten seconds. Then first one, then two, then three, then four police radios burst to life with loud static and codes and urgent words, and cell phones rang, and the hall phone rang, and stumbling footsteps crossed the floor in the day watch's bedroom, and doors opened, and there were tramping feet on the stairs, and people started talking all at once, loud and scared and horrified.

Reacher stepped out of his room and hustled down to the hallway. The four women cops were standing all together on the rug, two in uniform, two in night clothes, all talking on phones, all white and shocked and looking around wide-eyed in

291

helpless restless panic, all full of adrenalin, all with nowhere to go.

Reacher said, 'What?'

One of the cops said, 'It's Andrew Peterson.'

'What about him?'

'He's been shot and killed.'

# THIRTY-FIVE

THE GUY FROM THE CAR ON THE STREET CAME IN AND JOINED the confusion. Reacher had no doubt the guys in the other two cars were equally distracted. For the moment Janet Salter's security was worth exactly less than jack shit. So he kept half his attention on the parlour window and used the other half to piece the story together from the babble of voices. It wasn't difficult. The hard facts seemed to be: following Chief Holland's most recent orders, the department was still on high alert. Therefore mobile patrols were constant, and vigilance was high. No street was visited less than every twenty minutes. Every pedestrian was eyeballed, as was every car and every truck. Every lot was checked regularly, every alley, every approach.

A unit driven solo by the new guy Montgomery had nosed into a snowbound parking lot north and east of downtown and Montgomery had seen Peterson's car apparently empty and idling with its driver's window all the way down and its nudge bars pushed up hard against a blank brick wall. On closer inspection

Montgomery had found the car not to be empty. Peterson was sprawled across the front seats, dead from a gunshot wound to the head.

Reacher stayed at the parlour window, watching the silent street, thinking about Peterson, leaving the cops to their private grief in the hallway. He could hear their voices. They were passing through a short phase of denial. Maybe the story was wrong. Which Reacher considered theoretically plausible, but very unlikely. Operational reports called in from the field were occasionally unreliable. And head wounds sometimes produced misleading impressions. Deep comas could be mistaken for death. But ninety-nine times out of a hundred hoping for the best was a waste of time. Reacher knew that. He was an optimist, but not a fool.

The bad news was confirmed five minutes later by Chief Holland himself. He drove up and parked and came in through the cold. Three items on his agenda. First, he wanted to break the news to his crew personally. Second, he wanted to make sure they got their minds back on their job. He sent the lone male officer back to his car on the street, he sent the day watch women back to bed, he sent one of the night watch women back to the library, and he told the other to focus hard on the front door. His voice was quiet and firm and his manner was controlled. He was a decent CO. Out of his league, perhaps, in over his head, no question, but he was still walking and talking. Which was more than Reacher had seen from some COs he had known, when the shit had hit the fan.

The third item on Holland's agenda was something halfway between an invitation and a command. He stepped into the parlour and looked straight at Reacher and asked him to come out and take a look at the crime scene.

Janet Salter had gotten up because of the noise and was hiding out in the kitchen. Reacher found her there. She was still fully dressed. She had her gun in her pocket. She knew exactly what

294

he was about to tell her. She waved it away impatiently and said, 'I know what to do.'

He said, 'Do you?'

She nodded. 'The basement, the gun, the password.'

'When?'

'Immediately anything happens.' Then she said, 'Or before. Perhaps now.'

'Not a bad idea,' Reacher said. 'The guy is out there, and close by.'

'I know what to do,' she said again.

Reacher climbed into the front passenger seat of Holland's unmarked sedan. Holland backed up and turned and drove towards town. He made a left at the park and a right that led past the coffee shop and onward past the clothing store that Reacher had used. Then he threaded right and left and right again through back streets to a long block of two-storey brick buildings. They were plain and square. Maybe once they had been stores or offices or warehouses. Maybe once they had been the hub of Bolton's commercial district. Now they were decrepit. Most of them looked abandoned. Three in a line had been demolished to make an empty space. A gap, perhaps a hundred feet by forty. It seemed to be in use as a temporary parking lot, maybe busy by day but now empty at night. It was humped with frozen snow and rutted by tyre tracks made days ago when the surface had still been soft.

The empty lot was guarded by two police cruisers. Their red lights were turning. Their beams danced crazily and rhythmically across surfaces far, then near, then far, then near. Each car held a lone cop. Reacher didn't know either of them. They were just sitting there. There were no crowds to hold back. It was way too late and way too cold for rubberneckers.

Peterson's car was all the way on the left side of the lot. It was still idling. Its driver's window was still down. The short vertical nudge bars on its front bumper were pressed up hard against a blank brick wall. Which was the side of the next building along.

Holland parked at the kerb and climbed out. Reacher followed him and zipped his coat and pulled his hat down over his ears. The side street they were on ran north to south and they were out of the wind. It was cold, but not impossible. They walked together into the lot. No danger of messing up any evidence on the ground. No danger of obscuring tyre tracks or footprints. There weren't any. The rutted snow was like corrugated iron, but harder. And it was glazed and slippery. They struggled on and approached Peterson's car from the rear. Its exhaust pipes were burbling patiently. The whole vehicle was just sitting there, like a faithful servant waiting for its master's next command.

Sheets of ice creaked under their feet as Reacher and Holland walked to the driver's door. They looked in through the open window. Peterson's feet were in the driver's foot well, and his body was twisted at the waist. He had fallen sideways. His gun was still in its holster. His head was flung back, his neck bent, one cheek pressed down on the upholstery, as if he was staring at an item of great interest on the inside panel of the passenger door.

Reacher tracked back around the trunk, his knees passing through the small white cloud of exhaust, and back along the far flank of the car, to the front passenger door. He put his gloved hand on the handle and opened it up. Crouched down. Peterson stared at him through sightless eyes. He had a third eye in the centre of his forehead. An entry wound, perfectly placed, just like the lawyer on the two-lane to the east. Nine millimetre, almost certainly. Fairly close range. There were faint burns on the skin, and faint powder tattoos. About five feet, probably.

There was no exit wound. The bullet was still inside Peterson's head, crushed and deformed and tumbled. Unusual, for a nine-millimetre at close range. But not impossible. Clearly Peterson's skull had been thick.

There was no doubt he was dead. Reacher knew enough about ballistics and human biology and he had seen enough dead people to be absolutely sure. But still he checked. He took off his glove and put warm twinned fingers on the cold skin behind Peterson's ear. No pulse. Nothing at all, except the waxy feel of a corpse, part soft, part hard, both solid and insubstantial, already completely alien to a living touch.

Reacher put his glove back on.

The car's transmission was controlled by a lever on the steering column. It was still in Drive. The heater was set at seventy degrees. The radio volume was turned down very low. There were regular gasps of quiet static and occasional murmuring voices, all of them unintelligible.

'OK,' Reacher said.

'Seen enough?' Holland asked.

'Yes.'

'So what happened?'

'I don't know.'

'Why didn't he drive straight home?'

'I don't know.'

'He was looking for the shooter,' Holland said.

'You all are.'

'But that wasn't his job tonight. So he was freelancing. You know why?'

'No.'

'He was trying to impress you.'

'Me?'

'You were practically mentoring him. You were helping him. Maybe you were even pushing him.'

'Was I?'

'You told him what to do about the dead lawyer. All those photographs? You told him what to do about the dead biker. You discussed things. He was going to be the next chief. He wanted to be a good one. He was ready to listen to anybody.'

'I didn't tell him to go searching for the shooter all alone in the middle of the night.'

'He wanted to break the case.'

'You all do.'

'He wanted your respect.'

'Or yours,' Reacher said. 'Maybe he was trying to live up to the bullshit you put on the radio tonight. About the meth? You made him feel like a fraud.'

Silence for a beat.

Holland asked, 'What happened here?'

Reacher said, 'He saw someone in the lot. Almost certainly in a car or a truck. Too cold to be on foot. He drove in. A wide circle. He stopped, cheek to cheek. Pretty close. He turned down his radio and opened his window, ready to talk. But the guy just went ahead and shot him. He fell over and died and his foot slipped off the brake. The car drove itself into the wall.'

'Same basic setup as the lawyer.'

'Pretty much.'

'Was it quick?'

'Head shots usually are.'

They went quiet. Just stood and shivered in the freezing air.

Holland said, 'Should we look for a shell case?'

Reacher shook his head. 'Same deal as the lawyer. The shell case ejected inside the shooter's vehicle.'

Holland didn't speak. Reacher could see the question in his face. *Who was the guy?* It was right there in his eyes.

An awkward question, with an unappealing answer.

Reacher said, 'Now I see why you wanted me here. You wanted me to be the one to reach the conclusion. And say it out loud. Me, not you. An independent voice.'

Holland didn't speak.

Reacher said, 'OK, let's not go there. Not just yet. Let's think for a minute.'

They went back to the station house. Holland parked in the slot reserved for him and they walked between the garbage cans to the door. They went to the squad room, to the desk that Peterson had used. Holland said, 'You should check his messages. Voice mail and e-mail. Something might have come in that led him there.'

Reacher said, 'You're clutching at straws.'

'Allow me the privilege.'

'Did he even come here first?'

'I don't know.'

'Did he even have time?'

'Probably not. But we should check the messages anyway. Because we need to be sure, with a thing like this.'

'You should do the checking. It's your department. I'm just a civilian.'

Holland said, 'I don't know how. I never learned. I'm not good with technology. I'm old school. Everyone knows that. I'm the past. Andrew was the future.'

So Reacher puzzled his way through the telephone console and the computer keyboard. No passwords were required. No PINs. Everything was set up for fast and casual access. There was only one voice mail message. It was from Kim Peterson, much earlier in the evening, just after six o'clock, just after Reacher and her husband had hustled back to Janet Salter's house after watching the surveillance video from the prison.

Kim's recorded voice was suspended somewhere between panicked and brave and resigned and querulous.

She had asked, 'When are you coming home?'

Reacher moved on to e-mail. He opened the application. Two messages downloaded. The first was from the DEA in Washington D.C. An agent there was confirming his belief that there was no meth lab under the facility west of Bolton, South Dakota. Expensive satellite surveillance time proved it. Peterson was thanked for his interest and asked to get back in touch should new information come to light.

The second e-mail was a routine nightly round robin BOLO bulletin from the Highway Patrol. Statewide coordination. Be on the lookout. For, in this instance, a whole bunch of stuff, including any or all of three stolen cars and four stolen trucks taken that day from random locations around the state, a stolen snowplough taken from a highway maintenance depot east of Mitchell, a thing called an Isuzu N-series pump and a de-icing truck stolen by two absconded employees from a commercial airfield east of Rapid City, a stolen Ithaca shotgun from Pierre, four suspects believed to be at large in a 1979 Chevrolet Suburban after a messy and aborted burglary in Sioux Falls, and finally Peterson's own contribution, a bartender fleeing a suspected Bolton homicide in a 2005 Ford pick-up truck.

Reacher said, 'Nothing.'

Holland sat down.

'So say it,' he said. 'Let's go there now.'

'Three questions,' Reacher said. 'Why did the lawyer stop on the road with such total confidence? Why did Peterson stop in the lot? And why was he killed tonight of all nights?'

'Answers?'

'Because the lawyer felt safe to do so. Because Peterson felt safe to do so. And because you announced the meth bust on the police department radio net.'

Holland nodded.

'The shooter is one of us,' he said. 'He's a cop.'

Five minutes to midnight.

Four hours to go.

# THIRTY-SIX

HOLLAND AND REACHER HASHED IT OUT BETWEEN THEM, LIKE people do, searching for weaknesses in a theory, finding none, and thereby strengthening it to the point of certainty. A bent cop already in town explained why the watch for incoming strangers had proved fruitless. A bent cop in a car, flashing his lights, maybe patting the air with a gloved hand out a window, explained why a cautious lawyer would come to a dead stop on a lonely road in the middle of nowhere. A bent cop, hearing Holland's triumphant radio message earlier that night, explained why Peterson had died so soon afterwards. The guy would have realized the need for action before morning. *Start of business tomorrow he'll be calling the DEA in Washington with the details*, Holland had said. A no-brainer. And a bent cop parked in a lot, maybe waving urgently, explained why Peterson had come straight to his side, completely unsuspecting, completely unready.

And a bent cop hauled unwillingly away by the siren and the

crisis plan explained why Janet Salter had lived through the prison riot, all five hours of it.

Holland said, 'It's my fault. What I said on the radio got Andrew killed.'

'I might have done the same,' Reacher said. 'In fact, sometimes I did do the same.'

'I was trying to help him.'

'Unintended consequences. Don't blame yourself.'

'How can I not?'

'Why did he even go there? He wasn't on duty. He wasn't just passing by, because it wasn't on his way home.'

'He was always on duty, in his head, at least. And it could have been on his way home. More or less. I mean, it was a very minor detour. Two extra minutes, maybe. And that was Andrew, through and through. Always willing to give a little extra to the cause. Always ready to try one last thing, check one last place.'

Reacher said nothing.

Holland said, 'I'm assuming the Mexican is behind all of this. The one we keep hearing about.'

Reacher said, 'Plato.'

Holland asked, 'How long ago do you suppose he turned our guy around?'

'A year,' Reacher said. 'This whole business seems to be a year old.'

'Was it money?'

'Most things are.'

'Who is it?'

'I don't know.'

'A new guy, I'm guessing. I hardly know them. Not enough to trust any of them, anyway. The department is a mess. Which is my fault too, I guess. I couldn't keep up.'

Reacher said nothing.

Holland asked, 'Where do we start?'

'Tell me about Kapler.'

'He had problems in Miami. Nothing was proved against him. But there were rumours. It was Miami, and there was drug money around.'

'Terrific.'

'They were just rumours.'

'You should look at him. And Lowell. What happened to him a year ago? You should look at this guy Montgomery, too. People who are all alone when they discover crimes are sometimes the same people that committed them.'

'Should I bring them in?'

'Safest thing to do would be to bring everyone in. The whole damn department. Sit them down right here in this room, and you'd know for sure your guy was right in front of you.'

Holland said, 'Can I do that?'

'Sure you can.'

'Should I do it?'

Reacher said nothing. Any cop's most basic question: *Suppose we're wrong?*

Holland said, 'The crew at Mrs Salter's must be OK. They didn't go anywhere tonight. Did they? They weren't waiting in abandoned lots. They have alibis. Each other, and you.'

'True.'

'So I could leave them in place.'

'But you should warn them first,' Reacher said. 'If our guy senses the net is tightening, he might make one last attempt.'

'They'd nail him.'

'Not if you don't warn them first. A fellow cop comes to their door, what are they going to do? Shoot first and ask questions later?'

'They'd nail him afterwards.'

'Which would be too late.'

'It would be a suicide mission.'

'Maybe he's ready for one. He must know he's going to get nailed sooner or later. He must know he's dead whatever happens. He's between a rock and a hard place. Two homicides or three, either way he's going to fry.'

'He might not come in at all. He might disobey my order.'

'Then he'll identify himself for you. He'll paint a target on his own back. He'll save you the trouble.'

'So should I do it? Should I call them in?'

303

'I would,' Reacher said. 'It's any police department's basic duty. Get criminals off the streets.'

Holland made the calls. First came seven individual conversations, with the four women and the three men stationed with Mrs Salter. The subtext was awkward. *One of your fellow officers is a killer. Trust no one except yourselves.* Then he made a general all-points call on the radio net and ordered all other officers, whoever they were, wherever they were, whatever they were doing, on duty or not, to report to base exactly thirty minutes from then. Which Reacher thought was a minor tactical error. Better to have required their immediate presence. Which might not have gotten them there any faster in practice, but to set even a short deadline gave the bad guy the sense he still had time and space to act, to finish his work, and in ideal conditions of chaos and confusion, too, with cops running around all over the place. It was going to be a risky half-hour.

Holland put the microphone back on its rest, and picked up the phone again. He said, 'Kim Peterson hasn't been informed yet.'

Reacher said, 'Don't do it by phone. That's not right.'

'I know. I'm calling the front desk. Because I want you to do it. The desk guy can drive you. He can pick you up again in an hour. An hour should do it.'

'Are you serious?'

'I don't have time to do it myself. I'll be busy here.'

'I don't have standing,' Reacher said. 'I'm just a stranger passing through.'

'You met her,' Holland said. 'You spent a night in her house.'

'It's your job, not mine.'

'I'm sure you've done it before.'

'That's not the point.'

'I'm sure you were good at it.'

'Not very.'

'You have to do it,' Holland said. 'I just can't, OK? Don't make me, OK?'

*     *     *

304

Plato spent an hour in seat 1A, front of the cabin, left hand side, and then he got restless. Air travel at night bored him. By day there was a view, even from seven miles up. Mostly empty and brown, to be sure, but with enough roads and houses and towns to remind him there were new customers down there, just waiting to be recruited and served. But at night he couldn't see them. There was nothing except darkness and strings of distant lights.

He got up and walked down the aisle, past his men, past the last first class seat, into the empty space where economy class had been. He looked at the equipment on the floor. His men had checked it. He checked it again, because he was Plato and they weren't.

Food, water, all uninteresting. Seven coats, seven hats, seven pairs of gloves. All new, all adequate. The coats were big puffy things filled with goose feathers. North Face, a popular make, all black. Six were medium, and one was a boy's size. The submachine guns were H&K MP5Ks. Short, stubby, futuristic, lethal. His favourite. There were seven small backpacks, each containing spare magazines and flashlights.

Immediately Plato diagnosed a problem. The backpack straps would have to be let out close to their maximum length, to fit over the bulky coats. An obvious conclusion. Simply a question of thinking ahead. But it hadn't been done.

He was Plato, and they weren't.

The ladders were made by an American company called Werner. Aluminum, thirty-two feet long at their maximum extension, rated for two hundred and fifty pounds. They were all plastered with yellow warning stickers. They rattled slightly. They were picking up vibrations from the engines. They probably weighed about twenty pounds each. There were four of them. Eighty pounds. They would be left behind. Better to use the airlift capacity for forty extra glassine bricks than four useless ladders.

The same with the six useless men, of course. They would be left behind too. Nine hundred pounds of replaceable flesh and blood, versus four hundred and fifty extra bricks of meth? No contest.

Plato was already visualizing the return trip. He knew he would succeed. He had many advantages. Most of them were innate and overwhelming. His man on the ground was insurance, nothing more.

Caleb Carter was considered low man on the totem pole. Which he thought was richly ironic. He knew a little about totem poles, and Native American culture in general. He knew a little about a lot of things, but in a random unstructured way that had paid no dividends in terms of high school grades or employment opportunities. So he had turned to the Department of Corrections. The default choice, for his graduating class. Probably the default choice for many graduating classes to come. He had been trained and equipped with a radio and a polyester uniform and assigned to the night watch at the county lock-up. He was the youngest and newest member of a four-man team. Hence, low man on the totem pole.

Except that calling a new guy the low man on the totem pole was completely ass-backward. Totem poles were what? Twenty, thirty feet high? Native Americans weren't dumb. They put the most important guy at the bottom. At eye level. What important guy wanted to be twenty or thirty feet off the ground, where no one could see him? Like supermarkets. The eye-level shelf was reserved for the best stuff. The high-margin items. The big corporations hired experts to figure out stuff like that. Eye level was what it was all about. Thus the low man was really the high man, and the high man was really the low man. In a manner of speaking. A common misperception. A kind of linguistic inversion. Caleb Carter didn't know how it had come about.

Night watch was an easy job. The cells were locked before they came on duty, and weren't unlocked until after they had left. In practice Caleb's team had only one real responsibility, which was to monitor the population for medical emergencies. Guys could start foaming at the mouth or banging their heads on

306

the wall. Some of them weren't fully aware of what prescriptions they should be taking. Some of them tried to hang themselves with jumpsuit legs, all twisted up and knotted. They were a sorry bunch.

The monitoring process involved ten tours of inspection, one every hour. Naturally most of them got blown off. Sometimes all of them. Easier to sit in the ready room, playing poker for pennies or looking at porn on the computer or chilling with the ear buds in. At first Caleb had been disconcerted by the negligence. New job, new life, he had started out with a measure of energy and drive. He had been prepared to take it seriously. But any new guy's first duty was to fit in. So he did. After a month he couldn't remember what he had been upset about. What did the department want, for their lousy ten bucks per?

But the riot in the big house the night before had shaken things up a little. The watch leader had mandated three tours in the aftermath. He had even done one of them himself. Tonight he was looking for two, but four hours into the shift they hadn't even done the first of them, so clearly they were really on track for one only. Which was about due right then, and naturally Caleb would get to do it, because he was high man on the totem pole. Which he was OK with. He would do it, real soon, but not immediately, because right then he was occupied with clicking through a bunch of sites featuring naked fat girls and barnyard animals. Work could wait.

Reacher slipped out of a battered sedan at the end of the Petersons' driveway and stood and watched the desk guy drive away. Then he headed for the house. It was like walking into a white tunnel. Ploughed snow was piled five feet high, left and right. Up ahead was the Y-shaped junction, right to the barn, left to the house. The wind was strong. The land was flat and open. Reacher had never been colder. He knew that with certainty. A superlative had been achieved. One day in Saudi Arabia at the start of Desert Shield the noontime temperature had hit a hundred and forty degrees. Now in South Dakota he was suffering through minus thirty, which was more like minus fifty with the wind chill. Neither extreme had been comfortable. But he knew which one he preferred.

He made it to the Y-shaped split. He turned left, towards the house. The path was OK. The underfoot surface had been salted and sprinkled with grit. Maybe the last domestic chore Andrew Peterson had ever done. Ten minutes' work. He had made it easier to inform his widow of his death.

The house loomed up ahead. Red boards, red door, made brown by the blue of the moon. Soft yellow light behind the window glass. A faint smell of wood smoke from the chimney. Reacher walked on. It was so cold he felt like he had forgotten how. Like a stroke victim. He had to concentrate. Left foot, right foot, one step, the next, consciously and deliberately. Like he was learning a brand new skill.

He made it to the door. He paused a second and coughed freezing air from his lungs and raised his hand and knocked. The thickness of his glove and the way he was shaking turned what was supposed to be a crisp double tap into a ragged sequence of dull padded thumps. The worst sound in the world. After midnight, a cop's family alone in a house, a knock at the door. No possibility of good news. Kim would understand that in the first split second. The only issue was how hard and how long she was going to fight it. Reacher knew how it would be. He had knocked on plenty of different doors, after midnight.

She opened up. One glance, and the last absurd hope drained from her face. It wasn't her husband. He hadn't dropped his keys in the snow. He hadn't gotten inexplicably drunk and couldn't find the keyhole.

She fell down, like a trapdoor had opened under her.


Caleb Carter took a black four-cell Mag-lite from the rack at the door and checked his radio. It was turned on and working. The Mag-lite gave a decent beam. Batteries were OK. There was a clipboard screwed to the wall. There was a pen tied to it with a ratty piece of string. Caleb pre-signed for the fifth tour. The first four notations were bogus. No one looked up. He left the ready room and headed down the corridor.

In terms of jurisdiction the county lock-up was entirely separate from the state penitentiary, which in turn was entirely separate from the federal prison. But all three facilities shared the same site and the same architecture. Economy of scale, ease of operation. The lock-up was mostly filled with arrested local folks who either couldn't get or couldn't make bail. Pre-trial. Innocent until proven guilty. Caleb knew some of them from high school. About a quarter of the inmates were post-trial, found guilty and sentenced, waiting out a few days until the system moved them to their next destination.

A sorry bunch.

There were sixty cells, laid out in a two-storey V, fifteen cells to a section. East wing lower, east wing upper, west wing lower, west wing upper. At the point of the V there was a metal staircase, and beyond it was a single-storey mess hall and rec room, so that the lower floor was actually shaped like a Y.

All sixty cells had occupants. They always did. The money had come from outside of Bolton, and it was like the politicians in Pierre or Washington or wherever wanted their investment to be well used. It was widely accepted around the town that laws got tighter if there was a vacancy. And vice versa. If there was an empty bed, an ounce of herb in your car would get you hauled in. But if all sixty beds were taken, two ounces would get you nothing more than a smack on the head.

Law enforcement. Caleb's chosen career.

He started at the far end of the east wing lower. Walked all the way to the end wall, turned around, clicked his flashlight on, and came back slower. The cells were on his left. He overhanded the flashlight up on his shoulder, which not only looked cool but put the beam in line with his eyes. The cells had bars at the front, cots on the right, combined sinks and toilets in the back left corner, desks no wider than shelves opposite the cots. The cots had men in them. Most were asleep, rumbling, mumbling, and snoring under thin grey sheets. Some were awake, their narrow furtive eyes reflecting back like rats.

He turned the corner of the V and checked the west wing lower.

309

Fifteen cells, fifteen cots, fifteen men in them, twelve sleeping, three awake, none in distress.

He climbed the stairs to the east wing upper. Same result. He didn't know why they bothered. The place was a warehouse, that was all. A kind of cheap hotel. Did hotel staff check their guests every hour? He didn't think so.

Procedure was such bullshit.

He passed the head of the stairs to the west wing upper. He walked it a little faster than normal. The shadows of the bars moved as his Mag-lite beam passed over them. Cell one, empty space on the left, humped form under the sheet on the right, awake, cell two, empty space on the left, humped form under the sheet on the right, asleep, cell three, the same.

And so on, and so on, all the way down the row. Cell six had the fat guy in it. The one who wouldn't talk. Except to the biker in cell seven.

But the biker wasn't in cell seven.

Cell seven, west wing upper, was empty.

# THIRTY-SEVEN

REACHER WAS TOO SLOW TO CATCH KIM PETERSON BEFORE SHE hit the deck. He bent down awkwardly in his big coat and slid an arm under her shoulders and sat her up. She was gone. Fainted clean away. Absurdly his main worry was that the door was open and heat was leaking out of the house. So he jammed his other arm under her knees and lifted her up. He turned away and kicked the door shut behind him and carried her through to the family room and laid her on the battered sofa near the stove.

He had seen women faint before. He had knocked on plenty of doors after midnight. He knew what to do. Like everything else in the army it had been thoroughly explained. Fainting after a shock was a simple vasovagal reflex. The heart rate drops, the blood vessels dilate, the hydraulic power that forces blood to the brain falls away. There were five points in the treatment plan. First, catch the victim. He had already blown that. Second, lay her down with her feet high and her head low, so that gravity could help her blood get back to her brain. Which he did. He swivelled her so that her feet were up on the sofa arm and her head was below them on the cushion. Third, check her pulse. Which he did, in her wrist. He took off his gloves and touched his fingers to her skin, just like he had with her husband. The result was different. Her pulse was tapping away just fine.

Fourth point in the treatment plan: stimulate the victim, with loud yells or light slaps. Which had always felt unbearably cruel to him, with new widows. But he gave it a go. He spoke in her ear and touched her cheek and patted her hand gently.

No response.

He tried again, a little more firmly. Louder voice, a heavier touch. Nothing happened, except that above his head the floorboards creaked. One of the boys, turning over in his sleep. He went quiet for a moment. Stayed still. Silence came back. The family room was warm but not hot. The stove was banked. He took off his hat and unzipped his coat. Bent down and spoke again. Touched her cheek, touched her hand.

Kim Peterson opened her eyes.

Point five in the treatment plan: persuade the victim to lie still for fifteen or twenty minutes. In this case, easy. No persuasion necessary. Kim Peterson didn't move. She just lay on her back and stared up at the ceiling, inquiringly, speculatively, her eyes moving and narrowing and widening, as if there was something written up there, something complex and difficult to understand.

He asked, 'Do you remember me?'

She said, 'Of course.'

'I'm afraid I have bad news.'

'Andrew's dead.'

'I'm afraid he is. I'm sorry.'

'When?'

'Within the last hour.'

'How?'

'He was shot. It was instantaneous.'

'Who shot him?'

'We think the guy they've all been looking for.'

'Where?'

312

'In the head.'

Her eyes narrowed. 'No, I mean whereabouts did it happen?'

'I'm sorry. It was downtown. In a vacant lot.'

'What was he doing there?'

'His duty. He was checking something out.'

She said, 'He was a good man, you know.'

'I know.'

'I have two boys.'

'I know.'

'What am I going to do?'

'You're going to take it one step at a time. One day at a time, one hour at a time, one minute at a time. One second at a time.'

'OK.'

'Starting now.'

'OK.'

'First thing is, we need to get someone here. Right now. Someone who can help. Someone who can be with you. Because you shouldn't be alone. Is there someone I can call?'

'Why didn't Chief Holland come?'

'He wanted to. But he has a big investigation to start.'

'I don't believe you.'

'He can't just let it go.'

'No, I mean I don't believe he wanted to come.'

'He feels responsible. A good chief always does.'

'He should have come.'

'Who can I call for you?'

'Neighbour.'

'What's her name?'

'Alice.'

'What's her number?'

'Button number three on the telephone.'

Reacher looked around. There was a phone on the wall at the kitchen end of the room. A cordless handset and a black console. All kinds of buttons, and a big red LED zero in a window. No messages. He said, 'Stay right there, OK?'

He moved away from her and walked into the kitchen. Picked up the phone. It had a regular keypad, for dialling regular numbers.

It had a memory button. Presumably the memory button allowed the keypad to recall speed dials. Presumably buttons one and two were Andrew, office and cell. He pressed memory and three. The phone dialled itself and he heard ring tone. It lasted a good long spell. Then a voice answered. A woman, sleepy but concerned. A little worried. Maybe her husband was on the road. Maybe she had grown kids in another town. Late night phone calls were as bad as knocks on the door.

Reacher asked, 'Is this Alice?'

'Yes, it is. Who are you?'

Reacher said, 'I'm with Kim Peterson. Your neighbour. She needs you to come right over. Her husband was killed tonight.'

There was silence on the line. Then Alice spoke. But Reacher didn't hear what she said. Her words were drowned out by another sound. Sudden. Loud. From outside. Wailing and howling. Screaming and whispering. Rising and falling. The new sound rolled in across the frozen fields like a wave. It smashed against the side of the house and battered against the windows.

The prison siren.

Five minutes to one in the morning.

Three hours to go.

# THIRTY-EIGHT

REACHER SAW A CRAZY DIAGRAM IN HIS MIND, EXPLODING IN four dimensions, time and space and distance: cops all over town, all moving randomly north, south, east, west, all answering Holland's summons, all heading for the station house, all hearing the siren, all changing direction at once, the seven on duty with Janet Salter rushing straight out into the night, joining the confusion, getting set, heading for the prison, leaving Janet Salter all alone behind them.

All alone and wide open and vulnerable to a last-ditch swing by the bad guy before he either ran for his life or tried to blend back in.

*I know what to do*, Janet Salter had said.

Reacher hung up the phone and called softly to Kim.

'I got to go,' he said. 'Alice is on her way.'

He got the front door open and stopped. The siren howled on. It was deafening. The ploughed path was right there in front of him. Fifty feet to the split in the Y, fifty more to the street. Then a mile to town and another mile to the Salter house.

He was on foot.

No car.

He closed the door behind him and moved out and slipped and skidded and made the tight turn and headed for the barn. The old Ford pick-up was still in there. With the plough blade.

No key in it.

He hustled all the way back to the house. Pounded on the door. A long, long wait. He pounded some more. Then Kim Peterson opened up again. Shock was over. She was deep into her nightmare. She was slouched, vacant, detached. She was crying hard.

'I'm sorry,' he said. 'But I need the key for the pick-up truck.'

She didn't answer.

'Kim, I'm sorry, but I really need the key.'

She said, 'It's on Andrew's key ring. In his pocket.'

'Is there a spare?'

'I don't think so.'

'Are you sure?'

'It's a very old truck.'

'There has to be a spare.'

'I think it was lost.' She looked away and turned and walked back down the hallway. She staggered and put out a hand and steadied herself against the wall. Reacher put the door on the latch and stepped outside to wait. For Alice. The neighbour. South Dakota farm country was big and empty. Houses were not adjacent. Not even close together. Alice would drive. He could borrow her vehicle.

He waited.

The siren howled on.

Alice came on foot.

He saw her a hundred yards away in the moonlight. She was a tall woman, dishevelled after hasty dressing, hurrying, slipping and sliding on the ice, gloved hands out like a tightrope walker, wild hair spilling from under a knitted cap. She came right to left along the road, a pale face glancing anxiously at the Peterson house, arms and legs jerky and uncoordinated by treacherous conditions underfoot. Reacher moved away from the door, into the cold, down the path, to the split in the Y, and on towards the street. He met her at the bottom of the driveway. Asked, 'Don't you have a car?'

She said, 'It wouldn't start.'

He glanced left, towards the road to town.

She glanced ahead, at the house.

She asked, 'How's Kim?'

He said, 'Bad.'

'What happened?'

'Andrew was shot and killed. Some guy in a vacant lot.'

'That's awful.'

'You better go in. It's going to be a long night.'

'It will be longer than a night.'

'You OK with that?'

'I'll have to be.'

'Call her dad. She said he sometimes comes to visit.'

'I will.'

'Good luck.'

She moved on up the driveway.

He headed left down the street.

*I know what to do*, Janet Salter had said.

A minute later Reacher was a hundred yards short of the corner that would put him on the main east–west county two-lane. To his right, the centre of town. To his left, the boondocks. He wanted a cop to be living way out there. The maximum ten minutes. Someone he could trust. Not Kapler or Lowell or Montgomery. He wanted one of the majority. He wanted the guy at home, off duty, asleep, then waking up, getting dressed, stumbling out into the cold, firing up his cruiser, heading west.

He wanted to flag the guy down and demand a ride.

He got part of what he wanted.

When he was still seventy yards short of the turn he saw lights in the east. Pulsing red and blue strobes, a mile away, coming on fast. The reflectivity of the snow made it look like there was a whole lit-up acre on the move. Like a UFO gliding in to land. A

317

huge bright dancing circle of horizontal light. He hustled hard to meet it. His feet slipped and skated. His arms thrashed and windmilled. His face was already frozen. It felt like it had been beaten with a bat and then anaesthetized by a dentist. The cop car was doing sixty miles an hour, on chains and winter tyres. He was doing three miles an hour, on legs that were stiff and slow and unresponsive. He was slipping and sliding, like running in place. Like a slapstick movie. The corner was still fifty yards away.

He wasn't going to make it.

He didn't need to make it.

The cop saw him.

The car slowed and turned into Peterson's street and came north towards him. Bright headlights, electric blue flashers, deep red flashers, painful white strobes popping right in his eyes. He came to a stop and planted his feet and stood still and raised his arms and waved. The universal distress semaphore. Big overlapping half circles with each hand.

The cop car slowed.

At the last minute he sidestepped and the car slid to a stop alongside him. The driver's window came down. A woman at the wheel. Her face was pale and swollen with sleep. Her hair was a mess. Her eyes were red. He didn't know her.

He said, 'I have to get to the Salter house.' His words were unclear. His lips were numb. The upper part of his face was a frozen slab. The lower half was just as bad. The hinge in his jaw was hardly working at all.

The cop said, 'What?'

'I need a ride.'

'Where?'

'Janet Salter's house.'

Five miles away the prison siren howled on. There was radio chatter in the car. A dispatcher's voice, low and fast, trying not to sound urgent. Probably the old guy already back at the police station desk. There was alcohol on the woman's breath. Maybe bourbon. A nightcap. Maybe two or three of them.

She asked, 'Who the hell are you?'

318

Reacher said, 'I've been working with Holland and Peterson.'

'Peterson's dead.'

'I know that.'

'Are you the MP?'

'Yes. And I need a ride.'

She said, 'Can't do it.'

'So why did you turn in for me?'

'I didn't. I'm heading for my position.'

'The prison isn't this way.'

'We make a perimeter a mile out. I get the northeast corner. This is how I'm supposed to get to it.'

'What happened?'

'The biker escaped. His cell is empty.'

'No,' Reacher said.

'What do you mean, no?'

'Not possible. It's a fake. It's a decoy.'

'He's either in there or not, pal. And they say not.'

'He's hiding out in there. In a broom closet or something. It's a fake.'

'Bullshit.'

'I've seen it before. Two problems with escaping. Getting out, and then beating the manhunt. The smart ones hide first. Inside. Until the manhunt dies. Then they go. But this guy isn't going anywhere. He's doing the first part only. As a decoy.'

The cop didn't answer.

'Think about it,' Reacher said. 'Escaping is harder than it looks. I promise you, he's still in there. Tomorrow he'll get hungry and come on out from wherever he holed up. Big smile on his face. Because it will be too late by then.'

'You're nuts.'

'He's still in there. Believe me. Take a chance. Be the one.'

'You're crazy.'

'OK, suppose I am. Suppose the guy really is out. He was gone more than five hours ago. You know that. So what the hell is the point of a one-mile perimeter now?'

The cop didn't answer.

The siren howled on.

'Five minutes,' Reacher said. 'Please. That's all I need from you.'

The cop didn't answer. Just hit the button and the gas and her window thumped back up and the car moved off. He leaned towards it and it accelerated and the rear three-quarter panel smacked him in the hip and spun him around and dumped him down hard on his back. He lay breathless in the frozen snow and watched the acre of lights move away into the distance.

*I know what to do*, Janet Salter had said.

Reacher got up and struggled onward to the corner and the siren died. It cut off mid-wail and tiny brittle echoes of its last howl came back off the ice and then night-time silence swarmed in. Not the dull padded silence of fresh snowfall, but the weird keening, crackling, scouring, rustling hiss of a deep-frozen world. The thump of his footsteps ran ahead of him through veins and sheets of ice. The wind was still out of the west, in his face, hurling tiny frozen needles at him. He looked back. He had made it through a hundred and fifty yards. That was all. He had two miles ahead of him. There was nothing on the road. He was completely alone.

He was very cold.

He half walked, half ran, in the wheel ruts, his heels sliding wildly after every step until they locked into the next broken fissure, where a tyre chain had cracked the surface. He was breathing hard, freezing air burning down his windpipe and searing his lungs. He was coughing and gasping.

Two miles to go. Maybe thirty whole minutes. Too long. He thought, surely one of them had the balls to stay with her. One of the seven. One of the women. Damn the rules. Damn the plan. Peterson was dead. Still warm. Enough justification right there. Surely one of them would gut it out and tell the feds to go to hell. At least one. Maybe more. Maybe two or three.

Maybe all of them.

Or maybe none of them.

*I know what to do*, Janet Salter had said.

320

Did she?

Had she done it?

Reacher pounded on. One step, and another, and another. The wind pushed back at him. Ice fragments pattered against his coat. All the feeling had gone out of his feet and his hands. The water in his eyes felt like it was freezing solid.

Dead ahead was a bank. It stood alone in a small parking lot. The edge of town. The first building. It had a sign on a tall concrete pillar. Red numbers. Time and temperature. Twenty past one in the morning. Minus thirty degrees.

He struggled on, faster. He felt he was getting somewhere. Left and right there was one building after another. A grocery store, a pharmacy, party favours, DVD rental. Auto parts, UPS, a package store, a dry cleaner. All with parking lots. All spread out. All for customers with cars. He hurried on. He was sweating and shivering, all at the same time. The buildings closed in. They grew second storeys. Downtown. The big four-way was a hundred yards ahead. Right to the prison, left to the highway. He cut the corner on a cross street. Turned south at the police station. The wind was howling through the forest of antennas on its roof.

A mile to go.

He ran alone down the centre of the main drag. A solitary figure. Ungainly. Short, choppy steps. He was bringing his feet up and dropping them down more or less vertically. It was the only way to stay upright. No fluid, loping stride. The ice didn't allow it. His vision was blurring. His throat burned. All around him every window was dark and blank. He was the only thing moving, in a white empty world.

Reacher passed the family restaurant. It was closed up and quiet. Dark inside. Ghostly inverted chairs were stacked on tables like a silent anxious crowd all with upraised arms. Four hundred yards to Janet Salter's street. Forty seconds, for a decent athlete. Reacher took two minutes. The roadblock car was long gone. Just its ruts remained. Empty, like a railroad switch. Reacher picked his way over them. Headed on down the street. Past one house, past the next. The wind hissed through evergreens. The earth creaked and groaned under his feet.

Janet Salter's driveway.

Lights in the house.

No movement.

No sound.

Nothing out of place.

All quiet.

He rested for a second, his hands on his knees, his chest heaving.

Then he hurried up towards the house.

# THIRTY-NINE

REACHER STEPPED UP ON JANET SALTER'S PORCH. HER DOOR WAS locked. He pulled the handle for the bell. The wire spooled out of the little bronze eye. It spooled back in. The bell bonged, a second later, quiet and polite and discreet, deep inside the silent house.

No response.

Which was good. She wouldn't hear it in the basement. And even if she did, she wouldn't come out to answer it.

He hoped.

*I know what to do*, she had said. *The basement, the gun, the password*.

He peered in through a stained glass panel. The hallway lights were still on. He got a blue distorted view of the room. The chair. The telephone table. The stairs, the rug, the paintings. The empty hat stand.

No movement. No one there. No sign of disturbance.

All quiet.

Forty-three possible ways in, according to his earlier

calculation, fifteen of them practical, eight of them easy. He backed away from the door and recrossed the porch. Stepped down and floundered through deep crusty snow alongside foundation plantings, around the side of the house, to the rear. He knew from his earlier inspection that the lock on the kitchen door was a sturdy brass item with a tongue neatly fitted into a heavy escutcheon plate. The plate was set into the jamb, which was a strip of century-old softwood. It was painted, whereas the front door's jamb was a piece of lacquered chestnut, fine-grained and milled and exquisite. Harder to replace. All things considered, breaking in at the rear would be the considerate thing to do.

He stepped back and took a breath and raised his boot and smashed his heel into the wood directly under the lock. No second attempt necessary. He was a big man, and he was anxious, and he was too cold for patience. The door stayed whole, but the escutcheon plate tore out of the jamb and clattered to the floor and the door swung open.

'It's me,' he called. 'Reacher.' She might not have heard the bell, but she might have heard the splintering wood. He didn't want her to have a heart attack.

'It's me,' he called again.

He stepped into the kitchen. Pushed the door shut behind him. It hung within an inch of fully closed. All the familiar sounds and smells came back to him. The hissing of the pipes. The percolator, now cold. He stepped into the small back hallway. He clicked on the light. The door at the bottom of the stairs was closed.

'Janet?' he called. 'It's me, Reacher.'

No response.

He tried again, louder. 'Janet?'

No response.

He went down the back stairs. Knocked hard on the basement door.

He called, 'Janet?'

No response.

He tried the handle.

The door opened.

324

He took off his glove and got his gun out of his pocket. He stepped into the basement. It was dark. He listened. No sound, except the roar of the furnace and the squeal of the pump. He fumbled his left hand across the wall and found the switch and clicked on the light.

The basement was empty. Nothing but sudden shadows from the vertical baulks of timber jumping across a bare expanse of floor. He walked through to the furnace room. Empty. Nothing there, except the old green appliance loudly burning oil.

He walked back to the door. Stared back up the stairs over the front sight of his gun. No one there. No movement, no sound.

He called, 'Janet?'

No response.

Not good.

He climbed back up to the kitchen. Walked through it to the hallway. It was the same as he had seen it through the stained glass panel from the front. All quiet. The chair, the table, the rug, the paintings, the hat stand. No movement. No disturbance.

He found her in the library. She was in her favourite chair. She had a book in her lap. Her eyes were open. There was a bullet hole in the centre of her forehead.

Like a third eye.

Nine millimetre, almost certainly.

Reacher's mind stayed blank for a long, long time. It was his body that hurt. From thawing. His ears burned like someone was holding a blowlamp on them. Then his nose, then his cheeks, then his lips, then his chin, then his hands. He sat in the chair in the hallway and rocked back and forth and hugged himself in agony. His feet started hurting, then his ribs, then the long bones in his arms and his legs. It felt like they were all broken and crushed.

Janet Salter had not had a thick skull. The back of it was blown all over her favourite chair, driven deep into the split the exiting bullet had made in the stuffing.

*I'll have plenty of time to read*, she had said, *after all this fuss is over.*

Reacher cradled his head in his hands. Put his elbows on his knees and stared down at the floor.

*I am privileged*, she had said. *Not everyone gets the opportunity to walk the walk.*

Reacher rubbed his eyes. His hands came away bloody. The ice spicules driven on the wind had peppered his face with a thousand tiny pinpricks. Unnoticeable, when his flesh had been frozen. Now they were raising a thousand tiny beads of blood. He rubbed both palms over every inch of his face, like he was washing. He wiped his palms on his pants. He stared down at the floor. Traced each whorl of muted colour in the rug, one by one. When he reached the centre of each meandering pattern he stopped and raised his eyes. Janet Salter stared back at him. She was diagonally opposite him. A straight line. A vector. Left of the stair post, in through the library door, across its width, to her chair. A small comma had formed below the bullet hole in her forehead. Not really blood. Just ooze. Leakage.

Each time he looked at her for as long as he could bear, and then he dropped his gaze again, back to the rug.

*I don't like getting beaten*, he had said. *Better for all concerned that it just doesn't happen.*

*Protect and serve.*

*Never off duty.*

Empty words.

He was a fraud and a fake and a failure.

He always had been.


He sat in the chair. No one came. The house hummed on around him. It didn't know. It made its noises, oblivious. Water moved in the pipes, a sash rattled in a frame, the busted back door creaked back and forth as it moved in the wind. Outside the foliage hissed and the whole frozen planet shuddered and groaned.

He picked up the phone.

He dialled the number he remembered.

*You have reached the Bureau of Labor Statistics. If you know your party's extension, you may dial it at any time.*

326

He dialled 110.

A click. A purr.

'Yes?'

Reacher said, 'Susan, please.'

'Who?'

'Amanda.'

A click. A purr.

Susan said, 'Reacher?'

He didn't answer.

'Reacher? You OK?'

He said nothing.

She said, 'Talk to me. Or hang up.'

He asked her, 'Have you ever been hungry?'

'Hungry? Of course. Sometimes.'

'I was once hungry for six straight months. In the Gulf. Desert Shield and Desert Storm. When we had to go throw Saddam out of Kuwait. We got there right at the beginning. We stayed there right to the end. We were hungry the whole time. There was nothing to eat. My unit, I mean. And some of the other rear echelon people. Which we thought was OK. We sucked it up. A big deal like that, there had to be snafus. Supply chains are always a problem. Better that whatever there was went to the guys doing the fighting. So no one made a big fuss. But it was no kind of fun. I got thin. It was miserable. Then we went home and I ate like a pig and I forgot all about it.'

'And then?'

'And then years later we were on that Russian train. They had American rations. I was bored at the time. We got back and I made it a little project to find out what had been going on. Like a hobby. One thing led to another and I traced it all back. Turned out a logistics guy had been selling our food for ten years. You know, a bit here, a bit there, all over the world. Africa, Russia, India, China, anyone who would pay for crap like that. He was pretty careful. No one noticed, the way the stockpiles were. But the Gulf caught him out. Suddenly there was a huge demand, and the stockpiles just weren't there any more. He was shipping it to us on paper, but we were starving in the desert.'

'The general?'

'Recent promotion. He was a colonel most of the time. Not the sharpest knife in the drawer, but he was reasonably cautious. His tracks were well covered. But I wouldn't let it go. It was him against me. It was personal. My people had been hungry because of him. I was in his bank accounts and everything. You know what he spent the money on?'

'What?'

'Not much. He saved most of it. For his retirement. But he bought a 1980 Corvette. He thought it was a classic. Like a collector's item. But the 1980 Corvette was the worst Corvette ever made. It was a piece of shit. They junked the three-fifty and put in a three-oh-five, for emissions. It was making a hundred eighty horsepower. I could run faster than a 1980 Corvette. Something just went off in my head. I mean, starving for some kind of a criminal mastermind would be one thing. Doing it for a complete idiot was something else. A complete, tasteless, clueless, sordid, pathetic little idiot.'

'So you hauled him in?'

'I built that case like it was Ethel Rosenberg. I was out of my mind. I checked it forward and backward and forward again. I could have taken it to the Supreme Court. I brought him in. I told him I was upset. He was in a Class A uniform. He had all kinds of busywork medals. He laughed at me. A kind of patronizing sneer. Like he was better than me. I thought, you bought a 1980 Corvette, asshole. Not me. So who's better? Then I hit him. I popped him in the gut to fold him over and then I banged his head on my desk.'

'What happened?'

'I broke his skull. He was in a coma for six months. He was never quite all there afterwards. And you were right. I was canned, basically. No more 110th for me. Only the strength of the case saved me. They didn't want it in the newspaper. I would have been busted big time otherwise. So I moved on.'

'Where to?'

'I don't remember. I was too ashamed of myself. I did a bad thing. And I blew the best command I ever had.'

Susan didn't answer.

Reacher said, 'I got to thinking about it afterwards. You know, why had I done it? I couldn't answer. Still can't.'

'You did it for your guys.'

'Maybe.'

'You were putting the world to rights.'

'Not really. I don't want to put the world to rights. Maybe I should, but I don't.'

She said nothing.

He said, 'I just don't like people who put the world to wrongs. Is that a phrase?'

'It should be. What happened?'

'Nothing more, really. That's the story. You should ask for a new desk. There's no honour in that old one.'

'I mean, what happened tonight?'

Reacher didn't answer.

Susan said, 'Tell me. I know something happened.'

'How?'

'Because you called me.'

'I've called you plenty.'

'When you needed something. So you need something now.'

'I'm OK.'

'It's in your voice.'

'I'm losing two-zip.'

'How?'

'Two KIA.'

'Who?'

'A cop and an old woman.'

'Two-zip? It isn't a game.'

'You know damn well it's a game.'

'It's people.'

'I know it's people. I'm looking at one of them right now. And the only thing stopping me putting my gun to my head is pretending it's a game.'

'You got a gun?'

'In my pocket. A nice old .38.'

'Leave it in your pocket, OK?'

329

Reacher said nothing.

Susan said, 'Don't touch it, OK?'

'Give me a good reason.'

'A .38 won't necessarily get the job done. You know that. We've all seen it happen. You could end up like the general.'

'I'll aim carefully. Square on. I'll make sure.'

'Don't do it, Reacher.'

'Relax. I'm not going to shoot myself. Not my style. I'm just going to sit here until my head explodes all on its own.'

'I'm sorry.'

'Not your fault.'

'It's just that I don't like to think of it as a game.'

'You know it's a game. It has to be a game. That's the only way to make it bearable.'

'OK, it's a game. What are we in? The final quarter?'

'Overtime.'

'So give me the play by play so far. Brief me. Bring me up to date. Like we were working together.'

'I wish we were.'

'We are. What have we got?'

He didn't answer.

She said, 'Reacher, what have we got?'

So Reacher took a breath and began to tell her what they had, slowly at first, and then faster as he picked up on the old short-hand rhythms he remembered from years of talking to people who understood what he understood, and saw what he saw, and grasped what didn't need to be spelled out. He told her about the bus, and the meth, and the trial, and the jail, and the police department, and the crisis plan, and the lawyer, and the witness protection, and the riot, and Plato, and the underground storage, and Peterson, and Janet Salter.

Her first response was: 'Put your hand in your pocket.'

He asked, 'Why?'

'Take out your gun.'

'Now that's OK?'

'More than OK. It's necessary. The bad guy saw you.'

'When?'

'While you were alone with Salter in the house. He had five hours.'

'He didn't come. He was up at the prison the whole time.'

'That's an assumption. We don't know that for sure. He could have checked in, dropped off the radio net, slipped away, gone back. And do we even know that they really called the roll at all? A thing like that, sure, it's in the plan as written, but who's to say it actually gets done, you know, in real life, in a situation like that, right when the shit is hitting the fan?'

'Whatever, I didn't see him.'

'He doesn't know that. If he saw you, he's going to assume you saw him. He's going to come after you.'

'That's a lot of ifs and assumptions.'

'Reacher, think about it. What's to stop this guy getting away with it? He popped the lawyer, and Peterson, and Salter, three rounds from a throw-down pistol. He's saving a fourth for you, and then he's home free. Nobody will ever know who he was.'

'I already don't know who he was.'

'He's not sure of that. And he's not sure you won't figure it out eventually. You're his last obstacle.'

'Why hasn't he come after me already?'

'No safe opportunity yet. That's the only possible reason. He's going to be cautious with you. More so than with the others. The lawyer was a patsy, Peterson was a bumpkin, and Salter was a harmless old lady. You're different.'

'Not so very different.'

'You need to pull back to Rapid City. Hole up somewhere and talk to the FBI.'

'I don't have a vehicle.'

'You have a telephone. You're talking on it right now. Put it down and then call the FBI. Keep your guard up until they get there.'

He didn't answer.

She asked, 'Are you going to do that?'

'I doubt it.'

'You weren't responsible for those people, you know.'

'Says who?'

'All of this would have happened just the same without you. It's a million-to-one chance you were there at all.'

'Peterson was a nice guy. And a good cop. He wanted to be a better cop. He was one of those guys who knew enough to know he didn't know everything. I liked him.'

Susan said nothing.

'I liked Mrs Salter, too. She was a noble old bird.'

'You need to get out of there. You're outnumbered. Plato won't come alone.'

'I hope he doesn't.'

'It's dangerous.'

Reacher said, 'For him.'

Susan said, 'Do you remember as a kid, watching a movie about a creature in a lagoon?'

'Is that thing still in my file?'

'In the back index.'

'And you read it?'

'I was interested.'

'They got it wrong. And they took away my blade, which pissed me off.'

'How did they get it wrong?'

'I wasn't some kind of a genetic freak. I was born as scared as anyone. Maybe more so. I lay awake crying with the best of them. But I got tired of it. I trained myself out of it. An act of will. I re-routed fear into aggression. It was easy enough to do.'

'At the age of six?'

'No, I was an old hand by then. I was four when I started. I had the job done by the time I was five.'

'Is that what you're doing now? Re-routing guilt into aggression?'

'I took an oath. Same as you did. All enemies, foreign and domestic. Looks like I've got one of each here. Plato, and whoever his bent cop is.'

'Your oath lapsed.'

'It never lapses.'

She asked, 'How does a six-year-old have his own switchblade anyway?'

'Didn't you have one?'

'Of course not.'

'Do you have one now?'

'No.'

'You should get one.'

She said, 'And you should go to Rapid City and do this thing properly.'

'We're short of time.'

'You have no legal standing.'

'So put another tag on my file. Or save them all some effort. Just Xerox it. Three copies, FBI, DEA, and the local South Dakota people. Send them out overnight.'

'You're not thinking straight. You're punishing yourself. You can't win them all. You don't have to win them all.'

'They put you in charge of the 110th?'

'And I'll stay in charge. As long as I want.'

'This time it was really important.'

'They're all important.'

'Not like this. I'm staring at a nice old lady with a hole in her head. She mattered more to me than being hungry.'

'Stop looking at her.'

Reacher looked down at the floor.

Susan said, 'You can't change the past.'

'I know.'

'You can't atone. And you don't need to, anyway. That guy deserved to be in a coma, maybe for ever.'

'Maybe.'

'Go to Rapid City.'

'No.'

'Then come to Virginia. We'll deal with this together.'

Reacher said nothing.

'Don't you want to come to Virginia?'

'Sure I do.'

'So do it.'

'I will. Tomorrow.'

'Do it now.'

'It's the middle of the night.'

'There was a question you used to ask me.'

'Was there?'

'You stopped asking it.'

'What was it?'

'You used to ask if I was married.'

'Are you?'

'No.'

Reacher looked up again. Janet Salter stared right back at him.

He said, 'I'll leave tomorrow.'

He hung up the phone.

Five minutes to two in the morning.

Two hours to go.

# FORTY

THREE HOURS INTO THE FLIGHT, AND PLATO WAS GETTING TENSE. Unsurprisingly. His life was like a video game. One thing popped up at him after another. Each thing had to be dealt with efficiently and comprehensively. From the most important to the least. Not that even the least important thing was trivial. He spent fifteen hundred dollars a month on rubber bands alone. Just to bind up all the cash that he took to the bank. There were no small problems. And plenty of big ones. And his performance was judged not only on substance, but also on style. Drama was weakness. Especially for him.

The irony was that he had been large as a child. Until he was seven he was as big as or bigger than anyone else. At eight he was still fully competitive. At nine he was in the ballpark. Then he had stopped growing. No one knew why. No one knew if it was genetic, or a disease, or an environmental factor. Maybe mercury, or lead, or some other heavy metal. Certainly it was not a lack of food or proper care. His parents had always been present and competent. At first they had turned a blind eye. The assumption was that such a thing would correct itself. But it didn't. So first his father had turned away, and then his mother.

Now no one turned away.

His cell phone was switched on. Normal rules did not apply to him. It rang and he answered it. His man on the ground. Some fellow cop had found out too much and had been taken out. Plato didn't care. Collateral damage. Unimportant. Some other guy was sniffing around, too, and would have to be dealt with. An ex-military cop. Plato didn't care about that, either. Unimportant. Not his problem.

But then, finally, the big news: the witness was dead.

Plato smiled.

He said, 'You just saved a life.'

Then he made a call of his own. Brooklyn, New York. He announced the news. The last obstacle had been removed. South Dakota was now definitively a trouble-free zone. The title was impregnable. Absolutely guaranteed. The Russian agreed to wire the money immediately. Plato listened hard and imagined he heard the click of the mouse.

He smiled again.

A done deal.

He closed his phone and looked out his window. Seat 1A, the best on the plane. His plane. He looked down at America spread out below. Dark and massive. Strings of lights. He checked his watch. Fifty-seven more minutes. Then, once again, and as always, show time. Another challenge. Another triumph.

Reacher went upstairs and found Janet Salter's bedroom. It was at the back of the house, directly above the library. It was a pleasant, fragrant room that smelled of talcum powder and lavender. Its bathroom was directly above half of the kitchen. There was a medicine cabinet above the sink. In it was an array of basic toiletry items, plus the box of .38 ammunition, eighty-eight rounds remaining of the original hundred.

Reacher put the box in his coat pocket and closed the mirror. He went back down the stairs and stepped into the library and stood over Janet Salter and moved her book and one soft arm and took her gun out of her cardigan pocket. It was still fully loaded. It had not been fired. He put it in his own pocket and replaced the book and the arm and stepped away.

The cop who had killed the lawyer and the deputy chief and Mrs Salter sat in his car and stared out the windshield. He was in his designated position on the makeshift perimeter, personally responsible for the eighth of a mile of snow on his left and the eighth of a mile of snow on his right. Not that any escaper would use anything except the road, even in summer. In any season the terrain was too flat and featureless for concealment. The dogs would run him down in a minute. Going cross-country and hiding in ditches and culverts was strictly for the kind of old black and white chain-gang movie that gets shown late at night on the minor satellite channels. No, these days any sane fugitive would come straight down the road, strapped to the chassis of an empty delivery truck.

Not that there actually was a fugitive. Plato had been clear about that. There were all kinds of voids in the prison architecture. Overhead plenum chambers where ducts branched, underfloor matrices where pipes split. All kinds of inspection panels. All perfectly safe, because none of the voids actually led anywhere. But useful for purposes short of an actual break-out. A sandwich and a bottle to pee in, a guy could hold out ten or twelve hours.

Which would be enough.

The cop checked his guns. Habit. Instinct. First his official piece, in his holster, and then his other piece, in his pocket. Loaded. A round in the chamber, and fourteen more in the magazine.

He wouldn't need the fourteen in the magazine.

Reacher took one last careful tour through Janet Salter's house. He was fairly sure he wouldn't be coming back to it, and there were certain things he needed to fix in his mind. He looked at the front door, the back door, the basement door, the kitchen, the hallway, the library, Janet Salter's position in it, and the book on her lap. Somewhere between five and eight minutes, he thought, for her to get as comfortable as she looked, given that she had been starting out from a state of extreme panic. It would have taken her that kind of time to relax, even in the safe and reassuring company of a trusted figure like a town cop.

So, allowing a minute's margin for her protective detail to clear the area, someone had been between six and nine minutes late to the roll call up at the prison.

Someone would remember.

Maybe.

If there had been a roll call at all.

If the guy had even gone.

Reacher zipped his coat and jammed his hat down over his ears and covered it with his hood. Put his gloves on, opened the front door, and stepped out once again into the cold. It crowded in on him, battered at him, tormented him, froze him. But he ignored it. An act of will. He closed the door and walked down the driveway and made the turns and headed back towards the station. He stayed vigilant all the way, right up there in the kind of hyper-alert zone that made him feel he could draw and fire a thousand times faster than any opponent. The kind of zone that made him feel he could mine the ore and smelt the metal and draw the blueprint and cast the parts and build his own gun, all before any opponent got the drop on him.

I'm not afraid of death.

Death's afraid of me.

Fear into aggression.

Guilt into aggression.

The police station was completely deserted apart from the civilian aide back on duty behind the reception counter. He was a tall creaky individual about seventy years old. He was sitting glumly on his stool. Reacher asked for the news. The guy said there wasn't any. Reacher asked how long the department would stay deployed. The guy said he didn't know. The department had no experience of such a thing. There had never been an escape before.

'There was no escape tonight,' Reacher said. 'The guy is hiding out inside.'

'That's your opinion?'

'Yes, it is.'

'Based on what?'

'Common sense,' Reacher said.

'Then I should think they'll give it another hour or so. The perimeter is a mile out. Two hours is long enough to decide the guy is already through, or maybe not coming at all.'

'Tell me how the roll call works. For the department, at the prison.'

'I do it from here. By radio. I work through the list, they answer me from their cars or their collar mikes, I check them off.'

'How did it go tonight?'

'All present and correct.'

'No absentees?'

'None at all.'

'Misfires? Hesitations?'

'None.'

'When did you do it?'

'I started when I heard the siren. It takes about five minutes, beginning to end.'

'So they're self-certifying, aren't they?'

'I don't follow.'

Reacher said, 'You don't really know where they are or what they're doing. All you know is if they answer your call or not.'

'I ask them where they are. They tell me. Either they're in position or close to it. And the prison warden is entitled to check.'

'How?'

'He can go up in a tower and eyeball. The land is flat. Or he can tap into our radio net and call the roll himself, if he wants.'

'Did he tonight?'

'I don't know.'

Reacher asked, 'Who was last into position tonight?'

'I can't say. Early in the alphabet, they're all still in motion. Late in the alphabet, they're all already on station.'

339

'So they tell you.'

'Why would I doubt them?'

'You need to call Chief Holland,' Reacher said. 'Mrs Salter is dead.'

Reacher wandered through the silent station, the squad room, Holland's office, the bathrooms, and he came to rest in the room with the crime scene photographs pinned to the walls. The biker, and the lawyer. He sat with his back to the biker and looked at the lawyer. He didn't know the guy's name. Didn't know much about him at all. But he knew enough to know the guy was basically the same as Janet Salter. A man, not a woman, a frozen road, not a warm book-lined room, but they were both half-wise, half-unworldly people lulled into a false sense of security, tricked into relaxing. The shift lever in Park and the window all the way down in the door were the same things as Janet Salter's comfortable posture and the book on her lap.

*Understand their motives, their circumstances, their goals, their aims, their fears, their needs. Think like them. See what they see. Be them.*

They were both all the way there. Not partway, not halfway. They were completely trusting. They had opened up, literally. Doors, windows, hearts, minds. Not half worried, not half formal, not half suspicious.

They were all the way there.

Not just any cop could do that to them.

It was a cop they both knew, had met before, were familiar with.

Peterson had asked: *What would your elite unit do now?*

Answer: Reacher or Susan or any of the other 110th Special Unit COs in between them would put their feet up on the damaged desk and send a pair of eager lieutenants to map out both lives, to list all known acquaintances in the Bolton PD in order of intimacy. Then he or she or any of the others would cross-reference the lists, and a name would show up in common.

Reacher had no pair of eager lieutenants.

But there were other approaches.

340

*     *     *

A minute later Reacher heard footsteps in the corridor. Arrhythmic. The slap of one sole, followed by the scrape of the other. The old guy from the counter. He had a slight limp. He stuck his head in the door and said, 'Chief Holland is on his way. He's leaving his post up there. He shouldn't, but he is.'

Reacher nodded. Said nothing.

The old guy said, 'It's a terrible thing that happened to Mrs Salter.'

'I know.'

'Do you know who did it?'

'Not yet. Did anyone call anything in?'

'Like who?'

'A neighbour, maybe. A shot was fired.'

'Inside the house?'

'In her library.'

The old guy shrugged. 'Houses are far apart. Everyone has storm windows. Most of them are triple-glazed and on a night like this all of them are shut tight.'

Reacher said nothing.

The old guy asked, 'Is it one of us?'

'Why would it be?'

'Chief Holland called a meeting. Just before the siren. Can't see any other reason for it. Can't see any other way of doing it, either. The lawyer, I mean, then Mr Peterson and now Mrs Salter. The three of them, fast and easy, just like that. It has to be one of us. And then you asked who was last in position tonight.'

'Were you a cop?'

'I was with this department thirty years.'

'I'm sorry.'

'I'd like to get my hands on the guy.'

'You spoke to him tonight. At some point. Either just before or just after.'

'They all sounded normal to me.'

'Do you know them well?'

'Not the new guys.'

341

'Was anybody particularly close with Mrs Salter?'
'A lot of them were. She's a fixture. Was a fixture.'

Seven miles up and four hundred miles south Plato's cell phone rang again. The money he had taken from the Russian was hammering its way around the world. From one jurisdiction to another, shady and untraceable, an automated all-night trip that was scheduled to take seven hours in total. But it was always banking hours somewhere. The deposit flashed across a screen in Hong Kong and tripped a code that meant the account holder should be notified. So the clerk who saw it dialled a number that bounced through five separate call forwarding triggers before ringing out inside the Boeing high above Nebraska. Plato answered and listened without comment. He was already the richest man he had ever met. He always would be. He was Plato, and they weren't. Not his parents, not the Russian, not his old associate Martinez, not anybody.

The bank clerk in Hong Kong hung up with Plato and dialled another number. Brooklyn, New York. After three in the morning over there, but the call was answered immediately, by the Russian, who was paying more than Plato was.
A lot more.
The clerk said, 'I told him the money was in his account.'
The Russian said, 'So now reverse the transaction.'
The clerk clicked and scrolled.
'Done,' he said.
The Russian said, 'Thank you.'

From Brooklyn the Russian dialled Mexico City, a number deep inside a local law enforcement agency with a long name he couldn't begin to translate. A colonel answered. The Russian told him that all was proceeding exactly according to plan.
The colonel said, 'Plato is already in the air. He took off more than three hours ago.'
The Russian said, 'I know.'

The colonel said, 'I want fifteen per cent.'

The Russian went quiet for a moment. He pretended to be annoyed. He had promised ten per cent. A ninety-ten split was what had been discussed all along. But privately he had budgeted for eighty-twenty. Eighty per cent of Plato's business had been his aim. To get eighty-five per cent would be an unexpected bonus. A free gift. The colonel was a shallow, unambitious man. Limited in every way. Which was why he was a colonel, and not a general.

The Russian said, 'You drive a hard bargain.'

The colonel said, 'Take it or leave it.'

'You make it sound like I don't have a choice.'

'You don't.'

A long silence, purely for effect.

'OK,' the Russian said. 'You get fifteen per cent.'

The colonel said, 'Thank you.'

The Russian hung up and dialled again, a number he knew belonged to an untraceable cell currently located on a night table in a Virginia bedroom. After three in the morning down there, the same as Brooklyn. The same time zone. The untraceable cell belonged to a tame DEA agent who belonged to the Russian's cousin's friend's brother-in-law. The guy answered in Virginia and the Russian told him all was going exactly according to plan.

The guy asked, 'Do I have your word?'

The Russian smiled to himself. Office politics at their very best. The cousin's friend's brother-in-law's bent DEA guy had overruled Plato's bent DEA guy and had agreed that the Russian could take over the rest of Plato's U.S. operations just as long as he didn't take the government meth out of the hole in the ground in South Dakota. In fact if the government meth could just disappear altogether, then so much the better. Too embarrassing all around. Embarrassing that it was still there, embarrassing that it had been forgotten about, embarrassing that it even existed at all. Even bent guys had departmental loyalties.

The Russian said, 'You have my word on that.'

The guy in Virginia said, 'Thank you.'

The Russian smiled again at the absurdity of it all. But he would comply. Why wouldn't he? It was a treasure trove, for sure, but he had longer-term goals. And he wouldn't miss what he never had. And it wasn't as if he had paid for it, anyway.

He hung up again and composed a text message on another phone, and hit send.

Seven miles above Nebraska, three rows behind Plato, in seat 4A, a silent phone vibrated once in a pocket, a solid mechanical thrill against the muscle of a thigh. The fifth of the six disposable Mexicans pulled out the phone and checked the screen. He was the guy who had driven Plato in the Range Rover to the airfield. He showed it to the man sitting next to him, in seat 4B, who was the sixth of the six, and who had sat with him earlier in the front of the truck. Both men nodded. Neither man spoke. Neither man even smiled. They were both way too tense.

The text said: *Do it*.

A minute later Reacher heard Holland's car in the frozen stillness. He heard the low mutter of its engine and the soft crunch of its tyres on the ice. Then the sigh and the silence as it shut down, and the creak and slam of the door, and the sound of Holland's boots on the snow. He heard the lobby door open and imagined he felt the pulse of cold air coming in from the lot. He heard Holland's steps in the corridor and then he arrived and filled the doorway, stooped, bent, defeated, like he was right at the end of something.

Holland said, 'Are you sure?'

Reacher nodded. 'No doubt about it.'

'Because sometimes they can still be alive.'

'Not this time.'

'Should we check?'

'No point.'

'What was it?'

'Nine millimetre between the eyes. Same as the other two.'

'Anything left behind?'

'Nothing.'

'So we're no closer. We still don't know who it is.'

Reacher nodded.

'But I know how to find out,' he said.

# FORTY-ONE

REACHER SAID, 'IT'S GOING TO SNOW AGAIN SOON. THE RUNWAY is going to get covered again and the bikers aren't there to plough it any more. Weather is unpredictable, therefore time is tight. Therefore Plato is on his way, probably right now. Because he needs to get his jewellery out before the sale goes through. He's probably going to double-cross the Russian and take some of the meth, too. Maybe most of it. He's got a big plane. So my guess is he told his guy to be there to help. So the guy will pull off the perimeter at some point and head up there. Maybe real soon. All we have to do is get there before him. We'll hide out and see who shows up. He'll walk straight into our arms.'

Holland said, 'You think?'

'For sure.'

'We could be waiting there for hours.'

'I don't think so. Plato needs to get in and get out. He can't afford to get trapped in a storm. A big plane on the ground, no proper facilities, he could be stuck until the start of summer.'

'What kind of help would he need, anyway?'

'Got to be something.'

'He'll bring people with him. It's just walking up and down a staircase.'

'You don't buy a dog and bark yourself.'

'You sure?'

'They're going to land a big plane in the middle of nowhere. Someone might hear it. Anything might happen. A local cop is always useful.'

'We have to hide out up there? It's very cold.'

'Cold?' Reacher said. 'This is nothing.'

Holland thought about it for a minute. Reacher watched him carefully. Holland's mouth worked silently and his eyes danced left and right. He started out reluctant, and then he got right into it.

'OK,' he said. 'Let's do it.'

Five minutes to three in the morning.

One hour to go.

Holland drove. His unmarked car was still warm inside. The roads were still frozen and empty. The middle of the night, in the middle of winter, in the middle of nowhere. Nothing was moving, except the wind. They passed the end of Janet Salter's street. It was deserted. Holland was sitting close to the wheel, belted in his seat, his parka still zipped, its material stiff and awkward against him. Reacher was sprawled in the passenger seat, no belt, his coat open, its tails hauled around into his lap, his gloves off, his hands in his pockets. The ruts on the road were worn and wizened by the cold. The front tyres hopped left and right, just a little. The chains on the back whirred and clattered. There was a moon high in the sky, close to full, pale and wan, behind thin tattered ribbons of frozen cloud.

Reacher asked, 'How long are you guys supposed to stay deployed on the perimeter?'

Holland said, 'There's no set time. It will be a gut call by the warden.'

'Best guess?'

'Another hour.'

'So any cop we see before then is our boy.'

'If we see one at all.'

'I think we will,' Reacher said.

They made the turn on the old county two-lane parallel with the highway and headed west. Five miles, not fast, not slow. Wind and ice in the air. Then they turned again, north, on the narrow wandering ribbon, eight long miles. Then the runway loomed up, spectacular as always, imposing, massive, wide, flat, infinitely long in the headlight beams, still clear and dry. Holland didn't slow down. He just thumped straight up on the moonlit concrete and held his line and held his speed. There was nothing but grey darkness ahead. No lights. No activity. Nothing moving. No one there. The wooden huts looked black in the distance, and behind them loomed the stone building, larger and blacker still.

Two hundred yards out Holland took his foot off the gas and coasted. He was still upright, still close to the wheel, still belted in, still trapped and mummified by the stiff nylon of his coat.

'Where should I put the car?' he asked.

'Doesn't matter,' Reacher said. He was still sprawled out, no belt, his hands in his pockets.

'We should hide it. The guy will see it. If he comes.'

Reacher said, 'He's already here.'

'What?'

'He just arrived.'

The car coasted and slowed. It rolled to a stop thirty yards from the first line of huts. Holland kept his foot on the floor. Not on the brake. The lever was still in gear. The engine's idle speed was not enough to push through the resistance of the snow chains. The whole car just hung there, trembling a little, not quite moving, not quite inert, right on the cusp.

Holland asked, 'How long have you known?'

Reacher said, 'For sure, about three minutes. Beyond a reasonable doubt, about thirty minutes. Retrospectively, about thirty-one hours. But back then I didn't know I knew.'

'Something I said?'

'Stuff you didn't say. Stuff you didn't do.'

'Like what?'

'Most recently you didn't slow down and kill your headlights when we hit the runway. The guy could have been here already. But you knew he wasn't. Because you're the guy.'

Holland said, 'You're wrong.'

Reacher said, 'I'm afraid not. We spent an hour underground earlier tonight, and the first thing you should have done when we got back to the surface was call the Salter house. But you didn't. I had to remind you. Turned out she was OK, because the guy hadn't gotten to her during that hour. And you knew that in advance, because you're the guy. Which is why you didn't think to call. You should have faked it better.'

Holland said nothing.

Reacher said, 'I had a conversation with Peterson last night. He came over at eight o'clock, when we thought the head count at the jail was going to come up one short. We were worried. We were tense. He took me to one side and asked me, was I armed? I said yes. I told him Mrs Salter was, too. Obvious questions, in a situation like that. You didn't ask those questions the night before. You should have.'

Holland said, 'Maybe I assumed. I knew Mrs Salter had guns in the house. She asked me for advice about ammunition.'

'And it was good advice you gave. But you should have made absolutely sure those guns weren't still in the box that night. Verbally at least, if not visually. Anyone would have done that, except a guy who knew for sure they weren't going to be needed.'

Holland said nothing.

Reacher said, 'Right back at the beginning, we found you confronting those bikers on the street. But you weren't really confronting them, were you? You were listening to them. You were getting your instructions. A regular ten-minute lecture. Plato had decided. Kill the lawyer, kill Janet Salter. They were passing on the message. Then you heard Peterson's car behind you and you threw your gun down in the snow, just to give yourself a reason to be standing there so long. Then you shoved one of them and started a fight. All staged, for Peterson's benefit. And mine, I guess. And that thing about rolling the dice? No way could they have avoided random checks so long, unless you were calling them and tipping them off. You were all working for the same guy. Which is why you let them leave town without a word.'

Holland said nothing.

Reacher said, 'Then much later Peterson and I put you on the spot. We showed up here just when it was safe for you to get the key out of the stove. You knew where it was. But you hadn't figured it out. You had been told. You were there to set things up. But we all went downstairs together. Because you couldn't think of a convincing way of stopping that from happening. And so Peterson saw stuff he was obviously going to react to. So you put that crap on the radio so when you killed him straight afterwards there would be sixty suspects in the frame, and not just you. And then you lied to me about Kapler. You tried to point me in the wrong direction. There were no rumours about drug money in Miami. If there were, my friend in Virginia would have found them long ago.'

Holland said, 'I could have killed Peterson here. At the time. Underground.'

'True. But not me too. You knew that. You're scared of me. You checked my record with the army. The woman in Virginia told me that. Your tag is on my file. So you knew the lawyer and Peterson and Janet Salter were one thing, and you knew I was another thing. They were easy. You waited on the road and put your strobes on and waved him down and the lawyer stopped right there. Why wouldn't he? He probably knew you. A chief of police from the next county? You've probably had breakfast together half a dozen times. And Peterson would follow you anywhere. And Janet Salter was probably thrilled to see you. Until you pulled your gun.'

Holland said nothing.

Reacher said, 'Three shell cases. Two of them right inside this car, and the third picked up off Janet Salter's floor. I'm guessing

350

you dumped them in the trash cans right outside the police station. Should I call the old guy on the desk and ask him to take a look?'

Holland said nothing.

Reacher said, 'I'm guessing the fourth round is chambered right now. My round. Some kind of an old throw-down pistol. Maybe lost property, maybe a cold case. Or maybe the bikers supplied it. Want to empty your pockets and prove me wrong?'

Holland said nothing.

Reacher said, 'But my round is going to stay right there in the chamber. Because I'm not like the other three. You knew that. You sensed it, maybe, and then you confirmed it with the army. So you were cautious with me. As you should be. I notice things. You've been trying to get to me for the last three hours. Dragging me here, dragging me there, always talking to me, always trying to figure out how much I knew, always biding your time, always waiting for your moment. Like right now. Back in the station house, you were debating with yourself. You didn't want to bring me here, and then you did want to bring me here. Because maybe your moment might just come out here. But it hasn't, and it didn't, and it never will. You're a smart guy and a good shot, Holland, but I'm smarter and better. Believe me. Deep down you're just a worn-out old country mouse. You can't compete. Like right now. You're all zipped up and belted in, and I'm not. I could shoot your eyes out before you even got your hand on your gun. It's been that way for the last three hours. Not because I really knew yet. But because that's just the way I am.'

Holland said nothing.

'But I should have known,' Reacher said. 'I should have known thirty-one hours ago. The first time the siren went off. It was staring me in the face. I couldn't understand how the guy had seen me without me seeing him. And I knew he would have to show up in a car, on the street, from the front. Because of the cold. And he did exactly that. And I saw him. I saw you. A minute after everyone else left, you showed up. Bold as brass, fast and easy, in a car, from the front. You came to kill Janet Salter.'

'I came to guard her.'

'I'm afraid not. The riot could have lasted hours. Even days. You said so yourself. But you left your motor running.'

Holland said nothing.

Reacher said, 'You left your motor running because you planned to be in and out real fast. You figured you could afford to be a little late up at the prison. Like you were tonight, presumably. But I was in the house. You were surprised to see me there. You needed time to think. So you hung around, all conflicted. Mrs Salter and I thought you were conflicted about two competing duties. But really you were trying to decide whether I had one of Mrs Salter's guns in my belt, and if so, whether you could draw faster than me. You concluded that I did, and you couldn't. So eventually you left. You decided to try again another day. I'm sure Plato was upset about that. He was probably very impatient. But you did the job for him in the end.'

Holland was quiet for a long time. Then he said, 'You know why, right?'

Reacher said, 'Yes.'

'How?'

'I finally figured it out. I saw the photograph in your office. She looks just like her mother.'

'Then you understand.'

'She wasn't a prisoner. They made a half-assed attempt at hiding her, but she was there out of choice. That was clear. I guess she liked the lifestyle.'

'Didn't make her any less vulnerable.'

'No excuse. There were other ways of dealing with it.'

Holland said, 'I know. I'm sorry.'

'That's it? Three dead and you're sorry?'

Holland didn't answer. He just sat still for a moment longer. Then he took his foot off the floor and stamped down on the gas. The car leapt forward. Dry concrete under the wheels, a big V-8, twin exhausts, plenty of torque, heavy-duty suspension, not much squat, a fast rear axle, good for zero to sixty in eight seconds. Reacher was hurled back against the seat. They were thirty yards from the side of the hut. Ninety feet. That was all. The headlights blazed against it. It filled the windshield. It was coming right at them. The engine roared.

After thirty of the ninety feet Reacher had a Smith & Wesson out of his pocket. After sixty he had its muzzle jammed hard in Holland's ear. Before they hit he had his left hand hooked over Holland's seat back, his arm rigid, his shoulder locked. The front end of the car punched straight through the wooden siding. The airbags exploded. The windshield shattered. The front wheels kicked up on the hut floor and the whole car went airborne. The front bumper hit a bed frame and smacked it like a cue ball and drove it into the paraffin stove. The stove tore out from under its pipe connection and clanged away like a barrel and the car fell to earth and ploughed on and hit the bed again and smashed it into the next bed across the aisle. The header rail above the windshield hit the unmoored stovepipe and bent it with a shriek and its raw end scraped the length of the car's roof and then the car was all the way inside the hut, still moving fast, the chains on the back thrashing and grinding across the wooden floor. Reacher kicked Holland in the knee and forced his foot off the gas. The car crushed beds two deep against the far wall and punched out the other side into the moonlight and landed hard and came to rest nose down half in and half out of the hut in a tangle of bent iron frames and tumbling plywood sheets. Both headlights were out and there was all kinds of grinding and rattling coming from under the hood. There was hissing and wheezing and ticking from stressed components. There was dust and splinters all around and frigid air was pouring in through the shattered front glass like liquid.

The Smith's muzzle was still hard in Holland's ear.

Reacher was still upright in his seat, still braced easily against the back of Holland's chair. The passenger airbag had inflated against his squared shoulder, and then it had collapsed again.

He said, 'I told you, Holland, you can't compete.'

Holland didn't answer.

Reacher said, 'You damaged the car. How am I going to get back to town?'

Holland asked, 'What are you going to do with me?'

Reacher said, 'Let's take a walk. Keep your hands where I can see them.'

*I'll have plenty of time to read*, Janet Salter had said, *after all this fuss is over.*

*You reap what you sow.*

They climbed out of the wrecked car into the cold and the wind and stepped away into the narrow lane that separated the first row of huts from the second. Holland walked ahead and Reacher followed ten feet behind with the old .38 six-shooter held low and easy. It was the one Janet Salter had cradled through so many hours.

Reacher said, 'Tell me about Plato.'

Holland stopped and turned around and said, 'I never met him. It was all on the phone, or through the bikers.'

'Is he as bad as he sounds?'

'Worse.'

'What's supposed to happen tonight?'

'Like you figured. He's going to take the jewellery out and steal back some of the meth.'

'And you were supposed to help?'

'I was supposed to be here, yes. I have some equipment for him, and the key to the door.'

'OK,' Reacher said. Then he raised the .38 and pulled the trigger and shot Holland between the eyes. The gun kicked gently in his hand and the sound was the same as a 158-grain .38 always was outdoors in quiet cold air, a fractured spitting *crack* that rolled away across the flat land and faded fast, because it had nothing to bounce back from. Holland went down with a loud rustle of heavy nylon and the stiffness of his coat pitched him half sideways and left him lying on one shoulder with his face turned up to the moon. Thirty-eight hundredths of an inch was mathematically a little larger than nine millimetres, so the third eye in his forehead was a little larger than Janet Salter's

354

had been, but his face was a little larger too, so overall the effect was proportional.

Chief Thomas Holland, RIP.

His body settled and his blood leaked out and his cell phone started ringing in his pocket.

# FORTY-TWO

REACHER GOT TO THE PHONE BY THE THIRD RING. IT WAS IN Holland's parka, in a chest pocket. It was faintly warm. Reacher hit the green button and raised it to his ear and said, 'Yes?'

'Holland?' Practically a yell. A bad connection, very loud background noise, a Spanish accent, nasal and not deep.

A small man.

Plato.

Reacher didn't answer.

'Holland?'

Reacher said, 'Yes.'

'We're fifteen minutes out. We need the landing lights.'

Then the phone went dead.

*We?* How many? *Landing lights?* What landing lights? Reacher stood still for a second. He had seen no electricity supply out to the runway. No humped glass lenses along its length. It was just a flat slab of concrete. It was possible the Crown Vic's headlights were supposed to do the job, in which case Plato was shit out of luck, because the Crown Vic's headlights were both busted. But then, headlights couldn't stretch two miles. Not even halogen, not even on bright.

Fifteen minutes.

Now fourteen and change.

Reacher put the phone in his own pocket and then checked through the rest of Holland's pockets. Found the T-shaped key to the stone building's door, and a scuffed old Glock 17. The throwdown pistol. There were fourteen rounds in the magazine and one in the chamber.

His round.

He put the key and the Glock in his pocket and took another Glock out of Holland's holster. His official piece. It was newer. Fully loaded. He put his gloves back on and bunched Holland's shirt collar and jacket collar and parka collar all together in his fist and dragged the body to the nearest hut and all the way inside. Left it dumped in the centre of the floor. Then he hustled back to the car.

Thirteen minutes and change.

The car was canted down at the front, half in and half out of the hut. He squeezed along its flank and in through the hole in the shattered wall and stood where the stove had been and opened the trunk.

All kinds of stuff in there. But three basic categories: normal car stuff where the Ford Motor Company had planned it to be, regular cop gear neatly stowed in plastic trays, and then other things thrown in on top of everything else. In the first category: a spare tyre and a scissor jack. In the second category: a fluorescent traffic jacket, four red road flares, three nested traffic cones, a first-aid kit, a green tackle box for small items, two tarps, three rolls of crime scene tape, a bag of white rags, a lockbox for a handgun. In the third category: a long coil of greasy rope, an engine hoist with pulleys and tripod legs, unopened boxes of big heavy-duty garbage bags.

Nothing even remotely resembling a landing light.

Twelve minutes and change.

He pictured the scene from a pilot's point of view. An airliner, a Boeing 737, descending, on approach, dim blue-grey moonlit tundra ahead and below. Visible to some degree, but uniform, and featureless. The guy would have GPS navigation, but he would need help from the ground. That was clear. But he wouldn't be expecting any kind of mainstream FAA-approved bullshit. That was clear, too. Nothing was going to be done by the book.

What would he need?

Something improvised, obviously.

Fire, maybe?

World War Two bomber pilots landing in East Anglian fog were guided in by long parallel trenches pumped full of gasoline and set ablaze. Small planes landing secret agents in occupied Europe looked for fields with three bonfires arranged in an L-shape.

Was Holland supposed to have set fires?

Eleven minutes and change.

No, not fires.

Reacher slammed the trunk lid and kicked away debris from behind the car. He squeezed around to the front and hauled away tangled bed frames from under the fenders and dragged splintered plywood off the hood. The engine was still running. It smelled hot and oily and the bearings were knocking loudly. He squeezed back and opened the driver's door and dumped himself in Holland's seat and put the transmission in Reverse. Hit the gas and the car jerked and sputtered and dragged itself backwards the way it had come. In through the hole in the far wall, across the floor, out through the hole in the near wall. It thumped down tail first and Reacher spun the wheel and jammed the lever into Drive and headed for the northeastern corner of the runway. The top right corner, from the Boeing's point of view. He braked to a stop and slid out and opened the trunk again and grabbed the four red road flares from the plastic tray. He tossed three into the passenger seat as he passed and spiked the fourth into the concrete. It ignited automatically and burned fiercely. A bright crimson puffball. Visible from a long way on a road, presumably even further from the air.

He got back in the car and headed for the opposite corner. The top left. He had no headlights, but the moonlight was enough. Just. A hundred yards. He used the second flare. Then he set off down the length of the two-mile stretch. No fun at all. The windshield glass was gone and the wind was biting. And the car was slow. And getting slower. It felt close to stalling out. It smelled of burning oil. The engine was knocking and vibrating. The temperature gauge in the dash was climbing steadily towards the red.

Not good.

Nine minutes and change.

Two miles should have taken two minutes, but the wounded car took more than four. Reacher used the third flare in the south-western corner. The bottom left, from the pilot's point of view. He got back in the car. Backed up, turned the wheel, headed out. The car started juddering uncontrollably. It started losing all its power. The temperature needle jammed hard against its end stop. Steam and black smoke started coming out from under the hood. Thick clouds of it.

A hundred yards to go. That was all. One more corner.

The car made fifty yards and died. It just ground to a stop and stayed there, refusing to go on, hissing and inert, right in the middle of the runway's southern edge. The transmission was gone, or the oil pressure, or the water, or something, or every-thing.

Reacher got out and ran the rest of the way.

He spiked the last flare and stood back.

The crimson glow in the four distant corners was way brighter than anything else around it. And it came back off the shaped berms of ploughed snow twice as bright. Adequate, from the Boeing's flight deck. Looking forward and down from an oblique angle there would be no doubt about the shape and location of the landing strip. The car was dark and dead right across the middle of the near end, but it was no worse than an airport fence.

Two minutes and change.

Job done.

Except that Reacher was stuck two whole miles from where he needed to be, and it was a cold night for walking. Except that he was pretty sure he wouldn't need to be walking. He was pretty sure he could get a ride, if he wanted one, before too long. Maybe even before he froze. Which was good. Except that given the state of his current information it was highly likely his ride would get him to the stone building a little after Plato got there. Which was not good. Not good at all. And not even remotely what he had intended.

*Plans go to hell as soon as the first shot is fired.*

He hustled back through the frigid air to the dead car, and he leaned on its flank and watched the night sky in the south.

And waited.

A minute later Reacher saw lights above the horizon. Like stars that weren't stars. Tiny electric pinpricks that hung and twinkled and grew and danced a little, up and down, side to side. Spotlights in an airplane's landing gear, for sure, approaching head on, maybe ten miles out.

Then he saw lights below the horizon, too. Yellower, weaker, pooled on the ground, less stable, bouncing, moving much slower. Headlights. A road vehicle. Two of them, in fact, one behind the other on the wandering snowbound two-lane, approaching head on, crawling along, doing maybe thirty, maybe five miles out.

His ride.

Close, but not close enough.

He leaned back in the cold and waited and watched.

The Boeing got there first. It started out small and silent, and then it got bigger and noisier. It came in low and flat, all broad supportive wings and swirling heat shimmer and deafening jet whine and stabbing beams of light. Its nose was up and its undercarriage was down, the trailing wheels hanging lower than the leading wheels, like talons on a giant bird of prey ready to swoop in and seize the crippled car like an eagle takes a lamb. Reacher ducked and the plane passed right over his head, huge and almost close enough to touch, and the roiled air and shattering noise that trailed behind it threatened to knock him flat. He straightened again and turned and watched over the roof of the car as the plane skimmed and hung and deliberated and floated, a hundred yards, two, three, and then it put down decisively with a loud yelp of rubber and a puff of black smoke and then its nose tipped down and it ran fast and flat and true before the reverse thrusters cut in and slowed it in a bellowing scream.

Reacher turned back and faced south.

The road vehicles were still heading his way. They were moving slowly and carefully along the moonlit two-lane, cautious because of the curves and the ice and the bad surface, but relentless, a miniature convoy with a destination in mind. Their headlight beams swung left, swung right, bounced up, dipped down. The first vehicle was a strange open-frame truck, with a big coil of heavy flexible pipe wrapped over a drum immediately behind the cab, and then a pump built into a square steel frame, and then a second coil of pipe on a second drum. The vehicle right behind it was the same general size and type, but behind the cab it had a big white tank, and a cherry-picker bucket, and a long articulated boom arm folded up and tied down for travel.

The first truck was painted in the colours of the Shell Oil Company.

It had the word *Isuzu* across its grille.

The statewide BOLO bulletin: *an Isuzu N-series pump and a de-icing truck stolen by two absconded employees from a commercial airfield east of Rapid City.* Stolen on Plato's orders, presumably, so that his 737 could be refuelled from the underground tank and then flown away safely through bitter night skies.

Reacher pushed off the flank of the car and waited. The pump truck's headlights hit him, and it slowed, and then its lights flicked up to bright, and then it stopped dead. For a second Reacher was conscious of his dark pants and khaki hat and tan coat. The coat was old, but it still looked like Highway Patrol issue. And the dead Crown Vic was parked crosswise, as if to block access to the runway. And no one uses plain Crown Vics except law enforcement. But the Rapid City guys must have been told that a bent cop would be waiting there to meet them, because after just a brief pause the pump truck moved on again, with the de-icer close behind. Reacher raised his hand, partly like a greeting, partly like a traffic stop, and a minute later he was sitting in the warmth inside the pump truck's cab, riding up the runway towards whatever was waiting for him at the other end.

Twenty-seven minutes past three in the morning.

Twenty-eight minutes to go.

# FORTY-THREE

THE BOEING HAD TAXIED AND TURNED AND WAS PARKED AS NEAR as it could get to the first line of huts. Up close, it looked gigantic. A huge plane, high and wide and long, at temporary rest in the middle of nowhere, towering over the silent buildings behind it, hissing and whistling, an active, living presence in a passive, frozen landscape. Its engines were still spooling noisily and its belly light was still flashing red and its forward door was latched wide open. Lights were on inside. An aluminum housepainter's ladder had been extended down from the cabin to the runway surface below. It looked thin and puny and insubstantial next to the giant plane.

There were seven men on the ground. Or what looked like six men and a boy. There was no mistaking Plato. Four feet and eleven inches tall, but that abstract measurement did not convey the reality. He had a big man's heft and thickness and muscularity, and a big man's stiffness and posture and movement, but a small child's stature. He was not dwarfish. He was not a freak. His limbs and his torso and his neck and his head were all reasonably well proportioned. He was like an NFL linebacker reduced in size by exactly twenty-five per cent. That was all. He was a miniature tough guy. Like a toy.

He looked to be somewhere between forty and fifty years old. He was wearing a black goose-down jacket, and a black woollen watch cap, and black gloves. He looked very cold. The six men with him were younger. In their thirties, maybe. They were dressed the same as him. Black down jackets, black hats, black gloves. They were normal-sized Hispanic men, Spanish not Indian, neither short nor tall, and they looked very cold, too.

The pump truck drove around and parked close to the Boeing's wing and the de-icer parked behind it. Both drivers got out. They had no visible reaction to the abject temperature. They were Rapid City guys. They knew about cold. They had down jackets of their own. They were both white, medium height, and lean. Hardscrabble people, rural roots, worn down to the bare essentials. Arms, legs, heads, bodies. Maybe thirty years old, but they looked forty. Maybe a couple of generations off the farm.

Reacher stayed in his seat for a moment, keeping warm, and watching.

Plato was moving around inside a loose cordon formed by his six guys. No real reason for that. Maybe habit, maybe appearances. And Plato and his six guys were armed. They all had Heckler & Koch MP5Ks slung around their necks on nylon straps. Short stubby weapons, black and wicked. Thirty-round magazines. They rested raised and proud and prominent on the puffy coats. Butts to the right, muzzles to the left. All seven guys were right-handed. All seven guys had backpacks, too. Black nylon. The backpacks looked mostly empty apart from small heavy loads at the bottom. Flashlights, Reacher assumed. For deep underground. And spare magazines, presumably. For the guns. Always good to have. On full auto thirty rounds came out of an MP5 in two short seconds.

Sub-machine guns. A bullet manufacturer's very best friends.

Reacher climbed out of the pump truck's cab. Into the cold and the wind. The Rapid City guys were still doing OK with it, but all seven Mexicans were shivering hard. They had expressions of total disbelief on their faces. They had left a balmy evening knowing they were heading for somewhere cold, but understanding the word and feeling the feeling were two completely different things. Plato's gun was bouncing a little on his chest because his whole body was trembling. He was walking small tight circles and stamping his feet. But part of that might have been plain annoyance. He was clearly tense. He had a hard brown face and his mouth was set down in a grimace.

The Rapid City guys didn't read it right.

The guy who had driven the pump truck stepped up and spread his hands and smiled what he clearly hoped was a cunning smile, and he said, 'Here we are.'

A self-evident statement. Plato looked at him blankly and said, 'And?'

'We want more money.' A plan, obviously. Clearly discussed and pre-agreed with his buddy. Bar talk. Irresistible, over a third beer. Or a fourth. Show the guy the prize, and then yank it back and ask for more.

Can't fail.

Plato asked, 'How much more?'

Good English, lightly accented, a little slow and indistinct because of a cold face and the jet whine in the background.

The pump driver was used to talking over jet whine. He worked at an airport.

He said, 'The same again.'

'Double?'

'You got it.'

Plato's eyes flicked across three of his guys and came to rest on a fourth. He asked in Spanish, which because of the cold was slow enough for Reacher to follow: 'Do you know how to work this equipment?'

The fourth guy said, 'I think so.'

'Think or know?'

'I've done it before. With the fuel, I mean. Many times. The de-icing, not so much. No call for it. But how hard can it be? It's just a spray, for the wings.'

'Tell me yes or no.'

'Yes.'

Plato turned back to the Rapid City guys. Put his gloved hands on his gun and raised it up and machine-gunned them both in the chest. Just like that. Full auto. First one, and then the other. Two brief bursts of fire, barely separated at all. Nine or ten rounds each. An impossibly fast cyclic rate. Shattering noise. Searing, vivid, foot-long muzzle flash. A hosing stream of ejected brass. The spent cases bounced and skittered away. The two guys went down in a mist of blood from their ripped bodies and a cloud of feathers from their torn jackets, first one, then immediately the other, with ragged bloody holes in their chests big enough to plunge a fist in. They fell side by side, dead before they hit the ground, their hearts torn apart. They thumped down and settled at once, rags and flesh, two small mounds close together.

The gunsmoke whipped away in the wind and the sudden noise faded and the jet whine came back, low and steady.

Twenty feet above them the pilot looked out the Boeing's door.

Reacher was impressed. Long bursts, tightly grouped. Great trigger control, great aim, and no muzzle climb at all. With gloves on, too. Plato had done this before. No question about that.

No one spoke.

Plato moved his thumb and tripped the release and the part-used magazine fell out and plinked against the concrete. Then he held his hand palm up and waited. The guy nearest to him scurried around and dug down in Plato's own backpack and came out with a fresh magazine. He slapped it into Plato's waiting palm. Plato clicked it into its housing, and tugged on it once to check it was secure, and then he turned to Reacher.

He said, 'You must be Chief Holland.'

Reacher said, 'Yes.'

'Finally we meet.'

'Yes.'

'Why isn't the door open and the equipment set up for me?'

Reacher didn't answer. He was thinking: what equipment?

366

Plato said, 'Your daughter is still under my direct control, you know.'

Reacher said, 'Where is she?'

'She moved on with the rest of them. She's living her dream.'

'Is she OK?'

'So far. But my threat against her still stands.'

Reacher said, 'My car broke down. The equipment is still in the trunk.'

'Where's your car?'

'At the other end of the runway.'

Plato didn't answer directly. The sign of a good leader. No sense in fussing about what couldn't be changed. He just turned to one of his men and said in Spanish, 'Take the de-icing truck and fetch the equipment we need from the trunk of Chief Holland's car.'

The guy headed for the de-icer's cab and Plato turned back to Reacher and asked, 'Where is the key for the building?'

Reacher took it out of his pocket and held it up. Plato stepped through his human cordon. Reacher rehearsed two possible moves. Drive the key through Plato's eye, or drop it on the ground and drive a massive uppercut through Plato's chin and snap his puny neck.

He did neither thing. Plato had five MP5Ks right behind him. Within a split second seventy-five nine-millimetre rounds would be in the air. Most of them would miss. But not all of them.

The de-icer truck crunched into gear and moved away.

Plato stepped up next to Reacher. The top of his head was exactly level with Reacher's breastbone. His chin was exactly level with Reacher's waistband. A tiny man. A miniature tough guy. A toy. Reacher reassessed the uppercut. Bad idea. Almost impossible to launch a blow from so low down. Better to drive an elbow vertically through the crown of his skull.

Or shoot him.

Plato took the key.

He said, 'Now take your coat off.'

Reacher said, 'What?'

'Take your coat off.'

'Why?'

'Are you arguing with me?'

Six hands on six sub-machine guns.

Reacher said, 'I'm asking you a question.'

Plato said, 'You and I are going underground.'

'Why me?'

'Because you've been down there before. None of us have. You're our local guide.'

'I can go down there with my coat on.'

'True. But you're in civilian clothing. Therefore, no gun belt. The weather is cold and your coat is closed at the front. Therefore, your guns are in your outer pockets. I'm a smart guy. Therefore, I don't wish to enter an unfamiliar environment with an armed adversary.'

'Am I your adversary?'

'I'm a smart guy,' Plato said again. 'The safe assumption is that everyone is my adversary.'

Reacher said, 'It's cold.'

Plato said, 'Your daughter's grave will be colder.'

Six hands on six sub-machine guns.

Reacher unzipped his coat. He shrugged it off and dropped it. It hit the ground with a padded clank. The Glocks, the Smiths, the box of rounds, the cell phone. Plastic and metal and cardboard. Thirty degrees below zero. Windy. A cotton sweater. Within seconds he was shivering worse than any of them.

Plato stood still. Not long, Reacher thought, before the de-icer truck got back and the driver described the smashed-up Ford. Therefore not long before someone looked down the row and found the damaged hut. Not long before someone searched the other huts. Not long before someone started asking awkward questions.

Time to get going.

'Let's do it,' he said.

Twenty-seven minutes to four in the morning.

Twenty-two minutes to go.

# FORTY-FOUR

THEY WALKED OVER TO THE STONE BUILDING, SEVEN MEN, SINGLE file, a strange little procession. Plato first, four feet eleven, then Reacher, six feet five, then Plato's five guys, all of them halfway between the two extremes. Plato's sixth guy was still safely away in the de-icer truck, looting Holland's dead car. The stone building was standing there waiting for them, quiet and indifferent in the moonlit gloom, the same way it had stood for fifty long years. The stone, the slate, the blind windows, the chimneys, the mouldings and the curlicues and the details.

The portico, and the steel slab door.

Plato put the key in the lock. Turned it. The lock sprang back. Then he stood still and waited. Reacher took the hint. He turned the handle down sixty degrees, precise and physical, like a bank vault. He pulled the door through a short arc. The hinges squealed. He stepped in behind it and pushed it all the way open, like pushing a truck.

Plato stood still and raised his hand, palm up. The man behind him stepped up and dug down in his backpack and came out with a flashlight. He slapped it into Plato's palm, the way an OR nurse feeds tools to a surgeon. Plato clicked it on and transferred it to his other hand and snapped his fingers and pointed at Reacher. The guy behind him swung his own backpack off his shoulder and took out his flashlight and handed it over.

It was a four-cell Mag-lite. From Ontario, California. The de facto gold standard for man-portable illumination. Alloy construction. Reliable and practically indestructible. Reacher clicked it on. He played the beam around the bare concrete chamber.

No change.

The place was exactly as he and two dead men had left it more than four and a half hours earlier. The circular stair head, the two unfinished ventilation pipes jutting up through the floor. The stale dry air, the stirring breeze, the smell of old fears long forgotten.

'After you, Mr Holland,' Plato said.

Which disappointed Reacher a little. He had lost his coat, but he still had his boots. He had entertained the idea of letting Plato go first, and then kicking his head off about a hundred feet down.

But, obviously, so had Plato. A smart guy.

So Reacher went first, as awkward as before. Big boot heels, small steps, clanging metal. The sound of the whining jets faded as he went down, and he heard Plato issuing a stream of instructions in Spanish: 'Wait until the de-icer gets back, then set up the equipment, then start the refuelling. Get the other three doors open on the plane, and get the other three ladders in position. Figure out how the de-icer works and figure out how close to take-off we need to use it. And put a man on lookout a hundred feet south. That's the only direction we have to worry about. Rotate every twenty minutes. Or more often, if you want. Your call. I want the lookout alert at all times, not frozen to death.'

Then Plato stopped talking and Reacher heard his feet on the stairs above him. Smaller steps, more precise. The metal still clanged, but quieter. The two flashlight beams went down and around, down and around, always clockwise, separated vertically by twenty feet, and not synchronized. Reacher took it slow. He was Holland now, in more than name. He was improvising, and hoping his moment would come.

On the surface the de-icer truck got back with the necessary equipment all piled on and around the passenger seat. The engine hoist, the rope, the garbage bags. The hoist was a sturdy metal thing, with three legs and a boom arm like the jib of a small crane. It was designed to be set up at the front of a car, with the jib leaning in over the engine compartment. The pulleys would produce multiplication of effort, according to ancient mechanical principles, allowing a lone operator to lift a heavy iron block.

Three of Plato's guys carried the hoist into the bunker and set it up with the jib leaning in over one of the ventilation shafts. Like fishing from a barrel. They started threading the rope through the pulleys. No free lunch. More weight meant less speed. Pull the rope a yard, and with one pulley in play a light weight would move the same yard, but with two pulleys in play a heavier weight would move just eighteen inches, and with three pulleys in play a heavier weight still would move just twelve inches. And so on. A tradeoff.

They chose to thread two pulleys. A balance of speed and capacity.

The guy who had driven the truck said nothing about the Ford.

Two hundred and eighty awkward steps. Reacher completed seventy of them, a quarter of the way down, and then he began to speed up. He saw a window of opportunity ahead. *Set up the equipment, then start the refuelling,* Plato had said. Which meant that there would be some busywork up top before one of his guys came down to connect the pump truck's hose to the fuel tank. Five minutes, maybe. Possibly ten. And five or ten minutes alone with Plato deep underground could be productive. So he aimed to get to the bottom as far ahead as possible. To prepare. So he speeded up as much as he could. Which wasn't much.

And which wasn't nearly enough.

Plato matched him step for step. Gained on him, even. For a man of Plato's stature, the winding stair was broad and palatial. Like something from a Hollywood production. And his feet were dainty. He was nimble and agile in comparison.

Reacher slowed down again. Better to save energy and avoid busting an ankle.

The guy who had sat in seat 4A was standing with the guy from seat 4B in the lee of the pump truck, out of sight of the stone building, hidden from the Boeing's flight deck windows, invisible to the sentry a hundred feet down the runway. The guy from 4A had texted the Russian: *Cop car damaged. No getaway possible.*

The Russian had replied: *I will double your money.*

The guy from 4B glanced over at the de-icer truck. The guy from 4A followed his gaze. A diesel engine, a little clumsy, not fast, distinctive in appearance, and stolen. But it was a vehicle.

He said nothing.

The phone buzzed again against his palm.

The Russian had offered: *I will triple your money. Do it.*

Triple the money was a fortune beyond comprehension. But even that paled against the prospect of a life without Plato in it.

The guy from 4B nodded. He had just driven the truck. He knew it worked.

The guy from 4A texted: *OK.*

Reacher passed through the second of the oboe nodes. Two-thirds of the way down. The individual sounds of four separate feet on metal merged and melded into a keening ghostly song that pulsed up and down the shaft and hung and oscillated in the still dead air, like an elegy for a tragedy about to happen. Reacher shivered and kept on going down into the darkness, his flashlight held between gloved thumb and forefinger, his other three fingers spread and brushing the wall. Above him Plato's beam turned and jumped and stabbed. Reacher's heel hit the two hundredth step. Eighty more to go.

\*     \*     \*

The pump truck was basically a simple device. A relatively recent invention. In the old days tankers refuelled planes directly. In the modern world airports put fuel tanks underground, and skeletal trucks drove out on the tarmac and linked nozzles under manholes to nozzles under airplane wings. The hose on the reel directly behind the cab spooled out and connected to the underground source, and the hose on the reel at the other end of the truck spooled out and connected to the plane. In between was a pump, to suck fuel out of the ground and push it onward into the aeroplane's tanks. A simple, linear proposition.

The guys from seats 4A and 4B manoeuvred the truck as close as they could get it to the stone building's door, which put it about halfway between the tank far below them and the thirsty Boeing. One jacked the first nozzle on his shoulder and the other operated the electric motor that unwound the drum. The one with the nozzle on his shoulder walked the hose into the building and fed it down the second ventilation shaft, the one that the guys with the rope weren't using.

Reacher made it to the bottom. Same situation as before. He rested on the last step, nine inches off the round chamber's floor, its ceiling level with his waist, his upper body still inside the shaft, his face an inch from the curved concrete wall. Plato crowded in behind him, the same way Holland had before. Reacher felt the H&K's muzzle on his back.

Plato said, 'Move.'

Reacher ducked way down and got his shoulders under the ceiling and waddled forward, painfully, his legs hurting, his neck bent at ninety degrees. He dropped to his knees and folded himself sideways and sat down. He shuffled through half a turn and scooted away backwards, undignified, slow and awkward and claustrophobic, heels and knuckles and ass, once, then twice.

Plato stepped off the bottom stair and just walked straight into the chamber.

He took three confident strides and then stopped and looked around, erect, upright, with four clear inches between the top of his head and the concrete.

He said, 'So where's my stuff?'

Reacher didn't answer. He was adrift. The world had flipped underneath him. All his life, to be taller had been to be better. More dominant, more powerful, more noticed, more advantaged. You got credibility, you got treated with respect, you got promoted faster, you earned more, you got elected to things. Statistics bore it out.

You won fights, you got less hassle, you ruled the yard.

To be born tall was to win life's lottery.

Born small, two strikes against.

But not down there.

Down there to be tall was a losing ticket.

Down there was a world where the small guy could win.

'Where's my stuff?' Plato said again, with his hand on his gun.

Reacher took his own hand off the floor and started to point, but then there were twin ragged thumps behind him, and a slap, and another thump. He shuffled around and saw that three packs of garbage bags had been dropped down the ventilation shaft, plus the tail end of a greasy coil of rope. Things he had seen before, in the trunk of Holland's car.

Plato said, 'We have work to do. It's not exactly rocket science. We put the stuff in the bags, we tie the bags to the rope, they haul them up.'

Reacher asked, 'How much stuff?'

'The plane will carry sixteen tons.'

'You'll be here all week.'

'I don't think so. I have about ten hours. The biker will come out of his little hidey-hole in the jail just after lunch time. And I arranged with the warden that he will keep your whole department on station right up to that point. So we'll be undisturbed. And a ton and a half an hour should be possible. Especially with you down here to help. But don't worry. The hard work will be done on the surface.'

Reacher said nothing.

Plato said, 'But we'll do the jewellery first. Where is it?'

Reacher started to point again, but then a brass collar on the

374

end of a thick black hose dropped through the other ventilation shaft, right next to him. It thumped down on the floor and excess hose came tumbling down after it and coiled all around it. Then he heard feet on the steps way above. Distant tinkling and pattering in the stair shaft, getting louder, getting nearer. A man on his way down.

Refuelling was about to begin.

Plato asked, 'Where's the jewellery?'

Reacher didn't answer. He was estimating time. Two hundred and eighty steps. Somewhere between two and three minutes before the refuelling guy arrived, however fast he moved. And two or three minutes should be enough. It was a long time since Reacher had been in a fight that had lasted longer than two or three minutes.

A window of opportunity.

'Where's the jewellery?' Plato said again.

Reacher said, 'Find it yourself.'

The sound of feet on the stairs got a little louder.

Plato smiled. He pushed back his cuff and made a show of checking the time on the watch on his wrist, slow and nonchalant. Then he darted forward, fast and nimble and agile, and he aimed a kick at Reacher's side. From a sitting position Reacher swatted Plato's foot aside and came up on his knees and Plato stumbled away and Reacher pivoted up and lunged after him.

And hit his head hard on the ceiling, and scraped his knuckles, and collapsed back to his knees. Plato righted himself after a step and danced in and delivered the belated kick, a decent hard blow to the ribs on Reacher's back.

Then he stepped away and smiled again.

He said, 'Where's the jewellery?'

Reacher didn't answer. His knuckles were bleeding and he was pretty sure his scalp was torn. The ceiling crowded down on him.

Plato put both hands on his gun.

He said, 'You get one free pass. And that was it. Where's the jewellery?'

So Reacher used his flashlight beam and found the right

corridor. Even from a distance the reflection came back bright and lurid. Plato walked towards it, fast and jaunty, no problem at all, right up on his toes, like he was outside on the street with just the sky above him.

He called over his shoulder, 'Bring some bags.'

Reacher shuffled over and grabbed a pack of bags, and then he shuffled after Plato, hobbled, restricted, constrained, humiliated, following the little man like a giant caged ape.

Plato was in the right corridor. He was doing what Holland had done. He was playing his flashlight beam the length of the shelf and back again, over the gold and the silver and the platinum, and the diamonds and the rubies and the sapphires and the emeralds, and the clocks and the paintings and the platters and the candlesticks. But not with greed or wonderment in his face. He was assessing the size of the packaging task, that was all.

He said, 'You can start bagging this shit up. But first show me the powder.'

Reacher led him across the chamber, heels and knuckles and ass, low and deferential, all the way to the third of the three tunnels packed with meth. Still a staggering sight. Bricks stacked ten high, ten deep, a whole solid wall of them a hundred feet long, undisturbed for fifty years, old yellowing glassine glowing dull in the flashlight beams. Fifteen thousand packs. More than thirteen tons.

'Is this all of it?' Plato asked.

'A third of it,' Reacher said.

The feet on the staircase grew louder. The fuel guy was hustling.

Plato said, 'We'll take what's here. Plus more. Until the plane is full.'

Reacher said, 'I thought you sold it to the Russian.'

Plato said, 'I did.'

'But you're going to take it anyway?'

'Only some of it.'

'That's a double-cross.'

Plato laughed. 'You killed three people for me and now you're

376

upset that I'm stealing? From some dumb Russian you never met?'

'I would prefer you to be true to your word, that's all.'

'Why?'

'Because I want my daughter to be OK.'

'She's with those guys out of choice. And ten hours from now I'll have no further use for her, anyway. I'm never doing business here again.'

'You'll have no further use for me, either,' Reacher said.

'I'll let you live,' Plato said. 'You did well for me. Slow, but you got there in the end.'

Reacher said nothing.

'I am true to my word,' Plato said. 'Just not with Russians.'

Behind them they heard the last loud footstep on the last metal stair and then the first quiet footstep on the concrete floor. They turned and saw one of Plato's men arrive, like all of them about five seven in height, therefore stooped but not too much. He had his gun on his chest and a flashlight in his hand. He was looking all around. Not curious. Just a guy getting the job done. He found the fuel line and picked it up one-handed and pulled it out straight and jerked it and heaved serpentine waves into it to work out the kinks. He asked in Spanish where the tank was and Reacher waited until Plato translated the question and then he pointed his flashlight beam at the relevant corridor. The guy hauled the heavy hose after him and disappeared.

Plato said, 'Go start bagging the jewellery.'

Reacher left him communing with his stock in trade and shuffled the long way around. Five thousand gallons in a home-made tank. He wanted to be sure the connection was secure. He was going to be down there until Plato died, which was a minimum of a few more minutes and a maximum of ten more hours, and he preferred one thing to worry about at a time.

He found Plato's guy finishing up. The brass end of the hose was neatly socketed into a matching brass fitment brazed into the end wall of the tank. The guy was nudging it one way, nudging it the other, feeling for looseness or play. He seemed to find none, so he opened a tap on the tank side of the joint. Reacher heard the fuel flow into the hose. Not much of it. Three gallons, maybe four. That was all. Gravity only, into the length of hose that lay on the floor at a lower level than the tank itself. For the rest, the pump would have to prime itself and then suck hard and haul it all up and out.

Reacher watched the joint. A single fat drop of kerosene formed where two fibre washers were compressed. It beaded large and waited and then fell to the floor and made a tiny wet stain.

That was all.

No more.

Safe enough.

Plato's guy crouched a little and duck-walked back to the stairs and headed upward. Reacher shuffled on around the perimeter of the circular chamber and disappeared into a corridor far from the jewellery and far from the meth.

# FORTY-FIVE

*D*O IT. SHORT SIMPLE WORDS, A SHORT SIMPLE COMMAND. OR A short simple plea, or a short simple request. Or a short simple half of a bargain. A very attractive bargain. Do it, and get extremely rich, and live happily for ever with respect and veneration from your whole community. They would be the men who took down Plato. Saints. Heroes. Songs would be sung, tales would be told.

The guy from seat 4A looked at the guy from seat 4B. They both swallowed hard. They were getting very close to doing it. Dangerously close. A hundred feet south a new sentry had just rotated into position. He was facing away, alert and on guard. Way far beyond him the flares still burned at the distant end of the runway. Fifty yards the other side of the Boeing's tail the third flare still burned. Fifty yards beyond the de-icer truck in the other direction the fourth flare was still a bright crimson puffball. Blue moon, white snow, red flame.

The other three guys were working in the plane. Opening the doors, setting the ladders, working out a system for hauling the stuff hand-to-hand along a human chain and then getting it up into the plane and stacking it safely on the floor of the old economy section.

The guy from seat 4A hoisted the end of the second hose on his shoulder. The guy from seat 4B hit the switch and the drum began to unwind.

Sixteen minutes to four in the morning.

Eleven minutes to go.

Reacher heard Plato moving about. Heard him step out of the corridor into the round chamber. Reacher was sitting on the floor in the first of the curved connecting tunnels. In what he was calling the B-ring. Like a miniature Pentagon, but round and underground. The central chamber was the A-ring. Then came the B-ring, and then the C-ring, and around the outside was the D-ring. All partially interconnected by the eight straight spokes. More than seventeen hundred linear feet of tunnel. Twenty-four separate junctions. Twelve random left turns, twelve random right turns. Plus a total of ten hollowed-out bathrooms and kitchens and storage chambers.

A warren.

A maze.

Reacher had been in it before, and Plato hadn't.

No cell signal, his guys all busy on the surface, no possibility of reinforcement.

Reacher waited.

Plato called, 'Holland?'

The sound of the word boomed and echoed and took unpredictable paths and seemed to come from everywhere and nowhere.

Reacher waited.

Plato called, 'Holland? Get your ass over here. Our deal isn't finished yet. Remember, I'll cripple her and mutilate her and let her live for a year before I finish her off.'

Reacher said nothing.

Plato called, 'Holland?'

No response from Reacher. Five seconds. Ten.

380

'Holland?'

Reacher said nothing. The big gamble came right then. Right at that exact moment in time. Fifty-fifty. Live or die. A smart guy with a dawning problem would hustle straight up the stairs and send foot soldiers down in his place. A dumb guy would stay to fight it out.

But so might a smart guy overcome by ego, and arrogance, and a sense of superiority, and a need never to appear weak because he was only four feet eleven inches tall.

Fifty-fifty.

Live or die.

Plato stayed.

He called, 'Holland? Where are you?'

A trace of worry in his voice.

Reacher put his mouth close to the curved concrete and said, 'Holland's dead.'

The sound rode the walls and went all around and came back to him, a quiet-spoken sentence, everywhere and nowhere, conversational, but full of menace. Reacher heard Plato's feet scuffling on the concrete floor. He was spinning in place, trying to locate the voice.

Plato's feet went quiet and he called out, 'What did you say?'

Reacher moved along an empty spoke into the C-ring. A slow, silent shuffle. No sound at all, except the whisper of fabric when the seat of his pants hit the floor. Which didn't matter anyway. All sounds were everywhere. They hissed and sang and branched and travelled.

Reacher put his mouth to the wall and said, 'I shot Holland in the head. Now I'm coming for you.'

'Who are you?'

'Does it matter?'

'Tell me.'

'I was a friend of Janet Salter's.'

'Who?'

'The witness. Didn't you even know her name?'

'Are you the military cop?'

'You're about to find out who I am.'

381

A smart guy would have run for the stairs.

Plato stayed.

He called out, 'Do you think you can beat me?'

Reacher called back, 'Do you think bears shit in the woods?'

'You think you can beat me down here?'

'I can beat you anywhere.'

A long pause.

'Where are you?' Plato called.

'Right behind you,' Reacher said. Loud voice, booming echo. Fast feet scuffling on concrete. No answer. Reacher moved on, in the dark, his flashlight off. He heard Plato enter a corridor. A straight spoke. The sound of his feet narrowed and then bloomed and the tap of his heels came back from the right and the left simultaneously. Reacher scooted left, then right. Into a straight spoke of his own. Adjacent to Plato's, apparently. He saw the glow of Plato's flashlight as it passed the mouth of the C-ring. He moved on and stopped and lay down on his side, curled like a letter S, in the mouth of the straight spoke, just three feet from the main chamber. Down on the floor, to show a small target. Away from the vertical surfaces, because bullets rode walls, too. Not just sound. Any combat veteran would say the same. Narrow alleys, confined spaces, near-misses didn't ricochet at gaudy angles. They buzzed and burrowed close to the brick or the stone. Flattening yourself against a hard surface did the other guy a favour, not you. Counterintuitive, and difficult to resist, but true.

He heard Plato stop in the mouth of his corridor. Saw the glow from his light. He was facing into the main chamber. Two possibilities. One, he would turn right, away from the tunnel where Reacher was waiting. Or two, he would turn left, towards it.

Hide and seek. Maybe the oldest game in the world.

The guy from seat 4A walked the second hose into the stone building. He wrestled it across the floor and around the stair head and pulled it over to the same ventilation shaft the first hose was in. He put it up on his shoulder again and faced the void and kicked with his knee until the nozzle fell into the shaft.

Then he fed the hose down after it, yard by yard, ten feet, twenty, thirty, forty, like he was chinning himself backward along an endless monkey bar. When he had a good sixty feet in the shaft he ducked out from under it and laid it down against the lip. He kicked it straight on the floor and checked it for kinks.

All good.

Up the shaft from the tank, through the pump, and straight back down the same shaft again.

A simple, linear proposition.

*Do it.*

He walked back out to the cold and found his friend. Asked him, 'Can you hit the sentry from here?'

The guy from seat 4B looked down at his H&K. A four and a half inch barrel. A great weapon, but no more accurate than a fine handgun. And he was shivering hard. And not just from the cold.

He said, 'No.'

'So sneak up on him. If he sees you, tell him you're there to relieve him. Keep him talking. I'll hit the others as soon as they come this way out of the plane. Wait until you hear me fire, and let him have it.'

The guy from seat 4B said nothing.

'For your mother. And your sisters. And the daughters you'll have one day.'

The guy from seat 4B nodded. He turned around. He headed south. Slowly at first, and then faster.

Plato turned right. Away from where Reacher was waiting. A disappointment. Or perhaps not. Perhaps just a delay, and then eventually a benefit. Because the flashlight glow was dimming and brightening, then dimming and brightening, slowly and regularly and rhythmically. Which told Reacher that Plato was walking slowly around the circumference of the chamber, counterclockwise, playing the beam into one corridor at a time, pausing, checking carefully, and then moving on. No net loss. After all, in a circular space, turning right was ultimately the same thing as turning left. And counterclockwise was better than clockwise. Much better. For a number of reasons, which were about to be made plain.

To Plato, especially.

Reacher waited.

The flashlight beam moved on.

Then: from far above Reacher heard tiny sounds. Brief muted purrs. Four of them. Quiet enough to be close to the point of not being audible at all. Maybe the pump truck's starter motor turning over. Maybe the de-icer. Maybe something to do with the plane.

Maybe anything.

But if Reacher had been forced to guess worst case, he would have pegged them as triple taps from fast sub-machine guns.

Of which there were six on the surface.

Plato heard them too. His flashlight beam stopped dead.

Silence.

Nothing more.

A long wait.

Then the flashlight beam moved on.

Reacher saw Plato from the back through the circular lattice of steel that was the bottom five and a half feet of the staircase. He was twenty feet away. A hundred and eighty degrees opposite. His flashlight beam was horizontal in the corridor directly across from Reacher's.

Reacher moved his right arm. He cocked it behind him, ready.

Plato moved on, still counterclockwise, still slow. His body was facing forward, walking a perfect circuit. His head was turned. He was looking to his right at a square ninety degree angle down each of the radial spokes. The flashlight was in his left hand, the beam across his body. Which meant that the gun was in his right hand. The gun was still strapped around his neck. Which meant that the muzzle was facing left, which was fundamentally the wrong way, for a right-handed guy walking a counterclockwise circle. It was facing inward, not outward. A bad mistake. It would take a fast awkward flex of the elbow and a complicated tangle in the strap to correct in a hurry.

384

Reacher smiled.

Not such a smart guy after all.

Plato kept on coming.

A quarter-turn to go. Two more spokes.

One more spoke.

Then: vibration in the hose that led away from the fuel tank. The pump had started, way up there on the surface. Reacher heard the swish and rush of liquid as the pump primed itself and sucked air and created a vacuum and fuel moved in to fill it. He heard a hiss of air from the tank as it began to empty, quiet at first, then louder.

The flashlight beam moved on.

It arrived.

It played down the long tunnel, concentrated just above Reacher's curled form. But scatter from the lens picked him up. Plato froze, a yard away. Just a split second. Reacher sensed it. And used it to whip his right arm forward. Like a desperate throw from the outfield, bottom of the ninth, the opposition's winning run heading for the plate. The Mag-lite was a foot and a half long. Heavy alloy, four D cells. Cross-hatching on the body. Great grip. Ferocious acceleration. Tremendous leverage. Muscle, fury, anger. Geometry and physics.

Reacher's flashlight hit Plato butt-end-first square on the forehead. A solid punch. Reacher spun on his hip and scythed with his legs and kicked Plato's feet out from under him. Plato crashed down, flat on the floor. Reacher rolled on to his back, rolled on to his other side, rolled right on top of Plato.

And the world flipped again. Now the horizontal was vertical and the vertical was horizontal. No disadvantage in being tall. In fact, just the opposite. On the floor, the big guy always wins.

Reacher started hammering heavy blows into Plato's face, *one*, *two*, *three*, hard and vicious. Then he scrabbled for the H&K and got his hand on it just as Plato did. The two of them started a desperate tug of war. Plato was strong. Unbelievably, phenomenally strong for a man of his size. And impervious to pain. Reacher had his left hand on the gun and was using his right to hammer more blows to Plato's head. *Four, five, six, seven.*

385

Plato was bucking and writhing and tossing left, tossing right. Reacher was on top of him, smothering him, all two hundred and fifty pounds, and he was in danger of getting thrown off. Plato was snarling and biting, curling and rearing. Reacher jammed the heel of his hand under Plato's nose and smashed his head down on the concrete, *one, two, three*. Then *four*.

No result.

Plato started kicking for Reacher's groin, bucking, thrashing, like he was swimming backstroke. Reacher pinned the H&K and clambered off and smashed a right to Plato's ribs. Plato coughed once, coughed twice, and blood foamed on his lips. He jerked up from the waist and tried to get Reacher with a head butt. Reacher clamped a giant palm over Plato's moving teeth and smashed his head back down on the floor.

Plato's eyes stayed open.

Then suddenly: sloshing, gushing, pouring liquid. Loud, forceful, relentless. Like a fire hose. Like ten fire hoses. Like a hundred. Like a waterfall. Roaring. The stink of kerosene. Reacher kept his left hand on the gun and scrabbled with his right and found Plato's flashlight and jammed his elbow in Plato's throat and played the beam towards the sound.

Liquid was sheeting out of the nearer ventilation shaft. A flooding, drenching, torrential flow. Hundreds of gallons. A deluge. It hammered on the concrete and bounced and spattered and pooled and raced across the floor. Like a lake. Like a tide. Within seconds the floor was soaked. The air was full of fumes. The flashlight beam danced and shivered and swam through them.

Kerosene.

Jet fuel.

And it kept on coming. Like a giant faucet. Unstoppable. Like a burst dam. Gushing, sheeting, rushing, pouring, drenching. Plato bucked and jerked and twisted and got his throat out from under Reacher's elbow and said, 'What the hell is it? A leak?'

'Not a leak,' Reacher said.

'Then what?'

Reacher watched the flow. Relentless and powerful. And pulsing. It was the pump on the surface, running hard. Two hoses in the same shaft. One up, one down. One emptying the tank, the other wide open and dumping the contents straight back underground.

'What is it?' Plato said.

'It's a triple-cross,' Reacher said. His head was already aching from the fumes. His eyes were starting to sting.

'What?' Plato said.

'The Russian bought some of your guys. You're out of business.'

'They think they can drown me?'

'No,' Reacher said. 'They're not going to drown you.'

There was no possibility of drowning. There was too much floor area. Five thousand gallons would level out less than two inches deep.

He said, 'They're going to burn you to death.'

'Bullshit,' Plato said.

Reacher said nothing.

'How?' Plato said. 'They're going to drop a match down the stairs? It would go out on the way.'

Reacher said nothing. Plato wrenched away. Got to his knees. His nose was broken and leaking blood. Blood was coming out of his mouth. His teeth were smashed. One eye was closed. Both eyebrows were cut.

He put his hands on the H&K.

Then he took them off again.

Reacher nodded.

'Don't even think about it,' he said. 'The muzzle flash on that thing? With these fumes in the air? You want to do their work for them?'

Plato said, 'How are they going to do it?'

Reacher said nothing. He was thinking. Picturing the scene on the surface, running options through his head.

*See what they see.*

*Be them.*

Not a match.

Plato was right.

A match would go out.

*　　　*　　　*

The guy from 4B gunned the de-icer truck and spun the wheel and took off east towards the top right corner of the runway. Fifty yards. Forty. Thirty. Twenty. He spun the wheel again and slewed through a tight circle and the guy from 4A jumped out of the passenger seat and ducked down and grabbed the burning flare at its base and pulled its spike out of the concrete. He held it away from his body and climbed back in the truck and kept the door open and held the flare at arm's length in the slipstream. It burned brighter and it smoked and flickered. But it didn't go out. The truck raced back. Fifty yards. Forty. Thirty.

The deluge kept on coming. It was never-ending. It poured and sheeted and hammered. The ventilation shaft was like a bathtub faucet increased in size by a factor of a hundred. Reacher was on his knees. His pants were soaked. The fuel was already a good half-inch deep. The fumes were thick. Breathing was hard.

Plato said, 'So what do we do?'

Reacher said, 'How fast can you run up a flight of stairs?'

Plato got to his feet.

'Faster than you,' he said.

They were face to face, nose to nose, Reacher on his knees, Plato on his feet.

'I don't think so,' Reacher said.

*I'll have plenty of time to read after all this fuss is over.*

Reacher unleashed the uppercut from his knees. A colossal, primitive, primeval blow, driven all the way from the centre of the earth, pulsing through the wet concrete, through his knee, his thigh, his waist, his upper body, his shoulder, his arm, his wrist, his fist, every muscle and every fibre twitching just once, rippling fast in perfect propulsive sequence and harmony.

Plato's jaw shattered and his head snapped back like a rag doll. He hung motionless for a split second and then he splashed down, hard and vertical.

Reacher was pretty sure he was dead when he hit the floor.

Then he made absolutely certain of it.

He clamped his hands on Plato's ears and jerked his head one way and then the other until he felt the vertebrae pull apart and then he kept on doing it until he was sure the spinal cord was torn all the way to mush.

The deluge kept on coming, rushing, sheeting, torrential. The round chamber, once still and dry and ancient, was soaked with chemical stink and boiling with fumes, the fuel suddenly close to an inch deep, with small urgent waves racing outward from a frothing maelstrom directly under the roaring pipe.

*Surely everyone's afraid of death*, Janet Salter had said.

*Depends what form it takes*, he had answered.

He ran.

He splashed across the floor on his knees and ducked his shoulders down and got his head up inside the stair shaft and crawled and clawed and scrabbled to his feet. He leaned in towards the centre pole and took the stairs three at a time, galloping madly, his left hand sliding up over the steel, his right hand pawing crazily at the wall, batting and clutching and grasping at every extra second. The sound of his feet on the metal was drowned out by the waterfall roar of the fuel from below. He charged on, three at a time, four at a time, not breathing, anaerobic, up and up and up, round and round and round, not counting, just running, running, running, climbing, churning, hammering, straining, hurling himself towards the surface.

The de-icer truck jammed to a stop and K-turned and backed up and straightened. Directly behind it, the stone building. Directly ahead of it, the runway. The guy from 4A got out and ran crouched with his arm straight and the flare in his hand. He stopped in the doorway and turned and held the flare behind him and paused for a second and then swung his arm and lobbed it in. The flare tumbled end over end, a bright pink firework hissing through the air. It hit the unfinished lip of the ventilation shaft and kicked up and turned over once more and then dropped straight down and out of sight.

Five minutes to four in the morning.

Sixty-one hours gone.

# FORTY-SIX

I T WAS FOUR DAYS BEFORE THE SITE WAS COOL ENOUGH TO INSPECT.
By that point there was a long line of agencies waiting to join
the hunt. First on the scene were Homeland Security, the air
force, the FBI, the Highway Patrol, and a group of specialist
arson investigators drafted in by the government. The incident
had attracted intense interest. The North American Air Defense
Command had been the first to spot it. Their satellites had seen
a bloom of amazing heat and their computers had interpreted it
as either a missile launch or a missile strike. Their Russian
equivalents had seen the same thing. Within seconds the White
House had been on the phone, reassuring, and receiving
matching reassurances. There were launch silos in South
Dakota, yes, but not at that location. And in turn, no Russian
missile had been fired at America.

The National Guard was sent in to secure a wide perimeter.
Through it crept the waiting agencies, one by one. They set
up forward operating bases five miles out. They sent patrols
forward, as close as they dared. Then came news from the nearby

town of Bolton of a strange toxic cloud borne on the westerly wind. The patrols were pulled back. Hazmat gear was issued. Doctors were dispatched to Bolton. Reported symptoms were confusing. It was as if a light dose of a psychostimulant drug had been administered to the entire population. Temporary euphoria and excitement were reported, as was difficulty in sleeping and enhanced sexual appetite. The air was tested. No conclusion was reached. The wind had been blowing strongly for days, all the way from Wyoming. No symptoms were reported further east in the state.

The patrols crept inward again.

Their first discovery was a crashed vehicle four miles south of the epicentre. It was an airport de-icing truck reported as stolen from a commercial airfield east of Rapid City. It seemed to have been driving south on the old county two-lane leading away from the site. The road was snowbound and the surface was bad. It seemed that the truck had skidded off the road and turned over at least twice. It was an ungainly vehicle.

Two bodies were found close by. Two unidentified men of Hispanic origin, wearing dark suits apparently purchased in Mexico, under brand new winter parkas. The men had severe perimortem injuries, presumably caused by the crash, but they had died of exposure, presumably after crawling away from the wreckage. They were both carrying illegal fully automatic weapons. One gun seemed to have fired three rounds, and the other, nine. With that news, the Bureau of Alcohol, Tobacco and Firearms joined the roster of waiting agencies.

The patrols crept closer. By the middle of the second day the forward operating bases had been moved up to the southern edge of an old air force runway. At that new location they discovered a damaged and undriveable unmarked police car. It was positively identified by locals as the Bolton PD's property. It had been issued to the department's chief, Tom Holland. Holland had disappeared on the night of the fire. The Bolton PD was in disarray. It was dealing with three recent homicides, one of the victims being its own deputy chief, Andrew Peterson.

An observant fire officer taking a walk found the burned-out husks of two road flares, one in each corner of the old runway, apparently carefully placed. Which suggested the possibility of an unauthorized night landing. No flight plan had been recorded with the FAA. But through binoculars some agents claimed to see twisted wreckage just south of the epicentre that might or might not have been the remains of a large airliner. With that news, the National Transportation Safety Board joined the queue.

By the middle of the third day the Air Defense satellites showed the outer perimeter to have cooled to seventy degrees. The patrols moved up. The outer perimeter seemed to be about a hundred yards in diameter. Clearly some kind of fireball had bloomed, burned, and died back, but it had been brief compared to the main fire. The arson theorists began to run simulations on their laptops. Close inspection of the area inside the perimeter showed grievous damage. There was a dusting of ash a hundred feet out that might have been the remains of a human being. There was scorched and twisted aluminum that the NTSB claimed was the remains of an airliner, possibly a Boeing, possibly a 737.

The patrols moved up, into a dead world of twisted smoking fragments, some made of iron, some made of steel, some possibly from a vehicle, some smaller pieces possibly from weapons. Piled everywhere was debris from the plane. No attempt was made to quantify human remains. It would have been a hopeless task. Dust to dust, ashes to ashes, literally.

The only remotely intact structure was a small concrete stair head bunker disguised to look like a stone house. The air force claimed ownership. The original plans were lost, but anecdotally it was known to have been built fifty years previously, to contemporary blast-proof construction standards. It had stood up well. The roof was damaged. The interior concrete was blistered and spalled and calcified, but still reasonably solid. There were three circular shafts dropping down through the floor. It was surmised that once there had been steel casings for two ventilation ducts, and a spiral staircase probably also made of steel, but they had first melted and then vaporized.

Which proved, the arson people said, that the fire had started underground.

They donned protective gear and were lowered what turned out to be a total of two hundred and ten feet into the earth. They found a sequence of small tunnels and chambers, more blistered and spalled and calcified concrete, some ash that might once have been organic, and, amazingly, more than one thousand intact diamonds.

The arson specialists set up shop in the Bolton police station and connected their laptops wirelessly to their mainframes back home. They started work. They drew three-dimensional models of the underground facility. They made some guesses and assumptions. They knew from police records that a pump truck had been stolen along with the de-icer. So, if the aluminum had been an aeroplane, and if there had been an underground storage tank, then the accelerant might have been jet fuel. Which was consistent with their estimates of the fire's temperature, the upper limit of which they felt was defined by the survival of the diamonds, and the lower limit by the fact that the snow on the ground had been melted for two miles in every direction.

Major Susan Turner saw the news every evening on the television, and read it every morning in the papers, and followed it all day on line. She stayed in her office in Rock Creek, waiting by the phone. She slept in her visitor chairs, leaning back in one, her feet up on the other. The phone never rang.

After a week the arson theorists presented their best guesses. The fire had been a refuelling accident. Possibly due to undischarged static electricity arcing between the plane and the hose, more likely due to vapour build-up underground and a spark from a boot heel on concrete. The fire had burned mostly two hundred and ten feet below the surface, with enhanced thermodynamic characteristics due to a strange aerodynamic stasis in which a gale of air had howled down the stair shaft and the products of combustion had blasted up the twin ventilation shafts, in exactly opposite directions but with perfectly equal masses and velocities, in what amounted to a controlled and

393

everlasting explosion in a narrow vertical cylinder made of fireproof material. Like a rocket blasting off, but upside down, heading for the centre of the earth, not the sky. The roof damage was felt to prove it. Two temporary caps placed in the fake chimneys fifty years earlier had blown out and were found six hundred yards away. It was estimated that the narrow cone of flame might have reached a thousand feet above ground level, thereby mimicking the heat signature of a launching missile.

It was felt the initial phase of the fire might have lasted four hours. Then when the fuel load had depleted below a certain critical point the stasis had collapsed and a fireball had bloomed upward and outward, at a lower but still tremendous temperature, and had burned for an hour or so before collapsing again and finally burning out.

The toxic cloud in Bolton could not be explained. The air force admitted to storing surplus aircrew requirements from World War Two in the facility, all of it tanned leather in the form of helmets and boots and flying jackets, and it was felt that chemical residue from the tanning process might have been responsible for temporary adverse medical effects.

The presence of the diamonds was not explained, either. A theory was advanced that they had been stolen in Europe in the last days of the war, and entrusted to a quartermaster to be smuggled home, but had been mislaid and routed to the wrong destination.

After a series of discreet phone calls from the Pentagon, both the FBI and the local agencies in South Dakota concluded that in the absence of remains positively identifiable as human, no homicide investigation could be opened.

Two weeks later Kim Peterson moved with her children to a small rented house in Sioux Falls, to be nearer her father and their grandfather. Not exactly a teeming metropolis, but at least there were things to be seen from her kitchen window.

Four weeks later Susan Turner was deployed to Afghanistan. Elements of the 110th were operating there, and her presence was required. On her last day in Virginia she put Jack Reacher's old service file in a khaki envelope and marked it *Return to Human Resources Command*. She left it front and centre on the damaged desk. Then she walked out of the old Rock Creek office, and closed the door with the fluted glass window, and walked along the narrow linoleum corridor, and down the stone stairs, and out to her waiting car.

To be continued
30/9/10

**Lee Child** is British but, after he was made redundant from his job in television, he moved with his family from Cumbria to New York. All his novels feature the maverick Jack Reacher, and regularly top the bestseller lists in the UK and in the US.